tw
Post (where ....) and eight ... .
correspondent. His memoir, *Love in the Driest Season*, was
one of *Publishers Weekly*'s Best Books of 2004.

ALSO BY NEELY TUCKER

The Ways of the Dead

Murder, D.C.

NEELY TUCKER

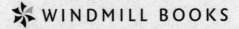WINDMILL BOOKS

1 3 5 7 9 10 8 6 4 2

Windmill Books
20 Vauxhall Bridge Road
London SW1V 2SA

Windmill Books is part of the Penguin Random House group of companies
whose addresses can be found at global.penguinrandomhouse.com.

Penguin
Random House
UK

First published by Century in 2015
First published in paperback by Windmill Books in 2016

www.windmill-books.co.uk

A CIP catalogue record for this book is
available from the British Library.

ISBN 9780099591733

Printed and bound by CPI Group (UK) Ltd, Croydon, CR0 4YY

In memory of Tommy Miller

One day I went to see the "slaves' pen"—a wretched hovel, "right against" the Capitol, from which it is distant about half a mile, with no house intervening. The outside alone is accessible to the eye of a visitor; what passes within being reserved for the exclusive observation of its owner, (a man of the name of Robey,) and his unfortunate victims. It is surrounded by a wooden paling fourteen or fifteen feet in height, with the posts outside to prevent escape and separated from the building by a space too narrow to admit of a free circulation of air. At a small window above, which was unglazed and exposed alike to the heat of summer and the cold of winter, so trying to the constitution, two or three sable faces appeared, looking out wistfully to while away the time and catch a refreshing breeze . . .

E. S. Abdy—Journal of a Residence and
Tour in the United States of North America,
from April, 1833, to October, 1834

MURDER, D.C.

ONE

SULLY CARTER HAD a pleasant little bourbon buzz going. It was a fine afternoon in the first spring of the twenty-first century. He'd been out on a fast boat in the Washington Channel, taking in the sunshine and the brisk spring breeze and the view of the dead body being pulled from the water. It was all pretty cool and mellow until he decided to go over to Frenchman's Bend and see if that's where the guy got popped.

He got there at a little after two in the afternoon, maybe four hours and change before deadline. Stillness. The wind tickling his ears, the sound of water slapping. Closed his eyes and the world was a warm yellow light behind his eyelids. Opening them again, it was almost . . . peaceful. He was walking past the first trees of the Bend, the buds tight along the branches, the faint scent of brackish water in his face, when he saw two enforcers for the drug crew that ran the place coming out of the apartment block to his right.

They let him pass, the little fuckers, let him walk deeper into the park, out toward the open grassy knob that stuck out into the channel like a thumb, and now they were sliding in behind him, cutting off his retreat. He did not have a clear view of either. The shorter figure came in behind him off his right, a too-big hoodie draped over his head. The other, taller, faster, but not in any real hurry, peeled off behind him toward the brick-wall boundary with Fort McNair, coming in off his left.

He could not hear them but didn't expect to, what with the wind in his face. Their appearance wasn't unexpected—it was the Bend, after all—but there was going to be some shit. There was going to be some shit now. Slowing his gimp-legged walk, dangling the motorcycle helmet from his right hand, the cycle jacket unzipped and open, doing his best white-man-without-a-clue impersonation. Under his breath, he swore at himself for getting involved in this two-bit homicide because now it was going to screw the entire day. He felt, somewhere behind his eyes, the bourbon beginning to burn off, his senses coming alive, calculating the moves of the men behind him without acknowledging their existence.

This was how your day went south without even trying.

He'd been having lunch with Dave Roberts and his crew from WCJT, having a gentleman's drink or three at the Cantina Marina, on the waterfront. Dave got a call from the station about tourist boats shrieking to 911 that they'd seen a body floating in the waves. Good people from Iowa come to take a tour of your nation's capital, starting out from the marina in Southwest D.C., just a few hundred yards from the cherry blossoms at the Tidal Basin, then heading down to Mount Vernon, George Washington's place, for a picnic lunch. Then bam, they get a view of how the other half lives. The body was floating just off the tip of Hains Point, at the confluence of the Potomac and the Anacostia, not even three-quarters of a mile from the marina.

The station rented a boat on the fly; Sully bummed a ride because, hell, it sounded like fun. A quick story for the paper and away they went, roaring out into the channel, all boys, giggling that this was a three-hour tour, *a three-hour tour,* the camera man swaying, trying to get steady B-roll.

Two police department launches were already out there, the station's boat skittering beyond them so that the camera guy could shoot back toward the city as a backdrop. The body was floating like a cork in a bathtub, tangled up with a clutch of driftwood. The police techs got a net under it and then the winch on the launch's crane creaked. The net pulled the body up and up until it was in the air, water pouring, long thick hair, dreadlocks falling away from the skull, the corpse in jeans and a jacket of some sort and one shoe. It lay there like a dead cod pulled off the bottom.

"What do you know, we just made the six o'clock," Dave said.

The camera guy spread his feet and the camera whirred, getting the focus tight, pulling the body into clarity. The police boats had a lot of guys in sunglasses and Windbreakers with DC MPD on the back. Dave talking to the camera guy, "You got the Monument in the background?"

"The money shot," the man said, nodding.

Cops crowded around the corpse and after a few minutes the huddle broke up. Lt. John Parker, the chief of D.C. Homicide, emerged, walking to the rail, hands on his hips, feet at the width of his shoulders, sunglasses, and a blue-and-black Windbreaker over his suit, glaring at them like they were walking on his lawn.

"Hey John," Dave called out, cupping his hands into a megaphone. "Any ID on floater man?"

"That thing off?" John yelled back, rolling a hand toward the camera, shades still down, that hard-ass cop look he had.

Dave sighed and nodded and the cameraman flicked the camera off and set it by his feet. The boats idled closer, pulling alongside, the sun splashing on John's bald head, his sunglasses.

"All off the record," John said, "and I mean, I don't want to hear 'police sources say,' 'a source familiar with the investigation,' no shit like that. All y'all hear?"

Everybody on the boat on the forward rail, leaning to hear him, nodded: Dave, the former Redskins linebacker turned local news personality; Sully, the alleged hotshot for one of the nation's great newspapers, nodding, yeah, yeah, whatever.

"No I.D., no name," John said.

"Courageous, taking that sort of bombshell off the record," Dave said.

"Was he still recognizable?" Sully chipped in.

"Mostly," John said.

"What does that mean?"

"He still had a face."

"Jesus," said Dave.

"Fish, shrimp, crabs get after them when they been in a couple of days," John said, "so I'm guessing our guy was a recent entry."

"Cause of death?" This was Sully.

"I'm just a homicide cop, and I just got my body five minutes ago, but I'm going to go out on a limb here and say the extra hole in his head, entry at his left temple, exit on his right, contributed."

"That's actually two extra holes," Sully said.

"Thank you, Pocahontas," John said.

"The head shot is on or off the record?"

"Did I stutter?"

"Theories?"

"Drugs, guns, pussy, turf," John said. "Take your pick. Brothers get popped like clockwork around here and you asking me, without so much as an ID, a motive?"

John was somewhere between irritated and angry, so when Dave said they were going to need to back the boat off and shoot some more B-roll, Sully just shrugged. He'd ask John more later, after the autopsy, in private, when he'd cooled off. The boats pushed back and the camera guy went back to filming the police boats at a distance.

Sully killed time by studying the D.C. waterline, about four hundred yards to the north, already having a pretty good hunch where this particular corpse would have come from, and no doubt John Parker did, too—Frenchman's Bend, which bellied out into the water like a limp dick, like a mini-Florida, about a half mile back up the channel. It was a bullshit city park, scrubby grass and beat-to-shit trees, sitting right before the pencil-thin strand of Southwest D.C. gave way to the brick walls and manicured lawns of Fort McNair, the small U.S. Army base that ran to the end of the peninsula.

From his vantage point, the fort's long row of precisely spaced waterfront houses seemed so close that you could almost tell if the drapes were pulled. The jonquils and tulips and pansies and begonias were coming up around the porches. The flowers were planted at each house in the same pattern. The exacting nature of this arrangement, replicated at house after house, made the fort appear monotonous if not robotic. And yet it was those startling bursts of red and yellow and pink and white that made the protruding knob of the Bend so identifiable and desolate by comparison: brown dirt and weeds too dumb to die and scraps of paper and brightly colored plastic bags, trash flitting across the scrub. No wonder there was a seven-foot brick wall running between the fort and the neighborhood.

The Bend, meanwhile, wasn't on any tourist map and was scarcely acknowledged by the city itself. It had been the District's most notorious antebellum slave market, its chattel packed into long-gone wooden pens, slaves brought from the farms lining the Potomac or the Anacostia, put on a platform, and sold off onto ships bound for cotton plantations down south. It had opened long before Washington was the capital but stayed in business for decades, the shame of the city, slaves force-marched through the streets in neck shackles.

Its stigma was so great that the land had never been built upon, not in the late nineteenth century when Southwest was a working-class address of the Irish and Germans, not later when it became a warren of blacks and Jews, not even in the post–World War II razing and building boom in that quadrant of the city.

For the past thirty years, it had been a yellowish scab, a drug park run by one crew or another, and nobody really seemed to give a good goddamn. If Sully hadn't been raised in Louisiana, an entire state of a yellowish scab still haunted by slavery, he might have thought the Bend was poisoned or cursed or defiled, a city block of malignant soil so infected by the sins of its past that it seeped into the souls of the living.

Now, twenty minutes after Dave had dropped him back at the dock, Sully was walking across this sorry expanse of real estate, seeing if there was anything that passed for a connection to the body in the water. The giddy high of the bourbon and fucking around with Dave's crew was fading into a headache and a slow burn. John Parker was right. This was going to turn out to be another drug shooting in a city that had averaged almost a homicide every day of every week of every month, all year round. For John, that likely meant another unsolved killing. For Sully, it translated as a fuckall story that was going to take too long and add up to not much.

He stopped a few feet from the water. He slid the backpack off his left shoulder, pulled the notebook out of the backpack, and then reached around inside it, looking for a pen. When he found one, he set the helmet and the backpack down, flipped open the notebook, and started writing down the basics of the park. No relevant details as to floater man jumped out at him, but he was after scenery, not specifics. The main atmospheric—the big picture that gave the place its sense of foreboding, even in the daylight—was the dearth of anything anyone would want. Across the channel at Hains Point, East Potomac Park looked like an emerald idyll, bike paths and the golf course and manicured roads. Over here, on the wrong side of the water, it was all packed dirt and broken glass and the hard hustle.

"Not buying," he said loudly, still writing, not looking up.

The footsteps behind him paused, then resumed and stopped again. He kept writing, idle observations about the desolation of the place and the meanness it gave off, like the scent of blood in a coroner's office. He had been here once or twice at night on crime scenes and thought it depressing and mean. The fresh spring disinfectant of daylight and a good breeze didn't do much for it.

"Working on a story," he said, still writing, but turning around, "about this guy who wound up in the channel last night? Shot in the head."

He looked up. Didn't recognize either of them. Foot soldiers. It wasn't like the Hall brothers, the identical twins who ran this turf, would stoop to checking out the loco paleface wandering into the Bend in the middle of the afternoon.

The one on his left, he dubbed him Short Stuff, the hoodie still pulled over his head. That tall drink of water on the right, he'd go with Lanky Dreads as a nickname, at least for now. They both had their hands in their pockets and regarded him with the dull, flat glares that a nobody like him warranted.

"Probably military," Sully continued, making it up as he went, selling it, gesturing off to his right, "from the fort? But it turns out you can't get in there. So I stopped off here to look around."

He'd never been to the fort in his life and had no idea of the entrance requirements, and he was guessing the same applied to these two half-wits, so it wasn't like they were going to be reciting U.S. military protocol to him.

"Man dead in the channel?" This was Short Stuff, his voice deeper than Sully would have thought, and he moved his guess on the man's age from eighteen to twenty.

Sully nodded, yeah yeah, sure.

"White man?"

"Nah."

"You police?"

A shake of the head. "Reporter."

Lanky Dreads, the tall one on his right, shifted his weight to his back foot, eyeing him, Sully recognizing the long gaze on the scars. Then Lanky Dreads said, "The fuck's with your face?" his voice raspy, like a grate, like somebody sandblasted his vocal cords when he was three. Short Stuff laughed. It sounded like a bark.

"It's a shrapnel tattoo," Sully said.

"It looks like shit."

"Good thing I got it for free."

The same dude, flicking a wrist forward at him. "Whyn't you walk right?"

"Same shrapnel."

"It hurt a lot?"

"Until I passed out."

"You military?" This was Lanky Dreads again, but Short Stuff flicked a glance over at his partner, irritated, not hiding it.

"Nope," Sully said, cutting his eyes between them, trying to figure out who was in charge. "Reporter, like I said. I was in Bosnia. The paper? Sent me over there. They had a war going on. I got blown up."

"They get the guy?"

"What guy?"

"That fucked you up."

"It was a grenade. There wasn't any guy to get."

"So why you down here?"

"Curious," said Short Stuff, flicking that glance at his partner again, "cut that shit out."

Lanky Dreads blinked, three, four, five-six-seven times, like he was processing the interruption, but he did not take his gaze from Sully. "Brothers get capped on the block all the time," he said, defensive, like he was justifying the line of inquiry. "Ain't no reporters show up."

Sully shifted his weight, time getting short. You could only talk to dickheads like this for so long before it got ugly, and the clock was about to strike half past. "I already done said. This dude floating out there in the channel? Had six holes in his head instead of the usual five. Seven, you want to count the exit wound. Tourist boat spotted him riding the waves, they freaked, so now it's all over television. Police? They figure he's military, went in the water off the fort over there. Turns out you got to have a pass to get in. Which I don't got. Like I said."

"Whyn't you think he didn't fall off a yacht?" *Yat.*

"'Cause that's not what MPD thinks."

Short Stuff snorted like he was about to hawk up a wad. "Like they know shit."

"John Parker," Sully said, cutting his gaze back to Shorty. "When I say MPD? I'm meaning John Parker."

He threw the name out there—the head of D.C. Homicide—to show he wasn't a fuckhead, right, and to see if they knew the name, to get a gauge of what level of the crew he was dealing with. Short Stuff clocked his head a quarter turn.

"Hey, Parker? *John* Parker? Hey, fuck him, fuck you," he said. "You know where you at, fool?"

"The Bend."

"Then you ought to fucking know better."

"So you saying you didn't see nobody down here last night, picking up a couple dime bags? Gunshots? Nothing?"

The two didn't speak or look at one another. But Lanky Dreads blinked again—three, four times, bap bap, just like that—and it gave Sully the idea that maybe Lanky didn't have the heart for what had gone down. That was all the confirmation he needed.

"MPD been down here?" Sully said, putting the top back on the pen, flipping the notebook shut. Short Stuff and Lanky were ten feet away, standing maybe three feet apart, between him and the rest of the park.

"Parker's your bitch," Short Stuff said. "Ask him." *Axt.*

Sully nodded, a half smile, not putting much into it. "Well. Yeah. So." He picked up the helmet and backpack, moving forward, right between them because going around would have been giving ground and if you flinched, hunched over, slowed, showed any sign of deference, they'd beat your ass into the dirt for being that weak. It was the same everywhere you went. Bosnia, Somalia, South Africa, Lebanon, the Bend. Dudes, half-cocked.

He got within two steps of them and Lanky said, "That your Ducati at the curb?" Sully got the smell of sweat, of flesh, of ganja, of closed rooms and broken mirrors and moldy carpet, the smell and feel of the projects.

"The 916. Yeah."

"Bring that out to the Cove. Run you for pinks."

Sully worked up a cough, laughing, the you-gotta-be-kidding-me thing, turning his shoulders to edge through, making sure he didn't bump either one of them. "For *pinks*? Nah, nah, you ride what, I'm guessing here, a 'Busa?" he said. "And it's an eleven-second bike in the quarter, some shit like that?"

"Ten-eight."

He was past them now, walking backward, keeping eye contact, keeping it light. "Doubt that. But the Duc ain't a straight-line bike. I'd be looking at your ass the last two hundred."

"Reporter man?" This from Short Stuff.

Sully kept walking backward, not slowing down but not going any faster than he had to, either, and now he switched his gaze to acknowledge who was talking. Short Stuff had shucked his piece down into his hand, which was now out of his jacket pocket, flat against his leg.

"Stop walking."

"I'm on deadline."

"I say stop walking."

Sully, still moving, looked at his watch, looked up and smiled. "I got an hour and fifteen. And I got to—"

Short Stuff flipped the pistol forward and brought it level, pointed sideways, gangster chic, aiming at Sully's chest.

Sully stopped, still smiling, but raising his eyebrows, giving the man the respect he wanted. He brought his hands up a hey-you-got-me motion. "Okay. What? What are we talking about here?"

"Don't be bringing that broke-ass bike back down here, 'less you want to float yourself. You feel me?"

"Yeah. I do. Yeah. Okay? I hear you. But you got to know MPD's gonna come down here in a couple hours, start sweating you, the Hall brothers, everybody? You know that, right? That throwing the dude in the channel didn't fool anybody with a double-digit IQ?"

Short Stuff brought his chin up. "Thought you said they made the floater for military. From the fort. Over there."

Sully, giving him that same shrug, moving backward again. "Me, myself? I don't trust MPD for shit."

TWO

"IT'S A FLOATER story, but I don't know how good," he was saying, back in the newsroom, back in the recycled air of the office, the quiet hum of the overhead fluorescents making him wish he was back out on the water, wishing R.J. would get up off him for a minute.

"Dead body in the Washington Channel, scaring the tourists, what's not to love?" R.J. said, leaning over the wall of his cubicle, an editor looking for fresh meat for the final edition. He was rubbing his beard, the paper's wise old man in high good humor, his still-black hair slicked back over his scalp, the bow tie knotted at the button-down collar, all but chortling about this one. "I saw it on the television a few minutes ago. It's all over cable now, did you know? Talking heads yammering about floating bodies, the nation's capital gone to hell in a handbasket."

"I sort of thought it did that a while back."

"And you got the tourists, right?" R.J. said, looking down at him, his eyes big and weird through the bifocals. "Yahoos from flyover, a-damn-mazed this happened in sight of the Capitol Building?"

"Yes. At the marina. They were quite upset."

"You'd think they'd read the papers before they got here," R.J. snorted. "We've been the murder capital since when, Bush? Reagan? Carter? You get anything great? Like, 'I had to cover my kid's eyes,' or—"

"Two of them said it was Clinton's fault."

"Any logic ascribed to that position?"

"Are you serious?"

"Like maybe they thought he tossed *Monica* in the water, and—"

"Floater was black. And male."

R.J. sighed, still with the beard. "Well. That's not very creative."

"No."

"That's going to put a dent in the story—I mean, not that it should, but you know—"

"I could just make some shit up."

"Nah," R.J. said absently, looking at his nails now, not getting it. "Nobody has a sense of humor anymore." He blew out his lips, looking around, coming out of a trance, realizing the hour. "We gotta do something for the daily."

"I know it."

"You got out on the water, talked to the cops?"

"With Dave, on the WCJT launch. I been thinking about getting me a little boat myself."

"Thrilled. Look, if you can get MPD to say it was drug related, that'd help. Could you do that? You know, 'Drug wars spilling out into tourist country,' yada yada. But what would be great, I mean give this thing some elevation, if he's some sort of diplomat, an attaché at an embassy, or an, an *operative*, with a couple of passports—"

"A diplomat in baggy jeans and dreads," Sully said, rolling back in his chair, propping his feet on his desk. "The Ambassador to the State of the Most High."

"Jamaican! He could be, like, an operative of—"

"—the dreaded Blue Mountain coffee mafia? Rastas don't get into the diplomat thing, R.J. And he might be a narc, but that's hardly your CIA henchman."

R.J., pulling off his glasses, polishing them, looking at his watch. "Yeah, yeah. Okay. Trying to get us somewhere. Look, unless we get some sort of ID on floater man? I'm talking twelve inches below the fold on the Metro front. Maybe even inside. A lost day."

Ah, shit, Sully thought. Little in the life of R.J. was worse than a lost day. He'd won two Pulitzers, been a finalist twice more, never mind the George Polks. The man was carpe diem and kick over the sandbox of life. Front page and cleavage or it was bullshit, that was R.J.'s take.

"Sometimes it's just vitamins, brother, not steak sauce," Sully said.

"Come again?"

"It's going to run on B-12, not A-1, no matter what we do."

"You southern people are so colorful. Well. Here's a thought. You've had a run of vitamin stories of late, lad. Pop out front. Try the steak sauce."

"We tie it to the Bend," Sully said, pulling his feet down, rolling up the chair to the desk, "we'll be getting somewhere. I went down there just now, two vampires show up, say they'll cap my ass, I come nosing around again. I say to you, I just stepped on a nerve. I say to you, floater man went into the water right there, in Frenchman's Bend. This is going to be the M Street Crew, the South Capitol Crew; they're always beefing in Southwest. The Hall brothers run the—"

" 'Vampires' being your term for drug dealers."

"Bloodsuckers. Yeah."

"They know anything about floater man?"

"Like they're going to spout to me? But yeah, one of them, this kid, he blinked."

"He blinked?"

"He blinked."

"You're fucking with me now, right? Just to have something to do?"

"He blinked a lot."

R.J. looked at him, hard. Then blinked. Three times.

"Clearly the man is guilty of murder. How could anyone doubt this? 'Blinker Man Kills Floater Man.' I say we go hard with it on 1-A."

"No, I mean, what I'm saying, he has this little affectation, this tic. He blinks *bam bam bam*, seven or eight times in a row. He knows something."

"Good tracking, Kemo Sabe, but that's not going to carry the water. Maybe you want to get your guy Parker to spout. He's the homicide director, right?"

"Chief. John Parker is the chief of MPD Homicide. He ain't going to say nothing until he knows for sure. There's not even an ID on the body yet."

"Maybe he could blink it to you."

Sully rubbed his eyes. "I shouldn'a gone out there. I knew it and did it anyway."

"Like blink blink, pause, blink. Blink. Morse code. You know?"

"I repeat."

R.J., running with it now. "A homicide cop, blinking like that, I'd say means they just busted Pablo Escobar down at Twelfth and—"

"Did you have any sort of point in mind or—"

"—they got—what? What did you say? Are you with me here? Without a reliable source with an ID for floater man," R.J. said, coming back to the point, opening his eyes wider, "we don't have any connection to the Bend, correct? All we got is that there was a man in the water and he—"

"Scared the tourists," Sully finished for him.

R.J. raised his eyebrows, mock incredulous. "Get the man the stuffed giraffe from the top rack! So we're seeing it the same way."

"Mas o menos."

"Unless you can work some sort of miracle before the five o'clock."

"Not happening," Sully said. "I'll send you something short and mean." He sat up straight in his chair and poked his head up over the divider, seeing Chris two rows down, filing something, stuck on the cops beat, dying to move up to something more glamorous. He plunked back down. "And could you smooth it over with Chris? That I just happened across this?"

"Don't want his panties in a twist because you bigfooted him again? Look. Get the ID. Then floater man becomes a Specific Dead Man, and Mr. Specific might just be a story."

And then R.J. badda-badda-bapped the top of the cubicle, a little drum roll, like he'd told Sully something he didn't know, and he was off, his loafers hushed on the carpet, going to talk Chris down off the ledge.

The clock on the wall was ticking past four. The newsroom at this hour was a place that if you didn't want a drink before, you did after. Editors with armpits about to break into a sweat, stories that were evaporating or that were taking too damn long or just *were* too damn long. Copy editors settling in to examine the belly buttons and lint of newspaper copy. Reporters with fixed faces and ties or blouses askew, legs crossed at the knees, feet pumping, leaning forward and slapping keyboards like they were percussion instruments, talking too damn loud into the phone. Sully could swear, actually swear, that he could hear the clock tick from twenty paces.

He opened a file in the paper's word processing system, tapped in a slug, *floaterman*, and then closed his eyes. The shrink. His shrink. Ah, Christ. He was supposed to have been there thirty minutes ago.

He picked up the phone and turned his shoulder into it so the words wouldn't travel to the next cubicle and tapped in the psychiatrist's number, and Gene Henderson himself picked up, surprising him.

"You're not here," Henderson said, his tone abrupt, no hi-hello, sounding exasperated. Sully didn't mind the man, actually liked him a little.

"Astute, even for a former military man such as yourself."

"Is there an explanation?"

"I'm working," Sully said back down the line, pleasantly. "This dead guy turned up in the channel. It didn't make sense to stop working to come talk about work, if you see what I'm saying here."

"You didn't call me beforehand to cancel."

"The dead dude didn't call me, either," Sully said. "That's the thing about dead people."

Henderson was talking then, taking that official tone, telling him that by the contract the paper had signed, he now was required to inform HR that Sully had missed the appointment and that this was the third one this year, three in four months, and that was way over the line of—

"Peachy, peachy, peachy," he said, cutting Henderson off. "Just be sure to tell them that I couldn't make your appointment because I was covering the murder of a young man and having other young men with guns say they'll shoot me if I come back and ask any more questions about it and, you know, if they'd like to cough up some combat pay for that sort of work I'd be pleased."

"Three times in four months," Henderson repeated.

Sully, looking in his desk for gum and not finding any, the worry about bourbon on his breath in the back of his mind. You'd think gum wouldn't be a hard thing to keep in a desk. "So you'll bill me for it," he said. "You won't go broke and neither will I."

"Next week, same time," Henderson said. "You'd do well to remember this isn't an optional program." The line disconnected. Sully looked at the phone and decided he liked Henderson a little less today than he did yesterday.

He slumped back in the chair so far his skinny ass was barely on the seat, stuck a pen in his mouth to chew, and proceeded to take the easy day-hit cheap shot:

Tourists aboard a sightseeing yacht in the Washington Channel were startled yesterday to see a corpse floating past their view of the Tidal Basin.

A few minutes later, across the way, R.J. hooted, reading behind him.

"My boy!" he exclaimed. "You're so subtle!"

THREE

AFTER HE HAD filed—*floaterman* was a dozen inches, buried deep inside Metro—it was still just six thirty, middle of the week. The day had clouded over and now it was starting to mist. Ta-dum ta-dum. It was happy hour somewhere. There was a baseball or basketball game on at a sports bar, sure, but it wasn't football so who gave a fuck? That left his late-night plans with Alexis.

She was back home for a couple of weeks, R&R from her posting in Cairo, in the middle of a photo project on the Israeli pullout from Southern Lebanon. Had he not been blown up in Bosnia, he mused, he likely would be in Jerusalem now himself, a room at the American Colony, a bottle of Basil Hayden's with his name on it at the bar, evening runs up the hill to the Mount of Olives and then back, the sweat and the chill evening air and the Garden of Gethsemane in the middle distance, calling up some hot Israeli chick, *Hey, we're just having a drink at the Colony and* . . .

As it was, here he sat, fucked-up leg, fucked-up story, fucked-up life.

He thought about calling Alexis, see if she could meet him early, but nah, she was supposed to have dinner with the brass: the publishers; Eddie Winters, the executive editor; the honchos running the foreign desk. The kind of evening that would start at the Palm and move to the bar of the Hay-Adams, going past the Washington witching hour of ten—amazing, how the powers that be in this town ran for home at that hour. Given that, he and Alexis had made plans for drinks at his place at eleven.

But that was what, four hours and change? To do, to do. Movie listings, flapping open the Features section, staring at the agate type: costume drama, rom com, rom com, horror. Christ. He didn't want to go to his row house on Capitol Hill and stare at his backyard thinking he should have mowed his tiny rectangle of grass last weekend, he didn't want—

He picked up the phone.

"John? Hey, Parker?" he said into the cop's cell-phone voice mail. "No shit. Need the ID of floater man, partner. Call me when you get it. Anytime."

He clicked off and looked around until his eyes settled on his murder map of the city. It was new for the year but there were already sixty or seventy pins on it, each marking a killing. The map—his oracle, his witchcraft, his guide to understanding the ways of the living by divining the ways of the dead—was a poster-sized replica of the city's seven police districts, with homicides marked in each.

There were already three in or near the Bend, each of them noted with black pins and little red crosses that he marked on the map at the place of the killing. The color of the pin denoted that they were black men. The red crosses, marked with a colored pencil, denoted that their cases were unsolved. White victims got white pins; Hispanic, yellow; women, pink. No matter the color of the pin, most of them had red crosses, too.

Solved cases, which were only about a third of the total, got black crosses.

Sully turned to the computer and began keying in the passwords to legal databases that tracked arrest records and court decisions. He opened the file drawer to his left, the one that housed the murders of the current year.

His filing system: Each homicide victim got their own manila folder, filed alphabetically, the name of the victim and a number that denoted the order in which they were killed in the upper right corner of the tab.

The police incident report, the PD 1099, was all that was in some, but it gave the essential details. Matching the numbers on the murder map to the numbers on the folders, he pulled out the folders of those killed this year in or near the Bend.

They were: suspected drug shooting (no arrest), suspected drug shooting (no arrest), argument turned into a shooting (no arrest). This was pedestrian crap. But after a few minutes, a pattern started to register, to coalesce, his mind already sensing connections between the pin dots.

On the map of Washington spread before him, the quadrants of the diamond-shaped city originated from of the Capitol—northwest, northeast, southeast, southwest—a daily reminder of the power that radiated out of that building; the entire city turned on its axis. Meanwhile, the cluster of red (unsolved) crosses, nearly all of them marked by black pins (black male victims), was a deluge across the Anacostia, in Southeast D.C.

By comparison, Southwest was just a scattered shower of red raindrops and black pins. This wasn't surprising because Southwest—a teardrop-shaped, north-to-south sliver of land below the Capitol—was by far the smallest of the city quadrants. The National Mall cut it off to the north, the Washington Channel to the west, South Capitol Street on the east. The Anacostia cut it off to the south. Another chunk of Southwest existed on the other side of the Anacostia, most of it taken up by Bolling Air Force Base and that stinking sewage plant, Blue Plains, but neither of those was civilian turf.

Southwest, Southwest, he mused, tapping the map with the butt end of his pen, you're just a civic bunion south of the Mall, drug houses, apartment blocks, hipster whites and sort-of-but-not-really-upscale blacks living in condos, the occasional Supreme Court justice who doesn't like a long commute, and whatever the fuck Fort McNair is. You're some hairy-legged women and ganja-puffing douches on houseboats at the Gangplank Marina. You're good for fresh seafood at the dockside markets, for the grown and sexy clubs up on the waterfront, but that's about it.

Most of the housing was that post-1960s modernist crap, or row houses that went back to the early twentieth century when it was a packed-dirt warren. Now, since the 1960s, as long as you hewed to the riverfront? There were four or five blocks of modern apartment buildings and condos, nice enough eight- to twelve-story things, sure.

But once you hit the Bend? Construction yards, one-story warehouses, empty lots, a power station, a bus parking lot, cheap wire fences, and some of the most brutal projects in the city, a reminder of the days when thousands of people lived in carriage houses that opened onto brick alleys. If you crossed over South Capitol, you were technically in Southeast, but it was still on the peninsula dangling below the belly of the city, and it was spiritually still Southwest—car washes, long-term storage lots, the Navy Yard, that block of gay clubs on O Street, dilapidated row houses and street corner drug markets.

He went to his file drawers and began to pull out the folders of the dead from near the Bend, not just this year, but from years past.

"W1 (witness one) reports finding deceased BM facedown at base of wall of Fort McNair, in the Bend," read the witness accounts of the killing of Henry Andre Douglas, a black male, dead in January of a gunshot wound to the head.

"W1 and W2 report hearing shots in the Bend at approximately 3:15 a.m. Feb. 12," another report read, quoting the two witnesses, "a body subsequently found at the base of a cherry blossom tree, roughly twenty yards from the waterfront." The body belonged to Curtis Michael Lewis, "shot twice in the back of the head."

He read further into the reports, the newsroom emptying out, the time passing and his concentration growing as the jigsaw puzzle deepened and opened before him. As the hours passed and his awareness of them dimmed, an oddity became apparent in the police paperwork: Officers on the scene often denoted the address of the slaying as the entrance *to* the park, there at the intersection of P and Fourth streets. But the police action reports, the 1099s, of, say, Lewis and Douglas? Those killings actually took place *in* the Bend.

Reaching beneath his desk, he pulled out the murder maps of previous years. He unfurled them, three feet tall by two feet wide, and pinned them to the wall of his cubicle, sequentially: 1996, '97, '98, '99 and now, the first few months of 2000. This was the murder chart of the deadliest big city in America, a place that had been so for more than a decade. Four hundred or so homicides in a city of 550,000 in the heyday of the crack epidemic. The display took up the whole cubicle, making him stand back to take in the effect. There were no pins in the rolled-up maps, but the red Sharpie crosses remained: red for unsolved, black for solved.

You put it together like this, with a street-map overlay, year in and year out—what was it, a longitudinal study—and then you could recognize the city's worst housing projects and neighborhoods over the course of time. Benning Terrace, right over there in Southeast; Sursum Corda, closer to downtown; yeah, you could spot those. So, stepping back, looking at it, going to get a cup of coffee from the copy editor's desk, and coming back, your vision better now, you could see the flurry of crosses in greater clarity. His eyes drifted, automatically, up to Princeton Place, the cluster of crosses that marked the killings that had taken over his life last fall, that had, in their way, ruined the relationship he'd been building with Dusty, then a bartender at Stoney's. She was long gone now—he wasn't even sure if she was in Baltimore or had gone back home to Miami, or Boca, or wherever.

He blinked and his eyes refocused on the murder map and he saw something so obvious he'd never really noticed it before. It was a view of comparison and contrast, available only when you splayed it out like this on maps encompassing more than twelve hundred homicides over five years.

Though Southwest had only a few dozen homicides each year, the Bend itself showed up as a radiant spot of red crosses—an effect enhanced when you moved some of those crosses from *near* the park, as the cops had listed them, and *into* it, where the killings had actually occurred.

He counted all the crosses from the past five years that were in or near the Bend, and just to get the visual, moved them into the map of the most current year. He counted, his lips moving slowly to be sure, and stepped back to look at it.

Forty-four.

Over the past five years, forty-four people had been killed in the Bend, a knoblike park of little more than an acre, and not one had been solved. No mass shooting to skew the body count. It wasn't a high-rise housing project. No one lived there. It was just open ground. It was where D.C. went to kill and be killed.

"Frenchman's Bend," he said softly, already seeing it on the front page, above the fold. "The murder capital of the murder capital."

The idea floated across his mind, there in his reverie, that maybe he was wrong and the land itself really was somehow cursed with the history of its past, a settling of accounts that didn't limit itself to the passing of time. The sins of slavery and degradation and depravity didn't disappear into the ether, he knew that well enough from back home.

Willie Baker had gotten shot one night outside the Club, the juke joint near his hometown of Tula, hard behind the levee. Sully was seven at the time and he remembered it, rightly or wrongly, as his introduction to murderous violence.

Both his parents were still alive then. Everybody in Tula spent Friday nights in the fall watching Willie come out of the backfield and run over, through or just plain past the players from other rural schools. Everybody knew he was going somewhere. It was a big deal, not that long after integration, folks from all over the county coming behind the team, them making it to the state semifinals. Willie, tall, lean, always with the laugh—he signed a game program for Sully, walking off the field after their playoff loss in his senior year, steam rising from his body in the early-winter chill. Then he went to the Club and came outside about one in the morning and took a chestful from a 12-gauge and everybody knew Carl Evans and his buddies had done it, because Willie had gotten a scholarship offer from LSU and Carl, who thought he was hot shit, had not. And the sheriff, whom Sully would come to know and hate later, never even interviewed anybody because he knew as well as they did that no jury in their postage stamp of a town was ever going to send a white kid to prison for killing a black one.

And Sully, at seven, looking at his program the next day, asking his momma if they could go to the funeral whenever they had it and her blowing out cigarette smoke, saying she didn't go to nigger funerals because it was a bunch of caterwauling that went on for three hours.

It would be easy, Sully thought, to label that sort of hypocrisy and fear and loathing and violence a white southern virus, but the world was much more complicated than that. The dark verities weren't cultural. They had been around so long that they had become genetic, worming their way into the very blood of the living, the flesh and the DNA of successive generations. They came to the fore over the millennia because the world is Darwinian and hatred and fear and loathing were not left out like a sixth finger or a useless appendage, but were adapted into the core of the species. They spawned from generation to generation to generation because they had proven themselves to be stronger, more resilient, and more vicious than other attributes. You could not kill hatred and fear and loathing. They were hardwired into the neural pathways. They found homes in the webs of the neocortex. In the gene pool of survival, nature selected them and it selected them because they had proven themselves to be an integral survival skill. They had earned the right to survive.

"Hey, R.J.?" he called out, half-distracted, his eyes dancing across the map. "I'm thinking we got something here."

FOUR

"**WILLIAM SANDERS ELLISON,**" Parker was saying, "floater man, known to friends and family as Billy. Twenty-one-year-old black male, son of Delores Ellison and the late William G. Sanders."

Sully, in his row house on Capitol Hill, half-undressed, twenty minutes to midnight, crooking the phone between his ear and his shoulder, scribbling it down on the back of the Chinese takeout menu from the place on H Street, the one you'd rather order from than pick up, as the pickup area was walled off with six-inch-thick plexiglass, people had robbed the place so often.

"All right, all right, give me a second here. . . . Any more holes in him than the extra one in his head?" he said, sitting up on the couch, careful not to knock over his drink on the coffee table, Alexis sitting up herself now, pulling her unbuttoned blouse back over that racy bra, not happy about him taking the call, smoothing her skirt back down over her fishnets, things just getting interesting when his cell had buzzed. She still had her heels on—he was fine with them staying on, even if he stripped everything else off—and she was looking at the blank television screen, listening to the Van Morrison he'd had on when she had pulled up in a taxi, reaching for her chardonnay now.

"Nah," Parker said. "Just the one. Untouched otherwise, toxicology pending. But, really, the name is more important than the cause."

"It is?"

"The Ellisons? This doesn't register for you?"

"Not, ah, at the moment, I'm sort of—"

"The Ellisons. D.C. black society, brother. The e-lites, as the missus would say. Quiet, respectable, old money, Jack and Jill, the Links, house on the Gold Coast, summer home on the Vineyard, first black this, first black that. Dad, he married in, he was a young turk in the Carter administration."

"They're like, what, the Quanders, the Hairstons?"

"Bigger. Or, well, richer. By a lot."

"And you still thinking junior was a coke freak, scoring down in the Bend?"

There was a pause. "I did *not* say that."

"You were thinking it, out there on the boat. Come on. That's how they do it down there. I looked it up. Three homicides this year in Frenchman's Bend already. All three got dumped in the channel. Floater man was a tourist, he fell off a boat? Somebody would have called 911 when it happened."

Parker sighed. "So you were the white guy who went down there asking questions. Our guys get to the Bend this afternoon, bracing the usual suspects, and they start popping off about some narc."

"They made me for a narc?"

"I don't think they could believe a civilian would have been dumb enough to walk in there like he owned the place."

"Flattered. So, young Billy had a drug problem."

"Possibly. They tell me it happens in the best of families."

"You don't sound all broke up."

"They're very wealthy people."

"Isn't that what this great country is all about?"

"Yeah, which is what I'm saying. The Oval Office has already called the chief, right? And our lovely congressional representative called me fifteen minutes ago, which, I conclude, was about seventeen seconds after she found out about it."

"The *Oval* Office? On a shooting in the *Bend*? Come on."

"You'd grown up here, you'd know. The family is your local institution. Major Democratic boosters, but not hostile to the party of Lincoln. Fund-raisers, society things. This is Delores's family we're talking about. Dad, William, got killed in a car wreck on the Beltway ten, fifteen years back."

"Well, wait. If Dad was Sanders, how come the kid has mom's last name?"

"Talk to them. This town, Ellison is the family name you want. Delores is on the White House social list, regardless of the administration. Dad worked for Shellie Stevens. Delores still does."

Sully paused, tilting his head slightly, thinking maybe he hadn't heard correctly. "*The* lobbyist dude, Shellie Stevens, what gets everybody out of trouble?"

"Himself."

"Wow."

"Which is what I was telling you—my phone is ringing."

"Any connection?"

"How you mean?"

"Did the kid, what, Billy, work for Stevens, too?"

"No, no. You got it crooked. Dad was a partner in Shellie's firm, back in the day. Now, Mom is some sort of 'strategist' at the firm. That's what she said in the interview. Told the detective she works for Shellie—he says, 'In what capacity,' and she says, 'I'm a strategist.'"

"Oh."

"Like it's a title."

"You go down to the ME's for the cut?"

"To make sure it didn't get fucked up, that we're covering our bases, showing concern, won't rest till the killer or killers are caught, yeah, sure."

"Who you assigning?"

"Jeff Weaver, the lead in 1-D, since it looks like it happened in the Bend. He was down there for the cut, too."

"I don't know him much," Sully said.

"The ace in Southwest at the moment. Or what we have that passes for an ace. You wouldn't believe this place."

"How's the overhaul coming?"

"You got jokes now? Slow. Remaking an entire department? Icebergs make better progress."

"Obvious leads on Billy boy?"

"None. But you got to remember we didn't make a positive ID until about six this evening. He was already dead something like twenty-four hours, coroner says. Mom didn't tell us anything off the bat that sounded fishy. He was finishing his junior year at Georgetown, going to go into law like his old man. Like that."

"So what is it she says happened to baby boy?"

"No clue. She tells us he was living in an apartment, not at home. Didn't know anything was wrong till someone called her up and said they saw this body being pulled out of the water on television and it looked like Billy."

"So Billy, no known enemies."

"This is his momma."

"She know he had a drug problem?"

"Said she was in shock when we asked her about him being at the Bend."

"They always are," Sully said. "And so, look, I was going through the files? That murder map I keep? And—"

"You know that thing's not gospel, right? You know how bad the record keeping is here? The way the previous administration was trying—"

"Okay, so, okay, stipulated, but it looks like to me that the Bend? It's got maybe the highest density of killings of anyplace in the city."

"I haven't run it like that, but it'd be close, yeah."

"Just so we're straight, I'm thinking about that idea for a story."

He was still scribbling on the menu and sensed movement out of the corner of his eye. Alexis was finishing her wine and standing up—Jesus no, that couldn't happen. He smiled and lightly grabbed her wrist, shaking his head, no no no. She looked down at him, a little peeved now, blouse still open, that body, god alive—Billy Ellison could wait.

"Your business," Parker was saying. "There'll be a little more evidence tomorrow. Turns out there was a report of a gunshot in or near the Bend last night. There's gunshots down there most every night, hey? But do not—are you listening to me?—do *not* go fucking around in the Bend. That's the Hall brothers. They don't play."

"So I've been told," Sully said, clicking off the cell and tossing it on the table.

"Okay, so," he said to Alexis, "that's done. Where were we?"

Alexis took a stance over his legs, her hips at his eye level, a wonderful sight. "You were getting me another chardonnay and groveling," she said, "for your appalling lack of class."

"Lack?"

"Taking that call? When we're involved? You got a priority problem."

"Hey, when there's a call, there's a call. If that had been a shoot, you would have taken it."

"Not now I wouldn't have." She smiled down at him, a little drunk. "I'm on home leave."

"I'm not."

"So this is what they've got you doing now? Cops and robbers?"

"I don't mind it." He thought about it. "Most days I don't mind it."

"When are you coming back?"

"Back where?"

"*Abroad*, big boy. Domestic reporting? *Metro?* Going to the *office?* You?"

"I sort of got blown up."

"I sort of didn't know it blew off your dick."

"It most certainly did not."

"Then stop acting like it."

"I think I got it pretty fucking—"

"Not any worse than a lot of hacks," she said. "I was there the day they choppered you out, remember? I *helped* them chopper you out."

"Actually, I don't remember that. Something about loss of consciousness."

"Yeah, well, look, it happens. Hrvoje, you remember, he was at the AP in Bosnia? Shot through the chest in the Congo, back on the job now, in where, I think he's in South Africa. Saw him in Addis. Santiago got airlifted out of Sarajevo, just like you. He's back. Ann got her face half–blown up in that café bomb in Amman. I was three blocks down. She had to fly to London, L.A., I forget which, for the plastic surgery. They're still picking little bits of glass out of her face. David got taken hostage. He's in—"

"Yeah yeah yeah, old home week, I hear you. But you're not seeing this right. One, I mean, I don't get to go back to another posting just because I want to. I'd have to convince them."

"Why would they need convincing?"

"Word is I got a drinking and attitude problem."

"This is new?"

"They seem to be taking it hard."

"The international press corps is a floating drunk tank, don't they know that? It's your crowd. Brits drink more than we do every day of the damn week. A hard-core drunk in New York is a social drinker in London. And the Italians! Don't even start me on my dad and his Italian buddies. The Germans, the French, probably the Spaniards, definitely the Dutch . . . remember that Polish television crew in Tuzla? Those guys were *funny*. Did you know that 'vodka' literally means 'a little water'?"

"Not everyone grows up the daughter of a globetrotting diplomat," he said. "The paper's perspective is a little more Puritanical Americana."

"Eddie just knocked back four glasses of cabernet at dinner. He—"

"We're getting off topic. I'd been bugging John to call me all day. He had some good intel."

"Yeah, well, this John person doesn't put on fishnets and heels and fuck you real good."

"He better not."

She bit her lower lip, looking down at him, a finger under his chin, eyes dilated. She softened, her back slumping, leaning over into him.

"Good. Thought you might have started playing for the other team, coming back home, finding some cute guy, planting flowers in the back, interior decorating—"

"You talking about my place?"

"It looks nicer than mine," she whispered, playful.

"Look here." He reached for his glass of wine, still on the table, making her sit up. "You can have mine, you want some more."

Moving his left hand from her waist to the small of her back, he pulled her toward him and leaned back on the couch, balancing the wine in his right hand. She came forward lightly, balanced, her knees on the couch now, straddling him, blouse still open. She took the glass from his hand and moved forward. She fluffed the skirt up so it wouldn't get caught in the bend of her legs, a movement that allowed him to slip his hands under the skirt and onto her ass, the skin so soft it made him blink. She could be so rough, one of the guys, knocking back shots in the hack hotel in whatever hellhole they were all in, and then make those little moves, so graceful, so feminine.

She reached down, with trickling fingers, to his belt buckle and zipper. She undid both, letting him free, stroking him, cupping him.

"Oh my," she said, "you got a package for me, Mr. UPS man?"

"Special delivery," he said, his breath coming short. "You can sign for this?"

"Kiss my neck," she said, "and give me the package."

Her throat humming against his lips, her back arching.

"Lower," she whispered into his ear. "Lower. Like I like it. You know."

Jimmy T's didn't have much of a crowd the next morning. It was overcast and dreary, one of those raw spring days when it was cold down to the bone and your nose itched, all that pollen. He opened the glass door of the place for Alex, letting her step inside before him, not even sure what time it was.

He had woken up just after eight thirty, gotten out of bed, and Alex said she was going to roll back over but then he said he had this rich-kid homicide to chase, and she groaned, "I am *not* even going to take a shower."

While she was getting ready, he made a call to R.J. at home, giving him the kid's name (R.J. and his longtime partner, Elwood, a painter of some distinction, recognized the family immediately), and then roughed out plans for a short daily to get the name on the record. Then he would go hard for a long takeout on the Bend, maybe for Sunday.

Alex had come downstairs then, her face puffy, hair bedraggled, wearing some clothes of his she'd pulled from the closet—sweats, rolled up at the cuffs, a T-shirt from the Chart Room in New Orleans, where he'd tended bar a million years ago. He gave her an Italian leather jacket (from Rome, when he'd been on assignment and it had gotten cold) out of the hallway closet and then they were ambling the three blocks down to Jimmy T's, the neighborhood dive tucked into a narrow old row house on East Capitol.

Alex slid around a vacant four-top right at the entrance, navigated the narrow aisle, and plunked down in a booth along the back right side. She looked around, taking in the cracked vinyl seats, the green Formica table still wet with the rings of glasses and coffee cups of the previous occupants, the tin ceiling stained colors not found in nature.

"It's so upscale," she said finally.

"I only bring the classy broads here."

Wanda came by and wiped down the table. "Wanda," he said.

"Morning, sugar. Waffle and coffee?"

"Yes, ma'am."

"What about you, sweetheart?"

"Is there a menu?" Alex asked, running her hands through her hair, pulling it back into a ponytail.

"Why don't you just tell me what you want?"

"Ah, an omelet? Onions and mushrooms, a little cheese? And toast."

Wanda, leaning over the table, finishing with the cleaning rag, "Drinking anything?"

"Orange juice. And water. Please."

Wanda nodded and left, sidestepping a chair behind her.

"And the staff is so charming," Alexis said, looking after her.

"Wanda's all right," Sully said. "Been here since Nixon. Or Kennedy. Doesn't give that good-morning, good-to-see-you bullshit."

"And you tip for this sort of service."

"My aunt works in a place like this."

"She does? Aunt who?"

"Mable. Still down in Nola. Not far from Tipitina's."

"And she's a classy broad?"

"Until you piss her off."

"Does that happen often?"

"By me? No. I got farmed out to her after my parents got put in the ground. My sister, she went to my dad's people, out in Tucson. There was not a lot of shit to give Aunt Mable, not if you had any sense. I was thirteen and change when I moved in and by the time I turned fourteen it was clear who was the chief and who was the Indian. Wonderful woman, once you get past the chain-smoking alcoholic thing, and I mean that. Love her to death. Plus, she had this fighting cock in the backyard, Rojo? You did not want to get Rojo pissed at you, either. Right here, the forearm? Rojo did that."

"You cannot keep a wild rooster in your yard."

"Who said Rojo was wild? And this was in New Orleans. You don't go messing with somebody's chickens. Marie Laveau'll turn up on your doorstep."

"You're making this up."

"You don't have to make shit up in New Orleans."

"You don't have an accent until you're drunk or start talking about back home, did you know that? Why do you say the name of the place like it's one word?"

"Because it is, *cher*."

He leaned over to brush a stray hair from her face, dangling over her right eye, smiling at her then, the sleepy eyes, the face without makeup, no earrings.

"Think anyone can tell I stayed over last night?" she said, smoothing out the ponytail.

"Whyn't you ask Wanda?"

"I don't think Wanda gives a rat's ass."

"And you ask me why I tip."

"I'm guessing you eat here more than at home."

"Breakfast, anyway. When I eat breakfast. So what's this project you're shooting? All I know is that it's about the Israeli pullout."

"Depends on the access." She shrugged, pushing back in the seat to let Wanda slide the plates in front of them and put down the coffee, juice, and water. She didn't say anything and was gone.

Alexis sliced her omelet with a fork, then took a bite. "Richard's going to write. It's going to be a three-day series, starting on a Sunday. I've been on the Lebanese side so far, the soft-tissue stuff, lives in transition, like that. Sabra and Shatila. Then you go out into the Bekaa and wonder how many people are looking at you through binoculars."

"The lovely Bekaa Valley, home to more spooks than anyplace on the planet," Sully said pleasantly, sitting back. "I's talking to this farmer out there this one time, way the hell out in this field? It's all open country, you know, the mountains in the distance. The side of the road we were on was just being planted. You can see, or be seen, for a mile in any direction. Hadn't been there five minutes and three cars pull up and stop at hundred-yard intervals. Guys get out of all three."

"Ah shit."

"I'm thinking I got to outrun these fuckers to the village or I'll get Terry Anderson's old room for the next six years. And then the guys start pulling out baskets. *Baskets*. They were picking fruit, this orchard the other side of the road."

"Sweet baby Jesus."

"Blood pressure dropped about eighty points in three seconds."

"You miss it, don't you?"

"Who wouldn't?"

"See, that's what I mean. We got to get you back out in the real world, doing real stuff. They got you doing what? A piece on some rich kid who got popped in the Bend? Tooting nose candy? So what?"

"The piece I'm doing, it's more on Frenchman's Bend. The rich kid's murder looks like the way in. The Bend, it turns out, is the murder capital of the murder capital. It's the deadliest spot, per square foot, in the deadliest city, per 100,000, in America."

"Well," she said, chewing her toast. "Wait a minute. Doesn't sound all that bad, you put it that way. You want me to shoot it?"

He was drowning his waffle in syrup and looked up. "You said last night the great Alexis de Rossi was on R and R."

"Yeah, well, maybe I could shoot a splashy something for you, for the Sunday takeout. I'm not running out there to do a daily on this rich little snot, I'll tell you that, but I wouldn't mind seeing what you're up to. Keep an eye on you while I'm here."

"How long is that again?"

"A week. Ten days. You know home leave. Doctor, dentist, bosses, shop-ops."

The thing he liked about Alex—well, other than she'd never ask him about Nadia, instinctively knowing not to intrude on the truly private, and that she looked fabulous with her clothes off—was that he didn't have to tell her the Bend was dicey, that it was violent, and ask her did she really want to do this. Alex, she'd done the civil war in Nicaragua, shit in El Salvador he didn't even want to *know* about, guerrillas in the jungle, and that was before he'd met her in South Africa. The Bend wouldn't come close to making her Top 10 Hellhole list.

"If they're eyeballing you to make sure you're good to go back abroad," she said, finishing off the omelet—god, the woman could eat—"then knock this story out of the park, pass Go and collect your two hundred. Maybe I get some art to help get them juiced. Nobody on Metro is doing shit, artwise, at least that I can see. And stop popping off at people in the office. Your name came up at dinner. Eddie said you were 'brilliant but erratic,' and I nearly spewed my pinot. You get crossways of Eddie? You are *so* fucked."

"Great tip."

"See? That. That's going to get you in trouble. Or more of it. Now. Today. Do some fucking work. Where you headed?"

"Track down the dead kid's mom, his friends, touch base with some folks in the hood, maybe the cop who caught the case."

"Good. You need to start wowing them again."

"Second person in two days to tell me that."

"They seem to be pegging you as more erratic than brilliant."

"Keep fucking with me, go ahead."

"Get this thing rolling, I'll swing down by the Bend tomorrow."

"Tomorrow? What is it you're so busy with today?"

"The Madison," she said, stifling a yawn. "I'll be very busy at the Madison's spa. I need a massage and a good nap. Some Cajun kept me up half of last night. What's with you and the bondage thing, anyhow?"

FIVE

BACK HOME WITH Alexis bundled off in a taxi, he went into the kitchen and made himself a morning mint julep. The pewter cup frozen, the tang of the herb, the frozen ice rattling—got*damn*. Bourbon. It was evidence there might be a benevolent God after all.

He sat down and looked at the phone. The night and morning with Alexis had cheered him, given him energy and a sense of calm, but there was no getting around looking at the worst part of the job: calling the mother of the recently and unnaturally dead.

Another long pull on the julep and the dread of punching the digits eased the tiniest of fractions, some tic in the back of his head faded, pressure being released from a valve. He blinked. He let out a long, slow breath, reminding himself to clean up any hints of his accent. Then he quit dicking around and punched in the number for the home of Delores Ellison and from that moment on, he knew it wasn't going to end until he could tell her what had happened to her son. You didn't wade into the realm of the dead unless you had a purpose.

The phone rang several times, and when it picked up he was about to start his spiel into voice mail when a woman's voice said hello.

"Hello?" he said.

"Yes, hello?" The voice sounded tired, exasperated.

"Hello, ah, I thought I hit the recording. My name's Sully Carter, I'm a reporter for the paper? And I was trying to reach Delores Ellison, in reference to her son, William Ellison."

Air.

Then, "Yes. This is his mother. This is Delores."

He blinked twice, rapidly, kicking into gear. He had thirty seconds, perhaps a minute to gain her trust or lose her. "Ms. Ellison, I hate to bother you, but it's my job today to write a story about William and who he was and, what—what—all you lost with him."

More air.

Then the woman's voice said, "Billy. We called him Billy. His dad, we called William."

"Yes, ma'am, Billy. I—"

"Everybody who knew him two minutes called him Billy."

"Yes, ma'am."

"His father's been dead fifteen years now."

"I heard about that, and I was sorry to have done so."

"I just—I just—thank you for your interest in my son. He was the last piece of me on this earth. He was the last of the family, of the entire Ellison line."

Medicated. She was laced on the stuff. The slowed speech, the precise diction, the world seeming to move at underwater speed, the world above water too painful to navigate, the crushing burden of sunlight.

"Yes, ma'am. You do have someone with you right now, don't you?"

"Yes—what? Yes. A lot of people are here."

"That's great. That's the best way to handle it. Ms. Ellison, I do not want to intrude in any way, but I have a very short period of time in which to write a story about who Billy was, and what he had going for him in life, and I hate—well, I just don't talk to people over the phone in this type of situation. I'd like to come by for a few minutes and sit down next to you for a minute and let you talk about Billy. Just as little or as much as you'd like."

He pinched one eye shut, hating how he sounded. Even working from a place of sincerity, cold-calling the relatives of the dead could only sound like a ghoulish pitch.

Still, you choked that down and you started with Momma. No matter where you went on the planet, if somebody under thirty got dead, the first thing any half-ass hack did was turn around to the next guy standing there and say, "Where's his momma?"

Dads were not terrible by default. You could work with Dad, if you could find him. But the problem was, when dads lost their children? They tended to be angry or stoic or ready to whip your ass just for showing up. Worst, the absolute worst of all, they'd break down crying, great gut-wrenching sobs that left them leaning on a woman's shoulder or bent over with hands on knees or—Sully'd had this happen—a grown man falling over on you, keening and sobbing, and you could feel the soul leaving the body, a great black blob that would then crawl over your skin and the flesh would shrivel and there was nothing to do but absorb it, let it go through you.

And the guy in HR asking him, Why do you drink?

Maternal grief was as terrifying in its own way, true. The absolute hollow to the eyes, the voice you had to lean forward to hear, the way they would reach for your arm as they stood up and it felt like a leaf, like a dry and brittle leaf that fluttered across your wrist. Still, this was more in the course of gender expectations. The hollow-eyed mother was a kind of shorthand for Grief Eternal. And since newspapers were a kind of societal shorthand, everyone just understood it better. So you wound up going for Momma.

Down the line, Delores Ellison was still considering his proposition, breathing lightly into the phone. Sully tried to picture the room she was in, what she was looking at—the refrigerator, the television on with the sound off, pictures of her dead son, herself in the mirror—and what was going through her mind.

"Ms. Ellison?"

"Yes?"

"Just making sure you're still with me," he said.

She coughed drily, and finally said, "I think it would be helpful if you came by and I explained some things to you."

Holding the phone in his right hand, he pumped his left fist, the interview he had to have, falling right in his lap. The tic in the back of his head loosened some more, and he felt himself coming into the groove of it, the mojo you had to have for a story like this.

"You want to come right now?" she asked.

"That would probably be best," he said.

"There are all these television trucks out on the street, but I don't think I want to go outside."

"No, ma'am. I don't blame you."

"But you'll come here? You can come to the front and ask for Ivan. He's from the funeral home. He has the list."

"The list?"

"Of people who can come in."

"Right."

"I'll tell him to put your name on it. You're not going to bring anyone else in with you, are you?"

"It's your house, ma'am."

"Okay. Okay. And what did you say your name was again? I'm sorry, I know you told me, but it's just flown right out of my mind. I can't seem to re—"

"Sully. Sully Carter."

"From the paper."

"That's me. I'll come look for Ivan, and he'll bring me to you."

"Right. Right. And when did you say you were coming?"

"Right now, Mrs. Ellison. What's the address?"

"The address. Of my house? It's ah . . . We moved over here years ago, it's a nice street. Could you ask someone when you get here? They can tell you?"

"Yes, ma'am. That won't be a problem. I'm walking out the door."

He hung up and then clicked the phone back on and dialed the paper's news research desk, moving upstairs for a change of clothes. Susan picked up as he made it to the top of the steps, and he said, "Hey, it's me, redhead," and then, "I need an address," and gave her Delores Ellison's name.

"Just a sec," she said, and he heard her keyboard clacking. "Why are you breathing hard?"

"I just came up the steps."

"Twelve stories?"

"My leg," he said.

"Get off your ass a little more," she said cheerfully. "Here it is—1729 Crestwood Northwest. You know where it is? The Gold Coast, just off Sixteenth?"

"You mean like Crestwood the street, not just the neighborhood?"

"Yeah. It's this half-circle thing. Go across that bridge on Connecticut, the one with the lion statues, hook a left on Shepherd. Crestwood is your first left."

The home of the Ellisons, D.C. society for a century, was among a tree-shaded collection of brick houses, well spaced, all along the right side of the street, with Rock Creek Park on the left-hand side, dropping away steeply down a hill, a forest in the middle of the city. A long line of black-hued limos and Lincolns and BMWs and Mercedes and Escalades and other Cadillacs lined the curb, people visiting Delores, the house with the hub of black-suited drivers congregating in the brick driveway, a pair of television trucks out front.

It was a handsome, two-story, acid-washed brick colonial, dark shutters, a two-car garage, manicured lawn, and arched windows. The add-on to the downhill side, also brick, featured a huge bay window. The open curtains allowed a view of a baby grand piano. He idled the bike past the house, away from the television trucks, and tucked it between a couple of the black Lincolns, killing the engine quickly, as even that seemed too loud for the address.

"Well-bred," he said softly to himself, taking the helmet off, strapping it to the bike. It was a well-bred, old-money kind of place. He wondered if anyone living on the street had considered the middle distance of the western prairie at sunset, driving at a million miles an hour due west, the warm Pacific somewhere ahead, the endless rolling Plains, and he decided they probably had not. This was the East Coast, closed in and sheltered, a narrow horizon, the idea of a world beyond the Beltway both obscure and insignificant.

The cluster of drivers at the end of the driveway eyed him up as he walked past, mostly black but some white, the guys who didn't speak much English standing off by themselves, propping their patent leathers on the bumper of a Lincoln, muttering in what was probably Amharic, if he guessed right. There wasn't anybody who looked like an Ivan, so he just nodded and they nodded back, looking at the bike and letting out on the exhale of a smoke, not giving a damn about who he was or why he was here. He headed to the house like he was five minutes late, not even glancing at the television trucks. He didn't want anyone over there calling out his name, piggybacking their way in.

The door was opening as he approached—people leaving—and he quick-stepped onto the patio. As he did, a sturdy black man appeared at his left. It was like he materialized, coming out from behind a column or something on the porch. His face was set in a grimace and he was dressed in a dark suit and sunglasses. He shot an arm in front of Sully's chest, like the rail across train tracks stopping traffic, and looking at him through the glasses, said, "No."

Sully took it with a smile, letting the man get in front of him, coming to a stop, raising his eyebrows in a gesture of expectation.

"Ivan?" he said, "Hey. Ms. Ellison said you'd be looking for me. I'm on the list."

The door, when it swung open again, he couldn't help but think *medieval*, it was so oaken, so heavy, the air behind it so dark, so dank. Ivan followed him in and closed it behind them, and the low murmur of voices came up in the crowded entryway, the drawing room set off to the right, also heavily populated. Ivan put a hand gently on Sully's back, guiding him down the hall through a knot of hushed, well-dressed people, most of them holding stemware filled with orange juice, half of them turning to look at him, a new face in the gloom.

They made their way off the hallway, through the drawing room, the house opening before him in warm earth tones, a stairway now directly in his path, heavy wooden spindles, another parlor to his left. The illumination was from a series of lamps rather than overhead lighting, the curtains drawn, adding to the funereal air. The paintings on the walls were oils of ancestors and seasides, an island with Cape Cod houses along the dunes, and it dawned on him, thirty seconds in the door, that the Ellisons owned rather than rented on Martha's Vineyard, a nice summer place of the type for which he could not afford a single mortgage payment. A Supreme Court justice, that one who always looked constipated, sat on a couch on his left, the No. 3 in the Justice Department conferred with a serious-looking woman in a suit, the head of the city council was to his right, a couple of congressional reps, a silver-haired guy who might be a senator, a lot of middle-aged men and women in expensive suits . . . Sully guessed they were from Stevens's law firm, Hill staffers, or corporate honchos he didn't know. Robert Barnes, the mayor, corrupt soul that he was, materialized out of the gloom, a flicker of a smile crossing his face. He took Sully's right hand to shake and patted his shoulder with his left as he passed, and Sully wondered if he learned that grip-and-pat move in some sleazy politicians' school.

They kept moving deeper into the house, passing more knots of people, Ivan's hand gentle but steady on his back. They stalled for a moment and a woman in black slacks, white shirt, black vest, and a bow tie glided up on his left, a silver tray with the glasses he'd seen a moment ago. He nodded thanks and took an orange juice—he always accepted hospitality in a subject's home—but it did cross his mind that Delores Ellison either had staff or had someone call a catering company within hours of finding out her only child had been murdered. That was pretty brutal social efficiency.

And suddenly there she was, a small clump of people parting, a tall, athletic rather than delicate woman, standing there like a monument, her hair pulled back in a mercilessly perfect bun, setting off the diamond stud earrings. She was standing beside a coffee table and wing-back chair, having stood to see her guests away. She was wearing a black pant-suit and when Ivan leaned forward and took both her hands in his and whispered in her ear, her gaze turned over the man's shoulder to Sully and the faintest of smiles etched the corners of her mouth. It did not extend to her eyes, which settled on his for a moment while she moved around Ivan to offer her hand. As she said hello and thanked him for coming, her eyes darted to the left and then right behind him, that Washington disease of looking for more important people in the room.

"Mr. Carter, thank you for coming so quickly," she said, her eyes finally coming to rest on his, Sully guessing there was nobody better to talk to for the moment. "I'm just not going to be able to talk later in the day. It's—it's—it's just so . . . overwhelming."

"I'll just stay a minute," he said. "It's kind of you to—"

"Billy was just here three days ago. Right here. Right in the house and now—now I don't even know where he is. They're doing something with him. They're doing something. Someone killed him, and now someone else is doing something to him."

"You mean at the funeral home?"

"Yes. I mean, someplace like that. The medical examiners, the coroner's, the funeral home, I don't even *know.*"

His eyes searched hers, seeking a glint of something that might tell him what they had her on, what chemicals were flowing through her brain. It would let him know if he could quote her or not, if she was in command of what she was saying or just babbling a brook of Valium-induced speech that she would never remember having uttered.

"It's a terrible day," he said. "It's not something I enjoy, having to intrude, to come by. But I think it's important we, the paper, mark Billy's passing. We can't just ignore it."

"Of course, no, no, of course. I would like to help—I—would you rather talk in the kitchen or the parlor?" she asked. "We can talk in either."

"Is this the parlor?" When she replied yes, he immediately said, "The kitchen." She nodded and turned that way, touching Ivan on his arm, dispatching him, and Sully was following her now. The kitchen was better because it was usually the most informal room in any house, and he wanted her to feel at ease. It turned out to be an elegant, well-appointed room, marble island, large pots and pans dangling from above. The kitchen would suit. It was empty, save for one woman in the same bow-tie outfit pulling things out of the refrigerator, which looked to be about half a football field away. Delores gestured toward a small table set near a window with drawn curtains.

"Billy," he said, sitting down, smiling softly. "Billy. I didn't know him, Mrs. Ellison. Not at all. Don't know what his voice sounded like, how he walked, if his smile was crooked or straight. I hate to barge right in here, but can you tell me some things about him like that? I don't mean where he went to school or that he wanted to be a lawyer."

She looked at him, appearing surprised at the nature of the question—she looked like she had a spiel ready to unload—and then she looked off to her right, to a clock on the kitchen wall, or something in the middle distance that he couldn't see.

"His—his—his—heart," she said. "Billy had such a good *heart*. Always had. When he was three—I think it was three; he might have been four—there was a tiny little frog in a puddle in the backyard. A tadpole, really, I guess, he couldn't even really hop. Something was wrong with him. Billy put him on a leaf and brought him inside and asked me to help the frog."

Sully smiled, writing furiously. "What a gentle little boy."

"He had tears in his eyes. He was crying."

"And he stayed like that, you say?" The gentle prompt for another story.

"Always. He didn't play sports, other than cross-country; he just didn't like hitting other boys. He played the piano. He loved to read. Especially history, black history, you know, sort of how we, the Ellisons, came to be."

"And Mr. Sanders died, what was that, 1984?"

"January 13, 1985. A single-car wreck. He was driving home from Dulles, late, after a flight coming in from Chicago. It had been snowing. Billy was six."

"And Mr. Sanders, he—"

"William. We called him William, and we called our son Billy."

"And, to be clear, Billy's last name was Ellison?"

She smiled, nodding her head, slightly off to the left, with an almost imperceptible hunch of the shoulders. "A little odd, people said, at least at the time Billy was born. Things have changed now. So many single mothers, I suppose. But yes. The Ellison name is, is rich in history, but not in male descendants. I am an only child, as Billy was an only child. He was the only one to carry on the name of Nathaniel Ellison, the patriarch, as I'm sure you know. William understood. We gave Billy the Sanders surname as his middle, to carry that along. But the Ellison name was his last."

"And Mr. Sanders—"

"Was from Georgia."

It left her lips like an indictment, as if that explained everything he needed to know. He was far more familiar with condescension from northern whites than blacks, but the tang of it was just the same. He wondered if Delores Ellison understood that she was, herself, from south of the Mason-Dixon.

"I see."

"He overcame so much. Served in the Marines in Vietnam. Then Harvard Law. He was only thirty-eight when he died, but already was the first black partner at the firm."

"He was—"

"Billy attended Sidwell, where he was senior class president. The first black child to do so. Then he went to Georgetown. Dean's list every semester. History major. He was planning to stay at Georgetown for law school, though he hadn't ruled out Harvard."

Sully was writing all of this down, letting her talk to the air, but he couldn't help but notice that in spite of his request for the intimate, when she ticked off the measures of her only child's life, the things she mentioned were items of achievement, name-dropping Sidwell, the private school the presidents' kids usually attended. These were the markers of her life that she felt worth telling and important.

"It's quite an impressive set of achievements," he said, playing along, looking up, making eye contact, crossing his legs at the knee. "It seemed especially tragic, a young man with so much promise. Just to check, have the police contacted you with any leads at all? Possibilities, suspects?"

"Why—what—why do you ask?"

"Well, because the police would tell you things they wouldn't necessarily tell the public, and that might keep me from making some sort of mistake in the paper. The police seem to think he may have been shot in Frenchman's Bend."

Her shoulders seemed to lock in place. "There's a great deal of information about Billy's death that isn't public," she said, choosing her words, "but it isn't at the precinct."

He waited, but there wasn't anything.

"And where would I find that?" he said finally.

"With Shellie."

It was a pet peeve when people did this, make an obscure statement and force him to ask a follow-up question because of the intentional vagueness of their initial response. He shifted on the wooden kitchen chair—hell, it was probably mahogany—and said, gamely, to increase her sense of control of the situation, "Shellie?"

"My employer. William's former partner."

"Shellie Stevens," he said.

"Yes."

"Ah. It's none of mine, Ms. Ellison, but since you mention it, why would your employer be in possession of information about your son's death?"

"Because he's conducting his own investigation," she said. "He's hired private investigators."

"Ah."

He eyed her pleasantly, as if this made sense, as if everybody's son got killed and their employer funded some sort of parallel homicide investigation. But the look coming back at him now was no longer so doe-eyed and confused. Her eyes seemed more black than brown, her manner more focused, more of an air of condescension.

Sully set his pen down on his notebook.

"Do the police know of this private eye investigation?"

"Of course. They seem to have no idea who killed Billy. It's shocking. You hear of killings, homicides, you expect the police to know the, the landscape. They don't seem to. No ideas at all. Shellie is trying to help. You can't have any idea of how it is, your only child a murder victim, and for all you know, the killer watching your house each day."

"No, ma'am."

"Shellie hired private investigators last night. They have more time and, if I may, more energy than the D.C. police force, such as it is."

"It's good you can do that. So many parents I talk to, in situations like this, they feel helpless."

She nodded emphatically, as if he were a slow student. "That's why I want you to ask Shellie anything you need to know. You'll need to ask him if it's okay that I talked to you, and ask him what I can be quoted as saying."

He had to work to keep the poker face. There was a conscious effort not to fold his arms—you had to make every gesture an indication of being open—but now he leaned back in his chair, making no move toward writing in the notebook. "I'm not following. Shellie Stevens is your employer, and you want to check with him if you can say something about your son?"

Delores Ellison leaned forward now, a half smile, indulging him but not dismissing him.

"Well, like everything else he does, if you know him, Shellie doesn't want any publicity. He's already met with the police, with the mayor's office, the DOJ, the coroner. I wouldn't want to just say something in the paper without him saying, you know, okay on that."

"So, you'd like me to ask him myself?"

"That would be wonderful," she said. "And could you do me a favor? Could you just not mention that you and I talked today? That you just came to his office and asked if you could talk to me?"

"Well." This was getting creepy. "Why would he be expecting me to ask permission to talk to you?"

"You know Shellie?"

"Of him."

"Interviewed him?"

"To the best of my knowledge, no one ever has, at least on the record."

"Then you know the value he puts on being invisible. On not having his name, the firm's name mentioned, at all. His whole practice is based—"

"On not leaving fingerprints," Sully said. "I know. So why would he talk to me about this?"

"Oh, he's not," she said. "He's absolutely not. That's not what I was saying. You'll contact the firm, leave a message that you'd like to talk to me off the record, about Billy, and that you're touching base with him out of respect for the firm's privacy."

Heat rose behind his eyelids. "The firm's privacy is a position they take to the rest of the world, particularly the media," he said, as evenly as possible. "That's not necessarily the position we'd take toward them. Look, it's up to you if you talk to us, no one else. If you're trying to tell me you're feeling some pressure from your employer not to talk about the murder investigation of your son, then the paper would take a very dim view of that and we'd—"

"Do you want to talk to me, and maybe see the files his investigators produce?"

"Of course," he said. Playing dumb.

"Then do it his way. Shellie's not going to say anything to you, but if it's okay, he'll tell me he got this call from you, and ask if I want to talk to you, and so on. Really. He's doing so much. You don't understand."

He nodded. The number of people in this town who lectured him, who told him he didn't know what he was doing, that he didn't understand, that . . . yeah, okay, whatever. It was endemic, this superiority complex, these fuckers—you give them some money, make them partner, a strategist, you get them close to a congressional committee on fuckall, they start acting like they legislated the goddamn world into being. He leaned forward in the chair now, picked up the pen, put it to paper, stuffing his contempt back down into a tube of social propriety.

"And what number should I call Mr. Stevens on, ma'am?"

SIX

SEVEN HOURS TILL deadline and he still had his dick in his hand. Jesus.

He made two calls, right foot tapping.

The first one, Stevens's secretary answered and said that the great man was not available until four thirty but she would pencil Sully in then.

The second one was to Jeff Weaver, the homicide cop John had designated to lead the investigation. Weaver said he didn't have any time and Sully told him that you got to eat sometime and the man said he would be down at the Bend, round about two, and if Sully wanted to try to catch him there then, well, hey, fine, none off his.

That gave him about two hours.

Billy had been a history freak, his mom had said, so Sully made a couple of calls to where he'd been a student, Georgetown's history department, sitting there in the chilly windless shade on the bike outside the Ellisons'. He got a receptionist on the line and it turned out Billy boy had been in the American Studies program, and the offices were right down on Prospect Street, near the top of the *Exorcist* steps. Fifteen minutes later, he was down there, pulling out his press ID, a little blue card on a lanyard, hanging it around his neck so everyone could see it, and then started pegging bright, fresh-faced students for intel. Of course, a rich dead kid like that on the evening news, one of only three black kids in the American Studies program—hey, man, *everybody* knew Billy.

The second guy he talked to said he knew Billy, liked Billy, had been to some parties with Billy, but that Elliot? Elliot, man, he *really* knew Billy, and Elliot, you could find him—wait, what time was it? Twelve thirty? Elliot always ate lunch in the cafeteria, like, every single day in the same place.

Elliot was sitting upright and alone, a skinny kid eating a tuna-fish sandwich out of a ziplock bag in the back right corner, looking down at a textbook. He half-stood when the kid made the introductions and left. Sully took the chair across the table and Elliot sat back down. He had glasses, square bifocals with black frames, and Sully wondered if that look had gone retro-hip, Elliot's flannel shirt and jeans, the brown shoes, the whole getup singing nerd.

Elliot said he'd heard about Billy last night—officially, because he didn't trust the television news and didn't know anyone who did—but that he had known something was wrong because Billy had not come to classes or lunch Friday or Monday and that was just so unlike him.

"Two days, no lunch, hunh?" Sully said. "I'm guessing he must have eaten with you most days."

Elliot regarded him blankly. "Who told you that?"

"Nobody," Sully said. "Well, you. You said he didn't come to lunch for two days. You would have had to be eating with him on a pretty regular basis to know he wasn't in his usual spot, right?"

Elliot thought about it. "I guess." And then he said, "Why did Ted bring you here?"

"Because, well, I don't know. Ask him. I was over there at the American Studies program office, you know, where Billy was majoring, and asking around, and Ted said that you knew Billy pretty well. Then he brought me over here, looking for you."

"I eat here every day," Elliot said. "I'm a senior. I'm in the ASP, too."

"Well, I guess that's why Ted brought me here. So Billy must have sat right here where I am?"

Elliot looked uncomfortable but took a bite of his sandwich and said, "Yes. The next chair over. No. To your left."

"So you guys were pretty good friends. How did you say you found out he had, ah, died?"

"The television, like I said. And then everybody was talking about it. Well, wait. First everybody was saying, 'Where's Billy?' 'cause he wasn't around for a couple of days, and that was weird. You'd usually see him. He was around. And then there was the television and then all the professors knew. They put out a statement."

"Before you found out he was dead, did you try to reach him? Since he didn't show for lunch, or class?"

"Oh, yeah, to see if he was at home sick or something."

"And he didn't answer?"

"Well, he was dead, so, no."

Sully flipped a page in the notebook and resisted the urge to lean right over and smack the little twerp, a line like that. "So a couple of days would have gone by before you called him, right?"

"I guess. It was the weekend. I wasn't looking at a calendar. He wasn't at class, wasn't at lunch, so I called his apartment. There was no answer."

"Now I'm with you. Remember the last time you saw him?"

"You're asking a lot of questions."

"It's sort of the job description."

Elliot squinted. "Thursday? Thursday afternoon. Lunch. I saw him at lunch on Thursday."

"Hunh. Right here? He seem upset about anything?"

Elliot shook his head, loose black bangs, a library reading-room pallor to his features, the kid reminding him of a young Lou Reed. "No. Not really."

"What'd you guys talk about?"

"My thesis. I'm wrapping it up. It's a senior year project. You have to have it to graduate in American Studies. It's a multidisciplinary degree. Arts, sciences, politics. You have to pick an era. So I'm near the end of it. Billy, he was asking about that, since he had his coming up next year."

"What was he going to do it on?"

"Something about black life in D.C. in the 1920s and 1930s, you know, the New Negro Movement, the Harlem Renaissance. He was researching it, tying it in to his family."

"Un-hunh," Sully said. "Where was Billy's place? His apartment?"

"It was . . . there—what is that, Thirty-fourth Street? I always just walked over, you know, you ever do that? Just walk someplace all the time and not know the streets? I don't even know the address. He had some parties, sometimes. It was before you get to Wisconsin. Lots of row houses. He was staying in one of those little old wooden places, you know that looks like a can of saltine crackers turned on its side? He was renting one of those."

"You guys hang out?"

"Some, I don't know. Maybe. What do you mean, 'hang out'? We had History 181 together. It's a req."

And then, with that same flat voice, devoid of inflection, not looking up, with all the other information he was going to get already in hand, Sully tossed out the real question, the reason he'd come. "So Billy was one of the campus hookups for a little ganja and coke, right?"

Elliot stopped chewing and looked at him. "Not that I know of."

"Hunh."

"Why do you even think that?"

"Well, the place that police think he was shot? It's a major drug market. Hard to picture him having another reason for being over there."

Elliot resumed chewing and didn't say anything.

"So, okay, any problems you'd noticed about Billy recently? Either last Friday or before? He angry, scared, upset? Anything at all?"

Dabbing a napkin to his lips, Elliot said, "No. Well."

"Yeah?"

"Well, what we talked about, not so much history, but what we talked about a lot, was him and his mother."

"His mother? Him and his mother? What about them?"

"Well, she was kind of, and don't print this, but she was kind of a pain. They'd just gotten in a huge fight on Friday night, the day after I saw him last. He called me, crying, really really upset."

"What about?"

"Ah, I don't know. She just came down on him so hard all the time. She was just so . . . negative."

Sully making eye contact, trying to draw something from the kid. "I could see how you could kind of say that."

"And Billy was so open with her, so honest, and she just—it was all about law school, the career, making partner, doing as well as his dad."

"Hunh. And Billy, he just wasn't—"

Elliot was looking over the table at him, a quizzical expression crossing his freckled face, his manner so earnest, god you had to love kids, they were just—

"I mean," he said, "you know that Billy was gay, right? That we were partners? That this is what we're talking about?"

SEVEN

THEY HAD PUT yellow crime scene tape up at the bottom of P Street, blocking off the sidewalk that led down to the Bend. There was a crime scene truck and one marked vehicle and three or four unmarked Crown Vics that might as well have been painted iridescent orange for all the good it did. A uniformed cop stopped him at the tape, but Sully showed him his ID and told him Weaver was waiting on him. The uniform rattled that off on his walkie-talkie, and a corresponding squawk—Sully had no idea what it said—led him to raise the tape, looking off in the distance, letting Sully under, not really giving a damn about it one way or the other.

Weaver, the detective, was way down there, one hand against the be-draggled cherry tree on the Bend's namesake knob of land, his tie flutter-ing off his chest and back down again in the wind. Weaver had dark slacks and an unbuttoned sport coat, the gun holstered on the right hip. His sunglasses were pushed up on his head and he was eating a sandwich still half in a plastic wrapper. In his left hand he held a can of soda.

It was five minutes after two. Five hours, more or less, till deadline.

"How you living, detective?" Sully said, raising his voice to be heard above the wind. There were two techs working around the set of small orange cones in the grass, more or less in a triangle, fifty feet forward, nearer the water. They looked up at Sully, then at Weaver, then turned back, poring over the grass, the dirt.

Weaver, still chewing, held a hand up, a stop sign, then rolled the fingers forward, as in gimme a minute, while he finished. "We got a location," he said, taking a slurp of the soda, "of a pool of blood over there. And a shoe, down by the water."

"So this is what John was talking about, the new evidence. They Ellison's? The blood? The shoe?"

"Got to wait for a match on either," he said. "Techs just scraped the blood this morning. It wasn't bad cop work. We'd foot-walked the place twice, missed it. It's over there near that red little flag, see that? Some grass, by that patch of dirt? Looks like somebody tried to kick dirt over it, bury it. The shoe was down in the rocks there, with some other trash, where you see the red flag with the number two on it. His mother IDed it as his, for what that's worth."

"It's been, what, two days now? Will they be able to match the blood?"

A breeze came up and it fluttered Weaver's plastic sandwich wrapper and he had to snap a hand out to catch it, shrugging off the question. Sully didn't know much about him, only that he was a uniform who had made detective four or five years back and had a solid rep, particularly down here in 1-D. Late thirties, a shade over six feet, serious time in the gym. If he hit you—and Sully didn't doubt he'd popped some noncompliant dudes upside the head—you'd stay hit. He was lifting the bread on his sandwich, looking critically inside, then replacing it. "This, what we're talking about, it's off the record, right?"

Sully rolled his eyes and nodded. "I won't attribute it to you. Just a law enforcement source."

"Good, good. Well, see, the blood will only match by type, so it won't say it was him, just indicate if it was somebody with the same type. It's good for excluding people, but not for positive ID. The shoe—now, that's better, but without the blood, it could have just washed up from when he was swimming. If we can match the blood, though, that, with the shoe, then I'm feeling good about saying he got popped right here."

"Sure."

"Yeah, but even then? We got a decedent and we know where he went down. Hooray for our team. But we got no wits, we got no weapon, we got no ballistics worth having, we got no prints."

"What about the ticktock? When was the last time somebody saw him?"

"That we know about right now, Sunday night. At his mother's. Leaves and then it's just into the void. Doesn't go to classes Monday. If that gunshot, the one that got called in? If that matches up with him, which I'm thinking it does, then he got popped about a quarter of midnight Monday."

"So he was dead when he went in the water?"

"Yeah. No water in the lungs, no aspirated anything."

"Any idea how long he was dead before he got tossed in?"

A shrug. "Long enough not to be breathing no more."

"Toxicology?"

"Not back yet."

"Jesus."

"I told you. You want to boost your closure stats, you catch a domestic with six wits and the dumbass still standing there with the knife. You catch the shooting at the McDonald's, the one on Pennsylvania right by the bridge over the Anacostia? You remember that, last year? The whole thing on video, the license plates, and we look it up, and they still got the Big Mac wrappers in the car?"

Sully, nodding, thinking to himself that what you really didn't want to catch was the competently carried-out drug crew execution, particularly when the victim was then tossed in the channel, which then buggered the autopsy.

"This thing, it's a bad case," Sully said.

"It's a bad case," Weaver said. "But, now, look here. We had another decedent right over there on the edge of the park, last week. Thursday, to be exact. Four days before the Ellison thing."

"Hunh," Sully said. "Didn't hear about it."

"This kid's momma wasn't rich," Weaver said, "so who did? One Demetrius Allan Byrd, twenty-two, known to law enforcement."

"For?"

A sigh. "Dee Dee was a regular in the M Street Crew, the Hall brothers' outfit. Tony and Carlos. The twins. Not exactly what I'd call a major player, but he wasn't selling no dime bags, either. More a runner to the runners, that level right in there. He starts acting up a month or so back. Telling people what to do, using product like he paid for it."

"Uh-oh."

"You fucking-A, uh-oh. And so Dee Dee, he gets to instigating with the South Caps, beefing for no reason. The way it breaks down, South Capitol Street runs north to south, right? And M Street intersects, east to west. Now. That South Cap–M Street intersection, about a block around it, that's open turf. It's the DM-fucking-Z. Otherwise, South Cap runs their avenue, M Street runs theirs, and the world spins.

"But Dee Dee, he goes up to that McDonald's on South Cap? Clear South Cap territory. *Clear.* He moves a little product out of his car, strolls on inside, gets, I don't know, a burger and fries and then gets his whip cleaned up right next door at Splash. Sitting out front, chewing on a toothpick, talking shit with the Mexican ladies, the ones that dry off the car, do the detailing. That's just asking for it."

"What happened?"

"The car came out of the wash clean and had three bullet holes in the side by the time he made the light at P."

"So his demise a few weeks later was not unexpected."

"Dee Dee was moving new product. Clean, nearly uncut. Would take the top of your head off. Plus, the way he was dealing it, the way he was acting—"

"Says that he was trying to start up his own operation."

Weaver nodded.

"So, the connection here," Sully said, "if there's any, is that Billy Ellison was what, picking stuff up to sell back in Georgetown? To his gay buddies up there on O Street?"

Weaver looked up at him then, the chin coming up a tick, the eyes holding.

"So you got that, too. The gay thing. Let's just say the investigation is wide open right at this point here."

"But, I mean, the Bend is M Street's turf, the Hall brothers?"

"Yeah. For years."

"Who's running South Caps these days? I don't even know."

"Terry Mungo. T-Money."

Sully, thinking it out, thinking that the issue was that D.C. didn't have proper gangs, like the Crips and the Bloods in L.A. or the Folks and People alliances in Chicago. Those were big-city crime organizations and what they did made a certain business sense.

D.C. was a small town and the drug business was run by neighborhood-based affiliations, crews, guys who had grown up together and had known one another since childhood. It was, in its own way, a brilliant business model: an enterprise that incubated for years of shared existence before the doors ever opened for customers. It was impervious to infiltration; if you weren't in when you were six years old, you didn't get in. Likewise, if you ever got busted and thought about flipping, testifying for the state? All your former friends knew where your momma lived, your sister and her baby lived. . . . Somebody in your family would be dead because of you. But the flaw in this business model was that since it was guys who had known each other since Head Start, shooting wars would take off from shit that happened fifteen years ago, and it would never make sense to anybody outside.

"You guys braced the Halls?"

Weaver snorted. "This morning. For what it was worth. Tweedle Dee and Dum. Didn't say shit."

"Which one of them runs the show, you think?"

"Tony does a lot of the business, can figure the profit margin on three keys of coke while he's snorting a line for the test. Carlos, he's not quite so bright like that, but the boy ain't simple, either."

"You—"

"They was looking—this was a couple years back now, I'm gonna say ninety-six—looking for this dude from Brookland who had stiffed them on a payment. They staked out his place but it was the dude's girlfriend what came home first. Jalinda. Girl's name was Jalinda. They grab her, throw her in the back of a van, drive her all over, take turns slapping her around, then, when she wouldn't tell them when the dude was going to be home, they rape her in the back there while they drive around the Beltway. She kept begging them to let her see her baby before they killed her—she had a one-year-old, over at her momma's—and they didn't take that, obviously. After they got tired of fucking her, they beat her to death with a pair of garden shears they had in the back of the van. Threw her body in a trash dumpster on the back end of Capitol Hill. So, you ask me, which one of them does what, I say to you, this is a distinction without a difference."

"Jesus," Sully said. "But, I mean, how do you know that?"

Weaver took a bite of his sandwich. "Driver. Dude driving the van."

"Good god, he talked?"

"I mean he talked to me, and he talked to me 'cause he went to Eastern High, two years before my little brother. I been knowing him since he was five."

"So why didn't you charge the Halls?"

"Cause Driver Man, he said he'd rather do the time for what we pinched him on, possession with intent, than flip. He wanted me to know why he wasn't flipping, and that was 'cause he had a sister."

Sully watched the water picking up into little whitecaps out in the channel, the wind coming up now, and he was reminding himself to write all of this down as soon as he left. He started writing this shit down in front of Weaver, he'd spook.

Weaver put a fist over his mouth and burped lightly. "Which is all to say, the Bend ain't for amateurs, and little rich kid Billy Ellison? He was in way over his head down here. Goldfish swimming with the hammerheads."

EIGHT

THREE HOURS TO deadline by the time he got to Shellie Stevens's office. This was cause for relief, so he let himself take a deep breath and roll his shoulders backward once, then twice, letting some of the tension go. Stevens wasn't going to give him more than half an hour, it wasn't even fifteen minutes back to the office . . . he'd have two hours. Plenty.

The office building—sleek, modern, stone and glass—fronted on Pennsylvania, America's Main Street. It wasn't the tallest building by any means, but it breathed the personality of its most fearsome inhabitant, which is to say it was polished, sophisticated, and inscrutable.

When Sully walked into the lobby, his hard-soled shoes clicking on the marble, he had to show his ID to the pair of guards in three-piece suits at the chest-high reception desk. The tile was white and spotless and being mopped by a guy in blue coveralls. The black-and-yellow-and-red abstract painting behind the desk, huge and sprawling, the only splash of color in the room, likely was worth more than his annual salary. The only sound was a stone and boulder fountain, in the corner, and even that rippled rather than splashed. He had the unconscious habit of summarizing places or people in one word, and now "muted" blipped across his brain. The entire effect was—

"Pardon me?" the guard sitting at the desk said, looking up at him, expectant. His partner looked at Sully, too.

"For what?" Sully said, coming out of his reverie.

"You just said something."

"I did? What?"

The sitting guard flicked a glance at the standing one, both looking like they were wondering if this skinny guy with the scars was going to be trouble.

"I don't know. That's why I said, 'Pardon me.' Because I didn't hear what you said."

"Hunh," Sully said, wondering if he'd been talking out loud again. "I don't think I said anything. Is Mr. Stevens in today?"

They paused, both sizing him up, wondering if he was a nutter or just on his way there, and then the sitting guy said, "The secretary will be down to get you. Go ahead and sign in?"

He did and then wandered around the lobby, the only person there, wondering what other firms or agencies or bloodsucking leeches leased space in this sort of monument to soullessness. That biblical thing about cleanliness being next to godliness, he thought, standing by the boulders in the fountain, still feeling like somebody was going to come up and charge him for breathing the air, was that in federal Washington, cleanliness was next to power (if that was different than God in Washington).

Cleanliness of reputation or at least cleanliness from scandal that stuck to the sole of your wing tips like dog shit; cleanliness from tarnish in the eyes of voters or the Securities and Exchange Commission; cleanliness from allegations; cleanliness from flavor, from funk, from style, from hair over the collar, from skirts above the knee. The entire goal of existence in these quarters seemed to be living your life as an unscented sheet of white paper. It wasn't enough to have money here—you had to have *juice*, you had to have influence on the bench and in the House and Senate and Oval Office, and to have that sort of juice and that sort of influence, you had to appear spotless, clean, scrubbed with the disinfectant of integrity and good judgment and decorum and the utter lack of any personality at all.

And if you were Shellie Stevens, the man in the penthouse floor of this place, you didn't even appear as this. You were the ether, the air, someone so above the fray, so above the act of cleaning, so as to not appear at all. This combination of traits made Stevens one of the most intimidating names in the city, the lawyer who made things go away for the rich and the unclean.

Sully was supposed to be professionally free from bias, yeah, he knew that, except that he could not abide the very idea of Shellie Stevens, and he would have felt bad about this professional lapse, really, except for the fact that he was one hundred percent certain the feeling was mutual. Stevens's contempt for the Fourth Estate was what passed for Washington legend.

The receptionist came to claim him then, swiping a card in the elevator to access the penthouse floor, and then, once there, swiping it to open a locked set of double doors. Once inside, there was light classical music in a cavern of wood-paneled walls and oil-on-canvas paintings of Georgetown from the water and the Capitol in the eyes of an impressionist, hues of granite and limestone and fading light. The floors were polished hardwood, draped with Persian rugs that bled money. There were no windows in this space, but when you stepped into Stevens's inner sanctum, a corner suite commanding views to the east and south, the windows ran from the floor to the ceiling, a dozen feet above. Watery winter light, as thin as weak tea, filtered across the room.

In the middle rear of this space, backlit, Shellie Stevens sat behind his oaken desk, elbows on the table, his interlocked fingers beneath his chin, eyes flickering only slightly to take in Sully's appearance. He did not get up.

"Mr. Carter," he said from the slight shadow in which he sat. The receptionist, almost invisible, walked gently backward, pulling the doors closed behind her on the way out.

"Mr. Stevens," Sully said, making his way across the carpeted room, sitting down in one of the heavy leather chairs across the desk. There was no question of a handshake. The man wouldn't have taken his hand if he gave it to him gift wrapped.

"How may I help?" Gravel-voiced, impatient, the words more a demand than a query.

Stevens was thin, approaching sixty, short silver hair slicked straight back, wearing his suit jacket at the desk, the white shirt and light blue tie setting off his eyes of the same color. He assessed Sully like he was a fish flopping on a pier.

"I'm at work," Sully began, "on a story about—"

"I know that."

"—and I—well, then you'd know how you could help. Delores Ellison said I should talk to you." He reached into his backpack for what he knew would be a fool's errand. "Let me get my notebook and recorder, so I can keep—"

"This is not an interview. No notes, no recording." Stevens still had not moved.

"Fine," Sully said, pulling himself back up into the chair. "An off-the-record chat. Delores Ellison said I should talk to you about her son, Billy. Why would she do that?"

Stevens blinked, finally, then looked at him blankly, as if he were slow of mind. He inhaled and let it out slowly. "Why would Delores," he said, "ask you to talk to me." He considered. "Because I told her to. Because this is a private matter. Because there is very little that needs to be in the public sphere."

"I see. And what is it that should be public? That I might print?" He was trying to keep his tone neutral, but it was already wobbling.

"That you might print?" Another pause. The shoulders still had not moved, nor had the elbows on the desk, nor the hands clasped at the chin. "I have a statement prepared. It will be given to you on the way out. A list of Billy's notable achievements, his schooling, his social memberships."

"I look forward to seeing it. But you're describing an obituary. I'm writing a crime story."

Stevens did not nod or indicate that he had heard Sully. "This situation is not in any way a public news event. The family would prefer not to have Billy's name mentioned in the newspapers at all. However, Delores recognizes her family's social standing, and that Billy's many, many friends and admirers would want to know of his passing. Also, to assure them that the police will, in due time, apprehend his killer. Therefore, a statement. But in this story of yours, you will not mention anything about Billy that is not mentioned in the statement given to you."

The instructive had never been one of Sully's favorite tenses, particularly when applied to him in this tone. He did not shake his head, and barely moved his lips. "He's a public figure," he said.

"A public figure?"

"You have echolalia, counselor? You hear me okay? Yes. A public figure. Billy. All homicide victims are. Police reports are public documents. As politely as I can put it, I do not need yours, or anyone else's, permission to publish what police officers write down on criminal reports. Surely you know that. Surely you know that includes the murder of the last heir of a prominent family in the nation's capital. So when you tell me that I won't print anything but what you write in a statement, you know that's bullshit."

"Your language, Mr. Carter. What is it you think you know of Billy?"

"That he was in Frenchman's Bend at about a quarter of midnight Monday when somebody shot him in the head at close range. Likely, this would indicate a drug deal of some nature, as that is what constitutes most killings in the Bend. Also, that he was gay."

Stevens unclasped his hands and sat back in his chair.

"Gay," he said.

"Queer," Sully said. "As fuck."

They looked at one another, the Washington game of the loser breaking the silence. Sully, playing on Stevens's turf, let him have a home-court win.

"Elliot Cane, his partner and a fellow student at Georgetown," he said, "says that Billy was quite familiar with that stretch of gay clubs down on O Street Southwest. Which is only a few blocks from the Bend. Which might also explain why he was there. If he was a thrill seeker who liked slumming—well you can get a blow job or a baggie down there after dark. All of that is, you know, public record, too."

Stevens's eyes were flat. You couldn't even see the wheels spinning, this guy.

"Billy was not just one of my employees' sons, Mr. Carter. He was my godson. I have known Delores's family for a very long time. You will not drag their name through the mud so that you can sell a few more papers. You will be given a statement upon your exit. It will be spelled out for you what may and may not be printed without legal action."

"I think you said that already."

"There is a sentence that states Billy was successfully completing 'recovery therapy,' which is the only allusion that will be made about his dependence on, and trafficking in, narcotics. Billy dealt drugs. In substantial quantities. It was his weakness, some sort of street credibility issue. He wanted to appear something that he was not, which was tough, worldly. It cost him his life. However, he was never arrested and there is no"—and here he leaned forward—"public record of it. Likewise, the police have not made a final determination on where the shooting took place. So you have no standing to report that he was in Frenchman's Bend. Libeling Billy—a dead young man who hurt no one—or his family, will be addressed appropriately. Swiftly."

"You can't libel the dead, counselor, but yeah, I kind of got the rest of that."

"This is the type of story that has gotten you in trouble before."

"I wouldn't say so."

"Judge Foy. It is a well-known incident."

"Judge Foy," Sully said, "is lucky to still have his job."

"An irony, for you to make the observation."

Sully smiled. This was starting to be fun. "How's your private homicide investigation going?" he said. "You an expert now on the M Street and South Caps? You realized yet you're out of your league?"

"Another ironic observation."

Sully stood to go. "This has been edifying, counselor. I bet you can spell that without looking it up."

Stevens did not rise. "If you contact Delores again, the firm will file a restraining order against you. I'm sure you're aware that restraining orders are also public documents, and, should they become known, that you so hounded a bereaved mother to take such—"

"You'll be on the phone, explaining all this to Eddie Winters before I get back to the office," Sully said. "So yeah yeah yeah. I hear you barking. But all of this is going to come out in any story about Billy's death, so save yourself the oxygen."

"It is?" Stevens raised an eyebrow, the first time his face had so much as moved. "Where? In what publication? Other than local television and the *Washingtonian* magazine, no one but you has inquired, Mr. Carter. Television will go away after a day or so. The *Washingtonian* will mention Billy's loss in a society column. The *New York Times* called but agreed to my request for non-publication of a family tragedy. So. You are the only reporter in play."

Sully shrugged. "Then what a lousy stretch of luck for you."

He hit the door downstairs a few minutes later, the statement tucked in a crisp envelope under his arm, the fresh air in his face, the spring sunlight washing over the Potomac. Crossing at the light and briskly now, walking for the office, checking his watch, composing the story in his head. Shellie Stevens's Washington was rarefied air, the federal enclave. But this was not Sully's Washington, and it was intoxicating to a different type of reporter. Yeah, the Sunday morning political talk show hosts and guests, the ones who name-dropped whose table they'd been sitting at for the White House Correspondents' dinner, the type of reporters who posed for grip-and-grins with the sitting president at the Gridiron dinner and then put them on their mantels at home—those were reporters who would go to Shellie Stevens's office and let a thing like the death of an employee's son pass, chalking it up to cultivating a source, thus keeping the lines of behind-the-scenes access open to stories of national power and scope.

But those reporters were not him, and one thing he didn't like, one thing he didn't like at all? People in this town thinking they were better than him, and that included menace-laden motherfuckers like Shellie Stevens.

NINE

THE STORY WAS glue. It was just flipping glue. A day hit, a little seven-hundred-word sashay down the journalistic boulevard of life . . . and the thing would not emerge on the screen in front of him.

Every time he started hammering out a lede and a couple more 'graphs, his fingers started sticking to the keyboard. Shellie Stevens, that little shit, was right: You couldn't just say Ellison *was* at the Bend, because the police didn't have the blood test back yet, and you couldn't say it *looked* like he was in the Bend because of the shoe, because it wasn't conclusive and because the police weren't *officially* releasing that the shoe had been found. You couldn't even say he was doing drugs because the toxicology wasn't back yet, either.

"How we looking there, Sullivan?" R.J., appearing over the cubicle, looming, not pestering yet, but not far from it, either. Sully didn't take his eyes off the screen or his fingers off the keys.

"Super most wonderful," he said. "It's all short skirts and cleavage."

"I was asking because I was looking at what you've got in the system so far. It doesn't look like cleavage. It looks pretty matronly, actually."

"That's because there isn't much. I told you. We're sailing the magical Sea of Inbetween, located between the continents of What We Know and What We Can Print. We *know* the kid was gay, doing drugs, and got shot in the Bend at about midnight on Monday night, by person or persons unknown. The only part of that we can *print* is none of it."

"So you're still thinking he, what, was hanging out at the O Street clubs and got into a coke deal a few blocks over?"

"I guess. You ever see him down there? The clubs?" And now Sully looked up and made eye contact, since he was asking his boss a question about his private life.

"El and I are a little long in the tooth for O Street," R.J. said. "They had bathhouses down there before the health department made them shut down, back in the eighties. The AIDS situation."

"Club Washington is still up and working."

"It's not a bathhouse."

"They got little booths and X-rated movies. They call it a twenty-four-hour gym."

"It's not a bathhouse per se."

"You sound pretty familiar for somebody who says they don't go down there."

"So do you."

"Would you ask around?" Sully said. "You're a society guy. Billy was society. It seems like you might could do a little reporting here."

R.J. shuffled his feet, rubbed the back of his hand across his nose. "I can tell you Billy wasn't out, if that's what you're asking. I know Delores, and an openly gay son would have been known in her circle. As a liability, I mean. Washington, conservative Washington—most particularly black conservative Washington—isn't fashion forward on the issue. But that doesn't mean anything. A lot of people are closeted, but it turns out this is a pretty big closet. Members of the closeted tribe are known to one another. They're also known to those who are out, who keep their mouths shut. The agreed-upon meeting zone, from the city to the cops to the most closeted of the closeted, is O Street. Now. I myself haven't been closeted since Stonewall. But, see, that's why the O Street clubs exist—you won't be seen by anybody who's not a member of the tribe. It's the social comfort zone for those both out and not."

"And this applies, white and black? Gay and lesbian?"

"Mostly white, mostly gay. But yeah. Everybody. Washington is too small, too buttoned-down for two gay strips."

"Ah."

"All this discussion of gay chic and you still haven't said what and when you're filing. Melissa, you remember her? The editor of the section? She is most interested to know. She still doesn't like you much, in case you've forgotten."

"Soon and not much. I have a very helpful statement here from Shellie Stevens. It mentions that young master Billy had 'been troubled by narcotics' but had completed a 'summer of therapy' at the Rosenthal Center, which is I guess what they're going to count as acknowledgment of his drug dealing."

"It sounds like a spa."

"Turns out it's this inpatient rehab center up in Bethesda."

"Never heard of it."

"Neither had I. Incredibly discreet. And small. Like, ten beds. You go in for your seventy days and tell people you spent the summer in Provence."

"So, okay. I say we write it short, just a straight bio, and hold our powder for the longer story on the Bend. That's going to need to run on Sunday. And Stevens really told you he'd hit you with a restraining order?"

"He really did."

"You have a way about you."

"It's a gift."

"So, so," R.J. said, patting at the chest pocket on his shirt, like he was looking for something that was usually there but wasn't this time, the focus going from his eyes, his shoulders shifting, losing their frame, losing interest in the conversation, "fine, fine. Keep it to fifteen and kick it to me soon." He turned and started walking off, still with the pocket thing, and then, with a graceful turn, he spun on a heel and came back. Leaning over the cubicle, his voice a whisper, his eyes suddenly alert behind the glasses, he looked like a bright-eyed owl with an attitude problem.

"Secrets has the only male full-nude striptease show on the East Coast," R.J. stage whispered. "Of course we've checked it out. We're not old queens sitting at home with our knitting."

———

Filing a basic story, a blip that would keep Melissa off his back and wouldn't piss off Stevens just yet—he wondered if they taught this in J-school, if you paid professors to teach you how to walk this tightrope:

> The slaying of Billy Ellison, the scion of one of D.C.'s most prominent society families, has local and federal investigators scouring the banks of the Washington Channel for clues after his body was found floating in the channel Tuesday afternoon. Ellison, 21, a junior at Georgetown University and the son of . . .

He made it back home just before eight, a light mist falling. He walked inside long enough to open the fridge, pull out deli slices of cheese and turkey, roll one slice around the other, and eat it standing up in the kitchen, staring at the little green clock numbers on the microwave. Then he did another.

If he called Alexis, that would be good to set up their reporting for tomorrow, but he didn't want to get stuck in a longer conversation. And if she said she wanted to have dinner, he'd have to go and he was too jittery for that. So he put some things in his gym bag and walked through the dripping streets toward Eastern Market, letting the rain bead on his forehead, the hush of an early evening on the Hill, the only sound his cycle boots on the narrow brick sidewalks, the orange glow of the streetlights filtered by the overhanging branches, walking from light to shadow and back again.

The natatorium was a nondescript concrete one-story building set back from the street, deep in the shadows, a few yards behind the long thin redbrick buildings of the market.

Inside, Henry the pool guy nodded, not even asking for his ID. The air was heavy with chlorine and a dank odor that he could never place, something that could only live in dim fluorescent light. Shucking out of his pants and shirt in the locker room, he pulled on his trunks and reemerged, dropping feet first into the heated pool, hurrying now. He pulled on the goggles and spit in them, wiping the lens clean, and then pushed off, closing his eyes, floating and drifting. The rain seemed to melt into the pool and he melted into the water, the idea soothing to his frazzled brain, the reason he came here, the escape. Billy Ellison couldn't find him here, nor could any of his bosses or the likes of Shellie Stevens, not the memory of Nadia or any of the other dead whose faces floated past him in sleep, the land of dreams a disturbing realm of blackness that held as many ghosts as it did waves of peace. He could never tell what lay in wait for him in bed each night, the nightmares or the black slate of nothingness.

He was the only swimmer this late, closing time swinging near, and he reached out with an overhand stroke now, then another, pulling himself through the water with a grace he did not possess on land. It enveloped him, the water, the empty pool, the one place where he did not limp, where his scarred face drew no stares, the hollow nervous burning in his gut gone, dissipated. There was only his breathing, the pleasant tug on the lungs, the peaceful blue monotony of the bottom of the pool, the vacant white ceiling on the backstrokes, the lovely numbness of it all, no thoughts of the past or the killings in the present and no idea of the future, and this reverie was broken only at the end of one of these laps, when he saw a man's hand dangle down in the water ahead of him, the fingers waving back and forth.

He pulled his head up, gliding to the wall, expecting to see Henry telling him they were closing up, that he'd lost track of time again. Instead, as his hand reached the tiled wall, he pulled his goggles up and found, through the lens of water spilling down his face, that he was looking at Sly Hastings, one of the deadliest men in the city, a killer and a sociopath, and perhaps his best source in town.

"Aquaman," Sly said, smiling down at him. "I hear you been busy."

They were the only two in the locker room, the only two still in the entire place, save Henry up front somewhere. Their voices echoed and bounced. Sully stuck his head under the shower to get the chlorine out, then was back out, getting dressed, Sly leaning against the peeling baby-blue paint on the wall, one foot crossed over at the ankle, the sleeves of his tracksuit neatly pushed up to the elbow. He took off his glasses, the little round ones, and polished them on the hem of his shirt.

"This place, why you come here? It looks like you going to catch something."

"Water's got enough chlorine to kill cancer," Sully said, pulling a shirt over his head.

"I don't mean just the water. Lookit this floor." It was a slab of concrete, stained in patches that looked red or brown or slightly orange. The metal lockers were dented and had chipped paint and looked like any good tug would pull them halfway out of the wall. The trash can was three-quarters full, one of the lights was out, and the faucet dripped.

"It's got character," Sully said.

Sly snorted, looking up at the ceiling, like a disease was going to fall on him. "'S what white people say when they slumming."

"You can't slum in your own neighborhood," Sully said. "And what white people is this you been hanging out with, to know what they say about anything?"

"I know some shit."

"Un-hunh."

"About you people."

"Un-hunh."

"You going to finish getting dressed or what? Never seen a man take so long to put clothes on."

"Watch men get dressed a lot?"

"You know, you can get on a motherfucker's nerves."

Sully, deadpanning it now: "The way white people talk, how men get dressed—I'm learning a lot about you, brother."

As he bent to pull on his boots, he saw Sly move toward the door out of the corner of his eye. He was finished, but dragged it out, letting Sly leave and go outside, allowing him a minute to take a deep breath and think, because dealing with a warlord like Sly was not something to do offhand.

He'd first met him shortly after coming back from the war, in Benning Terrace, better known as Simple City. Sly was an enforcer for the crew that ran the place, and Sully, just coming out of rehab and laced on painkillers most of the time, did not give a particular fuck about anything.

Sly had dragged the body of a police informant, one Kermit S. Allen, nicknamed Froggie, into the main courtyard of the project at high noon. The man was already shot twice through the chest and dying. A crowd gathered.

Sly pulled Allen's head up off the dirt, clutching him by his hair, Allen weakly trying to claw at the hand holding him. Sly bellowed two or three times—it depended on which witness you believed—that this was what happened to motherfuckers who talked to cops. Then he shot Froggie through the forehead, blowing his brains out into the dirt. When Froggie was flat on the ground again, Sly shot him twice more in the face. Then he looked up and asked the assembled if there were any motherfucking questions.

When police came, no one talked to them.

Sully went down there to write a story about witness intimidation at the height of the city's crack wars. He was walking down a crappy hallway in one of the crappy buildings of the complex when Sly emerged from a door, shoved him into a wall, put a Glock to his temple, and asked him if he wanted to die.

Sully answered in Bosnian, sounding bored, looking straight ahead. Sly, who didn't recognize the language, slowed down enough to tell him to speak the English.

"I said," Sully told him, "that if you don't get that piece of shit off my face, then a pair of Chetniks that I sponsored for immigration will slit you from gullet to crotch."

Sly lessened his grip just enough for Sully to know that this was over and said, "What's a Chetnik?"

Of such things friendship and respect were born.

He had not seen Sly in what, two months, maybe three, hardly at all since the series of killings last fall up on Princeton Place. It had included the murder of the daughter of the chief judge of U.S. District Court in D.C. and a gorgeous Howard University student and both had been nasty. It had also ended badly, leaving a bitter taste in Sully's mouth and business with Sly he needed to avenge.

This was easier said than done. By Sully's count, Sly was responsible for at least five murders and probably double that. He was manipulative and ruthless. He was also a product of a disastrous upbringing in the projects who wanted better out of life, had used his drug profits to buy a couple of small apartment complexes, and now read books on property management and stock-market investing. He was loyal to what was left of his family, not a bad guy to watch a football game with, and a terror at the *New York Times* crossword puzzle. A good source who had given Sully better street intel than the cops had, but would also play him for a pawn if it suited his larger purposes.

No way to pigeonhole, to typecast, to write off.

Sully sat up straight now, arched his back, and took a deep breath, letting it out, onetwothreefourfive, and then he was as good as he was going to get, standing up and grabbing his bag and flicking off the light to the locker room on his way out.

The pool area was dark and the lobby was dim, the sound of his footsteps coming back to him. At the glass-walled front entrance, Henry was at the door, waiting to let him out and close up.

"Night, Henry," he said, nodding, but the man didn't even look at him. His face was set in a grimace, looking stiffly out the window; Sully knew he had recognized Sly and knew him for who and what he was. Sly had that effect on people, like they'd just seen the dead arise, and not the dead ones you loved and missed, but the dead you feared and loathed.

The rain had stopped but it was still dripping off the leaves overhead. They were standing in the darkness by the side of the building, the street fifty feet ahead of them. Two of the three nearest streetlights were out. Sully could make out Sly's car, the yellow-over-black Camaro at the curb, engine idling, and he knew that Lionel would be behind the wheel, keeping an eye on the boss. A match struck and flared to his left and Sully moved toward it, picking up Sly's outline in the glow. He was leaning against the wall, under the slight overhang, cupping the match till it lit the cigarette. Then he shook it dead. The light from the roadway glinted from his glasses when he moved his head and spoke, his voice soft and deep, an unseen thing in the dark.

"The Hall brothers," Sly began, blowing out a stream of smoke, "are a problem of mine."

Sully's mind lit up, connections flaring, instantly looking for where this was going. So . . . so Sly knew he'd been in the Bend—that could have come from the article he'd written about the body in the channel. It didn't mean Sly had been tailing him. He kept it straight, looking up at the trees, the water dripping, rubbing a shoe on the slick asphalt.

"Yeah? How so?" he said. The strap from his gym bag was slung over his shoulder, the bag light, almost weightless.

"They been looking to expand out they turf, M Street, down there like that. But, see, the problem with things expanding? They got to expand into something else. You know chemistry? Like, ions? They reactive, they bounce into other little molecules, and well, they change that other thing. That's the Hall brothers. They been expanding into me."

"Hunh." Sully said, still waiting, not sure where this was headed. "I didn't do all that well in chem class. But I didn't think anybody did that sort of thing, expand into your turf."

Sly's shoulders hunched and released, a deeper shadow in the gloom. "People try anything now and then. This business here, though, they don't *know* they been expanding into me. Right? And it needs to stay that way."

Sully waited, not giving him anything.

"So," Sly said, after another drag on the smoke, "you been asking around about shit in the Bend."

Nodding now, taking it in, putting the fingers of his right hand into the palm of his left to pop the middle knuckles. Sly's home turf was up in Park View, just off Georgia Avenue, a few miles from the Bend. Sully was trying to make the connection. The Bend was south of the Capitol Building, cut off from the rest of town. It was small, low-end, sleazy, some of the lowest dregs of the trade. Not a profit center. Not in Sly's wheelhouse.

"Glad to see you read the paper," he said.

"That story wasn't shit," Sly said. "Scaring tourists. Bullshit. You down there 'cause that rich kid got popped and you put it together, you thinking, he got popped in the Bend. Ain't no other reason for you to be there. So. You gonna keep being down there looking at that, the way I see it, am I right? Yes. Yeah. Sure. And so, you see what I'm saying, this here is what I need. I need to know what the Hall brothers thinking about. That would be helpful to me."

Sully nodded, as if this were perfectly reasonable, that he could just walk up and start asking the Halls what their short- and midterm business plans might be. But, behind that, his sense of security was fading. Sly was way ahead. The story on the body being identified as Billy Ellison hadn't run yet, and even if Sly had heard it on the radio or television, nobody had reported that the Bend was where Billy got killed. And yet Sly Hastings, who didn't get things like that wrong, had just uttered both as facts.

"You want to know what Tony and Carlos are thinking," Sully said, shrugging, "whyn't you go ask them?"

"Smart-ass. Look, the play here, you see this? I need you down there, and I need whatever intel you'n get on the Halls—Tony, Carlos, both, either one, I don't care."

For the first time in the conversation, Sully began to see an angle for himself here. Sly had a need, he had come to Sully, which indicated, Jesus, that he had so little access or insight into the Hall brothers' operation that whatever little surface intel Sully could get was worth having.

"What am I looking for? It would help to know."

Sly let his cigarette drop and lightly stepped on it with his Nikes, the grinding sound on the pavement.

"There was this here brother named Dee Dee," he said, "down there in the Bend. Was my what, what do you call it? My mole. My, like, eyes and ears. We were starting to move product."

"Demetrius Allan Byrd," Sully said. "Yeah. Somebody capped him."

"That ain't no secret. Yeah. Dee got popped. What don't anybody know is that he was working for me."

"And you want to know, what, if the Halls were onto him?"

Sly smiled at him in the dark.

"They ain't gonna tell you that, nah nah nah. That's not the play. See, you gonna be asking all over down there about that rich boy like you do. You gonna be talking to the police, the feds, and hey, sure, maybe you'll drift by and talk to the Halls about it. That's good. That's real good. You just keep an ear out for what they all thinking, what they talking about, see if you hear my name, right? You see what the police will tell you about the Halls. What *they* thinkin' about Dee Dee, not just about the rich kid. What *they* know. What they say about who's moving what product down there in the Bend. You see?"

He pushed off the wall with his back, leaning forward, and then he was walking slowly, moving toward the street. Sully moved with him, walking alongside, the day finally settling over him, the weariness a ton of bricks, the rain still dripping. Ahead of them, out of the shadows and in the street, Lionel leaned over in the Camaro to push the passenger's-side door open for the boss.

"Yeah, I see. I see that just fine. What I don't see is how that helps me. I'm writing about the Ellison kid. How does this help me do that? You know who popped him? That would help *me*. That would help me a lot."

Sly put his hands in the pockets of his tracksuit, adjusted the glasses on his nose, coughed.

"That there is the problem with you reporters," he said. "Y'all always looking at the wrong thing, barking up the wrong goddamn tree. Woof woof over here, woof woof over there. Look here. Follow the money. Ain't that what y'all like to say? Follow that money. That's good right there. Cuz nobody cares who killed that little gay boy. Not nobody. Well. *You're* curious, and I bet his momma 'nem is all upset, but he didn't matter for nothing. No. What matters?"

He stopped walking, and Sully stopped to look at him. Sly came forward a step, tapped Sully on the chest, looked him in the eye, maybe a foot away. "Who. Killed. My. Boy. Dee. That was a power play right there. That's what happening in the Bend. Your gay boy, shit. He's going to turn out to be, like, collateral damage. Any of them crackheads down there coulda popped him for who knows what? A blow job? But whoever popped Dee Dee? *That* matters. That's what's happening in the Bend. Whoever killed Dee Dee, he's yanking some strings. He's making money change directions. He's moving in on *me*. You follow who killed Dee Dee. That'll take you to the end of the goddamned rainbow, little leprechauns and the motherfuckin' pot of gold."

TEN

"SO, WHAT YOU'RE telling me, Billy Ellison got crossways of the M Street Crew," Alexis was saying, "and they popped him for it." She was driving him down Fourth Street NE in her rental, midmorning, traffic light on the one-lane southbound, the row houses of Capitol Hill gliding past, heading back to the Bend, the Capitol off on their right. She had already been down there at dawn, for the light, the atmospherics, the mood and sense of place. She'd eaten at Jimmy T's, called him at the house, rousted him, and picked him up twenty minutes later.

"That's what I understand from last night," he said, still blinking, dry-mouthed. "Him or his connection or both. The way I got it, he was likely buying shit from this dude, Demetrius Byrd, goes by Dee Dee."

"Okay."

"And Dee Dee gets popped, right?"

"If you say so. When was this? Dee Dee getting shot."

"A week or two ago. Not long. So, my working theory here is that Billy, naive little fucker that he was, didn't see Dee at their usual hookup, which is going to be somewhere near the gay clubs down on O, and so he went down to the Bend asking for Dee Dee, not knowing he was even dead."

"So," she said, goosing the car to beat a yellow light, "when he shows up asking for Dee Dee, the Hall brothers realize that Billy was working with him on his side business, and they kill him so that—"

"Everybody gets the message. Yeah. Just shut the whole thing down. Probably dragged his ass out there and shot him in front of people. Real theater. I doubt they had any idea who Billy was. Family-wise. I mean, look, all this is just a working idea, but you know, I'm betting it's going to be something close to the real thing."

"And that fits into your story because . . ."

He turned to her, surprised she didn't see the angle. "Because it illustrates the power and the pull of drugs and the city's worst drug market, which happens to be a former slave-trading post in your nation's capital," he said. "Talk about blunt symbolism. If Billy Ellison, rich kid of this privileged family, is tied to a drug-running crew in the Bend? The fucking Hall brothers? Wow."

"And how do you propose to figure that out? You said you'll get hit with a restraining order if you talk to Billy's mother again. Those two guys in the Bend said they'd shoot you if you came back."

"I can be a charming little bastard."

She laughed and said, "If you mean a little charming and a lot of bastard."

He looked out the window and coughed twice and popped his neck, to the left and then to the right. He wasn't about to tell her about Sly, about the real way this was going to work. He was going to work the story of Dee Dee's murder, and in return Sly would eventually give him enough to peg Billy Ellison's killer. Questionable tactics, maybe, but if you want to know what the bad guys are doing, you find out from other bad guys. Same way the cops did it.

"So tell me about the art you shot this morning."

"It's opener stuff, atmospherics," she said. "Good light. Four or five guys were already out there, scoring some heroin. They took me inside that apartment building right off the park—"

"The Carolina, the two-story brick thing?"

"And inside, yeah, I think that's the name of it. Does it have a name on it? They shot up right there in the entryway."

"They let you shoot them?"

"Faces averted or tight shots, yeah, sure."

"Surprised nobody braced you."

"Well. We were there in the hall, me shooting the camera and them shooting the smack, and then the big kids must have heard I was there. Two of them came in from outside and saw us and that was that."

"One of these enforcer guys, he real short?" he asked. "And the other one tall, lanky, with dreads?"

"Now that you mention it."

"Them's my friends."

"The ones who said they'd pop you if you came back?"

"The same."

"Hunh," she said. "They just asked me if I needed any shit and I took the cue."

"That's because you're a girl."

"It's because I'm not a dick."

A weak sun was filtering through the clouds, the streets still a little slick. Traffic was light and now they were on K Street SW, the discount shoe stores and liquor joints and nail salons still shuttered behind iron bars. The grocery store was open, the buggies wet and dripping from being left out in the rain overnight, a couple of patrons rattling them toward the double glass doors.

"I wonder what the fruits and vegetables are in there." She slowed, not braking, just letting off the gas, and said, "You said get back to the neighborhood, on K."

Sully took a moment to blink, to assess. He flipped open his notebook, thick-fingered, bleary-eyed still—he'd just splashed water over his face and hair, stumbling into jeans and a lightly starched gray dress shirt, coming down the steps and into her car, rolling up the cuffs—and now he flicked his tongue around his lips, wondering if he'd brushed his teeth. He thought so.

"I did, I did, and here we go. . . . Where is it? Ah. Byrd. We're looking for the family of dear old Demetrius Allan Byrd, unknown to all but family and law enforcement. It's in the Dempsys, God help us, this housing project right here. Slow down. It's coming up. Your right. On your right."

The Dempsys, a mean little squadron of two-story tenements, appeared on the south side of the street, easy to see, the entrance marked as it was by a ragged collection of teddy bears, votive candles, grocery store flowers wrapped in plastic, and a hand-lettered sign on green construction paper that read, RIP DEE. Balloons, three shiny Mylar things, fluttered in the breezeway of the main building. Nobody looked out windows, nobody stopped walking, nobody said anything; Alexis just pulled alongside a parked car and put on a blinker to back into the space behind it.

"That's a hotel?" she said, waiting for traffic to clear, looking across the street at a stucco three-story with railings that leaned outward and a front office with the blinds down. A pole stood sentinel out front, but the sign it had once held was jagged broken plastic and exposed fluorescent bulb.

"Motel."

"The difference?"

"You park in front of your room at the latter."

"Americanos."

"You're one."

"By passport."

She backed in and parked at a street meter and they got out, Sully still coughing his lungs awake, Alexis pulling her gear from the backseat.

He blew out his breath through his lips, assessing their target, his face slack this early. The Dempsys were four apartments to a floor around a concrete stairwell with rusted iron handrails, set five or six blocks from Fort McNair. It fronted on K Street SW, which was the polar opposite of its better-known cousin, K Street NW, the heart of Power Washington. A few miles away from all that power, the Dempsys existed in a parallel universe—eight, could be ten buildings in all, surrounded by a head-high steel fence with spikes along the top. There was a central courtyard, packed dirt, and stubs of weeds.

The only thing that passed for green in the complex, even in the spring, when everything was blooming, was half a dozen anorexic trees, saplings, that looked like they had spent the winter with bags over their heads. The Dempsys had gone up in the eighties, Marion Barry–inspired urban renewal, built on the cheap and looking like it. Five or seven blocks from where Dee Dee had wound up dead. Sully wondered what was the farthest the kid had ever been from home and guessed the lockup down at Lorton, thirty miles south.

The buildings had no markers to tell you which one was which. They had fallen off or been ripped off. You had to live here or be the mailman or a public housing cop to know the difference. When they were halfway through the courtyard, a heavyset woman emerged from the building to Sully's right, leaning against a support pole, near the teddy bears, looking at them without expression, lighting a smoke. She was wearing jeans that were too tight and some sort of green blouse that was too loose.

Sully looked over but it was Alex who was walking toward her, three cameras around her neck. And she said softly, almost reverently, Sully catching up, "We're looking for Mr. Byrd's family?"

Sully was the only man in the room.

The grandma, wrinkled, freckled, sagging onto the sagging couch, feet in slippers, the heavyset woman they'd seen out front now sitting beside her. There was a rail-thin, light-skinned woman in the narrow kitchen, eyeing him as he sat down.

She was wearing too-big sweats and a pullover T-shirt that read BUS-TIN' LOOSE above Chuck Brown's visage, a cigarette in her nervous left hand. Two little kids, a girl and a boy, couldn't be older than three either one, half-hiding behind the couch, looking at him like an extraterrestrial had whiz-banged down into the living room. Alexis had, by the magic that photographers worked, gotten herself into a sitting position against the far wall, a Leica pressed to her face, all but forgotten.

"Why you think Dee got jumped?" the nervous woman said, looking at Sully like he'd said she owed taxes or something. He pegged her as Mom and a walking advertisement for the wonders of long-term smack use.

He'd told them their names and what they did when they'd walked in, Alex making busy with the kids. He made his condolences and asked them polite questions about Dee's winning personality and school record and then, jeez, did they have any idea about who might have wanted to harm the bouncing baby boy? This was the question that had given offense.

"You saying he was in the life?" the thin woman said.

"I think—"

"I'm out here looking, looking for work, a job or something, you hear me, trying to *get* something, my baby gets killed, and you asking me if he was in the life."

"I don't think, ah, I don't think I quite asked—"

"He don't even go *out*, you hear me?"

"I do. I'm trying to—"

"Somebody'd ask a nigga they'd know."

"—to—to—learn a little bit more about him. All I know is what the police tell me, and that's not a complete picture, you know? Court records aren't fair to anybody. I know it's—this is difficult. We'll leave if you want us to."

He had to nod toward Alex, she was that forgotten already, this *us* confusing the woman. Smiling slightly, fighting for this interview because he had to have it, taking the initial volley of hostility. You let people talk shit at you for five minutes and not take the bait, most of the time they calmed down. Most. "But what I was trying—trying to ask, and I'm sorry to be here like this, is if maybe you could tell me a little bit more about Dee Dee. That I wouldn't find in the police report."

They all looked at him. He said, "Which is what brought us here."

The skinny woman said, "Police already been here." Her lip trembling.

"I'm glad to hear that. Good. But the police are looking, they're only looking for who did this *to* Dee. I'm asking *about* Dee, to see what he was like, what he was doing, you know."

Silence.

"Ms. Byrd?"

"What?"

"You're Ms. Byrd? You're Dee's mother?"

The skinny woman pulled on her smoke again, looked over at her heavy-set companion, blew out the smoke, and rolled her eyes. "And he so smart, too."

The other woman smirked, eyes darting back to the television. Some square yellow cartoon character, tiny little arms and legs, standing next to a pink thing, underwater. The sound was blaring but the ankle biters ignoring it, google-eyeing him. A talking sponge in his underwear and him, the bigger freak. He heard Alex take three frames, *chikchikchik*, nobody moving.

Sully took two steps forward and handed Mom his card over the kitchen counter, then sat down on the edge of the couch next to Grandma without being asked. Grandma skirted her eyes over to look at him. The place was brown-paneled walls, a four-bulb fixture overhead with three of the bulbs out. Styrofoam food trays were scattered in the corner, like Chinese carryout. Green carpet stained, worn down to nubs.

"So, Dee Dee," Sully said, trying to kick-start things one more time, "can you tell me about what he was like, meeting him? I never got to, and I mean, like I say, the court file, that's just not a fair picture."

"Something like what?" Mom looking to go off, ready to detonate.

"Ms. Byrd." He smiled. This was going to be over soon if he didn't rescue it.

"Mmm-hmm."

"I'm looking in the room here, I see hurting people, a family. Good people. You were kind to let us in. We're not the police. We're not social services. We have no right to be here unless you want us to be. I'm not trying make your life unhappier right now than it already is. Sometimes families like to talk about the ones they've lost. Sometimes they don't. But I don't know until I—until we—come ask. There's no disrespect intended, and I'm sorry that us coming has gotten you a little bit upset."

They looked at him.

"My mom, my dad?" he said. "Both of 'em died when I's a kid. At the time, I would have liked to talk about them, if anybody'd asked."

"Somebody shoot *them*?"

"Not entirely, no, ma'am."

"Then you really don't know the fuck you talking about."

He stood up. "You're right. Sorry about this. I am."

He cut his eyes at Alexis—Christ, he was going to get up and leave and they were still going to forget she was over there—and his hand was on the doorknob when Mom said, "Dee was my baby. Firstborn, you know, the son? So he was special to me like that."

Stopping, he looked at her.

"When he was six, seven?" she said. "I would come home and kiss him when he was sleeping. Beautiful child."

"Yes, ma'am."

"Made the good grades. Not great. But good. He liked school. He come home from school, show me all the stuff they did that day. Maps. Like Africa? He'd put in all the lakes, the countries, the deserts. Even weekends, he was a little boy, he'd lay on the floor and color in maps. Atlases."

"Yes, ma'am."

"Church. We went to church more then. Dee, he'd add up all the tithes for his class, then all of the Sunday school classes. The treasurer. He was the treasurer. And the maps, you know, of Galilee and Jesus and Bethlehem. He'd tell me, 'Momma, it ain't as big as you think.'"

"Yes, ma'am."

"And then he started growing hair where boys do. Fell in with them boys out there. Dropped out school. Acted like he didn't want to know nobody in here no more."

He half-turned, not even thinking about bringing out the notebook. It would kill the connection. He held her eyes with his and said, "It happens like that sometimes. It's hard."

"And me, working all the time. You think I had time to sit around here with him after school every day?"

"Where do you work, ma'am?"

"Did. Where *did* I work. D.C. Parks and Rec. At the community center up the street."

"What did you do there?"

"Cook. Cleaned."

"And it sounds like you got laid off, something like that?"

"Fired. I got fired. Four-five years back. Don't put that in your paper."

"No, ma'am. Where did he go to school?"

"Bowen, the elementary. Jefferson, middle. He got in some time at Eastern, but mainly he was over to Oak Hill."

Sully risked the notebook now, nodding, just scribbling the names of the schools, Oak Hill the city's disastrous juvie-d facility. It meant Dee had gotten busted and sentenced to something, who knew what, before he was eighteen.

"Did he wind up with his GED from over there?"

"Not that anybody told me about."

"Okay. Okay."

"He was good with his hands. He . . . where is it, over there, that bowl over there, next to the cereal box? He made that in one of them classes." Sitting on the small dining table, with folding chairs pulled up to it, was a serving bowl, red and green, a little lumpy but not all that bad.

"He played ball in Pop Warner. He was good to his little sister. He used to go with Nana here to church, even after he got big."

She was free-associating now, the mind beginning to seize upon all that it had lost and finding no grips for the grief or the pain or the rage.

"The Hall brothers?" He said it softly, as if he were in church himself, the crux of the interview right here. "They run the M Street Crew. Dee Dee knew them, yes?"

She sat down and flicked her eyes over to him, her gut empty now, no answers, no attitude. She looked punched out, flat on the canvas, the world a frightening and terrible place that needed an anesthetic to be faced even when the sun was out. He recognized the slack-faced look because he had seen it looking back at him out of his own mirror after Nadia got her head blown off.

"Like they was his muthafucking family," she said.

"And a man named Sly Hastings? Did he know a Mr. Hastings, older? About my height, slim, tends to wear little round glasses?"

The heavyset woman turned to look at him, the mother's face froze, and the air seemed to leave the room.

"You need to get the fuck up out of my house," she said.

ELEVEN

YOU HAD TO run with the fever while it held you, that was the thing, and stories were fever dreams that came and passed through you and, later, left you looking back, wondering how the thing had possessed you so completely.

He moved up the street, walking quickly, leaving the Dempsys, limping up the block toward South Capitol. That's all stories were, and to catch them was an art akin to photography; you captured the image when it existed, or it was gone and all that was left were shadows and light and a vague feeling of unease that you were less than you had been before. Stories were what he clung to instead of religion, that having deserted him shortly after his parents had died, one after the other, his sister sent away.

Alexis skittered behind, having lingered with Mom for a last bit of conversation or photograph or some bit of alchemy known only to her.

"Why didn't you tell her your mom was shot?" she said softly, coming up alongside him. "Or even Nadia, I mean. It would have been—"

"It's not what she was asking," he said.

"She asked if—"

"She wanted to have the upper hand," he said, impatient now, waving his left arm, a windmill motion. "The question was just the staging. I told her my parents died, it gives her an opening to talk, to ask a question, to come up out of herself. She didn't. She didn't give a damn, and she shouldn't. It's her kid who's dead, not mine."

"But—"

"So, right there, you know she wasn't going to *bond*. She wasn't going to say, 'Oh, so you know, just like me,' and we hold hands and exchange Christmas cards. She wanted to tell me that I didn't know shit, and she wanted me to say I was sorry. I did. *Then* she told me about Dee. That was the transaction. Plain as day."

"Oh."

"You're not understanding how to ask questions."

"Apparently not."

"You're not seeing this. I mention the personal, you see that? My parents, her kid, now I'm talking family-to-family. I broke the journalist-to-source wall. It's not an interview. It's survivor-to-survivor. So she's got two options. She can hold my hand and tell me personal stories, or tell me to fuck off. She picked B. So I backed off, and then, hey, what do you know? She felt bad. So she told me personal stuff about Dee, once she had peed on my grief."

Alexis, walking, her cameras bouncing into each other, the only noise other than traffic and their footsteps.

"So you played her."

"Did I seem insincere to you?"

She thought. "No."

"Then how did I play her?"

"Because you had thought out that exchange before she did."

"I need people to tell me things. Personal things. So I encourage them to confide in me, and one of the ways to get people to feel instantly familiar with you is by mentioning one's less-than-perfect family."

"If you say so."

"*I* do not say so. It's an act of human bonding, don't you see that? I'm talking to her, I'm asking questions based on family relations. I'm not all, 'Vomit out your personal details for me to exploit.' I'm talking to her, person-to-person."

"Okay, okay," she said, looking over at him as they left the car behind, moving deeper in the neighborhood, toward the Bend. "I just hadn't thought of it that way before. No offense."

"None taken." He blew out a breath. He had not thought of his mother's killing in at least a week and it had rattled him.

"So what's the plan now?" she said, hitching her lens straps over her shoulder, them coming to the street to cross, pausing for the light to change.

"The gay clubs, the strip up here on O Street," he said, regaining some momentum, motioning forward and to his left, a low sling of the arm. "Our boy Billy was into it, or so says Elliot, his partner. There's got to be a connection between those and the Bend."

"What about Dee?" she said. "What was that back there? You mentioned a name and his mom threw us out."

"Threw *me* out," he said. "You were invisible. I said to her, I said, 'Sly Hastings.' I wanted to see what reaction it got."

"Well, great. Now you know. It killed the interview."

"Nah. I was done. Well. Since she knew who Sly was, *then* I was done. He'd been in that apartment. The way she looked at me? She'd seen him up close. And if she's seen him up close, she was not going to gab to us any more than she already had."

"So why'd you bring him up? You think he killed Dee?"

"Nah, see, no. Dee was in the M Street Crew. Everybody knew that. She didn't have a problem confirming that. But I threw Sly out there to see if she knew of him, if she knew who he was. She did, and that confirmed for me the level this is at."

"So this Sly." She stopped to pull out a cigarette and light it. "What crew is he in?" Blowing out the smoke, concentrating, absorbing it all.

"Sly," he said, "is in the crew of Sly. Those things are going to kill you, you know. Sly is, put it this way, like in South Sudan? He is the warlord of warlords. He is the dust, he is the shadow, he is the walking apocalypse. Dee was a secret employee of his. A mole. Somebody popped Dee and Sly isn't happy about it."

"So if somebody killed Dee, Sly's boy, why is Mom afraid of him? Seems like he would be on her side, looking for who killed his guy."

He shook his head, smiling, keeping up with her despite his gimp-legged walk. "You got to remember it's entirely possible *Sly* killed Dee, because Dee fucked up or shorted him or God only knows why, and now he's acting all innocent and shit."

"Why would he go to the trouble?"

"Who knows? I'm not a drug lord."

"You seem to know a lot about this Sly person," she said.

"He is known to me, and I to him," he said, trying to change the subject before she got too much into his business. "But what we're doing now, right, is legwork. We're heading up to the gay bars, the clubs, the dives on O Street. We need to know how some rich college boy got killed four days and about a hundred feet from a mid-level dealer like Dee. Billy was gay, he was at least semi-closeted. The only way he wound up in the Bend? My bet is that he had been down here in this neighborhood, in these clubs. Otherwise, he'd never have a reason to be within two miles of here."

"Yeah?"

"This isn't on the way to somewhere else, so, yeah."

It was the smart money, he thought. The gay clubs in the slum of O Street, like R.J. said, were not here by happenstance. They had been forced out of their old haunts on Fourteenth Street NW and shoehorned here, by both development there and the anonymity of the neighborhood here —old, decrepit, impoverished.

They were coming up on the corner, the only pedestrians, the road itself six lanes wide. It looked barren, left for dead, but they were still less than two miles from the Capitol dome.

O Street itself was a block or so of low-slung warehouses that had once been carpet-cleaning businesses or storage facilities or some shit like that. Now it was an industrial zone that housed some of the most explicit gay clubs outside of San Francisco or Key West. Sully didn't know all that much about the area, other than it was patrolled on party nights by gay ex-Marines from the nearby barracks on Eighth Street, who went by the nom de guerre GEMS (gay ex-Marines), and that nobody found these places by mistake.

"Let's start with the Emporium," he said, nodding toward a spot three doors down, the door painted lavender. "Might as well go door-to-door. You want to piggyback with me or split up?"

Alex flicked her half-burnt cigarette into the street and left it there, blowing out a stream of smoke. "After that bit with Dee Dee's mom? Seriously? Split up. You run people off."

The first two places were dead ends. The Emporium wasn't open yet and the bartender in Secrets, the only guy in the place, told Sully to go fuck himself, asking about customers. He waited twenty minutes for the manager of Ziegfield's to show, the guy finally coming downstairs and leading him up some narrow stairs to a cluttered office, offering him tea or coffee, then sitting down, listening seriously to him, and finally saying no comment. The guy eyeballing him, like he was gay and maybe just looking for a little action.

It was nearly an hour before he met Kenneth, the bouncer at Storm, who was bringing in cases of beer, wine, and whiskey from a truck parked out front. The place wasn't open yet—not for business, anyway—but Kenneth told him that he could ask whatever he wanted as long as he was carrying a case inside while he did.

Sully picked up a case of Amstel Light off the flatbed and stumbled inside. The lighting was dim, the walls were black, and the hallway narrow before you went through a curtain of beads and into a large room, a long wooden bar with a mirror-lined wall behind it, bottles of spirits on the shelves, all the way up to the ceiling. He set the case on the counter, looking around, the banquettes along the wall looking greasy, like they needed to be wiped down.

"So who is it you work for again? You're not with the cops?" Kenneth was talking, moving behind the bar, bottles clinking.

Sully pulled a card out of his wallet and flicked it across the bar. "D.C.'s finest already been here about the Ellison kid?"

Kenneth, looking at the card, fiddled with it. He shrugged. "I guess. I dunno. A couple of detectives were in here the other day, asking about Billy."

"What'd they ask?"

"They talked to the boss, upstairs."

"Right. When was this?"

"Yesterday."

"I think you're talking about the lead detective on Billy's killing. You know what he talked about with the boss?"

"I wasn't upstairs, so, hey, no idea. Other than I'm not supposed to talk to anybody about Billy. Nobody is. That's what he came out and said."

"Okay. So, ah, you're not worried about talking to me?"

"Long as you don't put my name to it. Boss is in Alexandria for the day."

"While we're chatting, anybody else been down here, asking around? Other reporters, maybe they look like private investigators?"

"Nah. It was the cops, the boss says, the cops want us to shut up; there hasn't been anybody else asking around. Well. This photographer lady stopped in a few minutes before you did, but she had a card from the paper, too."

"You didn't talk to her?"

"I don't like cameras."

Sully nodded—too bad for Alex—and waded in. When he asked Kenneth if he knew Billy pretty well, Kenneth snorted and said of course and that there were hardly any black guys in here anyway, much less ones with dreads. Kenneth had some sort of New York accent but Sully didn't have the familiarity to place the borough. He had this no-nonsense, confident manner, leaning forward slightly when he talked, heavy on the eye contact.

"Billy'd be in here Friday nights, Saturdays, sometimes Thursdays," he said. "He liked to sit over there." He motioned to the back corner away from the dance floor, a circular booth set into a corner notch.

"Okay, yeah," Sully said, "the party nights. People like him? He a pain in the ass, what?"

"Liked. Billy was liked. Sweet kid. He'd pull up in a Benz convertible, one of the old four-fifties, one of the classic ones, always a white boy on his arm. Like he was the Great gay fucking Gatsby. You couldn't miss him."

"So, he was dealing ganja, a little coke out of the corner booth?"

A full stop, pausing, looking at him. "Not that I knew about."

"Come on. You're the bouncer. He brought it in, you had to be taxing that."

Kenneth snorted again and stopped pulling wine bottles out of their cardboard cases and asked what it was to him, both hands on the bar.

"Nothing? He was doing nothing?" asked Sully. "I'm just trying to figure out if he used or dealt. Was he a big player or an end user? You see what I'm asking here."

"I'n see it fine, I just don't know why you're asking it," Kenneth said, going back to sorting the bottles. "There's a connection or two in here, yeah, sure, whatever. But it wasn't Billy."

Sully, rubbing his hand across his mouth, trying to square this. "Maybe he did at the other clubs?"

"Nah. Something like that, I'd have known. The bouncers, the bartenders, the owners—it's a small block. Now, hey, look, maybe Billy snorted a line or blew a spliff? But a dealer? No way."

"Okay. I'd had somebody tell me he was."

"They were wrong."

"Fine. Okay. No skin off mine. You know Billy's white boy?"

"Which one?"

"I was talking to one of his buddies, over at Georgetown, he seemed to think they were dating. Kid named Elliot."

"You want some advice?"

"Sure."

"Stop using people's names."

"Great. The white kid from Georgetown."

"I know who you mean."

"He seemed to think he and Billy were a pair."

"When Billy wasn't pairing with somebody else."

"You're saying Billy was sort of a slut."

"Not to speak ill of the dead."

"Hunh. But, okay, Billy, he bring in any fights, weapons, scary drug dudes?"

"He'd be banned for that, I mean, bounced hard. We got a license, right? You think we're going to get any love from the city council, police stage a drug raid in a queer bar?"

"So, Billy, what you're saying, wasn't a scary guy?"

"Billy made Little Richard look butch."

Outside, he turned a corner into an alley and there were two guys standing back there. One of them smiled and said, "Ten bucks?" Sully said thanks but no and went back into the street and Alex was pulling up in the rental, shades on, windows down, saying, "You getting blown off in the alley? Jesus."

He popped open the passenger door and plunked down in the seat. "I was committing journalism," he said, "not fellatio."

"In an alley?"

"That's not where I was committing it."

"The journalism or the fellatio?"

"Could you just drop me off at my house, Pocahontas? I got calls to make."

She accelerated, skipping through the light on South Cap, a light more red than yellow. "You get anything back there? Seriously, I got dick. The cameras. I got kicked out of Traxx. Nobody said sweet fuckall."

"I got a bouncer in the main club. Sounds like Billy was hanging out. Guy was saying Billy might have blown a joint, but he wasn't a dealer."

"So?"

"The family is making a big deal about keeping Billy's dealing out of the paper."

"So they paid the bouncer to shut up."

"Might be," he said, watching the neighborhood roll by, "but it wasn't the guy's vibe. He told me the cops had been down there. I asked about other guys, these investigators the family hired? Dude said he hadn't seen nobody like that."

"I repeat: He gets paid to shut up."

He bit his lower lip, squinting. "Yeah, but the thing is? I believed him a lot more than I believed Shellie Stevens, the family shill."

"Nobody believes lawyers. About anything. I did my will last year, did I tell you? I was running around the West Bank all the time and started thinking about it. Wanted to make sure my mom would get my payoff if I got popped, y'know? So I got this lawyer to draw it up, and the first thing I did? Hired another guy to review it. They're shit, all of them."

"So had the first guy fucked you over?"

"No, thank God, but who can tell? That's the point. With lawyers, who can ever fucking tell?"

TWELVE

MARCUS YOUNG, THE retired chief historian at Howard University, was a quotable son of a bitch, so when he picked up on the fourth ring, Sully skirted around the edge of the kitchen table, surprised at getting him so easily, balancing the phone in one hand and a Basil's over ice in the other, trying not to drop either or both.

"Dr. Young, hey now," Sully said, sliding into a chair, phone and bourbon safe, reaching for his notebook. "It's Sully Carter, at the paper. Calling about Frenchman's Bend this time. Slave depots in antebellum D.C. Working on a story. Talk to me."

Before he could get the top off the pen and open the notebook, Young harrumphed into the phone and said, "Is this about Billy Ellison?"

Sully squinted one eye shut. He hadn't thought before dialing. Young had been born in D.C., never left, studied at Howard, then taught there, still lived in the Shaw neighborhood, a nice three-story row house. Had known Ellington, been onstage at the March on Washington, was longtime friends with Shirley Horn. . . . He wasn't about to piss off Delores Ellison, who had probably given him a grant for half of his career, for a cause no better than a quote in a newspaper story.

"You read the paper," Sully said, rolling with it, trying to make it work. "Yes. Ellison. Sure. It's about Billy Ellison. And Frenchman's Bend. The history."

"Billy was killed in the Bend?"

"It appears so, though I can't quite print it yet."

"I feel badly for Delores," Young said. He was emeritus these days, worked out of his home office. Sully could hear the man stirring about. A microwave beeped and started humming. His standard morning tea, for which he was famous. "I met Billy once or twice. In passing, at one function or another. William, his father, was of course a wonderful man."

"Of course."

"Did you know that Delores's great-great-grandfather, Nathaniel Ellison, was founder of the Washington Trust Bank, in the late nineteenth century? First black-owned bank in the city, if not the region?"

"I had heard that," Sully bluffed, scribbling fast to keep up, working in a sip from the drink. "Seems to have made a mint."

"The richest black man in the city, in his day. One has to marvel at the accomplishment, a black making money when the controlling interests hated the very idea."

He paused, Sully hearing the microwave door click open, the scuttlings of saucer and tea and milk. "So they know Billy was actually in the Bend when he was killed?"

"Unofficially, yes. Officially, not yet. Blood tests coming back, they found his shoe there, you'd have to believe it washed up on shore by accident. . . . Look, the piece I'm doing, it's a nonstory if Billy wasn't killed there. This is for Sunday. The police will have confirmed it or not by then. I'm just legging it out here, and you're the guy who wrote all the books on the history of the city, so, I'm just looking for an informed source who can—"

"Can what?"

"—talk about, well, okay, slavery in the city, back in the day. All I know is that the Bend was a scary place, some sort of slave house, portal, what have you."

"Is that the sum total of your knowledge?"

"On this?"

There was a sigh, followed by a long pause.

"I'm sure it's old hat to you," Sully said, looking up at the ceiling, "but I really don't think—"

"The Bend was part of a very complex economic system," Young said, sounding tired, an *umph* escaping his lips, Sully picturing the man sitting down at the kitchen table. "So. As I told my students, the ones who knew even less than you. Take the black and white out of it. Don't confuse your modern thinking with yesterday's. This was about profit and loss. It was trading in livestock, like cattle, sheep."

"If you say so."

"I do."

"Okay."

"Write that down: This was about profit."

"I already did."

"Now. The Bend wasn't the only slave house in the area, that's primary. You can't think this was some special hellhole. There were several slave portals along the river and in the city proper. This is after 1807 and, for our purposes here, before 1850, you understand? It's important. The international slave trade was outlawed by the U.S. Congress in 1807. The importance here is that it made African Americans already here much more valuable, because there wouldn't be any more imported. Or not many, in any event. The *domestic* trade in slaves became all the more important."

"Right."

"So then. In our nation's lovely capital, the District, the domestic slave *trade* was outlawed, again by Congress, in the Compromise of 1850. Slavery *itself* continued to be legal in D.C. until the reign of Lincoln, until April 16, 1862."

"That's the Emancipation Proclamation?"

A sigh.

"No. That much misunderstood document—which did not, for the record, end slavery in the United States—was still nine months away. This is the D.C. Compensated Emancipation Act."

"Ah."

"But here we're talking prior to 1850. When one could buy and sell slaves in the shadow of the Capitol. There were several such facilities. There was one, in a yellow house just behind what is now Independence Ave., about where the Department of Agriculture sits, but the exact location is disputed. They had a fence of wooden slats around the perimeter. Passersby wrote letters describing the place, shanties and poles, fingers wiggling through the boards. This is in full view of the Capitol even now, particularly so then. It is, I would surmise, half a mile. Downhill. In plain view."

"Jesus."

"It is your people, not mine, who—"

"I thought we were taking the white and black out of it."

"—were trafficking in, no, you're interrupting. But to the point: No other portals, locally, compared to the Bend. Infinitely bigger, infinitely worse. It was a holding pen for slave ships. It was often used as an adjunct of Franklin and Armfield, the slave-trading outfit across the river in Alexandria. You know of Franklin and Armfield?"

"Just the name."

"One of the largest slave-trading houses in the nation. It's a museum now. Thousands of slaves they sold down south. They used ships for slaves headed far down the coast, around Florida, up to the Gulf states. Those ships often docked at the Bend. But the Bend, it was larger than that. It was a staging, a holding point, for other slave houses. You could have hundreds of slaves penned up there, waiting for weeks and months."

"Sweet baby Jesus."

"As I noted earlier, African-Americans were, at the time, high-priced cattle and hogs. You could buy them in a lot, you could walk up and buy them one at a time. They had auctions the first Saturday of every month."

"So there were trading blocks, like that?"

"Before 1850? Perhaps, but I don't know about actual blocks. It was more of a small wooden stage they'd have slaves stand on so that the crowd could see. The Bend was isolated, out from the other wharves, from other buildings or houses along the southwest waterfront. It was an open area blocked off by a very high brick wall, almost like the fort that exists today, to the south. Inside the Bend's perimeter wall were one or two brick buildings and a wooden shack or two, and a pier for loading ships. The slave narratives of people who were there are scattered but shocking, even for the period. Rape, sodomy, the most base forms of humiliation and violence."

"Who ran it? Franklin and Armfield?"

"No. A man named Delacroix. A merchant who immigrated from Paris. Hence the name."

"What became of him? The place, the business?"

"He died soon after the war started. The Civil War. The business had been all but killed by the Compromise of 1850, but even as a holding ground it totally collapsed after the war, of course. The outer brick wall was demolished shortly after Lincoln's assassination. The rest just rotted and fell apart."

"What about later, though? Why hasn't the city done anything with it? It would seem—"

"If every former slave port or auction block was a national landmark, you couldn't drive through most southern cities, Mr. Carter. You know that. D.C. being, in this context, a southern city. There is no marker for the slave house that was on what is now Independence Avenue. Who would want one? 'Here, in the symbolic city of liberty, five blocks from the Capitol, was a small and petty dealer in human flesh'? What member of Congress is going to vote for that?"

"Okay, okay. Right. No one. So—"

"I grew up here, Mr. Carter. For all of my life and before, the Bend and the area around it has been a rough-hewn, ugly scab on the city's rump. The race riots of 1919, the Red Summer—do you know of this, the Red Summer?"

"In general. Across the country."

"Well." Young sipped his tea, a slurp down the telephone line. The man's wife had died twenty years ago and his daughter lived in Chicago. Sully pictured him in pajamas and a bathrobe, Granddad at home in the morning, eyebrows out of control and the bathtub needing attention. "This will answer the rest of your question. It was just after the end of the Great War, 1919. The black soldiers of that conflict were outraged to come home to the same old Jim Crow laws that they had left.

"Now. The white soldiers and sailors, however, came home to find what they considered to be a bunch of uppity Negroes in Washington. Some blacks even had federal jobs. Clerk, messenger, the like. Nothing like today. This was menial employment. Well. There were thousands of unemployed white troops just back home, congregated and milling about in Washington that summer and here were all these well-dressed Negroes taking the trolley back and forth to work like they owned the place. Now. At the same time, the newspapers—there were four of them—had been making headlines all summer with wild stories about Negroes raping white women."

"Truly a southern tradition."

"Indeed. So it is mid-July, a Saturday night, the nineteenth. Can you imagine this city—a swamp between two rivers, the heat, humidity, mosquitos, the misery in that time? Word went out—who knows, from hospital worker to friends, from soldier to sailor over a warm beer in a saloon?—that a nigger had raped a white woman."

"Ah, shit," Sully said.

"Do we need to describe the rest? For details only. Around Ninth and D streets in Southwest—this is not far from the National Mall today—a white mob fell upon a man named Charles Ralls, who had the misfortune of both being a Negro and being out in public that night. Another Negro named George Montgomery was walking home with groceries. His skull was fractured with a stone, a brick."

"How big is this mob?"

"Attendance was not taken, regrettably. Multiple newspaper accounts of the time say about four hundred, which probably means it was about seventy-five drunks. The next day, The *Washington Post* published a completely fictional story about the previous night's incidents and announced there was a general muster call of soldiers for a 'clean-up operation' downtown, to start about nine p.m.—that's about full dark, that time of year—and all soldiers should report for duty. Well. Let us apply our imagination to that factual image. The heat, the drudgery, the utter lack of intelligence, the comedown from fighting the war to being back home, or to be pedestrian, the simple lack of diversion or other sport. It was something to do. So they did congregate, in actual crowds this time, and they set out on a proper rampage. Blacks were pulled off trolley cars, a girl was killed in her home. It went on for four days. Fifteen dead, more than one hundred wounded."

"Newspapers being handy for inciting race riots."

"You have not heard me through. The point here is, ironically enough, that more whites were killed than blacks. Ten of the fifteen corpses. The number of critically wounded was about equal. This is the part of the story I want you to pay attention to. This was not a white mob against cowering Negroes. Black men, many of them former soldiers themselves, brought pistols, brought shotguns, brought rifles, to counter the white mob. The records, at least deemed by body count and physical violence, are clear. Negroes shot and killed and beat white people. It became something of a point of pride in the black community here, Mr. Carter, that the Red Summer was when black Washington stopped taking shit from the white man."

"And now it's Chocolate City."

"Mmmm." He sipped his tea and cleared his throat. "So you ask me, a native Washingtonian, you ask me about slave chattel in the nation's capital before the Civil War, about one of the places where black men, women, and children were kept in pens like pigs, half a century before the Red Summer? One such pen has been obliterated and built over. Another—the Bend—has been ignored and shunned, finding life only among drug dealers and criminals. What do I have to say? I say you are wading, Mr. Carter, into a very dark place. It is no place good. It should be dug up, dumped into the channel, added as landfill to Hains Point. Frenchman's Bend, I would say, in its life before the Civil War and in the century and a half after it, is the antimatter of the American dream."

THIRTEEN

SHE OPENED THE door and was surprised to see him there. The half step back, the lips parting, the carefully threaded eyebrows lifting. Her left hand fluttered to her mouth, then went down, coming to rest on top of her right, both holding the door handle.

"Mr. Carter," Delores Ellison said. "I wasn't—wasn't expecting you."

"I know," he said. "I wasn't expecting me to be here, either. Could I come in? It's just one or two questions that are bothering me. It would help a great deal. I want the story I write to be accurate, and there is no one who can clear it up for me but you."

He was standing on her front step, the street out front empty of television trucks and black sedans, nothing but the manicured yard and the trees blossoming into life, shade from the sun that was coming through the clouds now. It was maybe an hour and change since he'd hung up with Young. He'd walked around the house and out in the yard, called Alex but gotten her answering machine, and then said, Screw it. The questions that had come to him that morning, the noninformation that was beginning to come through about Billy's non–drug dealing, was bugging him too much; he couldn't sit still.

"I—I—well, we are planning the funeral," she said, looking at him, much more uncertain than during his first visit. "It is tomorrow. There's so much—I thought you had spoken to Shellie."

"I did," he said, clasping his own hands in front of him, mimicking her posture as much as possible. He'd left the cycle jacket and helmet on the bike, standing there in black slacks and a blue dress shirt. "He gave me a statement, and I quoted just about all of it in the short piece I did. But I'm writing another, much longer piece, as much about Frenchman's Bend as Billy, and Mr. Stevens's statement, as helpful as it was, didn't address everything. So I came to ask you about it."

The house behind her was dark, quiet, empty. Her eyes had a vacant look as well, and he guessed she was still on some level of medication.

"Restraining order?" she said, a hand flicking up to touch her hair, coming back down, looking for a place to alight. "Shellie said something about a restraining order?"

"He said that to me, too. But Mrs. Ellison, unless you have been declared incompetent by the court? Someone else can't obtain a restraining order on your behalf. Mr. Stevens did not assert to me that he was acting as your attorney. He said Billy was his godson, and he's your employer. I took his interest to be personal, not professional. Plus, in no way is there a restraining order currently in effect. If *you* tell me to get off your porch, I'll wish you the best and leave right now. There's no need for paperwork to get that done."

"Why—why do you care so much about what happened to Billy?"

He nodded. People, they either wanted you to do more or to get the fuck out of their lives. You were wrong either way. "Because his death happened to come into my scope of work, and it seemed wrong to dismiss it. I could pay attention to it, or I could lump it in with every other killing in the city. I chose to pay attention to it, because something went wrong. Billy, I can't see a reason for him being in the Bend, but you know and I know he was there that night. And because the police, well, you can't entirely trust the police."

"You are persistent."

"It's why I get paid."

She opened the door a few inches wider and stepped back.

The house was dark, quiet. The bustle of the staff that had been so prominent the other day was gone. As they passed through the front room into a hallway, he realized she was leading him back to the kitchen.

"They're handling the funeral preparations at the office," she said, reading his mind. "It's at the National Cathedral and there's just so much involved to place an event there. A production. Shellie is taking care of everything."

"That's good. It's a relief—a small one, at least—not to have that burden."

"I don't think you two got along, from what he relayed to me. A shame. Under other circumstances, I think you would like him."

"I really sort of doubt that."

"Water? Coffee?"

"No ma'am, I'm fine."

She opened the refrigerator, pulled out a slim green bottle, and pulled down a wineglass from the cabinet. She held the bottle out as a question. He smiled but shook his head no and took a seat at the kitchen table. She poured herself a glass, filling it well beyond halfway, and sat at the kitchen table. "So what have you discovered about Billy's death, Mr. Carter?"

"That's sort of what I wanted to ask you. I can tell you what I imagine the police already have—that he almost certainly was killed in the Bend. That he was a regular at the gay clubs on O Street, which are only a few blocks away, and that probably had some connection to how he came to be in Frenchman's Bend."

Her face tightened, but she only nodded. "And . . . and . . . anything else?"

"Well. I know that gay business doesn't make you happy. But I'm asking about three things. One, Billy's school friends say he did not show up for that last day or so of classes, and apparently there had been some sort of family argument that last weekend. I was wondering if . . . if that was about his narcotics, ah, problem. Perhaps you were trying to get him back in treatment, something like that? Could you tell me what happened that last weekend?"

"You said three things."

"Ah, yes. Three. The other two were names. Did Billy ever mention the Hall brothers to you? Or perhaps a man named Sly Hastings?"

"I may have heard them. I don't know. Billy had a lot of friends. Many of them I did not approve of. Are they—they the type of people who go to those O Street clubs?"

"No, ma'am."

"Oh."

"They'd be more in the narcotics line."

"Well then I certainly wouldn't know them. But, ah, Billy, he . . . he thought drugs were glamorous. I don't know why. He was a wealthy, privileged young man. He was quite proud of that, of our family name. Every class project he wrote in school was about some aspect of our name, our heritage in this city, how my family had become wealthy so early on, the hard work and sacrifice. But—and this is all between you and I, yes? You'll not print any of this?"

"Not if you tell me I can't."

"Well. You can't. You . . . you agree?"

"Yes, ma'am."

"Okay. Then okay." A long breath.

"Billy was unstable," she said. "He was an unstable young man to begin with. You should know that. You absolutely must keep that in mind. He lost his father at six. I think he never quite found his footing again. He was different, lesser, after that. It broke my heart.

"There were meetings with counselors, with headmasters, to be sure they understood. His grades were good, if not excellent, but something underneath had cracked. There was . . . was a birthday party at the ice rink at Cabin John. He was ten? Eleven? It was a great success. Nearly his entire class came. I was speaking with one of the other parents when Shellie—he was his godfather, and was there for everything—came to get me.

"Billy was alone on the ice, skating. Everyone else had come to get refreshments. And yet, there was the guest of honor, alone out on the ice, going in smaller and smaller circles, some sort of concentric rotation. With the most absentminded, blank expression that I have ever seen. Like, I don't know. Like what you picture when you think of someone who has been lobotomized. Just skating, barely moving his feet anymore, these circles, just coasting . . .

"So I went over to the gate onto the ice and called him. He did not hear. Then one of the attendants realized something was wrong. He skated out there. There was a commotion. The other children knew something was happening.

"The man finally reached him. It could not have taken more than ten seconds once he was on the ice. Possibly less. But it seemed an eternity. He was saying, 'Son? Son? You all right?' He was right beside him and Billy said nothing. Did not stir, did not blink, did not react in any way. And then the man reached out to take Billy's hand. Just reached out and touched it. And Billy just . . . *reanimated*. He came back to life. He did not blink or startle or jump. It was like a mannequin taking on life, going from plastic to flesh. Billy was suddenly there, the light back behind the pupils.

"He skated right over to the plexiglass, waving at his friends, sliding to a stop by the gate, stepping over it into absolute silence. They all just *looked* at him. And he noticed it. You could see that he noticed it. It went over his face like a shadow. And then it went away and he was giggling, laughing, a ten-year-old boy at his birthday, and he said something about video games and there was a burst of activity and laughter and shouting; all of a sudden it was just ten-year-olds at a birthday party again.

"Then it started happening when he was fifteen or sixteen. Episodes like that. Depressive spells. Outbursts. Days when he could not or would not get out of bed. Would not look at, or speak, or acknowledge that anyone was speaking to him.

"It was eventually diagnosed as bipolar disorder. They tried lots of medications. Elavil, early on, when he was down, and then they stopped that. Lithium. Others. They mixed, matched. Therapy twice a week. But on the whole, we were able to keep this quiet. I would imagine some of his classmates wondered, but I don't think he really told any of his peers. He got into Georgetown. We did not think we were out of the woods, but we were beginning to think his future would be bright to very bright."

She paused, looking at him. He waited.

"And then he started playing with cocaine," she said, letting out her breath in a rush. "Apparently it made him feel just fabulous, at least for a little while. And with that, he started having relationships that—that were not healthy, that—"

"You mean to say he was gay."

"No. I would not say that. I would say he was experimenting."

"Elliot, his, ah, friend at Georgetown, says they were having sex for two years, and that Billy was experienced when they started dating."

"Elliot is a depraved sort and is not, in any sense of the term, reliable."

"Okay."

"It just got all confused in Billy's head. He wanted to be like, I don't know, rap stars or some such."

"So you argued about that last weekend."

She eyeballed him, turning her head slightly to the side, sipping her wine, which was, he noticed, already half-gone.

"Yes," she said, pausing again. "He was dealing drugs out of his apartment. I—I told him that had to stop. He was getting in, ah, deep. A lot of drugs. A *lot*."

He nodded sympathetically. "It doesn't sound like you were happy about the gay aspect, either."

"What parent would be? We are churchgoing people, Mr. Carter. The Scriptures are clear."

"Yes, ma'am."

"Does that make sense with what else you're finding? Are these Hall people, are they helping you? Are the police telling you that they have suspects?"

"Yes, no, and no. The Hall brothers don't help anybody. The police have a very difficult case because there is very little evidence to go on, and, at least so far, no witnesses. People don't go wandering into the Bend by accident, particularly late at night, so there probably aren't more than thirty or forty people who could plausibly have been in the Bend at that hour, virtually all of them already known to police. But which one of them might have pulled the trigger? Very little way to tell. Even if three witnesses identified someone, those three people are going to be drug users, sellers, prostitutes, or all of the above."

"In other words, nobody that any juror would trust."

He offered her a wan smile. "That's about it."

She was fighting to hold it together now, the jaw trembling, the chin coming up the smallest of fractions. The hands again, fluttering. Jesus, he hated this, putting a mother through this kind of pain.

"I . . . I . . . that place," she said. "That place where he was killed."

"Frenchman's Bend."

"What—what a terrible place. For Billy. For everyone."

"Yes, ma'am."

"And what is it you're going to print?"

"Only what's relevant. I don't have any interest in embarrassing your son or your family, Ms. Ellison. But somebody out there knows who killed Billy, and I'll give eight to five that at least two other people know who that person is. I'm not, by any means, giving up. I think I can find them. I may, I think, have even talked to them already."

FOURTEEN

"DETECTIVE WEAVER. TELL me something good."

"Who is this—Carter?"

"Your new best friend, yeah."

"Hunh."

"So, Billy Ellison."

"What about him?"

"Who you liking for this?"

"Look, Carter, I just can't—"

"Parker'll tell you it's okay," Sully said, back home now, just for a minute. He was pulling his racing leathers out of the hallway closet, the one in his narrow front hallway, right before the kitchen. "I don't burn people, least of all cops who are playing straight with me."

A sigh down the line. Jeff Weaver was at his desk, Sully could tell from the background clatter, probably with this case and a couple of others on the table, rounding up witnesses for a few shootings last year, this one, that one, the meat grinder aspect of it all.

"The coroner gave us almost nothing from the cut," Weaver said. "The wound was through and through. No fragments, nothing to trace. Ellison, the kid's phones were clean, no calls to anybody who looks to be in the life. His classmates at Georgetown, all they know is he got into a spat with his mother the weekend before he got popped. We've pulled in, or been by to see, everybody who's anybody in the Bend and hey, what do you know, nobody saw anything."

"What about the report of the gunshot from that night? Who called that in?"

"Little old lady in the Carolina, that apartment building fronting Water Street, right by the Bend. Where the Hall brothers tend to hole up. Now she says she's really not sure."

"Somebody told her to shut up."

"You think?"

"What did Mom tell you about the argument?" Sully asked.

"That it was about him using drugs, selling them out of his apartment. She says she told him she was going to stop paying the rent if he didn't straighten out. Says he told her he could pay it his damn self."

"Did he have a sheet?"

"Nah. Totally clean."

"Not even juvie?"

"Nada."

"It strike you as odd, all that dealing and not even a traffic stop?"

"We can't catch 'em all."

"So, you got nothing."

"Nothing is two steps *up* from what we got."

Sully sat there, looking at the phone after he clicked off, the silence of the house descending.

"Bullshit," he said softly.

FIFTEEN

ALEXIS PULLED ONTO Sully's block half an hour later, finding a spot on the street, a small miracle at this late hour of the day. She got out, two cameras and a small bag of equipment slung over her shoulder, walking fast.

"Racing?" she said, coming up on him hard, looking at the full leathers he had on now. "You called me over here to go *racing* with you? The Ellison funeral is tomorrow, or did you forget? I'm still developing—"

"It's Grudge Night at Leonard's Cove," he said.

"—film from—what? What are you talking about?"

"Leonard's Cove. Race track, about twenty-five miles south. Way out in the Maryland boonies. Grudge Night is when they let anybody—you don't even have to have a racing license—drag the quarter, a straight shot. You get a few hundred gearheads and greaseballs out there, mainly motorcycles. Guys bet like crazy."

"You're not drunk, are you? Because, look, I got some really good stuff today, despite you killing our interview with Dee Dee's family. I was in the office developing. But if you're just going to go dicking around after dark, cutting it off after an eight-hour day to run around on your go-cart, then—"

"Pipe down," he said. "I'm digging on Billy. Finding guys who don't want to be found."

"At the race track?"

"As previously stated."

"Who?"

"You remember those enforcers in the Bend, the ones who said they'd cap my ass if I came back?"

"The ones who politely asked me if I wanted to buy something?"

"The tall one, with the dreads? I'm betting he'll be at the Cove to-night. He said if I brought my Duc down there he'd run me for pinks."

"You're going to tell me this means something."

"Pinks. Registration papers. The title. It means you race and the win-ner gets the loser's bike."

"And you're going to *do* this?" her voice rising. "This is why you're wearing leathers? Are you fucking daft?"

"Whyn't you come with me and find out?" he said, smiling, already knowing she wouldn't—couldn't—say no. "You can hold the papers, you want. Be my good luck charm. Hey, the leathers don't make me look fat, do they?" Turning to the side, letting her look at the black outfit, the gold piping, the flashes of white, striking a pose.

"You are—"

"They told me not to come back to the Bend, but they *invited* me down to the Cove. You want to talk to people, talk to them where they're comfortable."

"I haven't even eaten. I don't know where it is."

"They got barbecue at the track. And cold beer. I got an extra helmet and a jacket. Come on. See this here? It's a custom seat, sort of jerry-riggged, but it'll work. Just for you. Now. You going to go back to the office like a good girl or come out and play with the bad boys after dark?"

Sully kept the bike at an even sixty tooling down Indian Head Highway, keeping it in the slow lane because the cops knew it was Grudge Night, too, this one patrol car easing up alongside the bike for a good half mile, the cop eye-fucking him before pulling ahead. Alex tapped him on the right hip when the cop was past, and he tilted his head back a quarter turn to hear over the onrushing wind.

"Prick," she shouted.

He smiled and reached his left hand back and patted her upper thigh in response.

The land unfurled in a series of low hills and easy curves, farmland and houses with mailboxes on the road, the occasional roadside motel, the gas stations, a country market. Alex rode easy behind him, two cameras in her backpack. She sat upright with a hand of each of his hips, not leaning up against him except in the turns, when she pulled tight and leaned as he did. The natural rhythm to her riding gave Sully a contented feeling, one that he'd not had in too long, feeling her body against his back. Her dad, an Italian national who'd moved to the U.S. as a child, had been a lifelong biker, a Moto Guzzi devotee. Alexis had been riding since she was six. She could probably handle the bike better than him.

After a while, he took a left turn in a small depression of the road—the track wasn't marked, you just had to know—and went east for about two miles, then turned onto the road leading to the track, the noise a vibration as much as a sound.

The parking lot was filled with trailers, trucks, sports cars, guys on scooters going from their trailers, parked at the back of the lot, up to the stands, up to the concessions. Women walked in pairs, tight jeans and low blouses. Fires glowed in grills farther down, the smell of smoke and beef rising. Music blared from speakers, the announcer on the PA system calling the sprint races.

"These bikes are *quick* tonight people *quick* bikes *quick* bikes my goodness," and, in reference to something going on in the bleachers, "I don't care who you are, that's funny right there."

Sully flipped his visor up and told Alex to keep an eye peeled for Lanky Dreads.

"How would I recognize him?" she said.

"You don't remember him from the other day?"

"He wasn't pointing a gun at me so, no."

They rolled at a slow idle through the trailers. The rows of them extended all the along the track's straightaway to the finish line. The lights over the track were daylight bright, but the lights in the parking lot were almost all out, making the shadows between the trailers deep. It was useless, this sort of trolling, so he finally parked the bike in a narrow gap between two vans, close behind the bleachers.

"Been a while since I've ridden that long," she said, smiling, shifting her backpack to hang off one shoulder. "That was fun. I'm liking this place. Atmosphere."

"It's a classy joint," he said, getting a little of her vibe, glad again that she'd come. She lightened his mood. She was fun. She was good for him.

"So the idea," she said, putting the backpack on the bike seat, unzipping it, already pulling out her gear, "is for you to find the guy with the dreads. Then what? You race him and lose your bike? This is good exactly how?"

"*We* find him," he said, "and I get him to intro me to the Hall brothers. That's who I need to talk to. I'd never get to them in the Bend. Out here, though, they're in open air. I can just walk up on them. They'll be tailgating outside one of those vans down there, one of those trailers."

"How do you know which one?"

"I don't. But Lanky's a lieutenant in their outfit, the M Street Crew. He also races for pinks. That means that the crew rides, at least some of them. And you don't have to ride to come out to this. It's a social event. The guys from Southeast, from PG, who drag? They'll all be down here. Weed, gambling, a cookout, babes in booty shorts. What's not to love?"

"The ganja. Riding through those trailers down there? Wow."

"It was a haze."

"But why the Hall brothers? Why do you think they'll talk to you?"

"Good looks and personality," he said, "have always worked for me."

She took the infield of the track, using her press card and a smile to get past the guard, and Sully took the bleachers. He went up the aluminum steps at the far end, away from the press box, one at a time, minimizing the limp. When he made the landing, he turned and scanned the seats. A scattered crowd, maybe two hundred people. Women sitting in clumps, dutifully watching their men go at it out there on the track. Kids running up and down the rows. Most of the crowd was back in the trailers, the parking lots.

He walked through the bettors against the fence, turning sideways to get through, moving sixty, seventy yards down, moving into the long shadows, now coming up on the long line of bikers waiting to race. They were lined up in a double row, side by side, each paired off against their competitor. The bikes were turned off, the guys astride them walking the bike a few feet forward each time the line moved up, leathers unzipped to the navel. There was some soft chatter, and a peal of laughter from up front, but mostly it was tense. Game faces. The man next to them was the man they had to beat.

And then Sully blinked and grinned. Sitting astride a lime-green Hayabusa, wearing black-and-silver leathers, his helmet strap looped around the left grip, sat Lanky Dreads. To Lanky's right was a somber-faced black kid, close-cropped natural, glaring, sitting atop an iridescent blue Ninja.

Sully went to the back of the line, turned, and came up behind Lanky on his outside shoulder, started talking before Lanky could see him.

"Do I bet on you or do I bet on him?"

Lanky turned, lips together, surprised as Sully came to the fairing of his bike and stopped.

"You the one with the fucked-up face," Lanky said. Then, taking in Sully's leathers, his face lit up, like a kid going to the Popsicle stand. "You bring that Duc? You run for pinks? I'll go you right after this one."

The kid on the Ninja looked over at him, eyes flat, sizing him up, then turning away, unimpressed.

"I bet you would. No, I'm asking right now, are you going to outrun this man on your right?" He flicked his eyes that way. The kid over there cut his eyes at him, then cut them back, staying out of this, probably pegging Sully for a narc.

"Ain't but a C-note we got on it," Lanky said, "but yeah. Put your money up, right now. You'll get it back. But what about me and you? What you gonna do?"

The line moved forward then, a groaning and rumbling of bikes, the track getting closer, the PA announcer hollering like a pig in shit, engines whining up ahead at earsplitting decibels.

"I'll run you, but not for pinks," Sully said. "I got a deal. A prop bet."

"Shit."

"No, listen. I'll put up three hundred, but I run solo. I break thirteen, I keep my money and you walk me back to the Hall brothers. They out here somewhere."

Lanky blinked three or five times in a row, like he'd done at the park. He leaned over the tank of the bike, looking at him like he was stupid. Which, Sully conceded, he might be. "Why'd I do that?"

"Because you don't think I can break thirteen. Do you?"

"On what? The Duc?"

"Yep. Street legal."

"And what if—you—you don't?"

"I pay you three hundred."

"Bullshit."

"Nope."

"Show it to me."

Sully reached inside the top of his leathers, his fingers finding the zippered interior pocket, and pulled out five one-hundred-dollar bills, fanning them quickly, then putting them back. That got another look from the dude sitting on the Ninja, interest perking up now.

Lanky gave him a derisive, low whistle, the bikes moving up again, now on the edge of the track.

"Three hundred or you show me the Hall brothers," Sully said. "Put up or shut up."

Lanky held his gaze now, not saying anything, thinking.

"What, you sweating?" Sully said, leaning in closer, so no one else could hear over the noise. "Look at me. You think the skinny white geek with the fucked-up face can't ride, right? Right? Because the question ain't the bike, is it? The Duc can break twelve. You know it, I know it. So it's the dude on top of it, that's the bet. And you think I ain't shit."

"You got a mouth."

"Not that I can't back up."

"Then put down all five."

Sully considered. "All right. Five. Or the intro to the Halls."

Lanky Dreads looked at him hard, flat. "What you want with Tony and Carlos?"

"My business. All you got to do is point me."

"And you pop me five C-notes, you don't break thirteen?"

"Just like that. No hard feelings. Me, I grew up in Louisiana? I'm a Saints man. Paying off when I lose ain't nothing I ain't done a million times before. Who's holding? I give him my money right now." *Rat now.*

The bike was all but bouncing under him, the throttle wide fucking open. He couldn't hear, smoke was billowing off the back tire, he was leaning so hard over the tank that the zipper in his suit was cutting into his chest. The light walked down from red to twin yellows and then flashed GREEN and he let go of the clutch, all at once, just popped it and let the throttle take it all at once. The vibration shot from his feet, which came off the ground, up his spine, and ricocheted off his skull. The grips yanked forward, his fingers clenching on by a knuckle, his body flat on the bike but pulling backward, slammed back by the detonation under him. He couldn't see shit, just blurred colors and darkness. The rear tire tried to slide to the right but caught and he was screaming into the helmet, the world coming into focus.

His feet found the pegs and he shifted shifted shifted, the wind a hurricane trying to rip off his helmet. The lights blinked and there was the emergency wall of tires and hay bales looming and he downshifted so hard it nearly threw him over the grips.

He circled back around, coming up to the outside of the booth, where the attendant was leaning out, bored, a gimme cap pushed back on his head, a ticket held out in his right hand. Sully took it from him without stopping, idling forward, looking down at the tiny numbers in the dim light.

12:95 seconds.

He patted the bike. *You angel, you.*

SIXTEEN

"THEY THE ONES in the white-and-black tent," Lanky Dreads was saying, sullen, pissed off but doing it anyway, his leathers half-unzipped and him stomping as much as walking. Bets were bets and if there was one rule at the track that trumped race, gender, and economics, it was the law of the bet. Losers paid. Period. That didn't mean it didn't suck, and Sully thought the dude was taking it pretty well, all things considered. "They back behind that trailer."

The parking lot ran parallel to the straightaway, and he and Sully were edging their way through tents, three hundred yards from the grandstand, the noise from the track still deafening when the bikes came by. The smell of hot dogs, of burgers, of ganja, of hundred-proof gasoline.

"By the Suburban?" Sully yelled.

"Fuck no. The Expedition. The Eddie Bauer package. The Redskins tent? One past that."

"Now I got it."

Lanky turned and then came back, grabbing Sully's leathers to turn him around.

"Keep me the fuck out of it," he said.

"Yeah yeah. Don't get your panties wet about it."

Lanky Dreads gave him a half shove and left, getting as far away from him as fast as possible. Sully was fine with that. A smile on his face, a hot dog in one hand and a Miller in the other. Gotdamn. A hot dog and cold beer on race day.

Feeling his oats, he called Alex from his cell, putting the hot dog between two fingers on top of the can of beer in his left hand, the phone in his right, walking between the dozens upon dozens of tents, trailers, pickups with ramps down the back to unload the bikes.

"You mean you *won*?" she yelled.

"You don't have to act so surprised," he yelled back.

"I'm not surprised," she said. "I'm fucking *shocked*."

"I ain't nothin' but a winner, woman," he shouted back, telling her where he was going and to meet him at the bike in ten minutes.

He clicked off, chomping the rest of the hot dog, happy as a clam. The deeper he went into the lot, away from the stands, the darker it got. It had gotten chilly now that it was full dark. Women sat with blankets wrapped about them, the tight jeans covered up, the stiletto heels poking out at the bottom.

In a spot by the back edge of the parking lot, set among dozens of other trailers, he walked up on the Redskins tailgating tent—open air, no sides, just the overhead plastic. Half a dozen men sat around a small blaze in a fire ring, six or seven bikes on racks behind them.

He walked past that and there, set off a few yards from the rest, was a tailgating tent, half-black and half-white (it actually looked silver, making Sully think it was maybe a Raiders thing). They had a fire blazing in a copper fire pit, too, no steel mesh over it, sparks flitting up in the air, lost and wandering until they flamed out, about head high. He counted seven men sitting, two standing. The bikes were in a trailer behind them, a light on in there, somebody working over a Ninja with the panels taken off.

When he got within five yards of the tent, walking in a narrow passage between trailers, a man slipped into his vision, standing right in front of him, hand out, like a point guard spotting him up, fingers touching his chest.

"Whoa," Sully said, pulling up, spilling beer out of his can at the abrupt stop. He held his own hand up, motioning toward his mouth, still chewing the hot dog. He spoke louder than necessary. "Just wanted to talk to Mr. Hall."

The man—hell, it was a kid, maybe nineteen, could be twenty—who had his hand on his chest eyed him up. Then he turned and looked at the men by the fire, who had stopped talking and were looking at Sully.

"Which one?" said the kid, looking back at him.

"Either," Sully said. "Tony or Carlos. It's about Dee. You know. The late Dee Dee."

"What about him?"

"That's what I wanted to ask them."

The kid turned around again and said something low. The Halls, seated between the two other men around the fire ring, leaned back in their camp chairs, scarcely looking at him. Then the one on the right, the one in the black leather jacket, looked up and held Sully's gaze, then nodded. Sully figured this had to be Tony, the man in charge.

The kid pulled his hand from Sully's chest and stepped to the right, allowing him to pass, but stepping in behind him and closing the distance by a step. Sully looked around the men, making eye contact with each, being sure he didn't disrespect anyone, a longer gaze with Carlos, his eyes settling on Tony.

"Gentlemen, gentlemen," he said, not coming too close, just standing where he was, finishing off the hot dog now, sucking a dab of mustard off his left thumb, the half-filled can of beer in his right.

"Hey now. Was out running the bike. Saw you guys over here, thought I might mix in a little business on Grudge Night." He took a sip of beer, keeping it light, keeping it easy, taking his time. "I'm Sully Carter. I work at the paper. I'm working on a story about the Bend, about Dee Dee and that gay boy what got killed down there the other night."

This was greeted with crickets.

"You was out to the Bend the other day," Tony said, finally. He was looking at the fire, not at him. "You got told to fuck right on off."

The others around the fire leaned back now, enjoying this, tipping their chairs back on two legs. Tony looked up at him, giving him the time, folding his arms across his chest.

"I believe," Sully said, "I was asked not to reappear at the Bend, which I haven't. And when I came by out there? I didn't know there were *two* guys who'd gotten shot. I was only asking about *one* body, the most recent, which I have come to find out was this gay boy, Billy Ellison. Now, tonight, I'm out here racing my motherfucking bike, I stopped by to ask you about Dee Dee. Demetrius Byrd."

"You spouted some shit about the floater being a sailor." Tony, still looking at the fire.

"Actually, I think I said—"

"I *know* what you said," said Tony, still not looking up, "and I don't give a fuck, cracker."

Two of the men laughed, now sipping their beer, the fun just starting. One of them said, "Whoo," and blew out the smoke from his joint. Sully didn't move and the air tensed, Tony not playing with him.

Sully smiling, rolling with it. "Crackers, slim, they ain't from Louisiana."

"That right?"

"Yeah. It is. It seriously fucking is. 'Cajuns,' that's what you're looking to say. 'Cajuns.' Not 'crackers.' Starts with same letter, so I can see how it fucked you up, but it's actually, like, a whole different word."

"Hunh."

"*Crackers*, they from south Georgia, north Florida, like that. *Cajuns*, they from Louisiana. It's, like, a whole 'nother state, a couple hundred miles off. Like here, I'd call you a Jersey boy. That's how bad off you are, geography-wise."

Tony looked at him full on now, glaring.

"So I'm just a Cajun in the big city, right—the fuck do I know? Sophisticates like you. I ain't even asked nothing over there in the Bend about Dee Dee. Me, I was asking about Billy."

"Nobody said that faggot got shot in the Bend," Tony said. "He was swimming out in the channel, what I heard."

Sully sipped his beer, trying to keep this going.

"That's right," he said, nodding. "Absolutely. But, and maybe I didn't say this already, I ain't asking about Billy. I'm asking about Dee Dee." They all looked at him. "Demetrius Byrd. Part of your crew."

Tony looked at him, then at the others, then at the fire. Carlos stared him down.

"I do believe," Tony said, "the white boy can't hear."

There was whoop-whooping now, the others getting into it, the smell of fresh meat.

"*Me*, can't hear? Lemme try this again," Sully said. He'd never taken his eyes off Tony the entire time, if nothing else learning who was in charge here and who wasn't. "Billy Ellison, you don't seem to hear. Dee Dee Byrd, you don't want to acknowledge. So let's try another name. Sly Hastings. When I say 'Sly Hastings,' you hear that?"

The whooping stopped like the name of Satan had been incanted. The rest of the crew looked down into the fire, or off into the night. Carlos had not blinked, as near as Sully could tell. Tony looked at him, hard eye contact right back.

"Sly Hastings," Tony said.

"Yeah," Sully said, nodding. "Now look at this, now you can hear. Sly."

"What about him?"

"That's what I was going to ask you. You're running your turf down in Southwest, fine, great, people get popped. Whoop-fucking-ti. Means nothing to me. Then Dee Dee gets popped. Then the Ellison kid gets popped. And then, what do you know, Sly Hastings is on top of it, asking what's up, what's going on, why can't those tampon-douche Hall brothers handle their business without all—"

The middle of his back exploded, a deep *whump* like a blow to a punching bag, dulled only by the thick leather of the cycle suit. His head whipsawed back and his torso shot forward, his knees buckling, the beer flying. He flopped forward, getting his right foot halfway out in front to brace the fall, him now on one knee. The baseball bat came down again on his back, *whump*, knocking the other knee from under him, sending him chest-down onto the pavement.

He got his hands above his head and rolled toward where he thought the blow had come from, gasping. Above him was some guy he'd never seen before, walking around in front of him now, rolling the bat one handed, like he was warming up, batting practice.

Tony Hall's face appeared above him, three feet away. "The next one is going to be across your ugly-ass face, *Cajun*. I'n imagine that one'll put your brains on the asphalt here." He leaned forward then, spitting a thin stream of beer onto the pavement by Sully's head. "Now hear me, nigga. You listening? Look at me when I'm talking to you. Yeah? Right? Get your punk—"

Lights flashed over Tony's face, pop pop pop, beams and bursts of illumination, the light bouncing off the back of Sully's skull. He closed his eyes, the roaring in his head getting louder, then rolled away from Tony, trying to draw in air.

When he opened his eyes again, the man with the bat wasn't looking at him. Tony Hall wasn't looking at him. They were both looking off to his left. The circle of men around the fire were all looking that way, some of them standing. Sully registered another pop-pop of light.

Alexis stood at the outer edge of the tent, camera and flash looped around her neck, the camera at belt level. The flash went off, that pop of light, and he felt sick again. She had her cell in the crook of her neck, talking into it, taking a picture every few seconds.

". . . misunderstanding of some sort," she was saying into the phone, glaring at Tony, at the man with the bat, not even looking at Sully. "These guys get a little too much firewater, officer, you know how it is, they get to horsing around and it looks like a fistfight. I get closer, they're just girl-friends finger-fucking each other."

It was quiet as Sunday church in the tent, the men all staring at her. She said, "De Rossi. Alexis de Rossi. Photographer at the paper, down here at Leonard's Cove, Grudge Night, you know? Doing a feature shoot? In this row of trailers toward the back of the parking lot. I'm looking at Tony and Carlos Hall, you know, the M Street Crew in D.C.? But you get a squad car out here, your guys could ask them. They're just looking at me, sitting next to each other, like a bunch of puds."

Another pause, and she said, "That soon? No problem."

She clicked off the phone but kept it in her hand, still eyeing Tony, the man trying to figure out a play.

Sully squeezed his eyes shut tight, trying to clear his vision, wondering if Tony or Carlos had ever seen a woman like Alex, who had dealt with men worse than them in a Central American jungle, absolutely unfazed by the situation. He wondered, briefly, if Alex had a snub-nosed .38 in her belt loop and figured she'd fucking-A better.

He shook his head and pushed himself to his feet, nodding to Alex, taking two woozy steps in her direction, his feet feeling wobbly and a long way off. When he got to the edge of the tent—it felt like he'd walked a mile—he gave a half-turn. Tony was going back to his camping chair, the other men sitting down, the dude with the baseball bat choked up on the handle, looking hard at Alexis. It was over.

A cough rattled up out of Sully's lungs and he spit, a tinge of blood hitting the pavement. He blinked and said, "You got a misunderstanding." He said this to Tony, lights dotting the air in front of him. "I was trying to give you a heads-up. You don't understand. I was trying to help. But so help me God, when Sly comes for you, now? Don't you come crying to me."

SEVENTEEN

THEY WALKED IN silence back to the bike, staying close to the bleachers, where it was more open, with more light, more witnesses, at least an illusion of more security. Sully got to the bike and then leaned over and vomited, the beer and the hot dog and whatever else, coughing, heaving, spitting onto the asphalt. He sat there a minute, hands on his knees, hearing Alexis zip open her backpack, and a second later she was handing him a half-empty bottle of water. While he rinsed his mouth and spit, she said, quietly, shoving her cameras in her backpack, "If you can get on this thing, it'd be good to go. Nine-one-one told me it'd be twenty minutes before they could get a car out here."

He handed her the keys. "Crank it for me," he rasped, "and unlock the helmets."

She did, the engine popping, then purring into life, smooth as a cat on a ledge.

He leaned over and vomited again, spitting mucus. After a minute he stood up, a ragged jag in his back as he did, a grimace shooting across his face. He wondered, in the instant, if this was what old age felt like or if it was even worse.

"We gonna fly home," he coughed, spitting again. "I mean it. No way I'm going to let these pricks roll up on us out there, some 'accident.' It's twenty miles of dark road before we get back to the Beltway. Cops pull us over, we'll have your call to nine-one-one to back us up."

"You get your money's worth?" she said. She eyed him up, palms backward on her hips, pissed off good and for real. "That was the whole point of this? You getting your ass kicked?"

"I was trying to make a play," he said. "The Hall brothers are the two people on this earth who know who killed Billy Ellison."

"And you thought they would just tell you?"

"No," he said, the taste of vomit in his mouth, "I wanted to see if they jumped when I said the name Sly Hastings."

"And?"

"They jumped."

"On you, yeah."

"I been kicked outta better bars," he said. "And that reaction? That tells me they're spooked. That they know Sly is making a move on the Bend. That maybe *they're* the ones who offed Dee Dee, 'cause they pegged him as a mole. And if they offed Dee Dee—"

"Then maybe your idea was right, that Billy Ellison went down there to the Bend, asking for Dee Dee, not knowing he was dead, and they offed him, too, as an example to all and sundry."

He nodded, leaning over to rinse his mouth again. After a while, she started tapping him on the arm with his helmet. He stood upright to take it, the world finally coming into clear vision.

"Back there, how'd you find me, anyway?" he asked. "I said to meet me at the bike."

"Lucky for your punk ass, I met the dude with the dreadlocks. Saw him coming back on the track after your run."

"And he just *told* you?"

"I think he kind of likes me."

"I don't know," he said, coughing again, "that I'd be advertising that."

The next morning, a pair of deep bruises bloomed across his back like malignant cherry blossoms. In the light of the bathroom, naked, he looked at them in the mirror and said, "Goddamn."

They radiated pain, making him blink when he touched them, delicately plying them with his fingers. A cracked rib? Two?

He decided not to be a baby and washed down three painkillers with a bourbon and a splash and took the bike up to Jimmy T's. He put his files in his backpack and went to the same back booth that he and Alexis had sat in and Wanda brought him the standard waffle and coffee. After a few minutes, Wanda refilled his coffee and put a receipt under the cup and didn't say a thing. He tipped her ten dollars and did not speak.

Using the booth as his desk space, he set out the files from the backpack. Manila folders, each with the deceased's name and dates across the tab, all recent homicide victims in Southwest. All the names but one were male, and all but one was black—the outlier being Latino. Each decedent's home address, the location of their slaying, and any relevant phone numbers were written neatly across the top right of the folder. He sorted them by home address, looking for doors to knock on. He wrote these names and addresses on the back of a spiral-bound notebook.

He had eight names listed in black ink when his cell buzzed. The caller ID, when he fished it out of the backpack, was that of Jeff Weaver, the homicide cop.

"Detective," he said, "how you—"

"We got a match," Weaver said.

"I'm sorry?"

"The blood. In the Bend. O negative. Same as Billy Ellison's. John said you'd want to know."

"Excellent. Hey, that's excellent. But, ah, isn't that, like, the most common? Like, half the population?"

"You're thinking O positive. O negative excludes ninety-six percent of the black population, ninety two percent of white folks. But we know—can I speak freely here?—there ain't no white folks down there, so . . ."

"And Billy's shoe, thirty feet away," Sully said.

"Yep."

"So can I use that? The blood match, the shoe?"

"Yeah. I mean, as long as it's 'a source familiar with the investigation.' Not me."

"What's your comfort level with how the shoe got there?"

"One hundred and forty-four percent."

"Fabulous. Suspects?"

A coughing laugh down the line. "Everybody wants to be a comedian. Nah. No. Un-unh. Look, Mr. Carter, Sully, we're giving this one an extra shake or two because of the family connection, right? But I got three open homicides on my sheet. He's number four. And I'm going to be catching another case soon, I can tell you that, because ain't nobody taking a holiday out there on the gangster front. This thing? Man, no wits, no ballistics. The one lady in the Carolina who called in the gunshot, like I told you, now she don't know nothing."

"So you sitting there with your dick in your hand."

"Glad to hear you been listening."

"The family, they said they hired a private investigation firm."

"My nipples are erect just to hear it."

"You haven't bumped shoulders?"

"No, and we better not. The guys, PIs, whatever, go dig up one wit—*one*—who says he thinks he saw something, they'll express-deliver him to the evening news, Channel 4 live at six, and whether he's full of shit or not, I'll get a captain crawling up my ass. I'll spend two days tracking the wit down, checking him out, and I'll find out he was talking about a gunshot the *previous* Saturday night. Which you guys will put on page B-thirteen, if you put it anywhere."

"I hear you."

"Which don't do shit for me."

"I hear you."

"People got to understand—and look, if you're going to do some big story on the Bend, don't fuck me on this—this Ellison case ain't the blue-light special. I don't care who his momma is. This ain't a child homicide. This ain't a momma raped and tortured on her way to work. You understand? I know he's from a rich set of people and all? Trust me, I'm getting that from up top. But this is, by all that's holy, this is another drug killing in a city with about three hundred, three hundred twenty every goddamn year. Maybe ten or fifteen of your homicides are going to get a special ride. This one, a little bit, but not so much."

"Any word on his drug connections?"

"Small-timer, if anything," Weaver said. He sounded tired, like he was sitting back in his chair, tie askew, reports to be typed and collated, filed, sixteen calls to make on four different open files, and the wife hassling him about picking up the kids after school once for a change. "He'd buy, maybe over at the gay club he hung out at, bring some blow back to campus, move it over there. Maybe. But very, very small time."

"So why's the family telling me he's John Gotti?"

"Maybe they think an ounce is a bushel."

"Who was he buying from?"

"Not known. This guy, that guy. He wasn't moving no keys, I can tell you that. Only thing I can find? A couple of uniforms were trolling O Street a few months ago and happened across boyfriend here. He comes out of a club, high, talking shit, they frisk him, like that."

"No arrest?"

"None."

Sully sat back in his booth, arching his back, trying to keep the pain at bay by stretching.

"What about any street buzz that he was tapping into some of that top-end coke that's been popping up down there? He involved?"

"No way. No fucking way. He was nothing like that high on the food chain."

On the other end of the line, there was a clunk, a noise, Weaver moving his phone from one ear to the other, getting impatient, and Sully said, "Hey, what if he stopped over at the Bend on his way to the clubs? You know, cut out the middle man? Slumming, something like that?"

"Maybe he sashayed over there," Weaver said. "He was, what do I want to say, classically gay? The kind you know it right off? And maybe some brother over there didn't like the swish aspect."

"Could be," Sully said.

Still, something stunk.

Stevens's private investigators were supposed to be out there kicking over rocks, and yet nobody had seen them. Not Sully, not Weaver, not the bartender at the club. Meanwhile, Stevens was doling out threats that the Ellison family did not want to read about their son's drug dealing in the newspaper. It didn't add.

And then it came to him in a rush: Weaver and MPD, Sully suddenly realized, were meant to be fall guys for the family. The chump representatives, the incompetents, the Keystone D.C. police. If the family wanted Billy's reputation exalted, he saw now, then it was in their best interest that his case never be solved—certainly not if he'd been shot in a drug deal gone bad. Better to have it unsolved, unknowable.

"So you there?" Weaver was saying. "You with me? You seein' why this one isn't going to get much push?"

People liked to get upset about homicide, Sully thought, phone in hand, acting like it was the worst thing ever done, something no civilized society would stand for . . . and yet most cases went unsolved because no one who knew enough cared to get involved. The shooters who got away with killings weren't brilliant. They just killed people nobody really cared about.

"I got it," Sully said. "I got it."

Now Weaver was going on about the other cases he had piling up, this mother calling him about her seventeen-year-old, killed three weeks ago outside Ballou High, and *that* case, as fucked up as it was, had better prospects of being closed than the Ellison thing. . . .

Sully listened, doodling, looking at the names of the dead on the folders in front of him, pulling Ellison's to the top, flipping it open to look at his notes. Sure, under different circumstances, the murder of a rich kid might have been a case to elevate Weaver's homicide career, a great big gaudy closure. The chief would have him right there by the microphones at the press conference, announcing the collar. As it was, this was dirty laundry that no one wanted.

"Hey, detective, tell me something," he said. "You ever brace somebody down there in the Bend, an enforcer kinda guy, dreadlocks, tall, raspy voice? Dreads got little highlights on the end of 'em?"

"You talking about Curious George?"

"I don't know," remembering how Short Stuff had called the man Curious.

"Light-skinned brother, can't stop talking sometimes? Blinks all the damn time?"

"Yeah. Him."

"Curious George. George Ferris. An assassin for the Hall brothers. Tends to run around with a partner, short dude, that's Antoine Gillespie. Why you want to know?"

"He was sweating me the other day, when I's down there."

"Yeah, well, you give him room, you hear? Curious'll pop a cap in your ass just to hear what it sounds like. He fucks people up just to see. There was this guy one time? They were in grade school together, and he wound up pissing George off? We found the brother in a hotel room, one of those dumps down there in Southwest. Half of him was in the shower. You don't want to know about the other half."

EIGHTEEN

BY MIDMORNING, SULLY was going up and down the streets and alleys of Southwest, case files in his hand or half-stuffed into his backpack, knocking on doors on this pile of bricks or that one, back and forth in the James Creek public housing project. Right in the heart of Southwest, anorexic two-story row houses mortared together, thirty or more to a block, all of them looking like staggering drunks leaning on one another. Them with their crappy front and backyards behind sagging steel link fences. In the yards, plastic play sets and balls with half the air out of them. In the alleys, bottles of OE 800, empty packs of smokes, wrappers from rib joints. All these lives slapped up against one another. It put you in a mood.

Rap rap rap, he went on the door of 1729 Carrollsburg Place, home of Curtis Michael Lewis, killed in the Bend last year.

He stood there two minutes, sucking on wind. Finally the door opened.

He gave his name, showed his press ID and a picture of Lewis, and asked.

"I don't know," said the girl—she couldn't have been more than eighteen—who answered the door, not opening it past the length of the chain lock.

"Miss, are you a relative of Mr. Lewis? I don't mean to pry, I'm—"

"Who are you again?"

"Sully Carter," he said, pushing a card through the narrow opening. "I'm a reporter at the paper, and looking—"

"You not a cop?"

"—into the—what? No, I'm a reporter, not the police, but I was—"

And he was talking to a closed door.

It was the same drill at the former residence of Henry Andre Douglas, one street and three doors over. The man was dead since January. A no-nonsense dude, pushing fifty, wearing a wifebeater, answered the door. A smoke was perched on the edge of his lips. He looked at Sully's ID and listened to about twenty-three seconds of his opening spiel and shut the door, drawing the bolt behind him.

The next file was one David C. Rennie, last known address a couple of blocks down at 1510 First Street SW. Sully cranked the bike and rolled down there. The address said apartment 322. Great. Top floor and a walk-up.

He waded through the ankle-high weeds, pulled open the door, paused, relieved there were no gang-bangers in the stairwell. Hoofing it up the steps, alone, the place smelling of greens and macaroni and cheese and Clorox.

The door looked like the rest: brown wood, beat to shit. Rapping with his knuckles, he felt the throbbing in his back and looked at his watch. Still just ten forty-five. Billy Ellison's funeral was across town at one o'clock. The eyehole darkened, then lightened, and a voice behind the door said, "What you want?"

"Hi, I'm a reporter? I'm here about David. David Rennie."

The door pulled open about six inches.

"Don't talk so loud," said the young woman, short, stubby, looking up at him. "They'll hear you."

"They?"

Her eyes, behind glasses, darted down the hall, then back to him.

Sully, handing her his card, stage-whispered, "Ah, okay. Could you let me in, so we could talk? I'm writing a story about the Bend. And I wanted to ask you some things about David."

"Why you care?" she hissed back, holding the card, not even glancing at it. "It's been two years. More. Two years, three months."

"Yeah. It has. But I'm just now getting around to writing about it. People keep getting shot."

Her face did not soften but she stood back enough to let him in, warily, like she might just pop him with a shiv. Squeezing through the small doorframe, he was talking, explaining himself, the place opening up as tidy, small, and with a window open in the kitchen to catch a breeze. It was hard to believe he hadn't stepped through a portal to a different realm. Wooden bookcases lined one wall—they were filled, top to bottom, with hardcovers and paperbacks—and there was a simple cloth couch and end table. On it rested an open textbook and a spiral-bound notepad. The place smelled nice. Grapefruit, he decided. It smelled like grapefruit.

"Homework," she said when she caught him peering at the open textbook.

"Ah. Where you in school?"

"UDC."

"In?"

"Graphic design."

"Could I ask your name?"

"You can, yeah, and it's Diamond, but we're not talking about me. You wanted to talk about David." She looked down at his card. "*Mister* Carter. What? They arrest somebody?"

"No, no, nothing like that," he said, apologizing, explaining the story one more time—a long feature on Frenchman's Bend, the slayings that happened there, how they were overlooked, and—"

"Your paper didn't do shit on them, either," she said. "I don't know what you talking about, like somebody else overlooked them, and here you are, riding to the rescue."

"No, no, you're right. I didn't mean to say we were."

"Well."

"But I am asking now. I'm interested. I am."

She eyed him up, taking his measure, and let out a breath.

"What you want to know?"

"About him. About what happened."

"This in the paper or not?"

"Whyn't you tell me happened, and then we'll decide what's in and out. For now, out. Unless you tell me okay at the end."

"Why I'm gonna trust you?"

He shrugged. "I dunno. You mind if I sit? My leg. It's jacked."

"Go ahead." A nod.

He sat at the table, in a straight-backed chair. "Thanks. Thank you. So, let's be straight, you don't want to trust me, don't. I'm not selling nothing. I'm just writing a story in the newspaper. Is it going to help you, your family? Find the shooter? Probably not. Check that, no way. It ain't. But I'm here. I got my notebook open. I'm trying to find out what I can."

"Hunh."

"Whatever that's worth, you tell me."

"About what I paid for it."

He held up his hands. "Stipulated."

She sat down, too. Not really giving a damn but running through it.

"Davey ran shit sometimes," she said, one elbow on the table, sometimes looking at him, sometimes looking at the television, which wasn't on. "Couldn't get a job worth the hassle. McDonald's? Splash, the car wash? Please. Where else he going to work? He dropped out in tenth grade like all his stupid-ass friends. So, he sold a little bit, not a lot, but then, hey? He got a job at a moving company. He was working. He just kept dealing a little herb on the side. 'Pocket money,' s'what he called it."

"Sounds fair."

"Yeah."

"And?"

"And he went to get some shit at the Bend and got his ass shot."

"Did the police ever—"

"No."

"I didn't get—"

"Don't matter. Cops didn't spend half an hour here. Detective called twice. Never heard nothing after that."

"You got any ideas about—"

"I don't sell shit, so, no."

"You miss him?"

"Is this the emotional part of the interview? Yes? Kind of question is that? Of course. Every day. He was a fuckup but he was my big brother. Why you think I got through school? 'Cause if you fucked with me, you bought Davey bringing a beatdown. He looked out for me. For my mom."

"She lives here with you?"

"Why you asking?"

"Okay, okay. I don't have to know. I—"

"Look, I don't mean to be rude. You seem all right. But I got an exam this afternoon. The problem with Davey, with most of the brothers out there, is margin of error. You hear? And let me tell you, the minute I get my degree in December and get me a job, Momma and me are out. *Out.* But the problem here is—and you know it—margin. Of. Fuckup. Bethesda, Potomac, white boy gets in drug trouble? Suspended, counseling, expunged. Puff, poof, bye-bye. Brother down here gets caught dealing? Arrest, record, expelled. And where he going to find a job then? Don't talk to me about a GED. Right. The CEO of Riggs Bank, he got a GED? That truck driver what married your sister and beats her ass when he get drunk? Yeah. *He* got a GED. So the margin down here, especially for a lot of the males"—here she held up her thumb and forefinger toward his face, the two digits with their red nail polish separated by the width of the side of a piece of paper—"is about like that. How you going to write that in your newspaper? How wide you going to call that?"

NINETEEN

BACK AT THE house half an hour later, a second round of painkillers and a fresh shot of Basil's had him feeling better, getting out of the shower, looking in the steam-covered mirror again at the twin welts across his back, deepening into something like a ripe eggplant. It didn't hurt as bad as it had when he got out of bed. Buttoning his dress shirt, buckling his belt, sitting down to pull on his socks, he conceded that maybe it *did* still hurt as bad, he was just too numb to feel it. Prescription medication and alcohol. God was a genius.

By the time he was knotting his tie, the taxi was out front.

"The National Cathedral, quick like," he said, sliding into the back-seat.

The driver pulled out—he had never paused talking on his cell, going on in a language Sully couldn't place—and Sully called the desk, the clerk putting him on hold while he went to hunt down R.J.

When the man came on the line, Sully jumped to it, looking out at the Capitol Building, rolling down the Hill on Constitution, crosstown traffic midday not bad.

"Carter? This you?"

"It is."

"Well now. Off to the funeral event of the year?"

"I am. In need of a little pick-me-up."

"How's that?" Turning his mouth to the side, talking to someone else in the newsroom, muffled, coming back, "Yes, so, say what again?"

"Young master Billy turns out to be a fixture down there on O Street, but he's not much of a dealer, looks like," Sully said, lowering the window a crack to get some fresh air. "But, hey, the Hall brothers? Dudes what run the M Street Crew? Knew him well enough to call him a 'faggot.' So, yeah, Billy boy was known over there in the Bend."

R.J. asked him to repeat it and he did.

"Ah, the dark underbelly of the American dream," he said, and Sully closed his eyes briefly and thanked the stars that he had an editor who Got It. They were as rare as purple unicorns.

"It's like *Blue Velvet*," Sully said. "You see that? The David Lynch thing?"

"The underlying horror of suburbia," R.J. said, "Dean Stockwell, 'In Dreams.' The severed ear."

"Exactly. So we're seeing it the same way. Horror Story in the City, as opposed to suburbia. It's about the tragic pull of the Bend, the promise of the easy high and the quick dollar, the allure of slumming even for—"

"A kid who's got it all," R.J. said. "But the kid has to be sympathetic in this thing, even if, you know, he actually wasn't."

"I know it."

"We can't bash him, for God's sake."

"No plans to."

"Who's the hero?"

"Billy Ellison," Sully said.

There was a pause.

"The dead kid is the hero? Gay, drug-user hero?"

"Absolutely."

"Spin it to me."

"In the tragic sense," Sully said, moving around on the seat, trying to get comfortable. "He's a charmer, this kid; he's on the ball, carrying on for his dad who died too young, left him alone with—"

"The mom, the mom. Yes. Delores. Good. Good. I like it. But why isn't she the hero? Mom? Soldiering on, despite the loss of husband and son."

"Because what we're really writing about is the Bend."

"Right. But moms are good. Readers like moms."

"Mom talked to me a little yesterday, but I imagine Shellie Stevens is going to break into hives when he finds that out, so it's going to be hard to make her the hero when we don't have sweet fuckall from her. She hasn't set up a memorial trust, gone on television to plead for help, so what, you know, am I going to use to make her heroic? Besides, she didn't get shot in the Bend. Him, Billy, he did. We've got the Lost Promise of Youth thing going."

"I see what you're thinking," R.J. said. He paused, then said, "What's with your voice?"

Sully, tensing—shit, he wasn't slurring, was he? "Nothing," he said, coughing twice, for the effect. "I was running the bike out at Leonard's Cove last night. Got in late. Up early. I don't get paid enough, I been meaning to tell you."

"Running the bike? You're out dicking around, we got this thing working?"

"What do you think I'm doing out there? Digging, brother. There's some of the guys near the Bend got bikes. They race down there at the Cove. I went out there to confab."

"Yeah? And?"

Sully thought for a second. "Like I said. We chatted. They didn't care for Billy boy."

"They say anthing else?"

"Ah, no."

"Hunh. So you *were* just dicking around."

Sully closed his eyes and pinched the bridge of his nose with two fingers. Editors. Did he just think R.J. Got It? Seriously? What would R.J. say if he told him about the baseball bat beatdown?

"You put it like that, R.J., it was sort of a bullshit night." He looked out at downtown passing by the window outside and bit his lower lip to keep from saying anything else.

"So where are we on the police investigation?"

"Dead in the water," he said absently, the taxi braking for a light.

"Like young Billy. Punny."

"It's not what I meant. Well, figuratively, it's what I meant. Police got nothing so far. Somebody thinks they heard a gunshot, that's about it. The lead detective all but said flat out that it's going to stay in red ink."

"Which means, not closed."

"Right. So, Billy, the kid, this guy, the way we write this, he's our hero with the tragic flaw. Golden Boy, Golden Life, but . . . the Achilles' heel. It's Greek tragedy, man, I'm telling you."

"All right. All right. Stop trying to sell me so hard. You'll have to go easy on the gay business."

"Wait, because why? I've got it solid. It's not in dispute. He wasn't all that closeted."

"Not to his friends, but to the rest of his mother's set, he certainly was," R.J. said. "And we've got to consider relevancy. He was gay, so what? What did that have to do with him getting killed?"

"Maybe some, maybe nothing. Tony Hall, I told you what he called him. Indicates malice, motivation, like, relevancy."

"Hall told you this on the record?"

Sully thought about it. "He knew he was talking to a reporter."

"Well. Possibly. I'll look at it when you get it in print. Which will be when?"

"In a taxi, brother, on the way to the kid's funeral now. I'll come in after that and get started. Need to round out some calls, some due diligence, and we'll slap this puppy onto the front page. It's going to kill. The Bend, I'm telling you—you want underbelly? You want nightmares? That place is *dark*."

The cars and limos were backed up onto Wisconsin Avenue when the taxi approached at five minutes to one. They sat in the line of cars, police directing traffic, Sully looking out the window at the mammoth stone edifice, its Gothic towers soaring into the air, dominating the modest skyline.

You could see them from everywhere, brooding, magnificent in the light of late autumn, cold and forbidding in the snows of January, resplendent in the haze of summer. If you were going to build a church, he thought, this was the way to do it, all those gargoyles and faces set into the lime-stone towers looking down on you as if they were God's personal repre-sentatives.

"Quicker if you walked from here," the driver said, taking his ear away from his phone. Sully looked over at him, startled from his thoughts. A Sikh guy, thick mustache and beard, salt and pepper, a light blue turban, looking at him in the rearview mirror, heavy accent.

"I know," Sully said. "I'd rather ride."

The man hunched his shoulders and turned back around, going back to his conversation.

They inched into the right-hand lane, the driver cutting in, waving thanks to the car behind. A patrolman held a hand up in front of them, toot-ing his whistle at the cars turning from the southbound lane, letting two, three, five cars pull in front of them, then stepping out of the way. It was ridiculous to sit here, but Sully, what with his face, that gimp-legged walk, would be easy to pick out of a crowd, and he was taking no chances in case Shellie Stevens had people looking to screen him. He walked a hundred yards of open ground to get to the front entrance? Any shark would chew him up like a slow-swimming seal.

Halfway through the circle, by the side of the church's preschool playground, a group of college kids, ten, fifteen of them, came walking through the cars. Sully pushed open the door. He pulled a twenty from the breast pocket of his suit and held it out over the front seat, tapping the driver on the shoulder with it, the man's brown eyes turning.

"Keep it," Sully said.

He made it out of the taxi two steps behind the group and tried to nestle himself in the middle of them. Walking, head down, he made it up the steps before he looked up. Ushers were extending programs to the incoming streams of mourners. Then he was into the opening of the mas-sive sanctuary, its grooved pillars shooting up and away into the overhead gloom, ushers steering the murmuring herd this way and that. He followed a man in a gray suit into the next-to-last pew at the very rear of the church.

The cathedral itself was ecumenical, but he was willing to bet the Ellisons were Episcopalians or Catholics or AMEs, certainly not the Baptists of the type among which he'd been raised in Tula, that tiny lost town just behind the levee, its shotgun shacks and ranchers set on concrete blocks.

"I want to welcome you all," a pleasant male intoned from somewhere up front, the assembled raising their heads, craning necks to see, the voice drifting around and past the flags hanging impossibly high in the nave above, floating to the rose window in the back.

When his family had gone to church, bleary-eyed and gussied up, Sully never really felt like they belonged. You had to go sometimes, at least sometimes, or be socially ostracized as the godless pagan white trash at the end of the road, so his mother clamped a smoke between her lips and pushed and bullied them out of bed every fourth or fifth Sunday. His father amiably stood for it.

"We gather here to mourn, yes, but also to celebrate," the voice said, startling him back to the present. "To give thanks to our God for his solace in our grief, for the joy in having given us the life of this wonderful young man for as long as he did."

Sully closed his eyes and saw his mother's beauty parlor after the robbery. It was on a side road off Main Street, which is what they called Highway 65 as it passed through town, all twelve blocks of it. The big plate-glass window of the shop was pristine, the yellow cursive lettering just like his mother had liked it. The three swivel chairs were still there in front of the mirrors, the three big, bulbous hair dryers at the back. Everything else was knocked over and broken, one of the big mirrors was shattered, and there was still a messy glop on the black-and-white-checked tile where his mother's body had fallen, shot twice in the chest and once in the head.

The sheriff, Mr. Evans, telling his dad all the money in the register was gone and they had no suspects and did he know anybody who'd have wanted to do Cindy any harm, anyone at all.

The morning after the funeral he'd been at the breakfast table in the half-light, weeping and snot nosed, moaning that he'd wanted to see his mother one more time but the casket had been closed, his father with a bourbon for breakfast, his sister stone-faced and unseeing, the old man himself seven months from the car wreck that would kill him, drunk out of his mind, the F-150 impaled on a pine tree on the side of the road, three miles from home and five miles from the roadside bar where he'd had six beers and six shots of Jack.

Sully had not attended a church service since.

A woman stepped onto the altar, Sully tilting his head to see her, tall and thin, black dress falling from her shoulders. The organ came in softly. And now she looked out over the assembled and opened her mouth and her voice began on the lower reaches, rolling out over them like the tide, like something unleashed more than performed.

"Ave Maria" rumbled all the way to the back, effortless, the held and released notes. And then she took a breath and moved into the higher registers, something hard to believe could emerge from a single human being, a thing that caught him below the ribs and made him hold his breath, a mezzo-soprano voice as pure as sunlight, as rich as mahogany. Now it soared into the vast reaches of the cathedral, high above them, unseen and untouchable, a thing that curled around and caressed them all. He felt something stir inside him, something lost and forgotten.

Twelve inches from his right ear, a clean-shaven white man with bull shoulders and a tiny microphone in his ear settled his left hand on Sully's shoulder, whispering: "Sir? I'm going to need you to get up and come with me."

They were outside, the bull-shouldered man behind him, two others flanking him now. There was a man in front of them all, pulling off his sunglasses, his double-breasted suit impeccable.

"Mr. Carter," he said, flat, toneless. It was unsettling, the difference between the operatic range inside and this nasal pecking sound, this ex–federal agent, this goon hired by Shellie Stevens to find the killers of Billy Ellison and, in their spare time, shut Sully up.

"Yeah," Sully said, "what's the rumpus?"

"This is a restraining order," the man said, holding out a folded sheet of paper. "It is signed by D.C. Superior Court Judge Michael G. Canon. It orders you not to come within two hundred yards of Delores Ellison, her home, or office, until such a time as the court orders otherwise. You were told by Mrs. Ellison's legal representative not to approach her again, and yet you have come to her son's funeral service. The court instructs you to desist at once or face arrest and prosecution."

"Up to and including the full extent of the law," Sully said, leaning off his bad leg. "You forgot that part."

The man reached out, took Sully's hand—he was bracketed by the suits on three sides—and slapped the folded papers into his palm, then took his fingers and closed them over it.

"You have been served," he said.

Sully took the paper, unfolded it, looked at the seal, the date, and looked off to his left. Somewhere, people thought this was a lovely spring day.

He wadded the paper into a ball and tossed it, lightly, back in the man's face, bouncing it off his nose.

"And so have you, pumpkin," he said.

He took the shove in the back and stumbled, nearly falling, out into the driveway, thumping into the side of one of the Lincolns, catching his chin on the glass, opening a stinging ribbon of blood.

They watched him walk off, none of them moving. Limping out to the street, he saw a familiar form push off a tree, where she had been leaning, long lens dangling from her neck.

"Lemme guess," Alexis said, approaching. "Those are some more guys you pissed off."

"I didn't do shit."

"Are you actually bleeding?"

"We're going to kick these guys in the ass."

"Which guys?" she said, trying to suppress a laugh. "This isn't even from last night," she said, sounding amazed, dabbing the cut on his chin with a finger.

"I got me a list," he said, pulling his chin back, "and it just keeps getting longer every goddamned day."

TWENTY

SOMEWHERE OUT THERE in this great country of ours, Sully figured, there were writers who labored from a place of love, some deep passion stirring them to heights of literature.

He himself wrote from a sense of fury, tapping into this well unconsciously in the very first newspaper story he'd ever written, a freelance feature piece for the *Times-Picayune*, a thing about oil well pollution in the Atchafalaya Basin, reported from the boats and tugs and shrimpers that had been his father's world.

These many years later, half the world's war zones in his rearview mirror, he sat at his desk in an office in a violent city, his back purple, his leg aching, and a narrow dab of dried blood on his chin, writing from the same pit of emotion.

Slouching in his chair, he slapped at the keyboard, the Bend looming as the backdrop, as the scenery for the city's waterside tableau to unfold. Lanky Dreads and Short Stuff and killers like them came onstage, bumping shoulders with the vibrant gay scene along O Street, coke on tables in dimly lit booths, baggies in the shadows of the Bend.

> *Billy Ellison, the bright and engaging son of D.C. society, had a brilliant future in front of him—Georgetown Law, wealth, personal and professional connections in the nation's capital, a seat at the White*

House on social occasions. The 21-year-old was popular at college, drove a stylish Mercedes convertible, and excelled at his studies. It was the stuff of the American dream writ large for the latest generation of one of Washington's most storied families.

So when he turned up dead in the Washington Channel last week, shot once in the head at point-blank range, it was as shocking as the apparent place of his killing—Frenchman's Bend, the packed-dirt and weed-choked knob of land and open-air drug market that juts into the channel along the Southwest Waterfront. Police records show the former slave pen is the deadliest spot in the city, the murder capital of the nation's murder capital, a place where drugs and homicide are as common as rainfall, and sometimes more so.

The manila folders on the desk beside him furnished names, numbers, statistics. He cold-called relatives of other young men who had been killed in the Bend, not getting anything from most but adding the names and their short lives to the narrative, likely the last times those names would ever be mentioned in a public document. His murder map gave him context and vision and geography, a spatial relationship of homicide relative to the population, and he looked at it from time to time to confirm his vision.

Jeff Weaver, the detective, was not answering his cell, so Sully called John Parker and kept calling him until he found him at home, and with him he verified details of Ellison's slaying, of what he could and could not say in print. He got on the record that the Bend was the focus of the investigation, that police had "little doubt" Ellison had been shot there, given the blood and the shoe, and Parker gave him permission to attribute all that information to him, not to "a source familiar with the investigation."

His notes—his hand-scrawled details and factoids, the life-sustaining capillaries of any story—gave him the details of Billy's relationship with Elliot. He called Elliot back to confirm details and the kid was spunky, telling him to put it on the record that he was Billy's "partner" in an act of spite toward Delores Ellison, who, further confirmed, had lambasted her son for his sexual orientation.

This admission was key, as it elevated Billy's relationship preferences from anonymous-speculation to attributed statement. Buttressed by the information from Kenneth, the bouncer from the bar, the information was solid, unimpeachable, and relevant because it put Billy in the neighborhood that eventually claimed him.

> Ellison was a corner-table regular at Storm, an O Street SW bar that caters to a mostly gay clientele, according to an employee who declined to give his name, fearing he would be fired for speaking with a reporter. "He was one of the fixtures of the club," the employee said, "particularly on weekend nights. It's not just that we recognized him. We even recognized his car."

The fax from Stevens he dutifully quoted: stellar high school performance, college success. Phone crooked into his shoulder, he called Georgetown's American Studies program and got lucky, the director of the program taking the call, saying what a great young man Billy was and so on, the man apparently oblivious of what Sully had on the screen in front of him. Sully kept the material about Billy's mental instability out of it, just as his mother had asked.

He worked the phones into the evening, went home, slept, came back, and took it up again the next day.

> The 19th-century family patriarch, Nathaniel Ellison, made a fortune in banking, and his financial prowess extended down the generations. His son, Lambert, followed his father into the bank as manager, as did his son, Lambert II, until it was consumed in a merger with the National Bank in 1965, under the management of Lambert III. Delores Ellison, his only child, now works as a strategist at the law firm of Sheldon Stevens, one of the most influential and seldom-seen power brokers in Washington. A long-established force in political operations, Stevens . . .

And then, the coup de grâce, his favorite part of the story:

Stevens, acting as family spokesman, declined comment for this story. Instead, he sent a two-page fax listing Billy Ellison's achievements. When a reporter from this newspaper attended Ellison's public funeral at the Washington National Cathedral, private investigators escorted the reporter from the service and served him with a restraining order in the parking lot. They then shoved him into the side of the hearse.

"Pucker up, Shellie," he said under his breath to the screen.

By that night, Friday, the five-thousand-word draft had made the round of editors, lawyers, and executives. Eddie Winters convened a meeting in his glass-walled office after the Saturday first edition had closed, but the suburban edition was still a couple of hours away.

"So the gay stuff—it's relevant? We're sure?" Winters was saying from behind his desk, the usual big-story crew assembled. Anytime you had the center-front Sunday lede on 1-A, you were going to get this kind of grilling, and you wanted it. You wanted everybody poking holes in your copy before it ran, not after.

Melissa Baird, the Metro chief, energetic, sitting on the near side of the desk, skeptical as always but listening; Lewis Beale, the attorney, sitting slightly behind Sully, off to the right, also head down, reading, underlining, circling; Sully and R.J. directly across from Eddie.

"Yes," Sully said. "The club, Storm, was a key transaction point. Billy was selling or scoring there or both. It's seven, maybe eight, blocks from the Bend. It puts him in the area in which police say he was killed, with a motive for being there. And we have multiple sources."

"Give me the background," Eddie said. "This is a kid from a politically connected family, with no record, and we're outing him. Plus we're saying he's a drug user and maybe a low-level dealer—

"There's some exposure here," cut in Lewis, the attorney. "We really want to be—"

"—careful," Melissa cut in.

"I didn't think you could libel the dead," Sully said. "I don't see that much exposure at all."

"Sources, please," Melissa said.

Sully gave it up. The family, first and foremost, on the drugs angle. Elliot, firsthand and on the record, on the gay thing. John Parker, firsthand and on the record, on where he was found. Tony Hall, firsthand and (this would be a surprise to him) on the record about Billy appearing in the Bend, complete with the homophobic slur. Kenneth, the bouncer, firsthand but off record. And another drug dealer, just as background, but off the record. This was Sly, and Sully did not want them to ask but of course they did.

"The street source—who's that?" Eddie aid.

"A guy who knows. Who knew Billy Ellison by name as a user down there. We're not quoting him or attributing any information to him. It's just one more confirmation."

"And what's his name?"

"Can't say. It's our agreement."

Eddie looked up at him, assessing.

"Why on earth would a dealer confess to you that he was selling drugs to or through a murder victim?"

"I wouldn't call it a confession."

"*Tell*, then. Why would he tell you?"

"Because, Eddie. Because this source tells me lots of stuff and the deal is, it never comes back to him, and officially I never spoke to him. Because this is what I do."

Eddie looked at him.

"You paid me to deal with warlords and psychopaths and mujahideen and Serbian and South African thugs abroad, and hey, I came home and found a few warlords here. I'm not quoting this dude. I'm not calling Billy Ellison a cokehead because he said so. Our main sources—that's two guys on MPD, the lead detective and the head of homicide. Another is the dead man's significant other, who also testifies to the fact on the record. Further, I backstopped this through the street, which led me to this guy, who is, in my experience, reliable. You want to throw him out as a source, great. We still have two sources on MPD, the boyfriend, and the head of the M Street Crew referring to Billy as a 'faggot.' It's zipped up tight."

"The family denies the gay angle," said Melissa. "Vehemently."

"Thank Shellie Stevens. You know he's called the White House on this? The fucking West Wing? The point is we're on solid ground. If you don't like it, don't print it. But what—just think—what are the odds that when I show up and ask, two cops, two drug dealers, and the bouncer in a gay bar all decide to say Billy Ellison was gay, all independent of one another? When, in fact, young master Billy was in the campus library the whole time?"

Silence reigned.

"Lewis?" This was Eddie, looking up now.

The lawyer squirmed in his seat, moving his bulk around. "The sexual orientation, as long as we don't put it up high, don't focus on it, doesn't worry me. It's not an inherent insult. It's not actionable on its own. But, looking down in the piece, do we need the scene where Sully gets served with the restraining order and shoved into the car? On the invasion of privacy issue. It was a family funeral."

"There weren't invitations," Sully said. "As stated, it was an open event, given wide public notice. I respectfully sat in the back pew and was pulled out."

Melissa uncrossed her legs, Melissa-speak for *Listen to me*. "But, I mean, what led to that?" she said. "Didn't Stevens tell you they'd hit you with that? And you went to her house anyway, then to the funeral?"

"Yes. Sure." The room was stale with recycled air, the window looking over a two-story parking garage, the upper deck open-air, half-empty now. "I went back to Delores Ellison after Stevens shut me down—but *before* the restraining order—and told her I would leave if she wanted me to, but that I had a couple of questions. She invited me in and answered them."

"But hadn't Stevens warned you about a restraining order?" This was Melissa again. The tone not accusatory, not just yet.

"People threaten all sorts of things."

She flared a half smile. "Stevens wasn't bluffing."

"Bully for him."

"This doesn't look good. A judge has got to have some grounds to grant—"

"I really don't think," Sully said, "a superior court judge is much of a pull for Shellie Stevens."

She sighed, looking like she had to pee, and flicked a glance at Eddie and said, "I'd feel better if we cut that scene. It's the only part where the reporter is inserted into the story."

Sully bit his lip, waiting for R.J. to take the bait.

Eddie looked from Melissa to him, then to R.J. Then back to him.

"Entirely relevant," Sully said. "Shows hostility, willingness to use legal and physical force, shows family desire to shut down unflattering information."

"Cut it," said Eddie, the sound of his pen scratching across the page loud, like a knife through muslin. "Delores lost her son. Give her some space."

Sully looked up. "Delores? We're on a first-name basis?"

Eddie looked back at him. "You're sitting here saying 'Billy' this and 'Billy' that, like you guys played racquetball three times a week. So, yes, 'Delores.' I've seen her at social functions, as has everybody else in town. You knew they didn't want you at the funeral, you went anyway—I'm not saying, as your editor, that you were wrong—and they kicked you out. Fair play, you ask me. I'm guessing there were words exchanged if they shoved you into the hearse. So, internally, privately, that's par for the course. Externally, no, we don't need to tell readers."

He looked around the room. People studied their printouts of the story, kept their heads down, letting the two of them have it out. "Then let's kick it over to the copy desk and let them get at it tonight and all day tomorrow. Sully, stay close for edits and questions."

"We have gotten," R.J. said carefully, "several television requests for interviews with Sully on Sunday morning, once it's run. Apparently our PR department has been active in this regard. How should we respond?"

Eddie looked at R.J. at Sully, leaning back in his chair. "Want to?" This, directed at Sully.

He shrugged. "Why not? We don't have anything to hide."

Eddie nodded, looked over the sheaf of papers again, and then stood up, declaring an end to the conversation without saying anything. He leaned over the desk, reaching out for Sully's hand, making eye contact, looking hard, looking sincere, looking, for everything he was worth, like a no-shit newspaper editor sitting on a story that was about to blow up.

"Fabulous work," he said, gripping Sully's hand, hard. The murder capital of the murder capital. Frenchman's Bend. Have you seen Alexis's art? Stunning."

TWENTY-ONE

HE WOKE UP Saturday morning in a room he did not recognize.

It was daylight outside but dark behind the drawn curtains—he could tell that much with one eye open. The other eye was closed against the mattress, the air floating over his skin turning his shoulders to gooseflesh. The sheet on which he lay was ironed, soft, and tucked in at the corner. Hotel, had to be. Raising his head, he looked to the other side and there was no one in bed with him.

By the door, there was a tray with several plates and glasses.

After a moment, there was a mild thump, a diminished sound. The water in the bathroom had been on, and now it was off. Shuffling followed, and then the bathroom door pushed open, Alexis wrapped in a towel, toothbrush in her mouth, foaming, hair wet, falling over her shoulders. She pulled the toothbrush out and looked at him.

"Good morning, cupcake," she said, radiant, way too goddamn cheerful. "I thought I was going to have to leave you here."

"Maybe you do. Where is here?"

"The Madison. My room. You don't remember?"

He slumped back onto the bed, closed his eyes. The Madison. Four blocks from the paper. "Of course I do."

"Liar," she said, turning back to the bathroom. "You helped me kill a bottle of wine at dinner, then another one here in the room, and then you were drinking bourbon. You wanted me to get one of my girlfriends to come over and get naked with us."

"Is that bad?"

"You always want a threesome when you get really drunk."

He rolled over, looking up at the ceiling, yawning, trying to remember.

"When did she leave?"

There was a peal of laughter from the bathroom and now she came back, sans toothbrush, still with the towel.

"Don't you wish. You barely could handle all of this."

"You liked it."

She leaned over and kissed him, letting the towel fall open. She walked over to the closet, dropping the towel on the floor.

"I've got one more portrait to shoot of families of the guys who got killed in the Bend. David Rennie's mom and sister, what's her name, Diamond? I'm shooting them at their place at noon."

"Diamond. God. Talk about an attitude."

"She was fine with me." Pulling on jeans now, buttoning a shirt.

"What time is it?"

"Eleven."

"Christ. The bulldog will be out in a few hours."

"I know. This is the last shot I'm adding. Then it's done. They're holding a spot for it. Are you going to go in and put the story to bed or lay here on the eight-hundred-count and stare at the ceiling?"

Twenty-four hours later, Sunday morning going into afternoon, the day the story ran on the front page and over two open pages inside, the day it created a Washington media sensation, Sully was doing the television show circuit. Pancake makeup and the green rooms, then talking to a camera, alone in a freezing booth with a blue screen backdrop. Or there were the in-studio hits, him sitting at a table across from his host, the lights bright, reminding himself to cancel out his accent and sit up straight.

"I think it's a story like Professor Young said," he said over and over, sticking to his talking points, "about the dark side of the American dream."

By the time it was all finished—how many shows, six, seven?—he went home, changed, and staggered over to Stoney's for an early dinner and drinks with Eva Harris, from the U.S. Attorneys Office. The sun was out, it was warm for a change, the first hint of summer humidity in the air. May wasn't a bad month in D.C.

They talked about everything but the story—her dad and his boat, the approaching summer—until they were finishing up. Then she said, by the way, that he was going to get shit for the Ellison story and he maybe should have thought twice about it. She said, sipping on her pinot, that nobody black in D.C. wanted to read something bad about the Ellisons, who were well liked and admired, and that the white folks didn't give a damn about some dead black kid anyway.

This analysis caused the glitz on his good mood to fade. Eva had lived in and taken the temperature of this city a lot longer than he had. Sitting across from her in the booth, he called his work voice mail, putting it on speaker, while she listened in, leaning over.

There were thirty-two messages.

The callers Sully would identify as white were sometimes positive—"a tragic story," one female caller said. But mostly they were bitter rants directed at the victims. Cokeheads, the callers said, who'd gotten it from their own. Thug A shoots Thug B, and this is news how? One guy went on a racist tirade so long that the call timed out on him and he called back, his next message consisting entirely of, "And fuck you."

The callers he would identify as black, who were the overwhelming majority, called him things like a "neo-racist" and a "sensation-seeking white idiot." The last one called him a "lying little crap weasel."

"I don't think anybody ever called me a crap weasel before," he said, eating a french fry. "I would have remembered, because I would have punched them in the fucking face."

"And he said you were a *lying* one," said Eva. "You've got to like the creative insult. But I told you. Nothing good ever comes out of the Bend."

She took a last bite of her salmon, kissed him on the cheek, and left for home. He went back through the calls. *Hatred, America*, he thought, *your glowing hatred*. God what a place this country was, the way people would talk when not looking at you, without any repercussions to their loathing. . . . He was deleting one call after another, but the last call was new, phoned in during the past few minutes.

"Mr. Carter? This is Delores Ellison," it began. Her voice sounded clipped, tense. "Shellie and I are conducting a press conference at seven o'clock. It will be outside of his offices. Please call me after that."

The call clicked off.

He looked at his watch: 6:55. No way he could get there and, he suspected, that was the point. They had set up a presser—TV heavy, no doubt—and skipped notifying the paper because they were going to lambaste him. If he was standing there, the assembled press corps would allow him to ask the first question as fair play, as theater, and then, when it was over, they would descend on him for comment. Stevens was too smart for that. The paper had their say that morning, and now he was going to have a response for the evening news.

"Hoo boy," he said.

He had all the sympathy in the world for Delores Ellison, he did—a dead husband and a dead son and an empty house—but it didn't mean he could rewrite the facts or change history, and now she and her lawyer were going to get their pound of flesh out of him. It came with the paycheck.

Going to the bar to get closer to the bank of televisions, he pulled out a stool and asked Dmitri, the bartender, to channel surf, head down to Channel 8, they'd be carrying it live. When he hit the right station— Shellie at the podium, Delores a step behind his right shoulder, the thing already under way—he waggled his hand back and forth.

"Turn it up, turn it up," he said.

". . . utterly irresponsible and pointless," Stevens was saying into the microphone, looking at the cameras in front of him, both hands firmly on the wooden podium. He looked and sounded like he'd just come down from Sinai, the lowered, serious eyebrows, the blazing eyes, the tone of righteous indignation. "This is purple journalism. It does nothing to bring a killer to justice. Instead it seeks to smear the name of a murder victim with innuendo and circumstance. It is"—and here he paused, looking at the cameras—"a low thing."

"Well played, counselor," Sully said under his breath, tapping his fingers, onetwothreefourfive, on the wooden bar top.

Delores, her hands clasped before her, in a somber black dress, looked at the back of Stevens's head, her face set in stone. In front of her, Stevens looked from left to right, as if surveying a congregation in the pews. "The reporter who wrote this story," he continued, "was so relentless, so probative and scandal seeking, that we had to serve him with a restraining order—at Billy's funeral, no less—and yet this hatchet job still appears, in the most prominent position of the most prominent edition of the most prominent media outlet of the nation's capital. It serves only to libel the Ellison family name and besmirch the reputation of Billy Ellison, who was nothing more than a victim in a crime of violence."

Watching it, listening to the rise and fall of the man's voice, the cadence and delivery, Sully couldn't help but be impressed. Stevens was full of shit but he gave fabulous television, and he was burying Sully in the court of public opinion. Nobody was going to contradict him at the end of this. The television stations would dutifully call Eddie for comment, and Eddie could only say something along the lines of "We stand by our story," which was what the lawyers were going to tell him to say, and it was going to sound weak and cowardly and lawyerly, and the good people of Washington were going to go to bed despising Sully Carter and the shit rag of a paper that employed him.

"We will pursue this issue with the full weight and heft of the law," Stevens said. "We will not sit idly by. This story, this libel, will not be just corrected. It will be *rectified*."

Stevens turned from the podium then, offering the crook of his arm to Delores Ellison. They retreated inside the building, and the camera moved to the reporter at a stand-up, holding a microphone to her mouth, repeating what Stevens had said, summing it all up, holding aloft the front of the paper.

Sully applauded.

"Sounds no good," Dmitri said, holding the remote out, switching to an NBA game.

"A non-denial denial," Sully said. "Did you hear him say anything was factually wrong? Did you hear him say Billy Ellison was not in the Bend when he got shot? Did you even hear him say that he was going to sue?"

Dmitri looked at him, one hand on the counter, his heavy black hair a tousle. "He say he will rectify you," he said, his Russian accent trilling the *r*.

"Gimme another Basil's while I think of my sins," he said.

"You are the angry."

"A little bit."

"He said he was going to bury you."

"Dmitri?"

"Da?"

"Bourbon?"

Dmitri shrugged and flipped the hair back from his eyes, getting a glass from behind the bar, reaching for the bottle in front of the mirrored backdrop. "One more. *Odin*."

"Oh, for chrissake."

"Boss says we got a law problem, drunks go driving."

Sully's cell, sitting on the counter, buzzed and illuminated, buzzed again. He punched it on and said, "Yes?"

"Mr. Carter?" It was a woman's whisper.

"That was the old man. I'm Sully."

"I'm so glad you answered," the voice said.

"Delighted to hear it," he said, sipping the whiskey Dmitri had put down in front of him, "but who's this?"

"Delores. Delores Ellison."

The whiskey caught in the back of his throat. He took the burn, feeling it in his nostrils, trying not to spit it out, swallowing it straight. He moved the phone away from his face, coughed. Pinched the bridge of his nose, between his eyes, a tear. He blinked several times and then coughed again, into the crook of his arm, and brought the phone back to his mouth.

"I was just—just watching you on television," he managed.

"Yes, yes," she said quickly, still with that staged whisper. "I'd left you a message to please call me after that. When the conference ended and you hadn't called, I looked up your cell, from the card you gave me."

"I got it, that call, the message," he said, the whiskey still burning behind his eyes. "I just hadn't had a chance to call you yet. That conference just—"

"That's what I wanted to talk to you about. That exactly. That was Shellie's doing. I didn't want to do it. Not at all."

"Ah. I see. Mrs. Ellison, not that it's any of mine, but why are you whispering?"

"Because I'm still in Shellie's office. He's going to come back any second now, and I had to talk to you."

The lady had gone certifiable. Vilify him on television and call him two minutes later . . . and it dawned on him, in his paranoia, that maybe Shellie was setting this up, coaching her from three feet away.

"Okay," he said, mind spinning, taking the idea that he was speaking into a tape recorder. He blinked and shook his head, trying to get the burn out of his sinuses. "What is it I can do for you, Mrs. Ellison?"

"Actually, a great deal," she said, as if the idea was just coming to her. "Are you going to be writing more about Frenchman's Bend?"

"I might, yes, ma'am, as time and space allows," he said, making it up as he went, feeling this out. "Fascinating place. A lot of history."

"That's what I thought," she said, and now her ragged breath came more quickly. He wondered if she was still on meds. "I mean, how I read that, it seemed like you knew a great deal about the place, that you were going to do more."

"Well. I did find out a great deal about the history of the Bend," he said, going with it, raising his hands, wondering where in the hell this was going, his mind alighting on the events Prof. Young had recounted, "the slavery, the postwar years. Much more than what I printed, sure. Fascinating stuff. Billy, I mean, I'm sorry, he was just—"

"That's what I thought," she said again.

"Well, I did my homework, I suppose. It's one of the—"

"You did?"

"—everything that—what? Yes. I did. Your family, the bank. I suppose I get a kick out of research. Billy must have, too. That thesis, he must have put a lot of work into it. And I'm terribly sorry, Ms. Ellison, I know a lot—"

"Billy's thesis? You saw that?"

"Well, I'm familiar with it, what he was working on, that—"

"I see, I see. The thesis. Yes. Yes. Do—do you think you could meet me there, in about an hour?"

"Where is that, ma'am?"

"Frenchman's Bend."

He snorted, a cough again, a hand slapped the bar involuntarily, causing Dmitri to turn, looking at him like he'd gone nuts. "The *Bend*? I'm sorry? What? Mrs. Ellison, maybe you're not aware, but Mr. Stevens took out a restraining order after I came to your house the second time. I really don't know that this call is even a good idea, since it sounds like he doesn't even—"

"*I* didn't want that," she hissed. "*He* did. *I* wanted to talk to you. *I* wanted to explain. Now it's all . . . it's all *out there*, everything, every-body knows, it's just all—all—and now all this time, and now it—"

It sounded as if she were sobbing, trying to choke it back.

"Ma'am? Ms. Ellison?"

"I need you to meet me," her voice more controlled, but still that whisper, urgent, "at the Bend. Now. I mean, an hour from now. Latest."

"Ms. Ellison, it's getting dark soon and the Bend is not a nice place even—"

"Oh, for Christ's sake!" she burst out, spittle-flecking furious. "You put my dead son on the front of the paper and now you act scared to even talk to me? I know about the Bend. Billy knew about the Bend. That's what I want to show you. *Now*."

She hung up.

He pulled the phone away from his ear and looked at it like it was going to blow up or melt into a little black pile of plastic. It didn't.

"Dmitri, brother, could you bring me one more of those?"

"That was last." With an upward tick of the chin.

"Yeah, but I just spit and spilt all of it."

This drew a long sigh, a blowing out of air from puffed cheeks. He took the glass, without nodding, and went to the bar, bringing down the bottle.

Sully, hands flat on the bar, *bap bap bap*. Then he nodded to himself, picked up the phone, and punched in R.J.'s number at home. By the time Dmitri brought back the Basil's, he'd rattled off what Delores had told him.

"You sober, Sullivan?" R.J. said.

"As a judge."

"And why, exactly, would she go to the Bend? Much less meet *you* there?"

"Got none. She has exactly zero business down there."

"Didn't you tell her that?"

"I tried to tell her that."

"And?"

"She said to be there in an hour. Or now. Something."

"For chrissake."

"*Emphatically* said to be there."

"She's off her rails," R.J. said.

"I think I gotta go," Sully said, rattling the ice in his glass. "What, she goes and we just leave her out there, that place? Jesus. Maybe she wants to get all emotional about the spot where Billy died. Maybe she'll tell me something about this shadow investigation that Stevens is financing. That's what I got my money on."

"Why wouldn't they have announced that at the presser?"

"She says, just now, that she has always wanted to talk, that Stevens wouldn't let her. Quite excited about that."

"So why doesn't she tell the police?"

"Who says she hasn't? Maybe she did and they sat on it. Look, at the political level? The West Wing, Senator whoever, flipping Main Justice? They're leaning on MPD to make a collar, but the case is a dog. So maybe Momma Ellison isn't thrilled about hearing that. Maybe she thinks MPD is blasé about another young black corpse. Now that we've put Billy boy's real life out there in front of God and everybody else, maybe she wants to get back at the cops."

"Fascinating," R.J. said. "But you can't go. The restraining order."

"Fuck that. She called me."

"What part of 'restraining' don't you understand?"

"The part that her boss served me with it, not her."

"He's representing her. Don't be dense."

"Without contradictory information, yeah, sure. But we just got contradictory information. A principal player in a story that's on today's front page, the story everyone in D.C. is talking about, just told me she wants to meet. How can I not go?"

"Have you called Stevens? To see if she's of, what, sound mind?"

"He didn't give me his home or cell. It's Sunday night."

"Then call him in the morning. Proceed in the sane light of day."

"She's going *now*. She said that she read our story, represented to me that she had not given authorization for any restraining order. That gives us good faith."

There was dead air.

"She just lost her son," R.J. said finally. "That press conference, that was pre-suit language."

"Which means maybe she'll call it off, I meet her down there, hear her out. Look, she said "now," or "in an hour," so it's sort of a thing. How can we say no? How can we let a grieving mother go out into the worst section of the city, alone, at night? We can't. You see that. We're ensuring her physical safety, at legal risk to ourselves, and we're not committed to printing anything. It's goddamn chivalrous."

Another pause.

"Eddie's on the train, coming back from New York. It's your call. But I'd say no."

TWENTY-TWO

THE BEND IN the gloaming of the evening was a semi-populated expanse of the desperate and the forlorn. Smack freaks, crack whores, smoke hounds, drunken assholes, the lowest forms of prostitution known to mankind. Lording over it, the Hall brothers' mini-empire of dealers and runners and enforcers, taking full control once darkness descended. There was not so much as a working streetlight.

He parked the bike a block up on Fourth, in tight between two cars, not wanting it to be spotted. As soon as he turned in to the weed-and-dirt expanse that ran from Fourth down to the Bend—between the Carolina apartment building on the right and the high wall of Fort McNair on the left—a gaggle of prostitutes emerged from the gloom, two of them bone skinny, the other a chunky woman, a solid contender in the lots-to-love category.

"Hey, baby."

"Ooooh, I *like* him."

"You want some of this sweet ass right here? Come to Momma."

Sully was pretty sure the second one was in drag, but he wasn't going to stop to chat about it. He said hi, hey, nodded, and kept moving. They turned, the maybe–drag chick raising her hands, palms up, calling out, "You don't got to be like *that*." They muttered and went on for a second with he wasn't quite sure what, but left him be and turned back to the street, looking for a john on a slow roll.

A hundred feet farther down, two guys leaned against the wall of the fort, dealers sizing him up, and it occurred to him the lack of light might be to his aid, the shadows obscuring his face, making him harder to spot, and this happy thought made him slow down and attempt to minimize his limp.

The last rays of twilight lay across the channel, a glimmering raft of waves, not even whitecaps, water that refracted and bent the light into rays of gold and orange and amber and maybe purple. Hains Point lay on the other side, green and dark, streetlights illuminating the waterfront roadway.

He made it all the way down to the knoblike Bend and still no Delores.

He drifted over to the concrete walkway that ran along the waterfront up to the Gangplank Marina and leaned against the railing. The white streetlights glowed across the channel, small dim orbs in the darkness. Daisy's pier, he thought. You make that light green, it's Daisy's pier, the Great Gatsby and all that lost promise, Fitzgerald in his study, writing the lines, making it real. The lights themselves glowed and they ebbed with the wind, and he wondered if it was ever that simple, light and dark, or maybe the world was just a shimmering glob of gray and it was up to you to pick between the sort of lighter and sort of darker, and then there was a soft, high, thin voice floating across the wind.

Delores Ellison stood maybe fifty feet to his left, a little farther down, out on the knob of the Bend itself—it was possible she'd been in the shadows the entire time—and it took him a second to recognize her. She had removed her wig or weave or whatever she'd been wearing each time he'd seen her. She stood there in a close-cropped natural, jeans, and a black T-shirt. It wasn't her look at all.

"Ms. Ellison?" he said, pushing himself off the rail, walking toward her, moving off the sidewalk and onto the grass.

"That's you, Mr. Carter," she said. "I see you."

In seven words he knew it had all gone to shit, the whole thing a mistake, her words slurred—ah, Jesus.

"Yes, ma'am, I was just wondering if maybe it would be better if I could walk you back to your car and we—"

"You know this is the spot where Billy died? The detectives told me about it." She walked a little farther out, away from him, toward the waterline.

He took one step, then two; she was still forty feet away and she was going on about where Billy had fallen, talking too damn loud—"Yes'm, but this isn't really the best time or place—"

"It's the perfect time and the perfect place," she said, turning as if on a pivot, looking up at him, stopping the weaving. "You were going to find out."

Her right hand rose from flat against her leg. The gun, the dull black gleam of it, coming up. He thought he was dead. She was going to shoot him right damn here and there wasn't a thing he could do about it.

"Ms.—"

Then her hand came past ninety degrees, and he knew.

He pushed off on his bad foot, stumbling, his hands clawing the air for balance, for forward momentum, and he found her name in his throat, a guttural bellowing and stop stop stop stop stop but the pistol was to her temple and she smiled and the blast was flat and loud and it blew a hole in one side of her head and out the other, brains and gore sailing into the night air, her body dropping in a heap, still three steps in front of him.

There were hands on him, rough, shoving. Angry voices. There was yelling and people calling out motherfucker and paramedics and lights in his face and he was still cradling her in his lap, the remains of her head, the weight of her upper body on his legs.

He did not speak or resist or fight or say anything. Everything was very far away. The men pulled at him and cursed him and they dragged him down toward the water and rolled him over and cuffed him and stepped on his back and then pulled him hard into a sitting position. There were more lights in his face and it seemed about three hours before one of the lights dropped and he heard a familiar voice say his name.

He looked up, out of the shell he was in, and he could see John Parker's face in front of him, incredulous, talking from behind a flashlight, "Carter? *Carter?* Can you hear me? The fuck?"

Parker, too, looked very, very far away. Sully understood he was yelling but his voice was not loud. It seemed to stand out in perfect clarity, like the words were glowing in the darkness. He could see them, hanging in the air.

"Get those things off him, the cuffs," Parker was saying. "Get him up, get him up."

Sully stood up and wobbled and a uniform turned him to the wall and unlocked the cuffs and he felt them drop away. He turned and looked.

The black plastic was already over the body. There were temporary lights set up and what had to be a dozen uniforms and plainclothes. Yellow police tape was already fluttering. Jeff Weaver stood by the body, looking down, speaking into a walkie-talkie, glaring over at him. A crowd of dopeheads was behind the yellow tape, taking in the show.

Sully turned his gaze back to Parker, the face bringing him back, the sounds now coming in clearer and clearer, and he said, "Is it the suicide capital, too?"

TWENTY-THREE

WEAVER DROVE HIM down to 1-D, the nearest police district station, after a while. It was on the Hill, ten or twelve blocks from his house. It was in an old house by the dog park. There were seven or ten patrol cars parked out front.

When he got out of Weaver's unmarked Ford, he felt his jeans and shirt stiffen and then crinkle when he stood, and he looked down at them. Dried blood and gunk. Gobs and streaks and smears. In the shifting streetlights from overhead, the shadows moving from trees in a light breeze, they appeared as Jackson Pollock splotches.

Weaver led them up the steps. He went through the door first. The sergeant at arms buzzed them through a locked door, a half-interested flicker across his face when he saw Sully, looking him up and down to assess whether the blood was his or someone else's. Figuring the latter, he went back to the paperwork.

Weaver led him upstairs to the second floor, the detectives' room, the place smelling of stale cigarette smoke and sweat and potato chips and an air that nothing good happened in here. There was one other guy, on the far side of the room, watching a small television on his desk. He looked over, raised a hand to Weaver, and went back to the show. The television had rabbit ears.

They walked on, Sully dimly following, and Walker finally stopped.

His desk was a heavy metal thing in a room full of them. It was cluttered with paperwork, a typewriter, two coffee cups, old newspapers.

"Sit, sit." He motioned to a metal chair, parked by the side. Sully did. Then Weaver went to the back of the room. He came back with a clutch of forms in his hand and asked him if he wanted to go to the bathroom. Sully shook his head.

"Your arms, brother. Your hands."

Sully looked down. The techs at the scene had wiped him down, but not really. Crusted red streaks on his forearms, his shirt, his hands coppery.

"I'll clean up when I get home."

Weaver sat down lightly on the chair, putting both hands on the table, and then said, "I'm not going to do this, you sitting there with blood all over you."

Sully sighed. "You got an old T-shirt?"

Weaver got up and went to a closet, pulled out a dark blue DC MPD shirt, and tossed it to him. "Back there, on your right."

Sully went down the row of desks, tapping on each one as he passed, his eyes idly skipping over the framed portraits of previous generations of officers on the wall, notices stapled to a bulletin board, a large chalkboard filled with what looked like a roster of active cases.

The bathroom had a toilet, a urinal, and a sink. He turned on the faucet to get the hot water going, then stripped off his black pullover. The caked sections stiffened and cracked as the shirt came over his head, little rust-colored flakes popping loose and drifting down to the floor. He dropped it in the trash and looked at himself in the mirror.

Hands streaked with blood, heaviest in the webs between the fingers, thick on his forearms. You could tell the sleeves had been pushed up to the elbow because the blood stopped there. His chest, with those railroad-track scars from Bosnia, had only a faint red tint in spots, from the blood soaking through. His face was streaked with it, he guessed from absently rubbing his hand across his brow, his cheek.

The water stung his face. He took the soap and rubbed his hands and forearms. He turned off the water and stood there dripping over the sink, the streaks of blood on his face melting away. He tapped the mirror twice with two fingers of his right hand.

"Don't," he said, "tell him anything."

"So I got to fill this out," Weaver was saying, Sully coming back, still drying his hands on a rough brown paper towel, Weaver nodding toward the typewriter, "and Darrell over there put on a fresh pot. Sugar's there, you want it."

He started tapping, without looking up at him, a hunt-and-peck guy. *Tired*, Sully thought. The man looked tired, worn down, ready to be done with this, his face slack, the dress shirt he had on wilted, the tie pulled halfway down his neck. A wedding ring. Somewhere a woman was wondering when he was going to come in through the door.

"Thanks," Sully said, adding two packets of sugar to the black coffee and plunking down in the chair. He smelled. The pants, the blood smelled. The coffee was hot and, he noticed after an exploratory sip, god-awful. He pulled his lips back from the cup and ran his tongue around his mouth. "But I already done told you what happened."

"Yeah." Weaver kept tapping, not looking up.

"So that was it. I mean, I got nothing else."

"Yeah, but—"

"If there's a yeah-but, this is the part where I say I want a lawyer."

Now Weaver looked over at him and leaned back in the chair, taking his hands off the typewriter.

"No, yeah, well—look, Sully, you can, but you're not a suspect here. You're a material witness."

"A material witness."

"To what appears to be a suicide."

"It appeared to be a suicide to me, too."

Weaver started typing again, a pen stuck in his mouth. "So all right, then. Let's get this done. Again, why did she ask to meet you at the Bend?"

"You know you haven't given me the Miranda."

"I do," Weaver said, looking up. "So why'd she call you?"

"You'd have to ask her."

"That's probably not going to work out."

"Then I don't know what to tell you."

"You said, back there at the Bend, you said something about her telling you that she had something she wanted to show you."

"That is correct."

"Then that's probably why she called you."

"If you say so."

"No idea what that was?"

"Apparently blowing her brains out of her head."

"And why would she want you to witness that?"

"I got none."

"You had just written . . . written this story right here." He shuffled papers around on his desk, found the previous day's A section. "Page one. Right there in the middle. Her son's case is the beginning what do—"

"Anecdote."

"—anecdote, right, yeah. And Billy pops up in the middle and then at the end, too. A lot of it is about him, in fact. You talk to her about this while you were working on that story?"

"It says in the piece she declined comment."

"That's the official version," Weaver said.

"That's the only version."

"Nothing, while you were working on the story, nothing on background?"

"The paper does not comment on anything beyond what's in print. If somebody asks me if someone in this department talked to me about an investigation," Sully said, looking at him evenly, "I'd say the same thing—we don't give up confidential sources."

Weaver shifted in his chair, the pressed slacks, the wing tips, that wrinkled dress shirt; Sully wondered if it was his regular shift.

"So, was that a 'get outta my face' no comment, or an 'I'd love to talk but my lawyer says I can't no comment?"

"It was a 'no comment' no comment."

"Where did this transpire?"

"At her house. The day after you guys fished Billy out of the channel. I went by there, she said she couldn't talk, said to talk to Shellie Stevens. He said no comment."

"He says, actually, a good deal more than that. He says—he was blasting the chief on this a half hour ago—that you went by there after that, that you were bothering the hell out of her and that they had to serve you with a restraining order."

From amid the papers on his desk, he moved things around again, picked up a coffee cup, tapped on a stapler, picked up a pen, and put it in the top drawer. "That's right here. A copy of which. This look familiar?"

Sully held his eyes on Weaver, not looking at the crisply folded paper. "Yeah."

"Well? A valid restraining order and we show up, she's laying in your lap."

"Then write me up. Go ahead. She asked me to meet her. Check her phone records, call my editor. I didn't do anything she didn't ask me to do. Told me the order was Shellie's bullshit, that she signed it against her better judgment. And, I mean, give me a break, the restraining order. Super court hands those out like Kleenex."

"Stevens says he told you not to include him in the story, and you— you included him anyway."

"It's called the First Amendment."

"Sounds like some bad blood. Like you were tweaking him."

"He's used to getting his way. Like most small children."

"So, today, she called you, did she say anything to you about the re-action to the story? Did she call you today and say that someone had called or threatened her about talking about her son's murder?"

"It was right after the presser, which I'm assuming you saw. Stevens raked me over the coals and then she called and asked me to meet her at the Bend. Period."

"You know what I'm asking. Lighten up. This is a prominent, well-to-do woman who just killed herself. It's all the hell over television. Cable is eating this alive. That means we're getting sweated, and shit, you know, flows downhill. Which means from me to you at this point. So. Now. I don't have any problems with the suicide. I'm asking, what I'm trying to get at, is maybe did her son's killers call or contact her in some way that resulted in this? You see where I'm going here."

"She said that her phone had been ringing off the hook, and she asked me to meet her at the Bend because she wanted to show me something."

"But she made no particular mention of any one call?"

"She did not."

"What did her state of mind seem to be? She crying, yelling, what?"

"Urgent, emotional, but controlled. It was weird, yeah, but she hung up pretty quick and, if nothing else, I didn't want her hanging out at the Bend by herself. I went by there to meet her, get her out of there, let her vent."

"Did you and she have a history?"

"The fuck does that mean, 'history'?"

"Did you and she have any sort of relationship? Did you sit next to her at the Ken Cen one time? Were you at the same cocktail parties?"

"Do I look like I go to cocktail parties?"

"Are you gonna help me out here?"

"I didn't ask for a lawyer, I'm—"

"Sully—"

"—a friend to law enforcement, puppies, little old ladies, and—"

"Answer the goddamn question."

Sully looked at him, tamping the rage back down. Down. He was going to keep it down. He was going to modulate his voice, his tone. He was going to get up and walk out of here and—

"Before this," he said, listening to his own voice, "I wouldn't have known her if she'd bit me."

"Okay," Weaver said.

"Okay."

"Okay. I'm just saying it looks extremely weird, her calling you up, this guy she barely knows, calling him to the spot of her son's murder, killing herself right there, wanting you for a witness."

"Stipulated."

"But you got nothing for me?"

"You think I'm lying, hey? Pull my phone records, do the legwork, I won't take it personal. But why did she do that? I'm a reporter, not a psychiatrist. Who knows why anybody does what they do? Nobody ever knows motive, detective. We only know what they tell us, and that doesn't mean shit."

They turned him loose about three a.m. Weaver walked him out the door, stopping at the top of the steps. Sully went down to the street. His bike was at the curb. He half-turned and Weaver said he'd asked a uniform who could ride to bring it up, as it would have gotten jacked at the Bend. He went back inside for a minute and tossed him the keys, underhanded.

Sully made the grab one-handed and then asked about the helmet and Weaver cursed and went back inside again, then came back out with it. Sully met him halfway up the steps. When he got on the bike, he gunned the engine twice and peeled, the rubber barking off the pavement.

He was going to get the shakes soon, and he wanted to be off the bike before they hit.

The shower, rinsing off the blood. The water ran from his chest to his stomach to his crotch and down his legs. Both hands were palms out, against the steaming tile, the hot water beating over his back. His mind ran in loops, flopped over, went elsewhere. He had never held Nadia like that, that's the thought that was circling around his head, that he was trying to keep out. No matter how hot the shower, how steamed the tile, he could not stay warm, and he felt the tremors start, back between his shoulder blades. He could feel the icy fingers of the Sarajevo morgue, the concrete and tile floor, the frozen light, Nadia among the other corpses, her black hair flowing, half her head gone.

You were going to find out, Delores had said. He stood there until the water ran cold.

TWENTY-FOUR

EDDIE WINTERS'S CORNER office, glass on two sides, was set on the southwest corner of the building. The Washington Monument rose in the near distance, the White House was just a few blocks over, and the Capitol was off to the east. On a morning in early May, with the sky overhead Carolina blue, it was easy to ignore the stalled traffic and alienation below and admire the austere lines of the federal city's profile.

"So they did or did not ask you to include the information about Billy's sexual orientation?" Eddie was saying. "Shellie Stevens was bellowing in my ear last night that you had promised that you were only including what was on the release they sent out. That you double-crossed him."

Lewis, the attorney, was sitting on the couch, looking like he had heartburn at nine in the morning. R.J. sat next to him, legs crossed at the knee. Melissa leaned against Eddie's bookcase, arms folded, studying the tops of her shoes.

Sully had not slept at all last night, coming out of the shower to put on sweats and a T-shirt and stare at ESPN, replays of baseball games watching him, until the sun came up. He had willed himself not to drink, knowing this meeting was coming.

Now, blinking back the sleep-deprivation headache, running on coffee and adrenaline, he tried to remember what Eddie had asked him. He was unaware of how long it had been since the question was asked, if people were staring at him or just looking. He brought his focus back from outside and returned Eddie's gaze with detachment.

"I was unaware, in Washington, that we published information only if the subject agrees," he said. "Certainly this would be news to our friends on the Hill."

"You didn't answer the question."

"I lost the thread. Who is 'they,' and which story are we talking about? Is this the story about Bill Clinton and oral favors from interns in the Oval Office? I believe 'they' asked—actually I think it was *demanded*—that we not publish. And you'll pardon the pun, but I believe we, and the rest of the Washington media, told them to suck it."

"Don't play games and watch your mouth," Eddie snapped. "Different stories, different standards. Compelling national interest versus none. Public figure versus private."

"Billy Ellison became a public figure the minute he got killed," Sully said. "We accurately reported material, primarily from official police documents. We established through reporting that he was killed in the Bend, a well-known drug market. We established that Billy was frequently in that area because of the clubs on O Street, and thus his sexual orientation was relevant. Plus, he is the member of a prominent family whose matron is sometimes pictured in this and other publications, and thus there is little doubt that Delores Ellison, and the family, are public figures. I reached out to his family to see if they wished to comment. Mr. Stevens, speaking for Mrs. Ellison, declined. Ta-da."

"Sully," Eddie said.

"Ask Lewis."

"Sully."

He uncrossed and recrossed his legs, in the chair, his knee beginning to throb. His back ached but he had skipped the painkillers, wanting to be clearheaded. "Shellie Stevens said I was to only include what was in the statement. I didn't agree to anything."

"He says you did. I would say he was close to unhinged about it. That would be better. *Unhinged.*"

"A Washington lawyer is having a hissy fit. This means what to me?"

"This means, smart-ass, did you ask any follow-ups about why he made such demands?"

Sully's eyebrows rose, and he looked to his left and to his right, but R.J. and Melissa were studying their fingernails now.

"Did you read the story?" Sully said. "Did we not have a meeting on this subject prior to publication? Jesus, man. If Shellie Stevens had a suicidal client, he should have said so."

Almost imperceptibly, R.J.'s left hand, on the chair arm next to him, rose and fell, rose and fell, a gesture of caution, of warning.

"So how did this meeting with Stevens end?" Eddie said.

"I thanked him for the intel and said that the death of the sole heir to one of the city's most prominent families in the city's worst drug park was news by any standard and we were going to print it. They could comment or not, and we would be happy to reflect either of her choices in the story."

Eddie turned toward the corner. "Lewis?"

The big man sighed, looking down at his notebook, then around the room. "This is terrible PR but legally speaking? Sully is correct. It's really attenuated. The woman's son was killed. They're going to convince a jury she was more upset about a newspaper story than the death itself? No. This ice is not thin. And, while we're on it, the dead have no legal rights to privacy."

This merry-go-round had been going on for nearly an hour. Sully had been expecting R.J. to pipe up early and often, but he had been almost entirely quiet, watching the ebb and flow. Sully, trying to fend off Eddie, had the growing impression that something had been put in place before the meeting ever started, that there was an agreement among the brass, legal, and probably HR, and what he was sitting through was a show trial in which he would be given a fair and equitable hearing and then taken out and shot.

"But just because we *can* report a fact or series of facts doesn't mean we *should*," Melissa said now. "Lewis mentions the public relations aspect—we're clear in the court of law, but I don't know about the court of public opinion. A grieving mother commits suicide in front of our reporter who published a story about her murdered son over objections? And our response is, 'Read the First Amendment'? I don't think that makes us look like we're comforting the afflicted."

There was a pause, the air in the room still, people looking solemn, and again, what struck Sully was the complete absence of anyone saying anything on his behalf. Other than Lewis, who had quoted the law, not Sully's judgment, as a defense.

In this conversational gulf, Sully turned to Melissa. "We're also supposed to afflict the comfortable. Who aren't exactly losing sleep about the murder rate in the—"

"Did you relay their—okay, Stevens's—request to your editors?" she said.

"Christ in a G-string!" Sully snapped. "They took out a restraining order. I think that makes it pretty clear they didn't want to cooperate. Everybody in here—including you—knew that."

"I don't remember hearing 'suicide risk,'" she said.

"Did I say that Delores Ellison would kill herself if we wrote this? No, because nobody told me that. Did I have any reasonable expectation that she would do so? No, because in nearly twenty years of doing this, I have written stories about thousands of people in dozens of countries and not a single one of them, or any of their family members, or any of their friends, or their mommas, or some guy they met in a bar this one time, shot themselves in the head after publication."

Melissa, softening her tone, maybe climbing down from her standard prosecutorial perch: "But you still met her, Sully, even with the restraining order."

"Because she asked me to, and because my editor said it was my call."

Eddie leaned forward. "Because you're supposed to be a pro. Because you've been in war zones for damn near a decade. You made right call after right call. Now, you come home, and it's like they took your common sense at customs. You know more than R.J. or any of us about this situation. You're *supposed* to know. You made the call. And it was wrong. When Stevens said 'family reputation' you should have asked. You should have made some effort to ascertain Delores's mental status."

"Like I told the detectives," he said, a ferocious headache coming on, "no one had any idea she was suicidal. I didn't, they didn't, Shellie fucking Stevens didn't. She said she wanted to show me something, that it was at the Bend and it was urgent. What, then, am I supposed to do? Let her go by herself?"

"And she didn't say anything?" Melissa said. "She just walked up and shot herself?"

You were going to find out. It ran through his mind again, as it had been all night, turning over and over, a riddle without a solution. His lower lip trembled, just for a second, and then he flicked his tongue around his lips, wetting them. He raised his hands and spread them. "I asked her what she wanted to show me, and she said something like, Yeah, I wanted to show you this. Bam."

Eddie coughed into his hand, tapping his pen on his desk.

"So what we're going to do, here, Sullivan, is try and head this off. We're—"

" 'This'?"

"—going to—this? *This* is a nasty protest against the paper. Stevens, three ministers, and two civil rights groups were in here at eight a.m. We are looking at the following optics: hundreds if not thousands of predominantly black demonstrators out front, railing against a powerful newspaper that drove a grieving black mother to suicide. You know how easy that'll be for the cable channels, the networks, to cover? With the background of the protests we had here in eighty-four? That time, we had the Urban League, the NAACP, the AFL-CIO, even Walter Fauntroy after our neck, and I *like* Walter. So we're not—"

"This isn't the same thing—"

"—not going to—what? No, no, you're right. It's *not* going to be the same thing. Because this time, we're going to do something about it before Shellie drums up whatever he's going to drum up. Notwithstanding your superb work from abroad, and on the Sarah Reese murder last year, there is still the Judge Foy matter, and that leaves a lasting mark, so—"

"There wasn't any mark before *you* put it there," Sully shot back. "You trusted a federal judge's word over mine. That federal judge was Sarah Reese's dad, David. You remember David? Now kicked off the bench? You want to clear up my reputation? Put the blame where it has belonged since jump street. On *you*."

Eddie's face flushed. The room, it was like no one was even breathing. Monasteries in Tibet made more noise.

"You're suspended, Sully," Eddie said softly. "For two weeks. While you're gone, you're going to go over your notes, you're going to write me a report on exactly what happened here, come back, and present it to me. This is your second suspension, and HR can go over this with you, but a third—"

"Suspending *me*? How about tell me what I did wrong, when the Ellison story was approved by everyone in this room, prior to publication, and it is without error? No one has asked for a correction. No one has said our premise was wrong. There's just heat from rich people because we published a story that they didn't like. So if you don't have the big-girl panties to deal with it, Eddie, just say you're looking for somewhere to stick it and I'm the only billy goat in the pen."

"You're suspended," Eddie repeated. "Two weeks. It was going to be with pay but you just talked your way out of that. Not only for this story, but for insubordination, just now. And for blowing off, what is it HR tells me, three of your required therapy sessions in the past four months. This gets out? The reporter on this Ellison fuckup had a drinking problem, was blowing off recovery? Good god. Two weeks, you go back to therapy. We clear? You clear?"

Smoldering, the veins in his temple about to pop.

"Crystal," he said.

TWENTY-FIVE

THE PHONE HAD been ringing and ringing but he didn't get off the porch to answer it. It was about half past dark and he'd been slowly but steadily drinking all day. He sat on the cold steel steps just outside his back door and looked at the cherry tree, the blossoms having faded and fallen two weeks back. They were still there, a pink carpet going brown. The pansies had come up from their winter hibernation, purple and white and yellow. The phone kept ringing and he took the bottle from between his legs and ice from the bucket he'd brought outside and poured another drink and watched the sky going from pale blue to black overhead.

He also had a fine view of the flat brick windowless sidewall of the neighbor's house behind him. And above his yard was a small nest of electrical and cable wires. He'd planted the cherry tree both for shade and as a means of breaking up this grim little tableau, but the yard and the narrow alley behind it were shielded from streetlights, leaving it a dark pocket in the middle of the city.

When he'd bought the house, beat-up as it was, the real estate agent had told him the Hill just had to come around, being a short walk from the seat of national government, but he didn't buy it as an investment. The neighborhood was two- and sometimes three-story brick row houses, lifted sashes and hardwood floors, no air conditioning and tin ceilings and fans in the hallway. They were a century old, places that people had talked and eaten and fought and fucked and died in, the bigger ones with carriage houses out back, the concrete alleys, where blacks had to live back in the day. You closed your eyes, you could hear the early years of the twentieth century the sound of trolleys and saloon music and women's laughter and breaking whiskey bottles and after-midnight foot-falls on the brick sidewalks, the broken moonlight floating down be-neath the trees, the local weapon of choice a razor rather than a pistol.

It was a place he felt comfortable, if not quite at home, this mixture of violence and family.

There had been a thumping on the street out front for several minutes before he realized it was somebody beating on his door and that he was perhaps a little drunk. He looked at the bottle and it was three-quarters empty.

The thumping stopped and he was glad whoever it was had gone away. He spilled some of the whiskey on the next refill, cursed, and then heard someone in the alley. He was surprised to hear a woman's voice blaring from the shadows.

"Sully! Sullivan *CARTER*! Damn it, you answer up or I'll put a brick through your window."

He blinked. "The downstairs windows got bars over them, Alex," he called out, "and if you get a brick upstairs? Buy you a beer."

She stopped, her head and shoulders discernible behind the wall, vaguely illuminated by the streetlights on Constitution. She put a hand over her eyes. "Where are you?"

"The steps."

She was at the steel gate to the backyard, rattling it, and then her shape became visible, smiling, her hair bouncing loose, spilling back over her shoul-ders, a tall, good-looking, athletic woman. She kissed him on the forehead and said, "I was knocking out front. I brought you this. From Schneider's."

A bottle of Basil's. He held his own bottle up, clinking it lightly off hers.

"I'll get you a glass," he said.

"No no. I'll work off yours." She sat on the step below him, found his glass, and took a pull.

"Wow," she said. "You going to cut that?"

He lopped in some ice cubes from the bucket. "Wait awhile," he said.

She stood, went past him and inside, got a plastic bottle of water from the fridge, and came back, this time sitting beside him. She poured the glass half-full of water, the whiskey sloshing.

"Too late if you're trying to water me down," he said.

She sat there beside him.

"Heard you had a rough day," she said after a while, her left arm going around his lower back, her right hand brushing the hair back over his forehead.

"Not as bad as Delores Ellison's yesterday."

"Well. Not that bad. But pretty bad."

"Pretty bad."

"How are you?"

"If I still had a dog I'd shoot it."

"That's pretty bad."

"It is."

"Eddie can be such a fucker."

"So much for the suspension being hush-hush."

"This is why you don't want to be in the newsroom," she said. "Nothing's a secret."

"So what's the talk?"

"That Eddie's pissing his pants about a protest, or a lawsuit, or both, and covering the paper's ass."

"Well."

"Let's go inside," she said.

"No no, not yet. I like it out here."

"You're a little drunk."

"Yeah," he said. Then, "She said something."

"Who? Said what?"

"Delores. Before she shot herself. She said, 'You were going to find out.'"

"What? What are you talking about?"

"She starts raising the gun, right, it's going up, I thought to Christ she was about to blow me a new one, and she says, 'You were going to find out.' And then blam."

"Find out what?"

He shrugged. "She asked me—this was on the phone, before—if I was going to be writing more about the Bend, and I said, well, maybe, whatever. I got there, she comes from over against the wall and says, 'This is where Billy died.' Then she says, 'You were going to find out,' and pulls the gun up."

"So did Eddie and Melissa assign somebody to track it down, what she meant?"

"I didn't tell them."

"Why not? Jesus, what's wrong with you?"

"Because she told *me*," he said, opening his eyes. "Because, because . . . it was supposed to *mean* something. She was telling *me* something, she thought something was obvious. That I was going to find out and put it in the paper."

"So she killed herself to prevent you from finding it out, or to take herself out of the consequences when you did?"

He spread his arms out, bumping into her, banging the other hand on the railing. "Or, did it to *help* me find it out."

Alex took a sip of his whiskey. "That's a mind fuck."

"Yeah. It is. It seriously is."

She let out a deep breath and put the glass down. "Now. Look. I want you to listen to me. Whatever it was, it's done. *Done.* I don't care what she meant. Let this one go."

He turned and looked at her, her shoulder against his.

"Why would I do that? Why would I ever possibly do that? The woman kills herself right in front of me. There's some moral responsibility here—"

"No there's not." She was speaking just above a whisper. "No. We come into people's lives for a few minutes, a few days, what are we to them? A voice on the phone, a sympathetic face? They see us as *those reporters*, those people who put that picture in the paper. They don't really know us and we don't really know them. This was an unhinged person. She projected that shit on you and that's her problem, not yours."

"*Was* her problem."

"I'm serious. Don't get caught up in all this D.C. crap, the office politics. Let Eddie cover the paper's tail. And keep your eye on getting back abroad. That's where you belong. Not in this . . . what do you even want to call Washington?" She laughed now, deep in her throat. "Soap opera? I've been back a week and I've already got the hives."

"How's the Middle East project thingy?" he said, switching the subject.

"I'm on a plane in thirty-six hours and change. I got a fixer who says he can get me into Hezbollah leadership if I get there quick. Now, come on in. Come on inside. Come on upstairs. I'm going to make you take a bath and get in the bed. Then I'm going out with the girls from photo. They're taking me clubbing."

"But you came here first?"

"I did."

"Because you just love me that much?"

"Because we are friends. With the occasional benefits package. And I like you even if may be I shouldn't. Now, stand up."

"You said 'package,'" he said.

"Hilarious. I did. Now, stand up."

She picked up the bottles, the ice bucket, the glass, pushing the door all the way open. "Get as drunk as you want tonight. Then you're going to take two weeks off, sleep late, and forget all about Delores Ellison and Frenchman's goddamn Bend. Right?"

He raised his chin and kissed her forehead and slung an arm around her shoulder.

"Right," he lied.

TWENTY-SIX

THE NEXT AFTERNOON, as required by the paper's HR department, he walked into the psychiatric offices of Gene Henderson. It was on one of the upper floors of an airless office building just off Eye Street downtown.

"You decided to come back," Henderson said, gray curly hair, a slight paunch, filling the doorframe. Sully walked past him into the office and sat down in the leather-upholstered chair facing his desk, slouching back, crossing his legs at the ankles.

Henderson closed the door and sat behind the desk. Sully looked at his degrees on the wall behind him: Morehouse, Princeton. The other framed items were three large photographs of land and water, a running creek in autumnal New England, a tropical beach, leaves dripping fat beads of rainwater.

There was a pause, the older man writing in some ledger on his desk, and Sully said, "Go ahead. Rub it in."

"No, no, that wasn't the point. Just that it is good to see you again."

"At ninety bucks an hour, I'd be glad to see me, too."

"Not everything is cynicism, Sully. This is your mode of conversation, of deflecting things. That's not what we're about here. It doesn't work."

"All right."

"Leave it at the door."

"All right already."

"You got suspended. I saw your story. I saw the woman killed herself."

"The woman?" Sully said. "You've lived here, what, thirty years? You knew the Ellisons."

"Of. They are not quite my social set."

"Were."

Henderson nodded, smiling, "Were."

"A real charmer, that broad. Killed herself right in front of me."

Henderson let that settle. "That is, that is terrible. Did you know her well?"

"No. We talked a couple of times, just about Billy. I sort of liked her, sort of didn't."

"What didn't you like?"

"Seemed to think her late hubbie was a yokel." Because he was from people who had to break a sweat when they worked. In Georgia.

"Perhaps he was."

"With a Harvard law degree? Doubtful. Plus, weird to make it so obvious, what, fifteen years later, to a reporter, just after your son was killed. I mean, who cares what I think?"

"The Ellisons, you must know by now, are—were—quite class conscious."

Sully waved a hand, dismissively.

"Your paper has said you were at the scene of her death. The cable channels said something about it, but I didn't catch it all."

"I was five feet away. Sat there with her head in my lap till the cops came."

"My god, man."

"I really don't want to talk about it."

"I would think you'd be in shock."

"Truly don't want to talk about it."

"Okay, okay." Henderson clasped his hands over his stomach and looked over the desk at Sully, a pleasant, comfortable smile across his face. "What shall we talk about, then?"

"I was thinking Nadia."

"Ah. Nadia. Our recurring theme." A hand raised, falling back over his stomach, the man swiveling in his chair. "You see the connection, do you not? Nadia, dead in Sarajevo, Ms. Ellison—"

"Spare me, Dr. Freud. How many women have you seen with their heads blown open? This is professional curiosity."

"I was in the military, you'll remember."

"Evasive response, Dr. Lecter."

"We are not here to discuss me."

"Zero. What I figured."

Dead air. The clock on Henderson's desk. The stillness of the sterile, refiltered air.

"Your mother," Henderson said, "was also a homicide victim, a gunshot wound."

"Three of them, if you want to get technical."

"One was to her head, as I recall."

"Yeah, Dr. Phil, I think that was the big one."

A long look with a grimace, a tightening of the lips, the lower jaw.

"Sully, your problem here is not depression."

"Hallelujah."

"It is not malaise."

"Preach, pastor."

"It is anger."

Sully looked at him.

"You are boiling with it. Everything you do, it cascades out of your eyes, your mouth, your pores. You are filled—"

"Do you even bother with calling yourself a doctor?"

"—with it, in—I am not answering attacks. It is your—"

"Because you—you went to school, you went to college, you went to *med school*, and this is it? Your genius diagnosis? *Anger?* That some prick whose mother was shot to death and whose girlfriend had her head blown in two—you, your professional opinion, is that this guy might just be a little pissed off."

"This—"

"I hope you can get your fucking money back. Princeton, my Cajun ass. I, I coulda told you that and I didn't even *go* to college—"

"Sully."

"—and I—*what?*"

"If you will calm down. It is very hard to learn anything while shouting."

"Which presumes I have something to learn from you."

Air.

"This event," Henderson said after a moment, "this matter with De-lores Ellison. It had to strike very close to home. You went to see Ms. Ellison that night for a reason. One that certainly is not known to your employers, and perhaps not even to yourself. You wanted to do some-thing for her. You wanted to save her."

"I wanted to do my *job*. She said she had something to tell me, some-thing about the Bend. *She* said I had to meet her there. I didn't go jumping on a white horse, I wasn't the catcher in the fucking rye. I was doing—"

"Did you try to stop her, once you saw the gun?"

"Who wouldn't? Look. I'm not doing this with you. Last time I was here, you asked me to write something about Nadia."

"What?"

"Nadia. You asked me to write about her."

Henderson blinked, his mind racing to keep up. "I think I—"

"Well," Sully said. "I did. A couple of weeks ago."

Henderson nodding, Sully saw, trying to figure out where this was going. "Right, right, yes. I asked you to write. Since you were having a hard time talking about her, about Nadia."

Sully nodded, exhaling. He unfolded the paper, taken from a sketch pad. Henderson, rattled now, leaned over the desk to take the paper from him, then pulled his bifocals down from his forehead.

the night wind slipped through the curtains
  leaving the lights of town below
  but I saw it flicker through your hair
  and felt the shiver of your skin

but now

i look at my hands
> *they look as they always did*
> *i look in the mirror*
> *but do not see your shadow in my eye.*

i lick my lips
> *to find no taste of your skin.*
> *i touch my chest but feel no*
> *trace of your fingertips.*

and yet

you are there, behind my eyes and
> *under my tongue in the weakness*
> *of my heart, for in memory*
> *love does not drown in the well of time.*

"It's expressive," Henderson said. "It's about the dead lingering in the physical sensations of the living. It gets at what has happened to you."

"A lot more happened to Nadia."

"This is true. But you are the only one still living."

"Another genius observation."

"Sully," Henderson said, attempting a smile. Trying to bring him down.

"So how wound up am I today?"

"A good bit."

Sully turned in the chair. "You should have a window for people to look out of or something."

"Let's slow down for a second," Henderson said. "Take a deep breath. Now, listen: There is nothing more to be done for Nadia, or for Ms. Ellison, or for your mother, or for any of the dead, for that matter. There is only tending to the part of them that still lives within us. But I want you to see this: It's not them we're helping, or tending, or nurturing, or even perhaps abusing. It is the part of ourselves that they still inhabit. That part may be smaller or larger, and it may be a positive force or a destructive one. But it is still the matter of the dead living within us."

"Whatever."

"Nadia is where she is, and that is all. You did all that you could for her, and yet you feel her moving inside your body."

Sully looked at his fingernails.

"If you sit in my chair, this is normal," Henderson said. "The dead have always been with us, Sully, and they always will be. It is one of the things that make us human. How *much* they are with us is the issue."

"Yeah, well, the thing is?" Sully said, shifting in his chair. "What I learned from covering war, open conflict? When you're done with it, it doesn't mean it's done with you."

Henderson nodded. "Yes. Yes. The past is not a light switch. You can't flick it to 'off' when you board a plane or cross borders. And yet you came home from war—you flipped that switch, yes—but now you cover . . . homicide."

"You want me to do the gardening column?"

"Again, the sarcasm. You could do other things at your paper, but this, this is the business you have chosen. You are familiar with Don McCullin, the combat photographer?"

"Everybody is."

"Belfast, Vietnam, Lebanon—black-and-white images of the worst places on earth. He went back home to the UK, eventually. You know what he does now?"

"Landscapes."

"Now he shoots landscapes," Henderson said, nodding. "Pictures of the earth, of nature."

"It's still pretty dark, you ask me," Sully said. "A lot of depth and shadow. A lot of weight. I wouldn't call it carefree."

"Fair enough. But he didn't come home and photograph more bodies and killings."

"You're saying my career has changed but I'm stuck in the same gear."

Henderson sat there, letting it play out, the artful silence of the inter-
viewer.

After several minutes, Henderson cleared his throat. "Sully? What are
you thinking now? We were talking about Nadia. About finding tran-
quility."

"You know what I'm thinking?" he said. "I'm thinking I'm not going
to sit here and second-guess what I do for a living. I'm not going to second-
guess that the loss of life through violence is an important thing, and that
it's worth covering. But Nadia? You asked me to write something about
her, so I did. And it told me something I've never said out loud."

"And what is that?"

"That I wish she'd leave me alone now. I don't want the ghosts anymore. She comes, she goes, the tremors come, they go. Half the time, it
feels like I'm not in control of it. That—that there's something *in* me that
is *not* me, and I can't get rid of it. I want that to go away. I want to make
them go away. All of them."

"I'm not sure I'm following. Who is 'them'?"

"Are you listening? The dead."

TWENTY-SEVEN

HE SAW ALEXIS off from the hotel the next morning. She looked fabulous: jeans and a light sweater against the early chill, the light of the day still soft, glowing. Her hair was pulled back, her skin holding a touch of sunlight that brought out the faint set of freckles along her cheekbones.

"I got a hangover," she giggled against his ear, giving him a hug. "We were out *late*."

"You got eight hours to sleep it off before Heathrow," he said. He held on to her longer than usual.

"Hey," she said, feeling it. "You're going to kick butt, right?" Pulling back to look at him, only a few inches shorter, her eyes searching his. She held his elbows with her hands, assessing, looking into him. She whispered, "You're going to take your two weeks, get some sleep, ride the bike. Then you're going to come back, smite some righteous ass, and come back overseas. Try to get the Cairo gig. It's going to be major."

A little shake of the arms and she stepped back, moving to the open door of the taxi.

"The Middle East has been big," he said, "for, like, the past two thousand years."

"Yeah, but no shit this time around."

"Okay, okay."

"I mean it. Hit me on the sat phone," she said. "They're so much better than they used to be. You have to get the hotel room facing wherever the satellite is—you can tell the foreign hacks, standing there at check-in with a compass on the counter—but it's reliable. Amazing. Sarajevo, only the AP and *Newsweek* had sat phones, going off at $18 a minute. Now—"

She kept prattling on, and he wanted to stop her, right here, right now. He wanted to say something to make her stay, to close the gap he felt yawning between himself and the rest of the world. It would be good to do that. He would say something funny and warm and she would look at him, taking him seriously, and the thing between them would deepen.

Two steps forward, three, and now he took her by the elbows as she had held him, and she didn't resist, let herself be pulled to him. Her face was inches from his, looking up at him, her head going slightly to the left, quizzical.

"Come back," he said softly, gripping her arms harder. "You come back to me."

She blinked and then leaned her forehead on his chin, let the weight of her body go fully into his. They stood there, the taxi driver behind the wheel, paying them no mind.

"You're a good man," she whispered. "Dig in. Don't quit."

"Okay. Okay."

"The bourbon, Sully, it's not your friend so much anymore."

She pulled back a final time, looked into his eyes again, searching, then put her fingers to his cheeks and kissed him, softly, on the mouth. And then she turned and got in the taxi and it was pulling away, taking her down the street and away from him, bound for the far side of the world.

He watched the taxi disappear into traffic, the ghost of her fingertips still on his skin, and the air around him cooled by a dozen degrees, he would swear it, and he shivered against the sudden chill.

For the next forty-eight, he laid low, taking her advice, trying to be good, staying around the house, wandering up to the corner store at Fourth and East Cap and shooting the shit with Jimmy, the Korean kid who worked the counter. His parents owned the place. One day Sully had breakfast at Jimmy T's and sat at the counter, watching Larry do the short-order stuff.

He went home and got the bottle down and reached for a glass and then looked at it and put it back, walking right back out the door, cursing under his breath. Ten minutes later, he was wandering through the tin-roofed main building at Eastern Market, fresh fish at one end, pastries at the other, vegetables and beef and chicken and sausage and handmade pasta in between. Without thinking—he didn't even realize what he was doing—he was picking up scallions and celery and parsley and then he understood that he was putting together a rémoulade. So then he picked up a pound and a half of shrimp and fresh-caught sea bass, the grizzled clerk with the stained white apron handing him the shellfish and the fillets wrapped in butcher paper across the glass-fronted counter, heavy in his hand.

He came home and put on some Zachary Richard. Went in the kitchen and dusted the shrimp with seasoning form K-Paul's and crusted the sea bass with a rub he'd cadged from Melvin, the sous chef at Brigtsen's. He set up the grill and the flame jumped from match to charcoal. Raking the coals out even, he set the sea bass over them, closing the lid, and stepped inside to make the rémoulade.

Lemon juice and oil and onion, the herbs, horseradish, mustard, ketchup, a splash of Tabasco, salt, pepper—it was a birthright; he'd never even seen a recipe. He pulled the fish off the grill, tossed a quick salad, and sat down on the back step to eat.

As he did, he read the paper. There was a story on the Metro front about the protest downtown, about Delores Ellison—they'd put the crowd at several hundred—but he skipped it and tried to be interested in baseball box scores.

That didn't really last, so he went inside and came back with a couple of books. He had the entire afternoon, the evening. He could lose himself in another world, the hours passing, and suddenly he would look up and it would be dark and he would feel rested, at peace.

The biography of the Laffite brothers lasted a few pages before he felt his mind wandering. The other, an old favorite, *The Soccer War*, by the brilliant Kapuscinski, didn't hold him, either, not even for a single coup.

By the time he finished eating, he was back into the paper, this time digging into the want ads. He found three boats for sale, small things that would get up and go on the Potomac or the bay. The one that caught his eye was a '94 Maxum 2400 SCR, a twenty-five-footer with a V-6 engine. The vinyl seats had a little sun damage and there was a long scratch along the right bow, but it was reasonable. Sully called the guy up and said that if he would tow it to the Gangplank—and if it handled the waves like a pony, not a mule, he'd take it, as long as the trailer came with it.

The next day, he took it out, the bow rising when he gave it some throttle, revving the engine on the Potomac's choppy waters, loving the speed and the sunshine.

He came back and wrote the man a check on the dock, then settled with the marina for a slip.

In the afternoon, he took it back out, slower this time, past Georgetown, the bluffs of Virginia rising on the left, the George Washington Parkway high up, the trees and brush coming in full, the bluff a mass of green. A bottle of wine, a baguette, the shrimp and rémoulade. Wine, he thought, turning to watch the wake, it wasn't as hard as bourbon, so that had to be better, right?

He smiled to himself at that, and then felt it fade. Alexis wasn't wrong about the whiskey. Perhaps she *really* wasn't wrong. Maybe it had slipped, unnoticed, from being his long and steady companion, his southern birthright to . . . what? A traitor? Something that had gone from propping him up to knocking him down? Was it possible, you know, that maybe the bottle was sucking the life from him rather than the other way around?

. A vicious little voice in his head had been echoing Alexis's words ever since she'd said them. Sure, the bosses had been telling him this almost from the day he'd gotten out of the hospital, the seventy-day re-hab . . . but they didn't know shit. They were corporate pinheads who followed protocols somebody somewhere else had written.

But Alex, she was no bullshit. He had always admired her judgment, whether it was to cross the checkpoint two clicks up the road or if this or that translator was going to be trustworthy if the shit hit. She could see him better than just about anyone else, could see past the scars and the limp and the chip on the shoulder . . . and she liked what was there. And still, she had seen something dark and ugly taking root inside him, a mean little animal burrowing under the rage and loss, feeding on it, growing. . . . After a while, he cut the engine and sat out there, just off Three Sisters, the boat rocking gently, watching the sun fade, letting the engine, like his mind, cool by degrees. He forced his mind elsewhere, only to find another dark little voice clamoring for attention.

You were going to find out.

Delores Ellison. From his problems to hers. Who could ever know the mind of the suicidal? She might have been completely deranged by then, driven over the edge by grief and sorrow. It might be a nightmare in her mind and nowhere else.

Still, shifting his weight on the seat, taking the corkscrew to the wine bottle, he didn't think so.

Delores had been clear that it was something *not* in the story that she thought he knew or was about to know. What could that be? Who shot Billy and why? Had *Billy* shot somebody and been much more of a thug than Sully or the police realized?

Or—and here he poured the wine into a plastic cup and recorked the bottle—maybe Billy, gay boy to the end, was slumming tricks down there, blow jobs as a means to his own debasement, and Delores felt the guilt, as a single parent, for him turning out that way. Maybe her suicidal rage was really directed at Sully. *This is the source of my shame and I will tie you to it forever, you fucking bastard.*

Ah. There it was. The nasty thought lurking in the basement of his own mind: Was her death on his hands, intentionally or not?

"Sorry, Alexis," he said out loud. "I got to do this."

He punched in the number of Sly Hastings on his cell and dipped the shrimp in the rémoulade.

"Tomorrow, about nine?" he said, still chewing when Sly answered. "Pick me up in the parking lot of the Gangplank. We have a mutual problem." He paused, listening. "Something like that. The Hall brothers. Turns out they're a special problem of mine, too."

TWENTY-EIGHT

"**SO MPD AIN'T** got shit about who killed your Ellison boy," Sly said, riding shotgun, slurping sweet tea through a straw, "but you gonna try to figure it out. Hero boy. White man come to save *all* us Negroes. Hoo."

Sully was riding in the backseat, watching the neighborhood roll by in the darkness, Lionel driving, keeping the Jeep Cherokee—Sly's second car—right at the speed limit. A little after ten. Sly had been twenty minutes late, then insisted on them getting carryout from Kenny's up on Maryland and Eighth, on Capitol Hill, then had been more interested in hearing about the whomping the Hall brothers had laid on him than the fact that he'd gotten suspended, or in Delores Ellison's sad and spectacular demise.

"I wouldn't go that far," Sully said. "You told me the key to finding out what was happening in the Bend was who killed your mole, dear old Dee. You said we figure that out, it's likely going to tell us who killed Billy. I got no other leads. Police got no leads. So let's find out who killed Dee."

"The South Cap Crew shot up Dee's car the week before he got capped—"

"Even MPD knows that," Sully said.

"—and I—you got to let me finish. That interrupting shit is rude, you know it? The Halls, man, you saw what happened when you walked up on them by yourself. They ain't got no home trainin'. So, we going to try to figure it out the other way. We going to go ask the South Caps if they the ones who killed Dee. You called me yesterday, it gave me the idea. That was good."

He looked down at his takeout, the Styrofoam container balanced on his lap. "Kenny can ace some ribs. Don't know what it is with that boy and the vinegar on them greens, though."

"It's too much," Sully said, finishing his. "The salt, too. So when you doing this thing with the South Caps?"

"Right now."

"*Now?*"

"You got something better? Yeah. Now. You called me, remember? We going to see Terry Mungo, T-Money. He run that crew."

They had been looping the Hill in an aimless circle, but now Lionel moved to the far right lane of Pennsylvania and turned, swinging right onto Eighth, the half-ass commercial block of the Hill—fried chicken places, check-cashing joints, the video store, the fire station, the marine barracks ahead on the left.

"I don't think I need to be—"

"I need me some bodies," Sly said, "that T-Money don't recognize. A little show—I'm not calling it force—but a little show of . . . of . . . what is it, substance."

"You got plenty of heavies," Sully said. "You don't need me."

Sly was looking out the window, studying the pedestrians on the sidewalk, the Jeep slowing. "Oh, but I need *you*, brother Sullivan. T-Money, he's gonna think you my connection on this new shit I been bringing in."

"And why is he going to think that?"

"'Cause that's what I'm going to tell him. You don't say nothing, right, but if you got to? Speak that Bosnian you talk. You know, that East European Mafia shit. The Russians! Man, you speak Russian?"

"*Nyet*, dipshit."

"Then just do that Bosnian thing. And put some bass in it. You'll scare the nigga to death."

"Sly, they had to already seen me walking around. I been all up and down South Cap."

"Perfect," Sly said. "You the foreign money, checking on the investment."

Then, without waiting for Sully to respond, he said, "There he go right there, Lionel, you see?"

Lionel slowed, stopping alongside the row of cars parked parallel to the curb. Sly pushed the button, the window going down, then waved an arm outside. Sully looked out to see a figure in a black hoodie turn and cut to the car.

The man got in the backseat alongside him and brought the door shut in a rush. Lionel accelerated away from the curb. The man pulled the hoodie back, dreads falling down his shoulders, turning to look at Sully, his eyes blinking three-four-five times in recognition, his mouth parting in surprise.

"This right here," said Sly, not even turning from the front seat, putting the window back up, "is Curious George Ferris. I think y'all done met."

Lionel eased down Capitol Hill, the building itself on the right, then turned left on Washington Ave., heading toward the Bend.

"How does this work again?" Sully said. "George here is the Hall brothers' chief ass-capper and—"

"Curious works for me," Sly said.

"*Now* I do," Curious said, that raspy voice. "Now I do."

"When did that start?" Sully said. "Down there at the track you—"

"Recently," said Sly. "Recently he started for me. The Hall brothers, he hasn't gotten around to telling them about his new employment opportunity."

Sully looked over at Curious, who was looking at him, then back at Sly in the front.

"He's your new mole," Sully said, "is what you're saying."

"If you like to say it that way."

"Jesus Christ."

Curious George had a broad, expansive face, his dreads perfectly maintained, the tips dyed reddish copper, the brown eyes looking hard at Sully. Nineteen, possibly twenty, could be twenty-one.

"After Dee Dee got popped?" Curious rasped. "Sly, then he approached me."

"Approached?" Sully said. "He *approached* you?"

"Don't get cute back there," Sly said. "We got business. Now, look here. T-Money, he's got no idea we're about to roll up. This how it's gonna work. Me, Curious, and you get out the ride. That's gonna look like me, the Hall brothers' enforcer, *and* the out-of-town money, all united. Shit. He gonna think we all done ganged up on him."

The car, now on South Cap, rolled them under the overpass, the McDonald's on the left, the park on the right, Southwest in all its paint-peeling, dime-bag glory. Lionel turned left again, east now, putting them in the South Caps' domain. At the stop sign, the ratty little row houses began, window units hanging ass out of the upstairs windows, men on porches, looking.

"Up here, right around the corner," Lionel said softly.

"Here we go," Sly said. "Nobody talks but me. We go inside, I talk with T-Money, nice and friendly, Lionel stays put in the ride." He turned to Curious George. "You got that Gat, yeah?"

Curious nodded, tapping the pouch of his hoodie.

"Keep that outta sight. Keep your hands out your pockets where everybody can see. Somebody bucks? I take my glasses off and wipe the lens? You see that, you open that Gat right the fuck up. Get whatever motherfuckers are at the door, between us and Lionel here. I'll take out T-Money and whoever's next to him." He looked at Sully. "You got that piece you carry? That thing from the war?"

Sully shook his head, no.

"That's too bad. Shit jumps off, you just run. I hope you quicker than you look."

T-Money's headquarters was a sagging brick row house, seven or eight guys out front on the sidewalk in the early May air, the dim orange glow of blunts and smokes in the gloom. When the Jeep pulled up at the curb, they converged, dropping smokes, grinding them underfoot. Two guys materialized from a parked car, three or four came off the porch, backs squared, baseball caps skewed to the side.

Sly got out and it looked like the freaking Red Sea. The guys on the sidewalk parted, the surprise registering on their faces, the man instantly recognized, feared.

"Hey now, hey now," Sly said, a toothpick working at the side of his mouth, pushing up the glasses on his nose, reaching out to slap palms. Then he stopped, stretched onto his toes, raising his hands up, stretching like he'd just driven in from Detroit, and unleashed a long, loud yawn.

"What is *up*, people," he said, bringing his hands down and pushing the car door closed. Curious got out of the back door, everybody recognizing him, too.

Sully pushed open his door on the street side and got out, the men sizing him up, the only white guy in twenty blocks, riding with Sly motherfucking Hastings.

When Sully got to the sidewalk, a chubby dude with an untucked flannel shirt was already bullshitting with Sly, like it was no biggie that Sly had rolled up unannounced in a place where he had no business and was not welcome. Chub Man looked over at Sully, furrowing his brow, saying to Sly, "Hey, fuckface over there—he rollin' with you, too?"

Sly nodded.

"What up," said Chub, still looking at Sully. "That face you got—what the other nigga look like?" And he broke up, killing himself here.

"He don't say much, speak the English," Sly said. "Nigga's from Yugoslavia, where they got that war? That shit's real over there, bombs and shit. Just *look* at him. I think somebody did that to him with a knife."

"Ah shit," Chub said, looking over at Sully. "No foul, though? Right?"

Sully nodded, hunching his shoulders.

"So, okay," Chub said. "Let's go see T-Money. Hey, Sly, brother, I know he wants to see you."

In the front room, the television was the only illumination, a pale blue glow falling over a sagging-ass couch, a couple of chairs, a beat-to-shit coffee table. By the time Sully edged through the crowd and got inside, the sound was off—it was some sort of rap music channel—and T-Money was sprawled on the couch, a black T-shirt pulled over his bulk, baggy basketball shorts, the man looking like Heavy D, making Chub look like a lollipop.

His legs were open, knees moving back and forth, a bowl of popcorn in his lap, a blunt on the sad-ass end table, smoke just barely smoldering off the end. Cans of Steel Reserve 211, the twenty-four-ounce things, littered the table. There were two women at the back of the room, moving off to the kitchen, when Sully finally got past the crowd.

T-Money looked up at him, the features registering at some level.

"Who this here?" Looking at Sully, but directing the question to Sly.

Sitting on the edge of the coffee table, pushing a pizza carton to the side, Sly turned and looked, like he had forgotten who all was with him.

"He's with me," Sly said.

T-Money looked at Sully, munching on some popcorn. "Does he talk?"

"When he's pissed."

"Hunh," said T-Money.

"So what I was saying," Sly said, "is that I understand. That's what I came to tell you. Dee got to being a real asshole. So I got no problems with him getting capped, you hear? None."

T-Money rolled his eyes back to Sly, the man high as a goddamn kite.

"We moving a little new product in from my skinny white Balkan brother over there," Sly continued. "I'm working with Tony and Carlos on it. It's all cool. But Dee, right? He started sampling product, couldn't handle the shit. Somebody had let me know about it, I'd taken care of it myself."

"Okay," T-Money said.

"I was thinking Tony and Carlos was on top of things," Sly said.

"Okay."

"So, what I'm saying is, I came down here—was getting dinner right up there on the Hill?—to make sure you knew I wasn't taking it as any disrespect or anything. You boys popping Dee. I got no beef. Full, straight-up respect."

T-Money blinked. "The fuck you talking about?"

"Dee. Don't be simple. Got popped two weeks ago in the Bend."

"I heard *that*, Negro. I asked, why you think I canceled his ass?"

"Come on, T," Sly smiling now, his manner easing, looking around the room, trying to draw a smile out of Curious, Sully, somebody. "Boy's car got shot up coming out of Splash, like, the week before he got capped. That's your turf—"

"Jordy, stick your hand up," T-Money said. "See Jordy over there? He plugged the car. Dumb-ass Dee was moving product in the Mickey D's, which is *this* side of the street. Jordy gave him a friendly little Gat to help him remember what's what."

The video on the television changed. Chicks at the beach on the screen and the sudden burst of illumination threw a wave of light across the room.

Sully kept his eyes on Sly and T-Money but took in the rest of the room: the men in the room all standing, save for Sly and T-Money, nobody leaning against a wall; limp curtains over the windows, catching the reflected light of the television. Sully risked a glance to his right at Curious George, who was staring at Sly but his fingers were working inside the pouch of his hoodie.

"Right, see, I'm with you," Sly was saying, forearms on top of knees, fingers making a steeple. "And Dee, he didn't get the hint, you know? So you had to cap him." He shrugged, rolling his shoulders. "I get it, brother. Like I say, it's none offa mine, asshole like that."

"Maybe you don't hear so good," T-Money said, his knees not jiggling back and forth anymore. "But Ima say it slow this time. We. Did. Not. Cap. Dee. The. Motherfucking. End."

Sly looked at him, his fingertips pressing together hard now. "You sure?" he said. "You, like, real sure, T? 'Cause if you didn't cap Dee, then it's a goddamn mystery. Then I got work. 'Cause I got to know who did."

The big man rolled from the back of the couch, his girth flopping over the front of the basketball shorts. "I ain't done shit," he said, his eyes taking on the glare of resentment now. "I ain't done shit, Sly. Believe that or go fuck yourself, walking up in my house like this. And you bringing product down here? To the Bend, Southwest? You best to remember where South Cap is, you hear?"

Sly, frozen in place now, like ice, like granite.

"Fuck *myself*?" he whispered back, lips peeling back to bare teeth. "Fuck *me*? I come down here, respecting your beef, and you say fuck *me*?"

Nobody moved, the room electric, ready to explode.

"I said we ain't done shit," T-Money said. "You heard it."

Sly pushed his glasses up the bridge of his nose, resetting them. For a half beat, Sully thought he was going to pull them off and wipe them and that he was going to die in this crappy hellhole, headlines in the paper, "Twelve Dead in Gun Battle in SE Row House."

But Sly only adjusted the glasses, then moved his hand from his face and pushed off the balls of his feet and stood up, rising to his full height, six feet and change, so that he lorded over T-Money and his fat ass on the couch.

When he spoke, it was a Miles Davis hiss, like the gates of hell had swung open and this was the sound of rust on the hinges. "I find out different, T-Money? Different in any way? I'm gonna start with your sister. You want me to say that slow?"

TWENTY-NINE

"THAT SEEMED TO go well."

Lionel was driving deeper into Southeast, turning right, the Anacostia appearing off to the left, black and silvery. Between the road and the river there was a long row of crumbling buildings, one- or two-story warehouses with loading docks, sprawling junkyards, a cement mixing plant, all hulking in a grayish gloom behind ratty chain-link fences.

"I'd drop it, I was you," Sly said.

"No, seriously. I'd say T-Money was open, receptive to new ideas—"

"Drop it, fuckface."

"You still think he did it? Or do we cross the South Caps off the list?"

They had been back in the car for five minutes, maybe ten, after stalking out of the house, game faces on, Lionel peeling off in a fuck-you squeal. Nobody had said anything, the dim lights and broken neighborhood rolling by, until Sully looked at Curious looking out the window, then started fucking with Sly.

"That ain't an easy question," Sly said. "T bet his existence on convincing me he didn't, I give him that. We don't cross him off, we don't clock him. He just stays in play."

"So, what you're saying is, we didn't get a damn thing done."

Sly harrumphed in the front seat, pushing his glasses back up on his nose, not deigning to turn and look at him. "We got his goddamned attention from off that TV set," Sly said. "He knows we're looking now. He knows some shit is ready to drop. We keep an eye on him the next few days, see what move they make. We did that."

His face was impassive, a finger tapping the end of his nose. The eyes themselves looked straight ahead, not left or right.

The car went silent, Curious George looking out his window at the crappy landscape rolling by, turning back west now, crossing South Capitol, back into Southwest, back into the Hall brothers' turf. The streets were dark, the same low-rent industrial eyesores, the long brick wall of Fort McNair, topped with razor wire. When the Jeep pulled to the curb at Fourth and P, at the top of the Bend, Curious George got out, wordless. The car didn't move.

"Go on," said Sly.

"I'm down at the marina," Sully said.

Sly, still looking straight ahead, said, "You'n get there from here. I got shit to do. Curious'll get you through the Bend. Ain't nobody gonna fuck with you."

This is bullshit, Sully thought, but he got out, hitch-stepping to catch up with Curious, the Jeep pulling off behind them, trailing a thin plume of exhaust.

They went down the gentle incline, beneath the trees, between the fort and the old apartment buildings, the channel down in front of them. The only illumination was dots of yellow light from within apartment windows, but there was sound. People murmuring or talking in the shadows, against the wall to the fort, the ravings of the high and the stoned, might be some sort of sexual thing over there to the left.

At the end of the park, as they made the waterfront, Curious stopped and snapped his head to the right. Materializing out of the gloom, a figure was coming down to them, a darker shadow moving in long, arrogant steps.

"The fuck you been at?" The figure moved closer, skullcap over his head, a leather jacket, and now Sully made out Short Stuff. It was addressed to Curious, but now he was looking back at Sully, his eyes opening wider.

"And this—this motherfucker *here*? You been somewhere with *this* motherfucker?"

Curious George glanced at Sully like he had forgotten he was there, then ticked his head back at Short Stuff. "He was up there at the top of the Bend. He started walking down here behind me, asking questions. I said whatever, man, it ain't none of mine."

"Ain't none of—this fool done been *told*. Carlos looking for you, you know that? You ain't nowhere, you not picking up your pager, and you show up with *this* bitch? No, motherfucker, no, this shit right here ain't *right*."

Curious kept his chin up, meeting the glare, shifting his weight from one foot to the other, sounding resentful. "I'n get a piece when I want. Little shorty up there off Prospect? Her momma wasn't home? She hit me on the pager. I ain't got to tell Carlos every time I get me a piece."

"Yeah? Frankenstein here? He waxin' that ass, too?"

"I done told you, he was up there at the head of the Bend. He ain't none of mine."

Short Stuff turned to Sully, the pistol coming out and up, and he shook his head, like a bull shark closing in on fresh meat. "You one dumb motherfucker. Get down there by the water. Get. Move."

Sully flicked his eyes at Curious but couldn't make out his face.

"What I'm gonna do," Sully said, looking Short Stuff in the eye, "is go where I been going, which is to my bike, which is at the Gangplank. I's up there at the O Street clubs, talking to them people over there about Billy Ellison and his coke, now I'm on the way back."

"Bullshit," said Short Stuff.

"I don't got a beef with you," Sully said, "but that's the way it went. Now I'm just on the way out."

He started walking, cutting in between Curious and Shorty, heading for the walkway that ran along the channel, up to the *Spirit of Washington*, the tour boat, and then the parking lot for the Gangplank. He needed ten steps, could be twelve, and it would be over. Shorty would yell at him, curse him, but he wasn't going to follow him.

But his third step put him between Short Stuff and the waterfront. Short Stuff stepped forward, bringing his hands up, and he shoved Sully at the shoulder, knocking him off balance, his bad leg not absorbing the load. He stumbled sideways, hands going down to the ground, trying to stay on his feet, staggering out onto the knob of the Bend.

"Can't even *believe* this motherfucker," Short Stuff said, shoving him again. The second blow sent him tumbling, his left shoulder crashing into the ground. He took the fall and rolled twice, the world spinning, the sound of the water close now, him getting back to his feet, the left foot finding purchase first, the right one stabbing the ground behind him for balance. It missed and he went down again. Short Stuff kicked him just below the ribs, an explosion in his gut, knocking him farther out to the water.

"He ain't worth it," Curious said, hunching his shoulders, watching, ambling forward. "Man, I ain't even in the mood for—"

"You shut the *fuck* up," Shorty hissed back. Sully rolled twice and made his feet, just in time for Short Stuff to walk right up on him. He shoved the gun to the back of Sully's head, poking him with it, Sully feeling it as a hard point of metal at the base of his skull. There was another shove in the back, moving him the last few feet to the edge of the rocks at the waterfront.

"You in deep *enough*," Short Stuff spit out at Curious. "Carlos finds out you been tapping ass instead of out here working? Shit. I spend twenty motherfucking minutes walking back and forth out here, hitting your damn pager, and now *this* bitch shows up. I guess he think we playing. I guess, what, motherfucker, you thought that beatdown at the track was as bad as it gets?"

He pushed Sully in the back again, sending him stumbling, taking three steps out on the rocks, the water splashing up around his shoes now. They were going to shoot him and dump him, that's what it was, he was going to be swimming in the channel, this is how it had gone with Billy Ellison, this right here, and the thought flickered darkly through his mind, *You wanted to know who killed him and now you know.*

There was the possibility, Sully thought, looking at the black water, the quarter-mile expanse over to Hains Point, that he could take five or six running steps and be in the water and dive and he'd swim.

The channel wasn't shit next to the Big River and his mind flashed to his old man, half-drunk but not mean, he'd never been mean a day in his life, making him swim the breadth of the river, right beside him in their johnboat, saying, *Swimming pools are for girls, a man come off a boat out here in the river currents branches cottonmouths nah they ain't no lifeguards out here this the only water you going to drown in boy this the water you got to swim in to live out here boy come on now we ain't but two hunnert yards out hell if it's nasty then stop swallowing it*, but he didn't think he'd ever make it three steps. He'd take two steps and the first shot would knock him down and the second one, Shorty would just walk up and put that one in his head.

This place, the Bend, it had been claiming bodies for more than a century and a half and it was going to claim his. The slaves, he thought, his mind ricocheting, they stood right here and got pushed onto boats headed down to the Carolinas or Georgia or Florida or on around Key West and back up to Mobile or Gulfport or New Orleans. Billy Ellison, he'd died right here, Dee had died right over there, so what difference did one more make?

He turned, his tongue dry and leatherlike and stuck to the roof of his mouth, time running out. He focused on making two moves at once. Drop down from the knees and lunge forward, hit Shorty low, get under the gun when it went off, and then go for his neck, his eyes, his balls.

There was enough light to see Short Stuff looking at him, the gun up at Sully's head, his features set in stone. Curious was five or six feet to the right, still ambling forward, lazily coming down to get a good look at the show.

"Hey, dog?" Curious George said.

Short Stuff moved his head a tic to the left, as if listening, and Curious brought his gun up and out of the hoodie and it exploded in a flash of orange and yellow light and he shot Short Stuff in the side of the head.

The man's gun went flying and he dropped like a freight train falling off a bridge. He went facedown. His foot quivered for a minute but then he was still.

The sound of the shot was a *pop pop pop* that skittered across the water like a flat rock tossed from shore. And then both light and echo were gone, darkness falling again as if nothing had happened. Curious put the gun back in the pouch of his hoodie and walked over, stooping down beside the body. He extended the sleeve of the sweatshirt over his hand and then nudged the shoulder with it. Then he turned the exploded head back toward him. He inspected the open skull cavity.

Sully, looking down, then up over the expanse of the park, expecting sirens, flashlights, running cops. There was nothing, just a light breeze coming in off the water. At the far end of the Bend, way back up toward Fourth, where they had entered the park, he could see three, now four figures moving hurriedly but something was wrong with them and he blinked and realized they were running away from the sound of the blast, not toward it.

"What—" he started to say, but Curious was saying something.

"You see where that gun went?" He didn't stop looking at the head. "His piece? You see it?"

Sully walked forward, his feet on the rocks, the water lapping at his toes. He bent down and looked in the water, over the rocks. And there it was, barrel down, wedged between a stone the size of a watermelon and a shattered bit of concrete block.

"Right there," he said, pointing.

Curious looked in that direction, then went back to the head, blood still oozing. "Hand it to me?"

Sully put his hand inside his shirtsleeve and leaned over, stretching the fabric, but picking up the piece only with the cloth touching the metal. It was lighter than he expected, and he stood back up and handed it to Curious, who, still kneeling beside the dead body, took it and put it in the pouch of his hoodie with the other one.

"Brains," he said, looking at Short Stuff. "You figure, you know, they'd look like something. But they just scrambled eggs, every time." He sounded disappointed and then he stood up. He kept his hands inside the sleeves of his sweatshirt and then kneeled back down and pushed the body over the rocks and into the water, giving it one more shove but being careful to stay on the rocks. The body moved out a foot or two but stuck there.

"Fuck it," he said. He took off his Timberlands and stepped into the water in his socks and then pushed the body hard, until it was floating.

Then he came back, his jeans wet halfway to the knee, and put on his shoes. They watched the body for a minute, facedown, slumped in the black water.

Sully turned to look at him. "What did—" but Curious was blinking, the lids going up and down rapid-fire, and he starting talking over him, cutting him off.

"Fucker forgot to look sideways," he said, watching the body, now ten feet out. "Sly said you was to get through the park okay."

He hit another blinking spell and it seemed to break his concentration. He turned to Sully and looked surprised to see him there, to see anyone at all, and he started walking back up the Bend, back toward the streets. There was a siren in the distance.

"I's you," he said, "I'd be getting my ass somewhere else."

THIRTY

THE THING WAS you couldn't run. You. Could. Not. Run. You want people to remember you? Start running after a gun goes off. *Then* they see you. Yeah, officer, this guy, he had this limp and he was hobbling down by the water, fast as he could gimp it. . . .

So he started walking right back up the Bend, no rush but not fucking around, either. Curious George was ahead of him, heading off toward the right, to come out at the top of the park right by the wall at Fort McNair. Sully could see his profile every now and then against the streetlights from way up on Fourth.

His breath was ragged and his ribs hurt but it was getting less with each step. When he got off the knob of the Bend, he broke off to the left, away from Curious, heading for the walkway along the waterfront. That would take him back up to the Gangplank and the bike. As soon as he got there, he'd be home free. Just another schmuck walking off dinner, for all anybody knew, another boat owner, a party guest, a bar patron.

He was picking up the pace when something flicked at the corner of his vision. Curious George, way up ahead now, skylined by the lights on Fourth, suddenly broke into a dead sprint, running like hell along the wall of Fort McNair.

Bright white lights exploded along the wall alongside Curious. Searchlights. A patrol *whoop whoop whoop*ing, the red and blue misery lights atop one, now the other setting off, whipping flares of light onto the trees, the buildings. A car alarm started bleating. Sully lost sight of Curious, but heard the spectral voice of a cop on the loudspeaker of the patrol car blaring orders, car doors thumping.

Now running seemed like a pretty good goddamn idea. He took two steps and a searchlight from a patrol car suddenly on the paved walkway in back of the Carolina, the apartment building. It shot out across the Bend, maybe twenty yards behind him, sweeping the other way. Raised voices, shouting, more car doors thumping.

He froze. God help him, he crouched and froze.

The searchlight swept back this way and he flattened out on the ground, the beam illuminating two, maybe three cops heading down the slight incline into the Bend, the smaller beams of their flashlights bursting into life. He could hear their voices, hear them fanning out, establishing a perimeter. No way out. They had cut him off.

He pushed up, found his feet, and turned and ran back out onto the knob of the Bend, away from the cops, not looking back. He stumbled and nearly fell face-first on the shattered brick and stones. He cursed, slowing, trying not to make any sound, wading into the water, feeling and not feeling the cold embrace of it moving up his ankles and now his knees, the body of Short Stuff bobbing in the shallows off to his left.

The searchlight swept back again and there were shouts behind him and he could not stop himself from crouching down in the water, turning to look. Half a dozen flashlight beams now, coming from the top of the park and the side, all converging this way, down onto the knob of the Bend.

Nothing else to do now. He moved two more steps, three, and the bottom disappeared beneath him. Blackness swept over his mouth, his nose, his eyes, and he was beneath the water. The iciness swirled over him, his balls shriveling and tightening. He felt his foot touch mud and he let both legs come down now until he was in a crouch, cheeks puffed out with oxygen, and he was in a tiny ball at the bottom of the channel.

He opened his eyes and they stung and there was only blackness and he snapped them shut. He shot his hands and arms out in front of him and pushed off. His arms moved the water from in front of him and swept to the side. Two strokes, three, the water getting colder by degrees as he moved into the deeper water. When he felt his breath going, he drifted and stretched an arm up above his head. After a while, he felt the tips of his fingers break the surface.

His lungs were burning, but he forced himself to slow, and slow some more, until he turned his body and pushed his chin up and away from his chest until his face was almost parallel to the surface and water was trying to shoot up his nostrils. Then he let his nose and mouth and forehead break the surface, gulping in the night air, his eyes still closed, his ears beneath the water. Then he tilted his head forward, keeping his chin above the water, looking back toward the Bend.

Flashlights swept across it, waving like the arms and legs of an insect on its back. Two patrol car searchlights also swept across the Bend, intersecting and parting again. The flashlights were not pooled at the waterfront. If there were voices he could not hear them. They had not seen him. They were not looking for him. They had not found Short Stuff yet, but they would soon and that would occupy them, absorb their time and attention. He wondered if Curious's gun had ejected a shell, if they had run him down.

The deep cold of the water swept over him again, raising gooseflesh. He put his face down in the water, pulling his right leg up, taking one shoe off and then the other, and he brought his face back up into the air. Beneath the surface, he tied each shoe tight against his belt.

The lights of Hains Point glittered across the water, but they no longer beckoned to him. The marina was maybe four hundred yards down the waterway on this side of the channel, an easy swim. There was no boat traffic and all he had to worry about was coming into the lighted area of the marina without being seen and pulling himself up onto one of the piers. From there, it'd be easy. Soaking wet, walking off the marina? Anybody asked, *Yeah, damn, tying up and dropped my keys over the side, had to hop in with a net to get them—Christ, I gotta get home before I freeze.*

He dipped beneath the water again, shooting his left arm forward, pulling it down and back toward him and then bringing the right arm over his head, reaching forward, taking the water again without slapping it, steadily kicking his legs below the surface.

Another stroke, and another, the muscles tight but they would loosen with the effort and the repetition, and then he was into a full overhand crawl, moving away from the Bend and toward the lights of the marina.

THIRTY-ONE

THE SUN WAS out on his back porch the next morning, warming his bones. He was in jeans and a thermal long-sleeve, eating the last of a monstrous breakfast—omelet, toast, bacon—and making himself drink the coffee he'd just brewed and not think about how he'd rather have the morning julep, when the phone rang. The receiver, where was it . . . here. Beneath the morning paper, the sections splayed out and flapping. He looked at the digits on the phone, picked it up, and said, "Why, John Parker. How good of you to remember me."

Wind was blowing on the other end. Parker was outside somewhere. "Why you not picking up your cell?"

"Enjoying a quiet morning at home, as a gentleman sometimes does."

"Things don't seem to be working out so good for you," Parker said, coughing, then bringing the phone back to his mouth. "Last time I saw you was with Delores Ellison. Now I hear you got yourself suspended."

"My employers are delicate little flowers."

Parker snorted. "I told the missus. She says she's worried about you. Wants me to get you to come over for dinner."

"Say when. As long as she's cooking. I've eaten yours before." He made a study of his toenails, working to keep his tone flat.

"Too bad you're not with the rest of us at the Bend, on this fine spring morning. That little fat guy what works with you was telling me the paper got on you about the thing with Delores."

"Chris?" Sully said, putting a note of surprise in his voice, like this was news. "What's Chris doing at the Bend?"

"Your job. You didn't hear? We got another body."

Sully left the toenails to their fate and reached over on the plate, breaking off a piece of omelet with his fingers, then popping it in his mouth. Keeping it light. "No shit? For real?"

"Body's out there in the water, not quite making it out to swim with the fishes. Your buddy Dave's down here with his television truck."

Sully sipped his tea and took another bite of toast, his gut tightening a little bit now.

"So who is it?"

"We're waiting on a family ID before releasing it, but I'm pretty sure it was one Antoine Gillespie, better known as Ant. Enforcer for the Hall brothers."

"Why 'pretty sure'?"

"Because most of the left side of his head is gone."

"Well there's that."

"Yeah. He's—was—a player in the M Street Crew, like his buddy Dee Dee, who got popped a couple of weeks back."

"This guy Ant, he kinda short, stocky, tends to run around with a hoodie?"

"That's him."

"Last time I saw him, he was threatening to kill me."

"That sounds about right," Parker said. "You want to come down and pay your respects? The techs are wrapping up, but they'll be here another hour or so."

"I think I'll pass. Let Chris handle it."

"Fine. You'll have another chance. This ain't the end of this shit. Some serious beefin' is cranking up."

Sully waited for a second, let some air in the conversation. "Any connection this guy Ant, Antoine Gillespie, had to Billy Ellison?"

"Could be, might be," John said. "All this is going to be tied to that new high-test blow we been seeing down here. Somebody's making a move. Three bodies in three weeks? That's not an accident."

"You catch the bad guys yet? Not the Dee Dee bad guys. The Ant shooter."

"Not yet. Foot chase between some uniforms and a suspect last night. Maybe one of them, anyhow. We had a couple of patrols up on M Street— this Korean nail salon place'd just got robbed? And we get calls about a shot or shots down in the Bend. So they roll down there, just to see if there's something to see, and soon as they pull up, some brother takes off running."

"They didn't grab him?"

"Lost him on the street."

"You thinking he might have been the shooter?"

"No way to know. Might have been some dude scoring coke, hears the shot from down on the water, takes off on GP."

"So this shooting, it was down by the riverside?"

"Yeah. The other units thought they saw somebody out there on the Bend, but nothing doing. They get down to the water, there's Mrs. Gillespie's bouncing baby boy, bobbing in the waves."

"Good god."

"I gave it to Jeff to take the lead on it, since he's working the other shootings down here, but we're getting the narcotics unit detailed, some help from DEA. We got uniforms canvassing every unit of the Carolina, that apartment building right by the Bend. You know how many helpful witnesses we're going to get?"

"Zero?"

"You got a genius for this business."

"Any forensics, shells?"

"None yet. But look, I got to jump. The Ellison funeral, that's today, and the chief wants a show of respect. I got to switch into a suit and get into traffic."

Sully blew out his lips into a raspberry. Christ. Delores. He hated funerals.

"You know they're having a daily protest out in front of your paper about your story?"

"I do."

"And that the funeral procession is passing by there on the way up to the cathedral?"

"I had missed that happy fact."

"I think they're trying to get you fired."

Sully nodded, but he wasn't sure if John meant the people outside the building or the people inside.

THIRTY-TWO

THE TAXI DROPPED him off at McPherson Square, four or five blocks from the paper. He had on jeans and a T-shirt under an old sport coat, plus a and a baseball cap and running shoes, so he didn't look like much, and the sunglasses covered part of his face.

By the time he made it to the block of the paper, there were several hundred people—no, more, at least a thousand—clogging the sidewalks, spilling into the street, holding signs, chanting. Every few minutes, a group of ten or twelve protesters would sling their rubber-band-bound papers at the building all at once, hitting the glass windows with percussive thumps, the better arms getting to the second and third floors.

"Hold on wait a minute / got to put some *bullshit* in it!" went the chant, morphing into "Take it back! Take it *back*!"

Television cameras at the intersection picked it up, the patrol cars and lines of police containing the demonstration, the west-bound lane in front of the paper blocked off. The crowd, mostly black but a good bit white, bobbing, weaving, roiling, bouncing against the police barricades, energized but not out of control. He worked his way toward the front of the crowd, walking along the yellow tape where the television crews were doing standups. Dave wasn't there. Surprising.

"Bitterly angry demonstrators," one reporter was saying, talking earnestly into the camera, gesturing to the crowd behind her.

"I wouldn't say they were enraged, David and Emily," another said into the microphone, talking to hosts back in the studio, "but I think it fair to call it passionate, this outpouring after the suicide of Delores El-lison, one of the city's most well-known socialites and philanthropists, which came less than twenty-four hours after a story on the front page of the paper, copies of which these protesters are hurling back at the paper that published this inflammatory . . ."

BILLY ELLISON DIED FOR YOUR SINS, read one sign.

Some of the others Sully could make out:

ELLISONS > HEADLINES

YOU HAVE BEEN CANCELED

TAKE IT BACK

RENEW THIS

In front of the crowd on the jostling sidewalk, a man in a somber black suit had a bullhorn, pacing back and forth. Sully recognized him as the pastor from the Capital City AME, a good-looking, charismatic preacher with a shaved head, exhorting the crowd milling back and forth in front of him, spilling into the street.

"We have labored all these *years*," he said, holding the horn close to his mouth, "to even be *recognized* by these types of media institutions." A little feedback and distortion during the pause.

"And *this* is what we get?"

"No!" yelled the crowd.

"And *THIS* is what we get," he came back, louder.

"*Nnnnooooo*," lowed the crowd.

"They can't hear you in there because they're counting *your* money!" he bellowed.

"NNNNNOOOOOOOOOOO!"

"Are you canceling your subscriptions?"

"YYEEESSSSSSS!"

And then, rising from the back, deep, booming, being picked up by the rest of the crowd until it was a resonating bit of rhythm cascading down the block, over all of downtown: "Hold on wait a minute / got to put some *bullshit* in it. . . ."

By the time Sully got up to the National Cathedral, the clock going on two, the second Ellison funeral in a week was already unfolding. From his vantage point across Wisconsin Avenue, his view partially obscured by the trees, it still looked like an affair of state.

The Veep was already inside; the guys in suits talking into their fingers were flanking the cathedral, all entrances, eyes up. Sully counted four black SUVs, rear doors open, a discreet M16 barrel poking out of one. There was probably a Supreme Court justice inside, certainly an undersecretary of state. Traffic on Wisconsin was impossible, a parking lot in both directions, cops with whistles and pissed-off expressions, arms windmilling, c'mon c'mon, or flat palms out, whistles blaring.

The pearl-gray hearse was parked just in front of the steps leading to the cathedral entrance. Three black limousines were behind it, parked, while others circled through, dropping off mourners. A man in a suit was rolling a heavy LOT FULL sign out to the road, telling people to forget the garage beneath the cathedral. Faintly, borne on the breeze, there was the sound of the organ. Television trucks and reporters outside, the antennae on the trucks rising into the air.

Chris was over there in the bank of reporters covering it, looking like a stuffed sausage in his suit, waddling up the sidewalk, talking to a few mourners along the way, stepping onto the grass to take down their names and remembrances in his notebook.

Sully stood across the far side of Wisconsin.

Another taxi had dropped him two blocks up and he had walked back down, now loitering in front of the Charleston, an art deco–era apartment building, watching the procession across the street, keeping tabs on the event for reasons he could not precisely name.

The guilt that coursed through him had grown into a snake of monstrous proportions. Billy Ellison and his mother had, less than ten days ago, been rulers of social Washington, the elite of the elite. Then Billy had died and Sully had written one story and then another, and now they were both in the ground, the Ellison family line wiped off the planet.

He had a small pair of binoculars but did not pull them up lest he draw undue attention, which, after the scene downtown, he was in no mood to do. As he leaned against a car, trying to affect an air of boredom, his eyes jumped around the perimeter, picking out Stevens's goons, standing separately, apart from the small knots of mourners. They were not the Secret Service guys, no, but they were keeping an eye out, looking for him, no doubt, looking to score points even after Delores was dead. Creating a scene would be a kill shot to his career. Stevens knew that as well as he did.

And suddenly there he was, Stevens, the man himself, emerging from behind one of the cathedral pillars, coming down the steps to the hearse, his feet shuffling along like he was wearing lead shoes. Sully tucked himself against the windshield of the car and pulled up the binoculars. Stevens had apparently asked the driver of the hearse for something. He was leaning against the rear of the vehicle, head down, hands on his knees.

Sully briefly panned the glasses down to the pavement to see if he had thrown up, but no, he hadn't. The driver came back, stopped short, a set of papers in his hand, and Stevens looked up at him and reached out to take the papers and then went back to his head-down posture, the papers trapped against a knee.

His head shook and the hand with the papers fluttered. The driver walked back to the front of the car. Stevens stood upright, but still leaning his right shoulder against the hearse. Then Sully could see his face. It was the color of shale, a great misshapen thing that settled above his collar as if in a choke hold. The eyes appeared as hard as ball bearings, gray orbs you could pull out of his head and still not be able to crack with a hammer.

"Jesus," Sully muttered.

Stevens stirred, coming back to himself, and Sully put the glasses back in the pocket of his sport coat and pushed himself up off the car, moving around a little bit, beneath the extended awning of one apartment building, and then back out into the sun.

He'd only been there a few moments when a thin young man in a suit stopped on the sidewalk dead in front of him. Sully pulled up short, nearly bumping into him. The face had said something. Christ, one of Stevens's operatives, what—and then Sully realized that the face was familiar, he'd seen this guy. Where, what—

"Mr. Carter?" the face said, smiling, brown bangs over his forehead, the Adam's apple bobbing. Reaching out to shake hands, his mind spinning furiously, it finally came to him.

"Elliot!" he said. "Elliot. Good god. Haven't seen you since the cafeteria."

"Yeah, hope I didn't interrupt. You were talking."

"What? Who? Who was I talking to?"

"Yourself."

"I was?"

Billy's onetime partner, a bow tie neatly knotted at his neck, moved back out of the middle of the sidewalk, standing beside Sully, so others could pass.

"Yeah," he said. "You looked preoccupied."

"Oh."

"When I heard you had been suspended," Elliot said, as if by way of explanation, "I was impressed. It told me that your story had really pissed Delores off, and that made you a friend of mine. I was hoping you might be at the funeral. So I came up. I saw a reporter over there and he said he was from the paper."

Sully folded his arms and bit on his lower lip, wishing Elliot would go the fuck home. "Chris. That's Chris. He told you I was over here?" If Chris could spot him, then, sweet Jesus—

"No, no. He caught me up on what was going on. I mean, I saw your story in the paper. Everybody did. Everybody was talking about it. Then it went around that Delores had committed suicide. That sounded bad."

Sully wondered which part of it sounded bad, but it pretty much all was, so he let it go. "Well, yeah, I mean whatever, so, thank you. It is. But I should let you get over to the service. I think they're starting soon."

He nodded across the street. They were shutting the doors to the cathedral. Two of Stevens's guys, in suits, stood tandem watch at the door, one on either side.

"Oh no," Elliot said, again with the hair flip, "I didn't come to go to the funeral. You'll remember Delores had a very low opinion of me. I mean, I'm sorry she's dead? But she made Billy miserable. I came because I thought I might find you. Your colleague said you weren't here and I was leaving and wow, I walked right into you."

"Me?" Sully felt his eyebrows arch, he couldn't help it. There was a headache building behind his eyes and Elliot, in all his earnestness, wasn't helping. Fucking kids, they got on his nerves, this lack of awareness of the rest of the world. "You put on a suit and tie and came to a funeral of a woman you can't stand because you wanted to find me?"

"I don't know that I would put it like that."

"Okay. Whatever way you like. What's on your mind?"

"Those morons his mom hired. Two of them are over there, guarding the doors."

"The private investigators?"

"That's dressing it up some, but yeah."

"What about them?"

"They tore up Billy's place."

"His place, what are you talking about?" Sully said, moving under the awning, Elliot following.

"His apartment. Billy's. They went through there and ransacked it."

"They . . . I guess, what, they were looking for the drugs, get them out of there, keep it from getting in the news."

Elliot's eyebrows knit together. "Drugs? No, I don't think that's what they were looking for."

"Why not?"

"Because they came to my house the next night, looking for the same thing."

"They—"

"But it's okay," Elliot said, nodding again, that Adam's apple. "I think I know what they were looking for. I've got it. You want to come see it?'

THIRTY-THREE

ELLIOT SAID THE thing wasn't at his apartment but at a friend's, and that this guy, he'd bring it to them. So they flagged a taxi and wound up in Georgetown, Sully letting Elliot tell the driver where to go. This turned out to be a bar called the Giraffe, on M Street, right on the main drag. They took a booth at the very back, set behind a partial wall of exposed brick. The waiter came, they ordered, and Elliot looked uncomfortable.

"The first time we talked?" he said, taking off his bow tie. "Right after Billy died, and you came to meet me at the cafeteria? I really wasn't all that sure who you were. I sort of held out on you. I mean, you didn't know anything. No offense, I mean."

"None taken," Sully said, wishing he'd smacked the little prick the first time. "I never know much about anything."

Elliot looked at him, nodding. The kid didn't even get sarcasm.

"But then? A day or two later? After Billy's funeral?" Elliot said. "They came by my apartment and asked if I had a key to his place, if I had been in there since he died, if—"

"They?"

"—if—they, those guys? The thugs Billy's mom hired. Or that dick-head she works for."

"We're back to the investigators now."

"Whoever. They wanted to come in and look around, can you believe it? In my place. I said, 'What are you looking for?' and they said, 'We'll know it when we see it.'"

"You didn't let them in."

"Of course not," Elliot said. "The way Delores treated Billy, the things she said about me? No no no. Of course I had a key to his place. We were partners for more than a year! You think I'm going to tell Delores that, just hand over my key?" He blew out his lips, getting worked up. "I told them to fuck right on off. One of them, the one with a shaved head, he called me 'faggot' and 'cocksucker.'"

"That's not good."

"It's insulting."

"This one with the shaved head, he have these big shoulders? Little pug nose?"

"Yeah. That's him. That's just the one."

"He's the one who shoved me into a car at Billy's funeral," Sully said.

"He did?"

"Yeah. They're sort of pricks, whether they think you're gay or not."

"He better be glad he didn't shove *me*," Elliot said. "Not in my—"

"So what happened? After he went all homophobic."

"They left. They were kind of disgusted. You could tell."

"No threats?"

"I don't think they're the kind who make threats," Elliot said. "I think they're more the kind that just do it."

"I think you're probably right."

The waiter came, set down a Basil's over ice for Sully and a Cosmopolitan in front of Elliot. The kid looked at it, then took an exploratory sip, leaning over and slurping from the martini glass without picking it up.

"They didn't come back, but I was pretty pissed," he said, puckering his lips after the drink. "Intimidation? Butch boys? Please. I've put up with that since high school. Football players. So, look, to get even, I went over to Billy's place the next day? With a couple of friends? We opened the door, took one step inside—and that was it. They had turned the entire place upside down. Bookshelves knocked over, furniture shoved around. We got out before we got blamed for it."

Sully added a tiny splash of water to his Basil's, took a respectable pull. God, it was fine. Quitting this . . . "Billy was dealing drugs," he told Elliot. "Maybe they were trying to clean it out. Or maybe one of his connections came looking for his stash after they shot him."

"Why do you keep saying that?" Elliot hissed. "What *is* this with the drug thing? You put that in that story, something about his rehab, drug problems—"

"He was a dealer, getting deep into it," Sully said. "Delores told me. Shellie told me. Billy got popped in the Bend. I mean, he was dealing, so—"

"Bullshit," Elliot said, shaking his head, tapping the table. "Oh man. Oh man. That's what they told you?"

"Yeah."

"You got suckered. No no no. Billy had—God love him—Billy had depression issues, sort of a bipolar thing—"

"Right, that's what they told me."

"And he was therefore *terrified* of drugs. *Mental* about it. 'I'm crazy enough as it is,' I can hear him now. Not a toke, not a toot."

"Maybe he—"

"I knew him since his freshman year," he said, shaking his head. "We dated off and on, more in the past two years, a lot this past year. Never saw him do anything harder than beer. He had friends from high school, Sidwell? And they'd say the same thing. Billy, he liked beer, at least sort of, but he was really very . . . fragile."

"How you mean, 'fragile'?"

"Delicate. He could be very giddy, a little loud at times, but there was a brittleness to it, if you knew it well enough to spot it. His moods, they'd fluctuate. Really not good self-esteem. He had weight issues, just mortified if he gained five pounds. Sometimes he stayed in bed and read all day. He wasn't, wasn't, really all that easy to know."

"His mom said he wanted to be a rap star."

Elliot rolled his head back and laughed, loud enough for the bartender to look over.

"So, I'm guessing—"

"*Billy?* Hip-hop? What, RuPaul does *rap*?" The laughter bubbled out of him, rolling across the place.

Sully sipped his bourbon and waited.

"I'm—" Elliot coughed, dabbing his eyes—there were little dewdrops at their edges—and he gave in to another round of it, squinching his eyes shut tight, waving his hand back and forth, then patting his chest, taking in air. "Okkkaaay. Sorry. Okay. Okay. I'm done. That rap business, though. Billy."

"You're telling me his mother lied to me."

"Yes, I, I am," Elliot said. "Billy was Tinkerbell with dreadlocks. He made Luther Vandross look like a middle linebacker."

"Somebody, guy I talked to, said Billy made Little Richard look butch."

"That would be somebody who knew Billy, yes."

It had always bugged him, getting hustled, getting played, and here it was, smacking him in the face. People lie right to your face and you got no idea. Jesus. He had sailed right by it, never doubting the rap star thing because it came from his mom. Rich, nice house, high on the social meter . . . and he'd gone for it, the circumstances coloring his vision, the weight he'd given her story. Would he have given Dee Dee's mom that sort of break? Nah. His own bias, assumptions, biting him in the ass. It was what you got for trusting anybody further than you could throw them.

"But why—why would she lie to me?" he said. "If everyone knew he—"

"Oh, c'mon, don't be dense," Elliot said. He all but snorted. "Delores didn't *want* to know Billy was queer, and she didn't want you to put it in the paper. She was so concerned with the family *image*, with getting invited to the White House each Christmas, with her precious clients. She wanted Billy to be a brand-new version of his dad. Who was, like, this Marine, a hard-ass, decorated, blah blah, then a lawyer. Billy wasn't like that. He was a terrible disappointment. They fought about it. She—"

A stocky young guy, had to be another college dude, sidled up to the table, holding a tote bag, THE STRAND emblazoned on the side. "Elliot," he said.

"Oh, Todd, hi." He stopped, looking at the bag. "You brought it. You wonderful man. You can just set it on the table."

Todd did. Two thick manila envelopes slid out, heavy things so stuffed with paperwork that the top of the envelopes could not be closed. Sully had to rescue his whiskey before it got toppled over.

"Sorry," Todd said.

"That's okay," Elliot said. "Thanks so much."

Todd nodded to them both and was gone.

"What's with him?" Sully said.

"He's just a boy I know. He was keeping this for me. After those goons came by, I didn't want to keep it at my apartment any longer."

"So this is it? What they were after?" It didn't look like much. Papers and, at the bottom of the bag, a square wooden box.

"I'm pretty sure. Billy brought it over to me the night before he was killed. He'd just had a huge fight with Delores, with Shellie. He'd been over at her house, he said, and he was very upset. Said he wanted me to keep it for him for a while."

"Like, bipolar upset?"

"Billy had stopped taking his medication a few months earlier. He had done it before. He didn't like taking it. I guess a lot of people who need that stuff don't want it."

"It dampens the highs, knocks them down," Sully said.

"Yeah. He said it made him feel dull. Like bread without yeast, that's how he said it. So he stopped taking the stuff and, no surprise, started getting weird. The racing thoughts, the rapid-fire talking? You know? It was something you had to learn to live with if you wanted to be his friend."

"So, him showing up at your house, a little wound up, wasn't that unusual."

"It wasn't an everyday thing, no, but it just seemed like another episode, another round with his mom. I thought he was just being a little paranoid."

Sully picked up one of the envelopes, pulled out a sheet. It was a copy of a property record over on Logan Circle.

"So what is all this?"

"His thesis."

"His thesis? He was hiding his *thesis*?"

"It was interesting for me to see all of the research, because he'd been very vague about what he was going to do it on, you know? He'd never tell me. But it turns out he was really focused. *Look* at all this."

Sully considered the heft of the envelopes. Why did people do this, after death? Pass along the writings or poems or letters of the dead, like it meant something to somebody else? And god, this stuff looked like it went a good five pounds.

"It's something about his family history," Elliot said. "Billy was terribly interested in all that. I think it was in some sort of order. But after he gave it to me at my apartment, I just put it in the bookcase. I didn't even think about it until after those creeps came looking for it. When I pulled it out, it all spilled on—"

He stopped dead still, looking toward the front of the bar, then slid to the back side of the booth. "Get the bag! Get over!"

Sully started to turn in the booth—his back was to the door—and Elliot kicked his leg under the table.

"It's those morons! Shaved head!"

Sully leaned over, pulling the bag with the envelopes on the seat beside him. The half wall of exposed brick behind them gave them shelter from the door, but they'd be in plain view if the men walked farther back.

"They *followed* us from the church," Elliot said. "The *fuckers*."

"What are you—"

"They had to be sitting out front, waiting on us to come back out, then saw Todd come in with the bag."

"Todd? They know Todd?"

"He's—he's—he was over at my apartment when they came over."

Sully started to say, This is ridiculous, they're not going to rob us in broad daylight, we call 911—and then got a mental flash of the *investigators* calling the police, charging *them* with theft. The cops would come, everybody would get hauled downtown, the bag would go into evidence and eventually be returned to the family—hell, it was Billy's property—and he'd get fired, harassing the poor Ellisons even when he was suspended.

His eyes locked on the narrow hallway a few feet behind them, lead-ing to the toilets. EMERGENCY EXIT, read the sign above the hall. Well.

He looked at Elliot—they both had their heads about six inches above the tabletop, leaning as far down as possible—and said, "Get up. Take your drink to the bar. They'll look at you, rag you some, but they can't do anything. That's going to give me a screen to run out the back with the bag."

"You don't look like you can run that fast."

"Fine. You take the bag and run and I'll—"

"No, no!"

"Do it then, before they come back here."

Elliot rubbed his hand across his face. "Call me," he said. He sat up, got his drink, and pushed out of the booth, walking bold as fuck up to the front. Sully, counting to three, decided he liked the kid after all.

"Hey! You, *Carter!*"

The voice bellowed when he was halfway down the hall, passing the restrooms. He hit the back door at full throttle, banging it open with his shoulder. He came out on a small deck with steps down to an alley. Covering that with an awkward leap, skittering on the loose gravel, he looked up to see garbage dumpsters, ten or twelve cars, the backs of stores. The alley narrowed and led to a street to his left.

Five seconds, ten, and they'd come out the door.

A Ford Explorer, a Cadillac, Nissan Sentra—maybe get under one of them or—another store door opened, thirty feet down. A guy carrying two trash bags emerged, heading to the dumpster. The bookstore. It was the back of that big-ass bookstore on the corner. Sully ran ten steps, getting to the door, the guy at the dumpster half-turning, Sully holding out his bag, saying, "Left my wallet upstairs," and ducked inside.

He found himself in a back storage room, books on pallets halfway to the ceiling. There was only one turn, though, and it led to a set of double doors into the store proper. Banging it open, he found himself in

Cookbooks and Home Entertaining. Moving, moving. Past Psychology and Science and Discounted. At the front of Bestsellers, he stopped and picked up one of store's cloth tote bags from a stand. He took it to the Magazine section and dumped the envelopes and the wooden box into the new bag. The tote from the Strand he stuffed behind the porn mags in their sealed plastic wrappings.

He picked up two motorcycle magazines, went to the checkout, and told the clerk he was in from out of town and was there a hotel nearby?

"Sure," she said, ringing him up. "If you're not looking for a lot of frills, the Monticello is just right there on the first street, once you get outside the door. That's Thomas Jefferson Way. Take a right and go down the hill."

"How far?"

"Maybe fifty or sixty yards? It's on the left. You'll see it, a green awning."

He started to go, then stopped. "What if I'm looking for frills?"

"Oh, that'd be the Four Seasons," she said with a smile. "A few blocks down, on M."

"Whoa, the Seasons? That's beyond my billfold. Look, do me a favor? A couple of buddies were supposed to leave work early and meet me here, like, twenty minutes ago. I guess they got held up. I'm going to go ahead and check in over at the Monticello there and then come back. If they stop by, looking for me, could you tell them where I am?"

"Sure, but what's your name?"

He gave her his best smile. "Just tell 'em that guy with the limp. They'll know."

By the front door, he waited until a taxi stopped at the light. He looked both ways, then quick-stepped through the revolving door and into the cab.

"The Four Seasons," he said, slouching down in the seat, the bag with the files tumbling to the floor at his feet.

THIRTY-FOUR

BY MIDNIGHT, WHEN Delores Ellison was beneath six feet of well-tended dirt, the files her son had left behind were a mass of disheveled paperwork spread over the floor of room 426.

It was a suite, actually. Sully splurged for the extra space, going for the in-room Jacuzzi. He figured he might be here a couple of days. If he was anything close to right, Stevens's operatives were over at his house right now, tearing it apart. That was okay. He could settle that score.

The nice thing about the Seasons was it had an honest-to-God bar. He'd had a bottle of Basil's sent up to the room with a big bucket of ice. Quitting cold turkey, he'd decided, might be a little much. He'd ordered oysters on the half shell, too, and cocktail shrimp, and now, the food demolished, he was deep into Billy's research, steadily working the bottle down.

He spread the paperwork over the small writing table, just to get it all out in the open, until it became clear that wouldn't contain the sprawl. So he moved the chairs and pushed the table against the wall, to give him space on the floor, only now the paperwork trail had spread into the adjacent bedroom in one direction and toward the front door in the other. There was a pile of pictures and booklets and other material he had yet to sort through on the couch. Still, he had to move the coffee table, grunting, to get more layout space.

Spot-reading this census report, looking through that Who's Who in Washington, squinting his eyes to read the tiny print on a handwritten property deed, he began sorting the piles in chronological order. There was a lot of stuff. There just didn't seem to be a point.

Finally, after two a.m., he refused to let himself refill the bourbon glass, not wanting the blur or the headache or lack of initiative, denying himself the relief from the ticking in his head. "What what what," he said aloud. "Billy, you sad fuck, what is the what here?"

Elliot said Billy had been unbalanced but coherent, and his research showed the same sort of bipolar fuckery. If it had been in any sort of order anyone else once might have understood, that had vanished when Elliot dropped the folder and scooped it all back together, helter-skelter.

So, okay, okay, he told himself. Find the pattern. Find the sustained thought. What was Billy after?

The general theme was black history in D.C. And yes, it was some sort of genealogical project. Incorporation papers of a bank, bylaws of long-forgotten social clubs. The Sons and Daughters of Moses. The Knights of Pythias. Pictures of the old Dunbar High School, faces circled in grease pencil. A program from a Saturday evening social hour at the home of Georgia Douglas Johnson, up there in Shaw, walking distance from Howard University. This caught Sully's eye. A reading from Jean Toomer—what was the year—yeah, before *Cane*, and then "remarks" from Alain Locke and W. E. B. DuBois. He whistled low. The family *was* plugged in.

Letters. Whole pouches of letters, held together with a rubber band, the missives still in the envelopes. He thumbed down through them, stopping at the return address of Mary Church Terrell. Inside, the cream-colored paper fading, the ink still there, was a thank-you note from the grand dame of D.C. black society to an Ellison whose first name Sully didn't recognize. It concerned a generous contribution to the Colored Women's League.

Scattered through these were property deeds for what looked to be houses or businesses in the city, or slim crisp copies from the National

Archives, detailing Civil War records—he imagined he was going to find that one of the ancestors had fought among the colored Union troops— and copies of D.C.'s Social Register. Stapled to these pages was a long-ago article from a black newspaper—the *Washington Bee*, likely—which boasted that seven black families had made the Register. The Ellisons, the Syphaxes, the Quanders et al.

Billy, you crazy bastard, you were way *down in the weeds*, he thought. It wasn't a sensation unknown to him, this kind of research piling up, getting out of hand, but with Billy's mental instability, this was teetering into madness.

Huge chunks of paperwork documented the life of Nathaniel Benjamin Ellison, the fabled patriarch, the founder of the Washington Trust Bank, the nation's first black-owned financial institution. Established in 1887, a copy of a newspaper ad stated, showing the five-story building standing alone, arched windows, hulking on its stretch of U Street.

On and on, Billy's obsession spilled out over the room, defying categorization. Property rolls, tax rolls, handwritten source documents. And it struck Sully suddenly, looking over these sprawling mounds of history of the city's black elites—the absence of political ambition.

Patronage jobs, yes. Federal staff positions, judgeships, a staff job at the Department of the Interior. But the city was a federal enclave, and the overwhelming majority of the black aristocracy, the homegrown Talented Tenth, seemed, based on what he was looking at, to have kept their vision on social climbing. They made calls, from the pulpit or the academic podium, for social integration and partnership, but mainly fought against segregation with the now quaint belief that by acquiring wealth, education, and social airs, they would be more palatable to white society. Adam Clayton Powell, the most powerful black man in Congress in the 1950s and 1960s, hailed from Harlem. Shirley Chisholm came down from New York, too. Their new black neighbors in D.C. neither had a vote in Congress nor governed their own city. They were presided over by the feds, as if an occupied people.

So, when the Civil Rights Movement swept into and over the city in the late 1960s and home rule took effect, the hands taking the reins of political power in the federal city were often the callused palms of the dispossessed and their champions, the interlopers from elsewhere, who galvanized the Slightly Less Talented Ninety Percent.

And thus, in a city of serious and sober black men of achievement and good standing for more than a century, the city's dominating power broker almost overnight became Marion Barry, the charismatic cotton chopper from the Mississippi Delta. Indianola. Jesus. Sully wondered how many people in D.C. had ever been to that place, or knew the difference between Greenwood and Greenville.

The Ellisons and their peers, embarrassed if not offended by Barry, kept to their pleasant smiles and good manners along the Gold Coast, invested in their children's futures, summered on the Vineyard, and slowly, steadily began migrating to the finer suburbs of McLean, Bethesda, Potomac, and maybe Silver Spring, watching the old neighborhoods of Shaw and Logan Circle and U Street melt into urban decay.

So this is the world Billy had re-created, seeking to bring his vanished family back to life. It appeared to be a labor of love, and Sully could not help but be touched by it. He followed the genealogy backward, laying out clumps of paperwork for each generation.

William Sanders, his dad, did not seem to have been of much interest to Billy, and certainly none of his ancestors had been, who were scarcely mentioned. William had come up from Georgia. High school football star, the son of a marine. William himself went on to serve as a marine in Vietnam, where he was decorated for combat bravery and heroism. Scholarships. Eventually accepted at Harvard Law, where he met Delores.

In the files, then came Delores and William's life together—some of their Jack and Jill connections, a copy of the deed for their house on the Vineyard (modest four-bedroom, two-and-a-half-bath, close to the waterfront but not on it). Press releases from when they were both hired at the Stevens firm.

Billy showed up in the records as an Ellison on his birth certificate.

Got his dad's first two names, took his mom's last. From the research, it appeared Billy had agreed with the emphasis on the Ellisons—there was almost nothing in the files on the Sanders of Georgia. It was like his dad had been reduced to a posthumous footnote.

"Daddy dearest," he said.

In the middle of the floor by the couch, he'd placed the records of Delores's parents, Lambert Ellison III and his wife, Ruth. They'd lived—and here a photograph was clipped to a weathered copy of a property deed—in a four-story Victorian off Logan Circle. It had also been, it turned out, the family home of Billy's great-grandfather, Lambert Ellison II, just a few steps from the gray stone and brick Gothic marvel of the Mount Gilead Baptist Church.

The next stack, moving backward in time, was that of Lambert Ellison himself. Born in 1879, married at twenty, a banker and the son of the founder of the empire, Nathaniel Benjamin Ellison.

Nathaniel himself seemed to come up from nowhere to found the Washington Trust Bank. He had been a founding member of Washington's black aristocracy—banker, financier, the heart of the community's ambition. He loaned, he built, he planned, he set his family up for a century of wealth and prominence. A photo showed him: light skinned, high forehead, thick eyebrows.

That appeared to be as far back as Billy had gotten.

The rest seemed to be documents regarding slavery in the city. There was one, from a Works Progress Administration project, that Billy had marked up in yellow highlighter:

> The District of Columbia, too small for slave rearing itself, served as a depot for the purchase of interstate traders, who combed Maryland and northern Virginia for slaves to buy and resell. Since the slave jails, colloquially known as "Georgia pens," and described by an ex-slave as worse than hog holes, were inadequate for the great demand, the public jails were made use of, accommodations for the criminals having to wait for the more pressing and lucrative traffic in slaves.

There were pens in what is now Potomac Park. More notorious were McCandless's Tavern in Georgetown; in Washington, Robey's Tavern at Seventh and Maryland Avenue; and Williams's "Yellow House" at Eighth and B street SW.

In Alexandria, the pretentious establishment of Armfield and Franklin, who by 1834 were sending more than a thousand slaves a year south to . . .

Scholarly articles from the Historical Society of Washington, D.C., the Library of Congress, the Smithsonian. A speech by one Joshua Giddings. The escape attempt by seventy-seven slaves aboard the *Pearl*, a schooner that made it all the way down the Potomac before being caught.

Finally, there was a cluster of papers about the Bend. Property records of Didier Delacroix, the man who owned the place. An 1830 census, listing the slaves held at the Bend:

One male under 10.
50 males 10–24
20 males 25–36
4 females under 10
50 females 10–24
20 females 25–36

"Working and breeding stock," he said out loud to himself. "Christ."

A traveler's description of the place in 1846, showed the population to have grown north of three hundred, crammed into an acre, and acre and a half.

Frenchman's Bend lies along the waterfront, a peculiar spit of land in the waters of the Potomac, well recognizable from quite a distance. The outer walls of the slave pen are brick in nature, rising at least ten feet. Outside this expanse are three buildings. Two are wooden, barn-like structures, dedicated to the keeping of foodstuffs and equipment particular to that trade. Leg chains, neck chains, manacles, well-oiled and kept, hang from long rows of wooden rails. The other building is a two-story frame house, white, set farther down, which the owner, Didier Delacroix, uses upon occasion, although his main residence is in the city proper.

The inside of the slave pen is largely open, a packed-dirt courtyard that is given over to mud and muck after rainfall. The door is well steeled and covered by a type of cantilevered awning, set higher above the wall and tilting back to it. It provides a type of shade or protection from the elements. The slaves themselves are kept in ramshackle structures, one-story in nature, divided by their gender, with long rows of slats for sleeping.

It is not an uncommon observation for those passing on the roadway or sailing on the waters to report hearing the strains of the lash and the cries of the afflicted.

Okay, good god, he thought, flipping through the papers, describing more of the land and the layout, his eyes glazing now. What ancestor was this about, Nathaniel's mother or father? Who had been bought or sold or brought here?

He was looking for a name when he saw it, circled, at the bottom of one page of financial records—and it began to glow on the page, red as the ink in which it was circled, one single name, for that's all the woman was listed as—Jeanne-Marie—and Billy's notation, "Nathaniel's mother."

And then he got it. He put two or three of the census records together, documents about Jeanne-Marie over a thirty-year period, and it all blew open for him, as it must have for Billy, and then he was ransacking the rest of the files, the paper, scrambling to find the rest of her awful history, the suffering and the misery, and it took him a full minute before he realized the ringing he heard was not in his head but was from the phone, someone calling him over and over again.

THIRTY-FIVE

THE CLOCK ON the nightstand read 2:47. Coming up on the witching hour, closer to daybreak than sundown . . . and still it kept ringing. He got up, padded around the room, looking—where was the goddamn thing? Why did they make them so small? It was . . . it was under the turned-back comforter on the bed. He snatched it, scowling at the caller ID, his temples throbbing. The number, he knew it, *Take a deep breath, calm down. . . .*

"Parker," he said finally into the phone. "John, what the hell, man, I didn't know you loved me this much, two in the morning."

John's voice, when it spoke back to him, was buried by static, by wind in the background, voices shouting, and there was a *whoop whoop* of a siren.

"Parker," he said, louder. "Where you at? Speak up."

There was a rustling and a clump and then the wind dropped out and Sully guessed he'd cupped a hand around the cell, tucked his chin down to his chest. "I said I'm back in the Bend, where you think?" he shouted.

"Why's that, brother? It's sort of late for—"

"Somebody just shot the Hall brothers."

"—this sort of bull—the *what*??"

"Both of 'em. Carlos, Tony. Dead as disco. Right down here at the waterline. Looking at 'em now. Hear that? That's me kicking Tony's foot.

Or is it Carlos? Can't tell 'em apart, facedown like this here. Why all the gangstas wear Timberlands?"

Sully slumped down on the bed, mouth half-open, running his free hand through his hair, pulling on it, this change of direction, trying to put together the angles, Sly, T-Money—

"What happened?" is what he got out. "What the fuck happened?"

"That's what I wanted to ask you, brother. You write a story about the Bend *maybe* being the murder capital and now it sure as hell *is*. Dee Dee, Billy Ellison, Antoine, Billy's *momma*, and now two heavyweights— I mean the guys *running* this place for six, seven years—all of 'em dead within what, fifty, sixty feet of each other."

"I didn't—"

"This some of your Louisiana voodoo?"

"It had started when I—"

"Yeah yeah yeah. Look, you coming to see these boys before we bag and tag 'em or what? I ain't going to be out here all night."

THIRTY-SIX

THE BODIES WERE, as promised, hard by the water, draped in plastic sheeting, illuminated by work lights the techs had set up. One right by the rocks, another a few feet over. The yellow tape was up at the street entrance to the park, at Fourth and P. There were no gawkers, the sidewalks and streets empty.

John Parker and Jeff Weaver were ahead of him on the right. There were two other men in Windbreakers, who Sully guessed were DEA agents. Three or four techs were milling about little orange cones marked 1 and 2 and 3 and 4, near the bodies; Sully was pretty sure those were designating ejected shells.

Both bodies were facedown in the clumps of grass, the packed dirt. The one on the right, whoever it was, one boot had come off. Sully couldn't help but think, *Shot right out of his shoes.*

John and Jeff looked at him as he stood at the edge of the light.

"Didn't a uniform stop you at the top of the hill?" John asked.

"I told him I was a friend of yours and that you had invited me special."

"You wearing a sport coat at three in the morning?" John said. "Where's the Ducati? And wait a minute, you found a taxi that would actually *bring* you here?"

"I paid him triple, cash up front, and told him I was meeting the chief of police at a crime scene. Plus, he dropped me two blocks up."

"You took a taxi from your house?"

"I was visiting a friend," he said.

"At three in the morning?"

"A special friend."

"She won't be thinking your ass is that special for long, running out in the middle of the night," John said. "Ask me how I know."

He was wearing what appeared to be jeans and a pullover shirt beneath a long black trench coat, the belt knotted, the tails flapping around his knees in the wind. Jeff, shifting his weight from foot to foot, jeans and a leather jacket zipped up all the way, a Yankees baseball cap tugged down. Everybody coming out here on the hotfoot, Sully looking dapper by comparison.

"So dear old Tony and Carlos, the talented Hall brothers," Sully said, looking down. "Four shells—two shots each? That's what we're talking about?"

"Appears to be," John said, moving to his left, between Sully and the corpses, kneeling to pull the sheeting back. "Gangland action. Carlos, he took one in the back of the head, close range, then another one in the side. Tony—here—took a pair, one behind the ear, one up there at the temple. See that? Damn."

The brothers lay facedown in the mud and dirt, the scrubby grass. Their jeans, already baggy, sagged well below their hips. Tony's T-shirt was hitched up in the back, leaving a stretch of his back and buttocks exposed. It was a pretty lousy way to die. Tony lay with his arms at his side. Carlos, his arms were thrown above his head.

"Tony got shot first?" Sully said.

John nodded and stood up. "Hey, you get a gold star. Tony had no warning, I'd say," flicking a hand toward the body. "Dropped like a ton of bricks. Ever see a boxer get knocked cold? He falls without getting his hands in front of him, just bam, facedown on the canvas? That's how Tony dropped."

He moved over a few steps, rubbed his eyes, and flicked the right hand again. "Now, Carlos, here, the way he fell, like he got in a step running before he got popped. Them arms out in front of him."

Sully walked around both bodies, staying behind Jeff, looking for anything that stood out as unusual. Seeing a lot of war killings—bombs, grenades, air power, machine guns, pistols, machetes—led to a certain detachment at the scene of a fresh kill. It was a crossword puzzle with gore.

The way to work a fresh murder was to sequence the action, starting out with the highest elevation, when everybody was standing up, because that's when everyone was alive and yet to be wounded. You started high and worked down low. Blood on the walls? Pick the highest splatter and that's likely where it started. Thin, watery streaks? That was going to be aspirated blood, meaning the victim had coughed or spit, and that meant they'd already been shot in the chest. When you had a body with three or four bullet holes, that sort of intel helped you sequence the shots.

But outdoor shootings could screw you over, at least if you were reading the body of the victim or their blood. Splatter just arced and fell on the ground, with no trace of the elevation from which it started. Fingerprints weren't going to be left behind on grass and dirt. You might get a footprint, but if it wasn't in blood, then it didn't help all that much, particularly in a public park.

All of these were reasons, Sully thought, why the shooter might have brought the Hall brothers outside, particularly in the Bend. Looking at how the bodies fell, and the location of the wounds, was going to be about all they had in order to try to re-create how it went down.

"You got to love the irony," Sully said.

"Come again?" This was John.

Sully nodded, coming closer now, tilting his head to look at just how they had fallen, five or six feet apart, both toward the water. "The Halls. Twins. Born at the same time. Died at the same time."

Jeff, nodding. "That's hard. That's hard."

"What's their momma say?" Sully asked. It was instinctive.

"We got somebody up at her house," Jeff said, "taking a statement.

She got a place up there in Brookland. They bought it for her, I guess. A little laundering. When things were better, going better for them."

Jeff looked down at the bodies. "Nobody thinks they ever going to die."

"Canvassing the Carolina, the apartment building?" Sully said.

"Two teams on it right now," John said, shrugging. He sneezed. "Like somebody in there's going to say something."

"What floor did Tony and Carlos stay on in there?"

"They had a couple of units, safe spots, girlfriends' places, you can't really say they lived here or they lived there," John said. "Stayed with their momma as much as anywhere. But they tended to hole up in 318 in the Carolina there. It's up there on the top right. Overlooks the channel."

"Mind if I take a peek?"

"When we're done here, I'll tell the unit up there you can look in the door. Can't let you in the place itself. All I need, this comes to trial, defense gets a list of people who been in that apartment and I got to answer for you."

"Did it look like they got rousted up there, then dragged down here?"

"Nothing one way or the other. Drug dealers, they tend not to be much on the housekeeping tip."

"But no blood, no holes in the wall."

"Don't I wish."

It didn't appear as if the Halls had planned to be outside long. The spring weather had turned chilly, but they had on short sleeves and no jackets. The way the bodies had fallen—well, if the bodies were hands of the clock, their feet would be at the center of the dial and their bodies would be at twelve and two, with Tony at twelve. The feet, what, maybe three feet apart? The torsos five. So they had been standing together, almost side by side, when they got shot. The shooter had to have been standing behind them, just off to their left, the shooter's right. The way he saw it: The gunman raises a right hand, the barrel almost touching the back of Tony's head, blam, then moves the barrel to the right, blam, shoots Carlos from three feet. Doesn't take a step. A second between shots. When they were both on the ground, he steps to both of them and puts one more in each brain. Whole thing, ten seconds.

"You roll them yet?" he asked, still circling.

"Yeah," said John. "Just a half-turn, see if there was more damage to the front. Wasn't any, so we laid them back till they get bagged. This right here is how they dropped."

"Ligature on the wrists?"

"None apparent."

"Knees muddy?"

"Nah. You thinking a classic execution, somebody ties their hands, brings them out here, puts them on their knees, blam blam. It didn't go down like that."

"So give me your scenario."

John tilted his head to the left, then to the right, studying the corpses, looking at them like something was going to materialize if he just stared hard enough.

"I'd call it they were standing together, a little bit apart, casual like," he said, finally. "Tony here gets the first one back behind his ear—the entry is clean, neat." He kneeled down next to the body now, pulling a pen out of his coat pocket, using it as a pointer. "The other one he got, right in front of his ear? That's just a kill shot. Look at the stippling."

"So the shooter was right on him for that."

"Barrel almost pressed the skin. Now, ask yourself: Is Carlos going to stand three feet away and watch his brother get shot in the head, fall down, and keep watching while the shooter puts the barrel to his head and shoots again?"

"Of course not."

"Of course not. So, the sequence. They came down to the channel, everybody looking at the water. The shooter is standing behind and to the right of Tony. Pops him right behind the ear. Tony drops, dead before he hits the ground. That's shot one."

"Okay."

"Now, shot two," John said, stepping around the first corpse to get to the second. "Our shooter takes a step over, like I just did. Carlos starts to turn. Shot two knocks Carlos down and takes him out of commission. See the one almost right in his ear? Like maybe he was turning toward Tony? Like he'd heard the first shot, turns and blam? So he goes down awkward. But the kill shot on him? Just like the one to Tony. At the temple. The stippling. Shooter had the barrel almost touching his head."

Sully, nodding. "So you figuring the cleanest shot was the first one."

"Wouldn't you?"

"The kill shots, the third and fourth ones fired, those come when they're on the ground."

John stood up, flexing his knees. "Like I said."

"So you're figuring one shooter."

John looked at him, then to the lead detective. "Jeff?"

Jeff held up his index finger, looking from Jeff to Sully. "One," he said.

"Talk to me."

"The initial shot comes from behind on both. Tony, Carlos, they don't fuck around. They come down to the water, take the breeze in the middle of the night, blow a joint, take a piss? Yeah, fine, their turf. One guy walking with them, maybe, drifts behind them when they all get down here to the water? Somebody they know? I can see that. But *two* guys? Right up on them like this? I don't like it."

"We'll know if it was one or two guns used when we get the ballistics," John said. "But look here. I can go one trigger man—but I don't know that our shooter was down here *alone* with them. Look at them both—short sleeves? Tonight? No, they weren't planning on coming out here. Or, if so, it was just for a second. Could have been a rival crew, the South Caps, somebody like that, got the drop on them up there in their apartment, rousted them down here and bam—so, yeah, you wind up with one shooter, but more than one guy involved."

Sully shrugged. "But why not just pop them up there in the building?"

"Too much attention. Too much noise. Too much chance of leaving evidence. Out here? Less evidence. Pitch-black dark, no wits."

"Okay, but yeah, if you go to all that trouble, why not throw them both in the water, like the rest? Dee Dee, Billy, Antoine—all of them got dumped. And these dudes, they not twenty feet from the waterline."

John shrugged, sniffling, sounding like he had a cold coming on. "Goes back to Jeff's one-shooter theory. It'd take too long to toss them. These brothers ain't little. Besides, we find Tony and Carlos Hall in the middle of the Potomac? We already know they got tossed from the Bend. It wouldn't fool nobody."

"But, you know, it'd help get rid of evidence, take longer to find the bodies, all that."

John shrugged. "You get a clean kill, you don't need it. And this is looking pretty clean."

"What time did this go down?"

"We got reports of gunshots about twelve thirty, twelve thirty-five, like that," John said. "We got the call from uniforms at one oh five that it was Tony and Carlos."

"So one guy gets Tony and Carlos to come out to the waterline after midnight on a spring night, cold and breezy."

John held up a hand, sneezing again. "I'm not saying that. What we know is that Tony and Carlos come down to the water, either with our shooter or were ambushed by our shooter. No sign of violence, of struggle. That's all the evidence says."

Sully, nodding, pointing to the orange cones. "So, the shells. I mean, they tell you anything?"

Jeff cut his eyes to John, just that quick, and Sully caught it. He turned to John.

"We off the record, Carter?"

"Yeah. I mean, same as always—you let me inside the tape, I clear everything with you before publication."

John let out a deep breath, the creases in his face working themselves out, then knotting up again, a man not at ease with himself.

"Okay. Okay. Look. Not for print or publication, attribution or deep background or whatever. But we got the murder weapon. Up against the

wall to the fort there. Down in the rocks by the water. Shooter man threw
it for the water but not far enough. Maybe it hit the wall and bounced off."

"Well, shit, that's going to narrow it down—you get the prints, the
serial—"

"Not in the way you're thinking. You know anything about guns?"

"They go bang. Some. I grew up with—"

"If I say, 'M1911A1 .45,' that mean anything to you?"

"Not really."

"Fucking civilian. It was the standard officer's sidearm in the U.S.
military from the nineteen twenties through the seventies, sometimes
used in the early eighties. You got police forces use it today."

"It was—"

"I made sergeant in Vietnam and I was proud of mine. But this piece?
Our murder weapon, bagged and up there in the tech van? This one is
your vintage World War Two model, a Singer, brother—a *Singer*. The
people what made sewing machines. Coltwood grips. The whole nine."

"I don't get this."

"Because you're a civilian. Look, before and during World War Two,
they were making guns as fast as they could. You had three or four man-
ufacturers of the forty-five, Remington being the biggest. And I'm
talking, like, a million units. But the piece we picked up over there by
the water—four rounds gone from the magazine, it's the murder weapon—
was manufactured by the Singer company. Only a few hundred ever
made."

"You're telling me somebody shot the Halls with a, a, what, sixty-
year-old gun?"

John sneezed, bent, put a hand over his nose, coughed. "Gonna get a
cold out here. Can feel it coming on, you know? That tickle you get, the
back of the throat? No, no, that's not just what I'm telling you. I'm telling you this pistol is a collector's item, something you only see in gun
shows. It's worth something like ten grand, no, this one, I'd go fifteen."

"You're fucking with me."

"Not at all. I myself have never handled one until today. They're like purple unicorns. Always talked about, never seen." John coughed again, deeper in the chest now. "I got to get inside now. Jeff, you keeping an eye on this till they bag these guys? The ME's been waiting on us. Good. I'll meet you down there at the cut."

He started walking back up the park, Sully raising a hand in farewell toward Jeff, catching up to walk alongside John, the wind at their backs now. He sneezed again, Sully said, "Bless you," and John waved it off, walking fast up the incline, the park deserted, the yellow tape across the entrance, the lone cop still standing there, hands in pockets.

"Now, what we're going to find?" John said. "We'll run a trace, see if somebody has reported this thing stolen. But I'm guessing all the military officers around here, maybe right over there in Fort McNair? One of those vets had this thing. Somebody from the hood goes over the wall, breaks in someplace, pulls that gun back over here, sells it, somebody else resells it and it eventually gets used to clock the Halls. That's my first thought. My second one is that it's going to be some dumb fuck who had no idea—no *idea*—of the gun he was holding."

They stepped over the yellow tape.

"So, you got somebody rousting the South Caps?"

"Right now, you damn straight," Parker said. "Maybe we'll get somebody to roll over on somebody else. But, you know, that's a death sentence so, I'm saying, probably not."

"Probably not," Sully said, the scene from the other night in T-Money's house blossoming anew in his mind.

"So when you writing something about this?"

"I got suspended, John, you remember? Not necessarily at all. I don't know. The paper will do something on Tony and Carlos getting shot, yeah, but that won't be me."

"Fine. Whatever, whenever, you decide to write? You talk to me before. Because look. This is the Hall brothers. The *Hall brothers*. This is not your garden variety hit. This, this here, changes business."

And then he walked off, a curt wave, his Crown Vic three or four cars down. Sully stood there on the sidewalk for a minute, watching Parker pull out, the muscles under his jaw cramping up. He rubbed it, gingerly, opened his mouth, worked his jaw around.

The minute Parker had described the murder weapon it had hit him who killed Billy Ellison, as bright and clear as a spotlight in the dark. He'd had to keep it off his face, keep his jaw steady and his eyebrows level the whole time, just standing there, nodding, acting like the world hadn't just blown up.

THIRTY-SEVEN

YOU HAD TO secure the beachhead first, make sure you had a safe base of operations, communications, resources. This was his mantra of working in war zones—keep your supply and communication lines open behind you, make sure whom you could trust before wading out into open conflict where all sorts of shit could happen, most of which you could not see coming and none of which you could control.

It really wasn't any different now. The people he could trust, with Alexis gone back abroad, were zero. The base of operations was the hotel, where nobody could find him. And his source of power, of influence, was Billy Ellison's golden fucking thesis. Well. The research for it, anyway. The kid never had the chance to write it.

He didn't risk going by his house, not even in a taxi. He was willing to bet dollars to doughnuts it had already been ransacked by Stevens's investigators and was almost certainly being watched.

It was a long goddamn walk, a mile or better, before he got back up to the National Mall and found a taxi, the driver on his way home, picking him up as a last fare, Sully promising him a $20 tip.

The first thing he'd thought he'd do, upon getting back to the room at the Four Seasons, was take a shower and fall into bed. But Billy's research and notes were spread over everything; you could barely walk in the place. It looked like, when he opened the door to the suite, he had gone as mad as Billy. Stepping over one pile of documents and between another two, he found himself looking down at it all, then lying on the floor to read back over some of it, and when he blinked again daylight was streaming through the windows. His back hurt. When he rolled over to sit up, he got a whiff of his body, a stale, dank odor of sweat and meaty flesh.

A shower sounded better now, and that was his definite destination, right up until he lay back down—just for a second—and sleep overtook him. His last thought, before darkness fell, was of Alexis, the way her hair bounced on her shoulders, the way she called his name, the taste of her skin, beneath her shoulder blades, above her buttocks. Just to put his mouth there.

"Sly Hastings. Brother. *Digame.*"

"Carter? That you?"

"You expecting Avon?"

Down the line, he could hear Sly moving, walking somewhere, had to be inside because there was a slight echo. Maybe his basement apartment over there in Park View.

"You got jokes, hunh?" Sly said. "That why you call me? Work on your material?"

"Where you at?"

"This duplex I got over in Southeast, the rentals. On Halley Terrace."

"Your sister still working those for you?"

"Not so much anymore. I had to get more involved. These bathrooms, man, people will put *any* damn thing in the toilets."

Sully was lying flat out on the bed in the Seasons, a place that probably went for as much a night as Sly could rent one of his junk boxes for a month. He had to call downstairs, ask them where they got these sheets. Thread counts were a real thing.

"I was wanting to ask you," he said into his cell, "about what the fuck happened last night."

"I really just don't know what you talking about. I'm a businessman with apartment buildings to manage."

"This was at a different apartment building. Two tenants."

Silence down the line. Then, "We gots to talk."

"You don't say," Sully said.

"That brother who can't cook his greens? Meet me at his place."

Sully smiled. "In forty-five."

Kenny's was in an old redbrick row house, three tables and takeout, the cook in the back behind the glass display cases, the cashier on the right. The house had been there probably eighty or ninety years, eight blocks from the Capitol, seven from the Supreme Court, and now it was a no-frills joint trying to bridge a couple of demographics, the neighborhood being what white people called "in transition." Close to the Capitol, in the 300 of Massachusetts Avenue, you had institutions like Schneiders, the tiny liquor store, on a corner. A few doors down was La Loma, the Mexican place, in an old row house, dining rooms upstairs and down.

But, just a few hundred yards and five blocks back, it was another world. Here, you had Customer Base A, the older black folks who had been living on these streets for decades. Customer base B, the young palefaces who were moving in, fixing up the century-old places, turning them into well-heeled showplaces.

Gay, straight, Hill staffers, journalists, IT consultants. All these new residents, couples with young kids, turning up at Lincoln Park on Saturday mornings, walking their lapdogs. Thirty-one-year-old first-time home buyers who didn't blink at dropping fifty thou on rehabbing the kitchen and bath.

Their row houses shared a brick wall with the older black couple next door who'd lived there forty years and kept plastic sheeting over the front-room furniture. Who went to one of the neighborhood churches every Sunday morning. Who bought their groceries at Murry's on H Street, where the riots had gone crazy in 1968, before half of their new neighbors were out of short pants.

Sully had been sitting on what passed for the front patio of Kenny's for twenty minutes, watching the comings and goings of the quick mart catty-corner across the intersection, the old dude panhandling out front. He was picking at a meat-and-three in one of the cast-iron chairs, which was chained to the cast-iron table, which was chained to the cast-iron fence.

Sly materialized from behind him, a Styrofoam container of his own, rattling another chair out from under the table to sit beside him.

"I was looking for the bike," Sly said. "Lionel and me made the block three, four times before I saw you sitting here."

"The bike's at home," Sully said.

"You walked over here?"

"More or less."

Sly opened his container, the pork plate, but just sucked on his sweet tea and sat back in his chair.

"I don't know, if that's what you asking me," he said.

"You moving in on the Hall brothers," Sully said, getting to it. "They get capped, and you want me to believe you just don't know."

"I said I did not know."

"Then you must be one scared motherfucker."

"I wouldn't say that, neither."

"Police come tap-tap-tapping on your door?"

"About five this morning, yes they did."

"They have a warrant, or was this a social call?"

"Hey, I'm a hardworking black man who has left his difficult youth behind, you hear? Earning an honest living in real estate. Low-income units. Sometimes? They elements in the police force, I don't want to call them racist, but they got this cynical view and do not believe in, what do I want to say, my basic integrity. Sometimes these motherfuckers come by my house. 'Cause they too dumb to know the shit theyselves."

"So, no warrant."

"Not even."

"And what did you tell them about the situation, this double homicide?"

"That I didn't know shit and they ought to get up off my porch."

Sully took a bite of his greens, using the little white plastic fork. "Hey Sly, you remember Noel Pittman? That fine sister who went missing on Princeton Place last year?"

Sly cut his eyes to him now, hard.

"You told me you didn't know nothing about her, neither," Sully said.

"I didn't and I don't," Sly hissed.

"Then good luck with the Bend," Sully said. "You going to need it."

He came in his backyard through the alley, walked up the steel steps to the back door, his breath catching short, even though he was expecting it: The window on the Dutch door was broken. None of it outside. When he walked up and peeked in, he saw it all shattered on the kitchen floor. The deadbolt was pulled back. Door wasn't locked.

He pushed it open with a knuckle and the smell of bourbon was everywhere. They'd taken his stash in the kitchen and poured it over the floors, the walls, the furniture. The plates and glasses were raked out of shelves and onto the floor, shards everywhere. The dining room table was knocked on its side. Broken glass, he saw, stepping into the front room; they'd smashed the bottles against the marble of the fireplace mantel, breaking off a chunk of it in the process. The couch upended. CDs pulled out of the racks, dumped on the floor.

Upstairs was worse. Sheets ripped off the bed, books pulled off the shelves, clothes pulled out of closets. File cabinets pulled out and dumped on the floor. A puddle of urine on the bathroom tiles, just a little smooch on the cheek. The sense of violation was there, the fury, but it was in check until he went to the bedroom window, the one fronting Sixth Street, and looked on the street outside.

The Ducati lay on its side, the rearview mirrors knocked off, the panels dented, the paint keyed.

"You motherless little bastards," he whispered. "You sister-fucking freaks. I will *find* you."

For fifteen minutes he walked the place, checking out the basement (equally trashed), his mood oddly calm. Nothing appeared to be taken. It was just a calling card, a cheap shot to let him know they could get to him.

After a while, he went back upstairs. He pulled open the folding doors to the hallway closet. He'd had it lined in cedar, one of his little upgrades, and stood on the lower shelf, where he put his sweaters. That gave him access to unlatch the small trapdoor into the attic. Reaching his hand up there, he found the small velvet pouch.

Sitting on the edge of the bed, unfolding the cloth, he felt the weight of the Tokarev M57, a gift from the Bosnian commander that night on the mountain. He pulled the last fold of cloth back and it lay open before him, black, dull, and deadly. He popped the magazine open, checked the rounds, and then ratcheted it back into place.

He dropped it in his jacket pocket and picked up the phone, calling news research at the paper.

"Hey gorgeous, it's me," he said, getting Susan, thank God. "I need an address and a home number this time."

She talked.

"Of course, it's off the books," he said. "I got suspended, didn't you hear?" Then he said, "Sheldon Stevens. The home, not the office." And, "Wait. Lemme get a pen."

Six minutes later, the phone rang down the other end. Shellie Stevens picked up.

"Hey motherfucker," Sully said. "Love what you did with the place."

There was a pause. "What I did with what place?"

"When you see me coming? Counselor, I advise you to run."

"Run? Is this you, Carter?"

"You hear me? I *know*. What you know? What Delores knew? What Billy found out? Counselor, *I* know. That sound you hear? It's the dirt thumping on your coffin."

THIRTY-EIGHT

THE FOURTH FLOOR at D.C. Superior Court held, just to the right of the escalator, the pending- and past-records room, the history of the city's crime and criminals in thousands upon thousands of folders and case files.

The reception area to the records room was a grimy little rectangular space, with an ever-present line of unhappy people waiting to get to the counter. A good many, like those today, were there to get an official records search on themselves. To get a stamped document for a prospective employer that showed they were no longer on probation, or parole, or that the arrest that had shown up on their record was actually, like, long since closed, or that some other dude had been arrested for it, only he had a similar sort of name, you see that right here. Or there were women trying to track down men they wished they had not dated, or fucked that one time, or married, or ever seen once in their goddamn lives, and is that son of a bitch locked up down at Lorton.

The floor was peeling linoleum and the tiled ceiling had brown spots of water damage. It smelled like disinfectant and felt like the waiting room for the end of the world.

One wall held a printer, and against the opposite wall were two public-access terminals for computerized record searches. One computer was out of order and the screen was dark. Seated at the second one was a fat-ass PI with a bad haircut and a yellow notepad filled with a long list of names, potential employees for some company or another, running them through the system. He had a Styrofoam cup of coffee from the cafeteria downstairs and talked a mile a minute into his cell. When he got a hit on a name on his pad, he scratched a line through it and went to the next. After a while, he looked over his shoulder and acknowledged Sully by holding one finger aloft, as in, "just a minute."

Twenty-two minutes later, the dude got up, pulling his notepad and briefcase with him, still gabbing, giving Sully a pat on the shoulder as he left. Sully took the still-warm seat and winced at the sensation when he sat down, moving his ass to the edge of the seat, then rolling the chair up to the terminal.

He only had one name: Ferris, George.

He punched it in, the machine thought about it and spit out one match: George Mercury Ferris. Date of birth August 16, 1976. Police Department ID number 673214. Aliases: Curious.

"Bingo," Sully said, hitting the button to call up the case histories.

More computer humming, and then lines and lines of green type popped up, filling the screen. Assault with a deadly weapon (baseball bat); assault with a deadly weapon (shod foot); possession of narcotics (marijuana, less than one ounce); possession with intent to distribute (cocaine); public intoxication; breaking and entering; robbery; robbery; simple assault. Nine arrests, and the man had been an adult all of five years.

A couple of taps on the computer, deeper into the records: Most charges had been no-papered the day after the arrest, meaning the cases were immediately dropped. A plea on the possession with intent; six months probation.

That meant there would be an intake form and a pretrial assessment. He stood in line to fill out a card with a request that it be pulled from the file room. After a while, Sully drumming his fingers on the countertop, the clerk returned with it, the slim manila folder handed back to him across the counter. You could step over to the left, review it, and ask for copies.

Sully moved down and flipped the folder open.

When you got arrested and were headed for trial, one of the indignities suffered was that you had to be interviewed by a social worker, who worked up a case report and put all of your personal business into a little history that was, to those who knew where to look for it, public record.

George's file wasn't very thick, his report on a fading printout on pulp paper, the kind with tear-off perforations on each side. You had to unfold the connected pages to read it. George, one of two children, the only boy, born to a single mother who'd worked at a gas station, then a grocery store. The family moved every other year or so, but only a few blocks each time, always staying in Southwest, the grandmother living with them. This was not, by local standard, a particularly hard lot in life. George had the opportunity to turn out okay. A report from a school counselor, entered into the school record, recorded a concern in sixth grade that George had begun to be disruptive in class and had fought on the playground. Seventh grade, another report that George often did not come to class. The next year, another report, this was about a dog being shot on school grounds. Several students said George had done it, although no gun was ever found and George denied it, but he was invited to attend a different middle school. In ninth grade, there was another incident, involving a cat, its mangled body left by the school's front door. By the tenth grade he was a dropout.

"Juvenile record under seal," was the line that explained that.

The social worker's psychological evaluation: Average intelligence, narcissism, anxiety disorder, antisocial personality. Treatment recommendations: probation, therapy, and possible medication. Last known address, the James Creek projects in Southwest D.C., his mother's place. A subsequent arrest, last year, held the notation that none of the recommendations had been followed through.

Sully wrote down the address of his mom and the name of his sister and handed the file back to the clerk.

Later that afternoon, he was on Half Street SW at the James Creek row houses, low-income public housing, the flat-faced two-story brick ovens sagging into one another since World War II. The front doors were fifteen feet off the sidewalk. No awnings, no porches, a few trees and gasping shrubs out front. Steel bars covered every downstairs window of every house on the block, and some had upstairs bars, too. There were tiny backyards to each, like his own, marked off from one another by rusty steel fences. He found himself knocking on a green door in the middle of the block. This pleasant-faced gent, about sixty-five, opened the door about six inches. Wearing jeans and a tucked-in dress shirt, sporting a close-cropped beard, he heard Sully out, nodding, then said he didn't know shit about whoever he was asking about and never had and he would be happy as hell if Sully left.

Sully apologized, saying he didn't blame him, and went out to the curb, hearing the door and the bolt close behind him. He called back Susan in news research.

"Hey, sweetheart," he said.

"Hi, darling yourself."

"I need another address."

"I need a date."

"I don't know any good guys," he said.

"I'm lesbian, stud."

"Oh. Forgot. You hot redheaded Irish les, you."

"An irresistible combination to women the world over."

"Well. I dunno any hot women, either. That I'm not dating myself."

"Did you call for a reason or just to fuck with me?"

He gave her Curious's name and asked for the address of his sister. She said hold on and set the phone down. Waiting, waiting, looking at his nails, the scuff on his cycle boots, wondering where Alexis was by now . . . Susan came back on the line.

Sis, it turned out, lived in Clinton, out in Prince George's County. He rode out there in half an hour, coming into a nice neighborhood, small brick ranchers, two-car garages, basketball hoops in the driveway. People mowed their yards, trimmed the hedges. He got off the bike. No dogs barking. No engines gunning. Suburbia. It was kind of nice, though the burbs tended to give him the hives. There was quiet and there was too quiet.

When he knocked, a slender, attractive young woman came to the door and asked what it was about.

"George," he said, and she started to slam it shut.

"Wait," he said, sticking a foot in front of the door, keeping it a few inches open. "I'm not the police. I'm not an investigator. I'm just a reporter, at the paper? I don't want to bother you. I'm sorry to be here. Just tell George, next time you hear from him, that I know. Okay? That I know. About what happened with Billy Ellison. That I've got intel from MPD on what happened with the Hall brothers."

He put a card on the floor, and moved his foot. The door slammed shut.

Two nights later, when he had finished trolling through the Bend on his scratched-up and beat-to-shit bike and was back on the Hill, on Pennsylvania Avenue, some idiot started gliding alongside, a hoopty Chevy slow-rolling past the shuttered little restaurants and bars, pulling even with him at the stoplight on Fourth.

They were the only two vehicles out and he ignored it when the driver's-side window came down. It wasn't until the car jerked slightly in front of him that he looked over.

Curious leaned out of the window, tilting his head back up the street. "Come on up here," he said, that rasp, "and leave my sister the fuck out of it."

They parked on Seventh SE, a dark, narrow little street of row houses, about halfway between Sully's place and the James Creek projects, which is to say, about three-quarters of a mile from either. Curious had killed the engine, sitting there behind the wheel, blowing a spliff with the window rolled down. Sully was sitting on the passenger's side, window rolled up, cycle helmet at his feet. He waved a hand in front of him, clearing the cloud, and told Curious one more time that if he wanted his information about what the police knew about the Hall brothers shooting, then he was going to cough up some intel, too.

"You wanted to know what happened, you shoulda gone down there and asked them," Sully said. "That's work *I* did. So, hey, you want me to talk to you, you talk to me."

"That what you do with Sly?" Curious rasped. The man's eyes were red, bleary, his mind floating off somewhere, high as a kite.

"Go ask Sly, you wanna know his business," Sully said. "You want to know what John Parker and MPD know, what he *told* me he knows, anyway? We trade. Capiche?"

"Whatever." A wave of the hand.

"What I got for you," Sully said, "the first part, is that they got the murder weapon on the Hall brothers killing."

Curious looked down, remembering his joint, sucking in another toke, blowing it back out, slow and easy, the sodium-vapor streetlight up the block casting an orange glow into the car. It caught him about the shoulder, leaving his face in the gloom.

"Yeah?" he finally grunted. "Well, good. Good. T-Money and them, rolling up on Tony and Carlos. That shit's wrong. Two and two, even MPD can see that's four."

"That right?" Sully said. "T-Money shot Tony and Carlos?"

George nodded, rasped, "Straight up."

Sully didn't hesitate, because this was it right here, right now. He rolled down his window to let the smoke clear.

"Bullshit," he said, waving an arm again, clearing smoke, "and you know it. T-Money don't have a thing to do with this."

Curious looked over at him. "That right?" That low rasp, sandpaper over steel, mocking him.

"Yeah," Sully said. "It is. It totally is. I'm interested in, like, actual facts. So I want you to tell me, you know, about something you *do* know about. I want you to tell me about the night Billy Ellison came down to the Bend and shot himself. Right in the head. You were there. You watched him do it."

There was a long pause in the car, the air heavy with tension and ganja. Curious, playing it straight, not giving him anything, looking out his window, away from him.

"What make you say that?"

"Because, Curious, he shot himself with the same gun, the *very same damn gun*, that was used to kill the Hall brothers. That's weird, don't you think? One gun, three shootings, same place? Plus, that piece is something like sixty years old. Didn't you notice, when you picked it up after Billy shot himself, that it was an antique? It was his granddad's gun from the military. I mean, I don't know that I would have thought about it, right up until I saw you you pick up Antoine's gun after you shot him. You did the same when Billy shot himself. Picked up the dead man's gun."

Another long, dry, dark silence. The night spun out, slow, dark, eternal, threatening.

"Dude didn't say shit till the end," Curious began, the buzz taking him over, scrunching down farther in the seat, talking for three minutes, now five, the sound of his voice low and steady in the silence of the car, him looking up and out the windshield, like there was something up there in the overhanging trees, going on and on in an endless monotone.

"And he was a skinny little motherfucker, you know that? Not big. Not that big at all. He just come down there that night, looking around. Went down to the water, came back up, went back. The Bend, people do weird shit, crack fiends, man, but this . . . it was like"—he took another toke, pressing his mind for some sort of reference—"like a dog, you know what I'm saying? Looking for something he buried? Like that."

"And he wasn't saying nothing?"

"Not shit. That's what I'm talking about. Like he didn't even *see* nobody."

"How long had he been coming down there?"

"Never seen him before in life. Me or Antoine either one."

"He hadn't been scoring down there at *all*? Wasn't buying quantity?"

"You can't hear? What did I just say?"

"Family tells me that he was moving coke, weed."

"Not from the Bend he wasn't."

"Okay, so."

"Okay, so, Antoine?" Curious licked his lips, worked his tongue up against his teeth, like he had something stuck on the top side and was trying to push it out. "He was pissed about the boy coming down there to start with, you hear? Like he could just show up? Like he owned the place? We walked up on him when he was way down at the water. The way we did you, that time you showed up. Brother man don't even turn around. Antoine, he says, Hey motherfucker, I'm talking to you. Shoves him, knocks him two steps, nearly in the water. *Then* boyfriend turns around and he was *crying*, just—"

"Billy cried because Antoine shoved him?"

"—*crying* and—what? No, see, nah. He's already snotty nosed. Boy was touched, you ask me. So, Antoine, this just pisses him off, the boy acting like a little bitch. He shucks out the Glock and says, Get your ass up and outta here before I clock you, you know? And brother man says, he says, I got my own goddamn gun! And then pulls it out and blam, right in the head. For fucking real. Shot hisself about three seconds before Ant woulda done it for him."

Sully was steadily looking at him, assessing this. Curious was still slouched back in the seat, the blunt almost gone, the death of Billy Ellison recounted—sad, desolate, forlorn, possibly the only time anyone would ever hear it. Sully did not doubt a word of it.

"Then y'all threw him in the water," Sully said.

"Ant kicked him two three times, 'cause he was pissed off, but yeah. Tossed him. Nobody wants five-oh walking around up in the Bend, poking their snouts where they don't got no business."

"And that left his gun right there."

Curious flicked a glance out the window, yawning, tired of this. "Where else would it go?"

"And you picked it up."

Curious cut off his yawn, looking over at him, his eyes bleary in the gloom but a glint underneath the haze.

"Somebody picked it up," Sully said, "and used it to shoot the Hall brothers. And since Billy's gone? And since you shot Ant in the head the other day? That leaves you, Curious. Who else could have plausibly picked it up?"

That did it, the glint in the eyes sparking into malice, his face tightening, Curious sitting up in the seat, the shadows in the car moving, shifting, his face hard to make out.

"The fuck you say."

"The fuck I don't. You wanted me to tell you what the police knew. I did."

"You said they found the piece. You ain't said—"

"They found the piece just like you wanted. You flipped it over there in the rocks, dropped it there, somewhere it looked like somebody tried to get rid of it. That was good. That was smart. You wanted them to go chasing a gun that couldn't be traced, some crazy-ass old gun that looks like it belongs in a museum."

"I done—"

"You're taking over the Bend, Curious," Sully whispered. "It's you."

Silence. Curious eye-fucking him *hard*, the ganja haze burned away now.

"You been doing it for a solid month," Sully said. "Dee Dee shot his mouth off about being Sly Hastings's boy. About being Sly's muscle for moving in on the Bend. Ha. Dumbass. You saw that opportunity for yourself. It was just sitting there, once he'd pissed on the South Caps and they'd shot up his car. You had free license, man. Everybody was going to think it was them. So you popped Dee and you went to Sly and said, Hey, *I'm* your man. Moved right on up."

Curious just looked at him, glaring,

"First time I saw you and Sly, that's what Sly says, you're his man. Then you capped Ant, right in front of me, so you can tell Sly you were getting me through the park all safe and sound. That was a nice little play there. Two down. And then the big kill, the Hall brothers. You get them to come outside, who knows what for, and bam bam. Who else would they have trusted enough to come outside on the spur of the moment, and let walk behind them?"

"You—"

"You're Michael fucking Corleone, laying waste to the five families. You run the Bend now. Does Sly know? 'Cause I'm thinking he'll cancel you out just for popping Dee without—"

"You think you know this." That rasp coming at him in the half dark. "And you ain't—"

"I didn't know it until John Parker told me about the pistol they found. He thinks it's a big-time clue, bless his heart. I like the man. But it's just going to throw the cops off, because it's never going to be traced. They want to trace it so bad, peg it to one of you lowlifes down there in the Bend. But they can't. Never will. You're going to walk, Curious."

"You talking out your neck."

Sully took a breath and let it out. It was all so clear now.

"That gun Billy used, that fossil? It belonged to his grandfather, in World War Two. It was some sort of collectible. Maybe Granddad got it issued to him on the luck of the draw, or maybe he was a collector and bought it. But when he died? Billy's dad inherited it. It was a big deal, a family heirloom. Billy's dad, he couldn't get over it. I read all about it in the family papers. Told Billy all about it, like this was his birthright. Supposed to be a, a, what, a man-to-man thing. Kept it in a velvet-lined box on the top shelf of his walk-in closet.

"Then Daddy died, in a car wreck, and Billy's mom, she kept it right up there on the same shelf. Told Billy all about it. Like it was magic. A birthright. Which is where Billy plucked it from, two nights before he came down here and shot himself. He was going loco at the end. He'd stopped taking his meds. He liked the mind-fuck historical aspect of his own suicide—putting an end to his family's bloodline with a family heirloom."

"You—you—there ain't no way you know—"

"Sure I do," Sully said, opening the car door, getting his cycle helmet off the floor. "I've got the case the gun was in. It's a little wooden box. Billy wrote the whole thing down—the gun, taking it from his mother's house, all that. He just didn't know I was going to be the one to wind up with it. He thought it would be Elliot."

He got out then, closed the door behind him, felt his knee twinge on him and bent it, and just that fast the passenger door swung open behind him. Curious had slid across the seat, pulled out a gun, and had it up and pointed, his jawline set.

"That gun, what you saying, the family's going to ID as soon as they hear about it," he said, "and you saying that's gonna lead them right back—"

"No no no, you not listening," Sully said. "That's your break. The family has known it's been gone since the night Billy shot himself. They've known it was suicide, the gun he used, the whole time. They found out Granddad's gun was missing? Then they set him up, you hear? All that 'Our Billy was a drug dealer' routine? It was bullshit, to protect the family's history. They sold him out. So trust me on this. They don't want anybody to know anything different. They ain't never, *ever* going to ID that gun."

He took two steps, then turned back.

"And, hey, motherfucker? You point a gun at me one more time? Ima tell Sly you capped Dee Dee. Your sister, George? You know what Sly'll do to your sister?"

THIRTY-NINE

IT TOOK SOME convincing with Sly to backstop him on the move he had set up. It took another mention of Noel Pittman and what he knew about it. But after a few days of no-bullshit hardball, and a few more days of scouting, Sly Hastings and Lionel reluctantly drove Sully out to Shellie Stevens's house in Great Falls, the Virginia suburb of the posh and posher, late on a Sunday afternoon, neither of them wanting to be there.

They were all riding in a black Lincoln Town Car with stolen plates. Sly had borrowed the car for the afternoon from a guy who owed him, then jacked the plates. They'd picked up Sully a few minutes later. Sly started to explain the whole situation and Sully said he didn't even want to know.

"You got to admit, it's a pretty good cover," Sly said. "We roll up on the man's house, looking like we just got out of a private jet at Dulles."

"The last thing anybody in Great Falls is going to look at," Sully said, "is a white man getting out of a chauffeured Town Car."

Sly, riding shotgun, turned to look at him in the backseat. "I didn't even know you had a suit. You got your piece in there?"

Sully tapped the coat's outer left pocket. "I'm not gonna need it."

"What about his wife? Kids?"

"Wife goes to the Kennedy Center every Sunday afternoon, this classical concert series. She's an official patron. Kids grown and gone."

Shellie Stevens's house was a monstrous stucco thing on a leafy street full of them. It was set back from the road on several acres. It was three stories, set among towering oaks with evergreens lining the drive. Lionel pulled up in the circular driveway, right around the fountain, and parked. Wearing a black suit and a chauffeur's cap, he walked to the front door and, using what appeared to be a suction cup and a glass-cutting knife, sliced a quick circle in the glass, pulled it back with the suction cup, reached in, and turned the dead bolt. He poked his head in the door, called out, heard nothing, and then walked back to the car. He opened the rear passenger door. Sully, wearing a black two-button Versace suit and carrying a leather briefcase, got out and walked smartly into the house like he was ten minutes late.

Sly and Lionel pulled out of the drive. They would tool around the neighborhood until Sully paged them. Then they'd circle back through and he had better be there when they did.

The house was lovely. He liked it. He really did. Stevens—or more likely his wife, or even more likely her decorator—had good taste, you had to give that up. The piedmont red in the dining room gave him ideas for his own place. The hallways were wide, the wooden floors polished to a scream.

Sully went to the kitchen—big as a tennis court—found the crystal, got a glass, and used the ice maker in the fridge for four, then five cubes.

The liquor took a minute to find but it was in a built-in cabinet between the kitchen and dining room. Stevens, pretentious little prick that he was, apparently drank mostly Scotch. But there was a bottle of Maker's Mark, its red wax seal peeking out from behind the Scotch and in front of the mixers. Not Basil's, but it would do.

He poured two fingers over the ice, picked up the briefcase, and went to the living room, setting the ice-filled glass on the coffee table—he was guessing teak here—so that it would be sure to leave a water mark. Then he opened the briefcase and sat back to wait.

A little before five, the garage door opened. He walked to the windows and saw a black Jaguar pull in. He settled back on the loveseat. A few minutes later, Stevens came in through a side door from the garage, wearing ridiculous golf pants and a light green knit shirt, visor still on his head. He had taken his golf spikes off and was holding them in his hand, padding across the floor in his socks.

He went to the kitchen and poured something from the refrigerator and was about to walk up the stairs when he rounded the corner, looked up, and saw Sully. The glass dropped from his hand, liquid and ice sloshing out, glass shattering on the floor.

"Counselor," Sully said, with a slight nod.

"How did—how did—"

"The same way your assholes got into my place," he said. "But I didn't fuck up your car, like you did my bike, and God knows I didn't waste your whiskey like you did mine. I just had one. Well, two. Since you took so long." He held up his glass, nodding. "You should really drink better shit. Not that there's—"

Stevens, ashen, moved across the room. "The police will take care of this. Of you. I can't—"

"Which 'this' are we talking about? You want to tell them about 'this'?"

He took the wooden box that had held the Singer .45 from his briefcase and set it on the coffee table in front of him. He lifted the lid. It was, of course, empty.

Stevens stopped short, his eyes going from searching for the phone to the pistol case.

"You been looking for this so hard," Sully said, "since the night Billy argued with you and Delores and ran out of the house with it."

"You—"

"Billy took the pistol out of this case," Sully said, "and shot himself in the head with it. You knew that from the beginning. His last little fuck-you to the both of you. Going to the Bend so you'd be sure not to miss the point. Like you could possibly."

Stevens's eyes had gone to the case, not seeing anything else.

"So, you want to call the police, partner," Sully continued, "you go right the fuck ahead. You call John Parker, head of D.C. Homicide. You tell him you found evidence that Billy Ellison was a suicide, not a homicide. Then you tell him the same weapon was used to execute the Hall brothers in the Bend a few days ago. Closing out three homicides—brother, I can't tell you how happy he's going to be to hear *that*."

Stevens stared, his lower jaw starting to tremble.

"Come on, Shellie. You repeat the end of everything I say. That would be 'Hear that.' Or do you want to sit down and let me explain the end of your professional life to you?"

"You—you presume to know things," Stevens said, "that you couldn't possibly—"

"Shut the fuck up," Sully said. "MPD found Lambert Ellison III's gun down at the Bend the other night, where it was used to kill two major-league drug dealers."

Stevens's face, the eyebrows starting up, the mouth moving.

"Billy also wrote at least a partial draft of the note he left you and Delores," he said. "Which I happen to have with me."

He pulled a single sheet of paper from his backpack and slid it across the coffee table.

Stevens's face became very still, the tension in his forehead absolute and frozen, his lips paper-thin slits, his fingers reaching out to pick up the slip of paper. He brought it to his face and said, briefly, "This is just a copy of something. It's not even—"

"I have the original," Sully said, softly. "We're using it for layout in the story."

Stevens looked at him across the sheet of paper, which was quivering ever so slightly in his hand, but his face was still holding, Sully saw, for the last time in his career, keeping it together, not yet aware of how completely all of this—the power office, the lunches, the deference he was accustomed to and thrived upon—was about to end.

"The thing that was always bothering me," Sully said, "was these investigators you hired. You told me they were to help out with the homicide investigation. 'To make sure justice is done,' that's what you said in your statement, how they were going to help track down the killers.

"But look at me. I been down there in the Bend, the gay clubs on O

Street, talked to the cops? Nobody saw these guys investigating any-thing. Nobody. I thought that was pretty strange, but I was thinking you guys had the drop. I figured that maybe we were in the wrong place—maybe Billy had been shot somewhere *else* and brought to the Bend to make it look like a drug deal, right, and your investigators had tracked down the *real* place of the killing? And that the police and I were just that dumb and that you guys were just that smart?

"Well. I *was* dumb, but not in the way I thought. You hired investi-gators to track down Billy's *research*, not his killer. You know the only people to see your investigators? Elliot. And his new partner. Who don't—and couldn't possibly—know sweet fuckall about the Bend. You couldn't possibly have been trying to find out who killed him because you *already knew*. You already knew he killed himself, and why, because he told you all of that in a note just like that one you're holding. You ran upstairs, looked in that velvet box, the gun was gone, and you knew.

"And yet you and Delores blew right past that, past your grief or what have you, and you hired those goons to find Billy's research, his thesis, and get rid of it. You and Delores—and really, just you—created this story about Billy being some sort of drug dealer, like *that* was the dark family secret. A wannabe rap star, right? Wasn't that it? So that everybody would think he was shot by another dealer. Then my story about the Bend ran. Delores panicked and thought I was onto the whole thing—selling her son out like that, the family reputation gone to hell—and it ate her alive. So she called me up and said, 'I got to show you something.' She was eaten up with guilt. She wanted me to know that she went along with it, but that it was your idea. You told her that it would fix everything. But it didn't."

"What—what is it, Mr. Carter, that you think you know," Stevens said, sitting now, taking a wing chair across the room, "that would prompt such actions on our part?"

Playing it to the end. Sully admired that. It was fucked up, but he admired it, in the way he admired how a snake's head would bite you even after it had been severed.

"What I know," Sully said, "is that the foundation of the family fortune, the basis of the empire, was not dear old Nathaniel Ellison and his bank. It was his mother, Jeanne-Marie."

Stevens looked at him, and Sully could see everything inside the man melt and slide away from its moorings, like a wax figure melting from inside.

"Jeanne-Marie," Sully said, "co-owner of Frenchman's Bend, one of the largest slave-selling markets in the United States. She was at first the mistress, then business partner, of Didier Delacroix, the Frenchman himself. Delacroix's wife, that was Lisette; she died in the 1840s, the consumption, which is what they used to call tuberculosis. They had one child, Joshua Steven, but he was just a tot. So, to help run the empire, who did Didier turn to? Who else? Jeanne-Marie, his black mistress. Who was French. She was the overseer, the one who split families apart and sold off black children like livestock. They were almost all teenagers, the stock at the Bend, did you know that? And she sold them all.

"It was good business, if you had the stomach for it, but then there was the war and all that unpleasantness. Two years after it ended—this is 1867—Didier up and died. A widower, he left half of everything to Joshua and half to Jeanne-Marie. Overnight, she became, very likely, the richest black woman in America. Whatever her last name had been, she changed it to Ellison, stayed in the shadows, and gave *their* child, Nathaniel, the inheritance. Which he had the good sense to launder and start a bank. And so the Ellison myth of American ingenuity began. But the *real* source of their wealth, like so many others of the era, was slaves. They kept it hidden for nearly a century and a half. Till Billy dug it up. Imagine what it did to him, a kid already beset by depression, mania—"

"This—this—"

"The Ellisons were never slaves, not a day in their lives, you knew that, right? Jeane-Marie came across on the boat with Didier from the old country, gay old Paris. She'd been his mistress for years, under the family-servant guise or nanny or whatever. When he went into the slave business, she was the one who dealt with the slaves, decided who to buy and sell, as she had the more native eye for it."

Silence, the mouth coming open, a small and tiny O.

"You know all this, Shellie. You've known it all your life. Didier Delacroix is your great-whatever grandfather."

"I—"

"Didier fathered Nathaniel by Jeanne-Marie, yeah, but don't forget his, what should we call him—legitimate son?—dear old Joshua Steven Delacroix. By the time Josh was in his late twenties—after the war ended—the Delacroix name became inconvenient to have around here. Lincoln assassinated, vigilante groups, freed slaves—it was a nightmare. Both his parents were dead. So he dropped the surname and added an *S* to the middle. And appeared to vanish.

"But Billy found him, in that deep hell of research he was into. Joshua moved to New York. Invested in mines and railroads. And when *his* son moved back to D.C. during World War One, he was just another rich New York lawyer.

"Three generations later"—Sully spread his hands, encompassing the house, the grounds—"here you sit, counselor. The progeny of the Frenchman himself."

FORTY

IT TOOK STEVENS a moment to gather himself—like Lee at Gettysburg, Sully thought, doomed but taking the offensive to the end—and he rallied.

"Many people owned slaves, Carter," he said. "My ancestors, Delores's. It's nothing to be proud of but in the context of the day it was not shocking. People, all over the South, descendants carry on without shame. Her family and mine shared a common bond, known to each generation but never aired in public."

"You don't say."

"It was a sort of cultural affiliation, the sort of which I would not expect someone like you to understand, with your inherent loathing of the wealthy. You wear your white-trash roots on your sleeve, like it's some sort of badge of honor instead of being the disgrace that it is. When my legal firm—which I took over from my father—hired William, everyone thought we took him as the star and that we brought Delores, his wife, on board as extra compensation. In fact, William was the token. Delores was the hire, keeping the bond between the families."

"I couldn't give a fuck about that, counselor, and neither could you," Sully said. "That your family and Delores's traded in slaves is one thing. But you lied about it. Hid it. And that gave the past a power it never would have had otherwise. You two could deal with it, keep your self-superior faces on, but it destroyed Billy.

"Imagine it. Nice kid, a little fragile, starts doing a thesis about his wonderful family, the thing in life of which he was most proud. A paper that would further burnish the Ellison name. Instead, he finds slavery and a century of mendacity, including his own mother and godfather. He comes to you two, upset and shouting, and you both tell him to shut up and sit down. So what, in his mental illness, can he do about it? Why, he can end it. He can end the whole thing. He gets the family gun and goes to the Bend, the source of the family wealth, and kills himself. How very symbolic. How very obvious. No wonder Delores panicked, thinking I would discover it. You know the last thing she said, counselor? 'You were going to find out.'"

Shellie looked up at him now, his face crumpling into the ruination that Sully, in a flash of insight, realized would define his features for the rest of his life, that would carry him to the grave. He did not speak, just sat there with a hollow-eyed stare, a vacant expression that was perhaps not too far removed from the one Billy Ellison had that day on the ice.

"Delores didn't kill herself because her ancestors, and yours, dealt in slaves," Sully said. "She killed herself because the two of you cooked up a false story about Billy. You two came up with this slander about him being a drug user and dealer, portraying him as the racist stereotype of his generation, in order to keep your secret. Delores killed herself because of what she'd done to her son *after* he was dead. You knew it. That's why you were almost sick outside her funeral. You knew what you'd done to her."

Stevens looked at him.

"You're going to—to publish this?" It was a whisper.

"On the front fucking page."

"But to—to what end?" Stevens said, the air hissing out of him. "Delores is dead. Billy is dead. You'd destroy her name just to expose me? My family?"

Sully hit his pager to summon Sly and Lionel.

He put Billy's papers and the pistol box back in his briefcase. He snapped it shut. The bourbon wasn't finished, so he took care of that, then threw the glass on a long arc into the dining room, where it shattered.

Using his good leg first, he stood up and came across the room and leaned over Stevens sitting in his wing chair, still wearing the ridiculous visor and golf slacks. His tone, it was almost a whisper, like a priest intoning a benediction.

"You'n ask your God for mercy, absolution, forgiveness, all you want," he said. "I'm not in that line of work. I will bury you, counselor, without mercy and without a second thought. You fucked over Billy Ellison, your godson, your emotionally damaged, frail, and vulnerable godson. And you, so help me Christ, will answer for it."

FORTY-ONE

Billy Ellison was not a homicide victim. He neither dealt in nor used narcotics. He was not in Frenchman's Bend, the city's most notorious open-air drug market, on the night of his death to settle business in that trade.

Instead, an investigation by this newspaper has found that Ellison, 21, committed suicide—with his grandfather's handgun—as a desperate last measure to call attention to his family's long-concealed ties to the former slave-trading post on the District's leeward shore.

The story took shape on the screen, line by line, steady and assured. It laid out everything. It attributed the groundbreaking research on the Bend to Billy's thesis. It came with speed and confidence. There was no bourbon involved, which, Sully thought, would make Alexis proud.

He wrote in a public file so that Eddie and the rest of management could read it as it took shape, but there were few interruptions. R.J. came by midafternoon and rapped on the top edge of the cubicle.

"The firm, it's officially the Stevens Group, not the Stevens Firm," he said. "And let's make it Sheldon Stevens on first reference, instead of Shellie."

Sully nodded.

"Also, after you file? Eddie wants you to stop in his office. I think he's going to ask you to go to lunch. There's going to be, I wouldn't call it an apology, but there's going to be something like it. A note in the personnel folder, retracting the suspension, reinstatement of lost pay, like that."

"Okay."

"Don't be a prick about it."

"Okay."

"Don't say, 'I told you so.'"

"All right already."

R.J. left and he went back to work.

After a while, Sully called John Parker. John listened to what he'd found out, cursing twice, and then Sully asked him for comment.

There was a pause, and then John said, "Okay, let's go with this. 'One of our first lines of inquiry was suicide, and the Ellison family and their attorney, Mr. Stevens, repeatedly assured us there was no such possibility. There was no mention of Billy Ellison's mental instability or of a suicide note or of a pistol taken from the family home. Mrs. Ellison and Mr. Stevens informed us they were hiring private investigators to assist us, in whatever fashion possible, with solving Billy's murder. That was the term they used repeatedly. 'Murder.' We will take these reports into account and revisit our investigation.'"

When he finished, he told Sully he was going to talk off the record and Sully said sure.

"I'll get that prick's law license for this," he said. "He's an officer of the court. I could go for obstruction of justice, but that would go to trial and take forever and he'd probably beat it. But the law license, that's a matter before the bar. That's going down."

"What about the other thing?"

"Which other thing?"

"The gun. Billy's gun. It was used to kill the Hall brothers."

John jumped on that.

"Yeah, no shit. Somebody had to pick it up after Billy used it. That means, it happening in the Bend, that it couldn't have been the South Caps. It means somebody already in the Bend, in the M Street Crew, picked it up, threw Billy's body in the water. That same person then used it to kill the Hall brothers. Which means it was an inside job."

"That give you a suspect?"

Another pause.

"By name, for me to tell you, right now, even off the record? No. But whoever turns up running the Bend in a couple of weeks, it's going to be him. That's not a long list of people. Didn't I tell you all this was going to tie into this new stuff getting piped in down there? Well. There you go."

"The way all that worked out," Sully said, "it's curious, isn't it?"

There was a long pause.

"Yeah," John said. "Curious, brother. It is. That's just what I was thinking."

By late afternoon, with deadline looming, he was down to the kicker of the story. It wasn't difficult. Sorting through the papers scattered across his desk, he retrieved the partial note the late Billy Ellison had left behind. It wasn't the final note, no, but it was a rough draft, and that was good enough. Elliot had come down to the paper and verified it as Billy's handwriting.

Sully just quoted it.

So, Mom, I don't know why you've been lying about this all this time. I don't know why you hate who I've become. I can't do anything about that. But I can do something. I can end it all. I am the last of the Ellisons, and that is one thing that—

The page was torn at that point, leaving the rest of his thoughts to himself.

He was only wrong about one thing, Sully thought. His mother had been the last of the Ellisons.

Had Sully been the type to weep, he might have. He thought Billy Ellison a good man. A young one, but a good man. They died all the time. They always had.

AFTERWORD & ACKNOWLEDGMENTS

THE PRECEDING IS a work of fiction.

Washington, D.C., did indeed have a series of slave pens in the antebellum era and some of those factual accounts are included herein. The epigraph and the horrific accounts of the Williams and Robey slave pens in the city, and the Franklin and Armfield place just across the river in Alexandria, Virginia, are taken from historical accounts, as is the journey of the *Pearl*. The Red Summer of 1919 took place largely as presented.

Frenchman's Bend, however, is cut entirely of fictional cloth. Neither it nor its proprietors and descendants ever existed.

The careful reader will notice that, as in *The Ways of the Dead*, I have taken small liberties with other D.C. timelines and geography.

This book is affectionately dedicated to the late Tommy Miller, my old professor, mentor, friend, and one of the western world's most underappreciated newspaper editors. He taught me how to think and write and how to make a living with a pen and a notebook. I miss him, as do so many others.

Many, many thanks are extended to the people who supported the writing of this book and who read, edited, and thought aloud about how it could be better. Most of the mostest is my adorable spouse, the belle of Jamaica, Carol Smith Tucker, my first reader, critic, and watcher of the kids when I am locked in a small room with the keyboard. Also, lookin' at you, Lynn Medford, my most boss at *The Washington Post*; Elyse Cheney, agent extraordinaire; and Allison Lorentzen, my very most wonderful editor at Viking. Thank you, ladies. Take the rest of the day off.

NEELY TUCKER

The Ways of the Dead

The body of the teenage daughter of a powerful Federal judge is discovered in a dumpster in a bad neighbourhood of Washington, D.C. It is murder, and the local police immediately arrest the three nearest black kids, bad boys from a notorious gang.

Sully Carter, a veteran war correspondent with emotional scars far worse than the ones on his body, suspects that there's more to the case than the police would have the public know.

With the nation clamouring for a conviction, and the bereaved judge due for a court nomination, Sully pursues his own line of enquiry, in spite of some very dangerous people telling him to shut it down…

'*A great read … I can't wait for what's next.*'
MICHAEL CONNELLY

'*It's got the plot, a brilliant lead character and a bucket-load of suspense.*'
SUNDAY SPORT

'*The very best in gritty, hard-edged suspense. Complex characters, taut dialogue, and a riveting plot all add up to one extremely excellent novel.*'
LISA GARDNER